desire lines

Also by Christina Baker Kline

FICTION

Sweet Water

The Way Life Should Be

Bird in Hand

Orphan Train

NONFICTION

The Conversation Begins:
Mothers and Daughters Talk About Living Feminism
(coauthored with Christina Looper Baker)

Child of Mine: Original Essays on Becoming a Mother (editor)

Room to Grow: Twenty-two Writers Encounter the Pleasures
and Paradoxes of Raising Young Children (editor)

About Face: Women Write About What They See
When They Look in the Mirror (edited with Anne Burt)

desire lines

A NOVEL

CHRISTINA BAKER KLINE

WILLIAM MORROW

An Imprint of HarperCollins*Publishers*

DESIRE LINES. Copyright © 1999 by Christina Baker Kline. All rights reserved. Printed in the United States of America. No part of this book may be used or reproduced in any manner whatsoever without written permission except in the case of brief quotations embodied in critical articles and reviews. For information address HarperCollins Publishers, 195 Broadway, New York, NY 10007.

HarperCollins books may be purchased for educational, business, or sales promotional use. For information please e-mail the Special Markets Department at SPsales@harpercollins.com.

A hardcover edition of this book was published in 1999 by William Morrow, an imprint of HarperCollins Publishers.

FIRST WILLIAM MORROW PAPERBACK EDITION PUBLISHED 2014.

The Library of Congress has catalogued the hardcover edition as follows:
Kline, Christina Baker, 1964–
    Desire Lines : a novel /Christina Baker Kline.—1st ed.
        p.   cm.
    ISBN 978-0-688-15107-2
    I. Title.
PS3561.I478D4   1999

92–54717
CIP

ISBN 978-0-06-056694-4 (pbk.)

14 15 16 17 18   OV/RRD   10 9 8 7 6 5 4 3 2

FOR MY PARENTS—

path seekers and finders

There are years that ask questions and years that answer.

—Zora Neale Hurston

PROLOGUE

The night Jennifer disappeared, fireworks lit up the sky above Bangor, Maine, for nearly an hour. Down in the harbor, graduating seniors on a boat anchored to its moorings danced to a rock band until the steely light of dawn washed over the Penobscot. In the shadows of Little City park, away from the buzzing streetlights, kids in leather jackets and awkward ties passed around a joint and tossed their mortarboards back and forth like Frisbees. Young couples fumbled in dark bedrooms in the rustic camps that ringed Green Lake, listening to the lapping of the waves on the rocks and the panting of their friends through plywood walls. Several teenagers, unaccustomed to the excitement or the alcohol, threw up, passed out, and found themselves at daybreak stretched out in the backseat of somebody's brother's Buick, or curled in a beanbag chair in a musty basement rec room, or tucked into their own beds—not knowing and not wanting to know how they got there.

The night Jennifer disappeared, a car full of seniors going up Essex

Street hill on the wrong side of the road swerved to miss an oncoming truck and plunged into a row of mailboxes, landing in a ditch. They stumbled out of the fractured car bruised and shaken. The driver, Tommy Green, called his father collect from a phone booth near the overpass. "Everybody's fine, Dad," Tommy said into the stunned silence on the other end. "We're okay, Dad. Honest. Are you there?"

The night Jennifer disappeared, she told her best friend a secret that her best friend didn't understand. They were lying on the hood of Kathryn's red Toyota, handing a bottle of wine cooler back and forth and watching clouds pass over a bright crescent moon. Below them, the black water of the Kenduskeag gurgled over a shallow bed of rocks.

"Did you ever do something—and you knew that even if it didn't seem so weird at the time, someday it would change everything about you?" Jennifer said.

"What do you mean?" Kathryn turned to look at her.

Jennifer sat up slowly. "And you know there's a path you're supposed to be following in life—but that somehow, maybe because you wanted to, or maybe because it happened so slowly you didn't even realize it, you've moved farther and farther away from it?"

"You mean, like, college?"

"Not exactly." She looked down and scratched a spot on the hood with her fingernail.

"What are you saying?"

Jennifer looked at her distractedly. For a moment, it seemed she was trying to form the words in her head. Then she turned away. "Nothing, I guess."

Kathryn took a deep breath and exhaled, puffing out her cheeks. Even now, all these years later, she doesn't know whether it was the wine, or the giddiness of graduating, or some deep unconscious fear about what her friend might reveal, but something in her arose, impatient. "Come on, Jen," she said. "Don't get deep on me. We're supposed to be celebrating."

When the rest of the group showed up, they built a fire down by the river. Will, Jennifer's twin brother, picked at his guitar, Rachel poured vodka and orange juice out of a Thermos and passed plastic cups around, and Brian and Jack played hearts for quarters in the flickering yellow light, moving closer to the fire as the air grew cool.

After an hour or so Jennifer stood and stretched. "I guess I'll be going," she said.

They squinted at her lazily. "You can't be serious," said Will.

"I'm really tired."

"It's a federal offense to sleep the night of your graduation," Brian said.

She gave him a wry smile.

Kathryn sighed and struggled to her feet, pulling out the car keys. "Come on, then," she said. "I'll take you."

"It's almost midnight—much too late to be roaming around by yourself," Jack said. "Stay here with us, just a little longer. Here." He patted the ground. "You can share my blanket."

"It's okay," she said firmly, backing away. "I'll be fine. It's not far. The walk will clear my head."

"Jennifer, you pain in the ass," Will said.

"*Will.*"

"I could walk you home, I suppose . . ." he started.

"I kind of want to be alone," she said, and smiled. "Really. Don't worry. I'll be fine."

THE NIGHT JENNIFER disappeared, her four closest friends and her brother sat around a pile of dying embers and watched her walk out into the darkness.

I'll be fine. Those were the last words she said—or the last anybody ever admitted to hearing.

PART ONE

HOMECOMING

Sitting in a window seat near the front of the tiny plane, staring out at the evergreen expanse below, Kathryn twists the gold ring on her finger. She eases the ring off, feeling the cool weight of it in her hand, and then slips it back on. She holds her fingers out to look at it. Turning her wrist, she glances at her watch. Then she leans back and closes her eyes. The plane will be landing in fifteen minutes. In half an hour she'll be home.

The night before, in Charlottesville, Virginia, sitting on the floor of her almost-empty apartment and trying to stuff every piece of clothing she owned into two suitcases, Kathryn had heard a knock at the door and then, suddenly, there was Paul. She hadn't seen him in almost a month. He looked different; his dark curly hair was clipped close to his head, like a shorn sheep. When they were together, he'd always worn it long. Looking around at the bare walls and the clothing stacked in piles on the floor, he held up an envelope for her to see. "Just in time, I guess," he said.

She skimmed the divorce papers quickly, straining to make out the fine print in the light from the single bulb overhead. Paul leaned against the wall, watching her. When she got to the last page, Kathryn could see that he had already signed it, and something about seeing his signature like that, firm and steady and sure, made a lump form in her throat.

"Listen, Kat," he said, seeing her hesitate. "We don't have to do this now."

"No. It's fine. Just give me a second, all right?"

"I know this is a busy time. You've got a lot to do, you're trying to leave. Why don't you send the papers to me when you get there? It'll just take a little longer."

"It's okay," she said, a bit more sharply than she intended. He fell silent. She signed the papers carefully, spelling out her name in a distinct, mannered script that bore scant resemblance to her usual scrawl. Then she folded the papers and handed them back.

"How about a hug, for old times' sake?" he asked, holding his arms out.

She shook her head. "I don't think so."

He nodded, joining his hands and bending them back at the knuckles. "Sure. I understand."

She bit her lip, and he looked at her closely. She could tell he was trying to see if she was going to cry. Then he smiled. "You're all right, you know that?"

"Yeah," she said, "I'm all right."

After he left she got the last of the Dickel from the cabinet above the fridge and slid down against the wall. It had been almost two years to the day since she and Paul were married. They had already been living together, in this apartment, for several months, and Kathryn remembers the strangeness of coming back after the ceremony to dishes in the sink and their unmade bed. They had wanted to pretend that getting married didn't change anything, but she knew in her bones that wasn't true. The stakes were higher now; they had made promises, they had expectations.

Even the apartment seemed different to her—smaller, somehow, as if the rooms had shrunk.

Paul had insisted on carrying Kathryn, in her white slip dress, in the driving rain, up the crumbling flagstone walkway and the creaky front steps and over the threshold. By the time he staggered through the door and collapsed on the couch, still holding her in his arms, they were both soaking wet.

Gazing down at her, he'd brushed wet confetti out of her hair. " 'Birth, and copulation, and death,' " he said. " 'That's all the facts when you come to brass tacks.' "

She frowned. "Are you quoting Eliot again?"

"Yes," he said.

She looked into his eyes. " 'I am measuring out my life with coffee spoons.' "

" 'Have measured.' That's the only line you can remember, isn't it?" He laughed.

She nodded. "But I know all the words to 'Paradise by the Dashboard Light.' "

They imagined it would be a story to tell their kids someday—how they met in graduate school and against their own better judgment fell in love. They were so different: He was a born-and-bred New England WASP, she a scrappy nonpracticing Catholic. He was focused and ambitious, she wasn't certain what she wanted to do. He liked to stay out late in jazz clubs, she was happy at home curled up with a book. But they believed there was enough to make it work. They both loved Monty Python and rice pudding; they shared a similarly deadpan sense of humor. And when she told him about what had happened to her best friend, how she had disappeared on the night of their high school graduation and never returned, he offered a story of his own, about a friend from college who was hitchhiking in a snowstorm and was blindsided by a truck. "He's still in a coma, so we can't even mourn," Paul said. "He's just—gone. It's like he disappeared; I've always thought of it that way."

It had seemed to Kathryn that Paul was the only one who really understood. But later, after things began to fall apart, she realized that, in truth, he didn't. He was impatient with her moodiness; he couldn't see the point of dwelling on the past. "There's nothing you can do. You've got to let it go and move on," he insisted. She tried, but it was no good. In the end it was easier to let go of the marriage than let go of the melancholy that grew slowly inside her like a tumor, obliterating everything else.

Alone in the empty apartment now, she got up and put Bob Dylan on the portable CD player. With the first strains of "Tangled Up in Blue," Paul's favorite song, the tears she'd been holding back rose in her like an undercurrent, dredging up the pain that had settled just below the surface.

When she couldn't cry anymore she wandered into the bathroom and looked at herself in the mirror. Her large, gray-blue eyes, usually her best feature, were swollen and bloodshot, and her light-brown hair hung limply past her chin. She'd lost weight in the past few months; her face was all angles and hollows. Plenty of guys over the years had told her she was beautiful, but she'd always dismissed it as romantic hyperbole. "You are beautiful, but not in a conventional way," Paul said once, with his usual blunt candor. "There's something . . . arresting about you." *Arrested*, perhaps, Kathryn thought, studying her reflection, but not arresting. Not anymore.

On an impulse she opened the medicine cabinet and rummaged through it, looking for the box of hair color she'd bought a few weeks before on a special promotion. "Autumn Glow." She studied the woman on the front of the box, her auburn hair smooth and shining, eyes sparkling, mouth wide in a smile. Then Kathryn opened the box and pulled out the instructions, ripping the plastic gloves off the paper, and lined up the little bottles filled with potions on the shelf above the sink.

The next morning, boarding the plane, Kathryn was numb, hungover, drained of emotion. The chemical smell of her newly dyed hair was making her nauseous. As the plane lifted into the air, she watched Charlottesville recede into the larger patches of landscape, and it occurred to her that she was leaving not only a marriage but a definable identity. She might be going home, but it felt to her as if she was heading into new and unfamiliar territory. She didn't have a compass, a map, or even a decent sense of direction. She wasn't certain she would recognize herself.

AS THE PLANE starts its slow descent into Bangor, Kathryn feels a tap on her right shoulder. She turns to look. Through a crack between the narrow seats she can see a vaguely familiar man behind her.

"Kathryn?"

She nods.

"Jeez. This whole flight I've wondered if it was you," he says in a heavy Maine accent. When he smiles, the hard brightness of his teeth filling the bottom half of his face, she has a vague memory of high school. *High school.* He has wide hazel eyes, a straight nose and firm jaw, sandy brown hair. An athlete, she decides. Trip . . . Skip . . . Flip . . .

"Chip Sanborn," he says, offering his hand over the seat. "It's been ten years—can't blame you for forgetting."

"No, no, I knew. Of course," she murmurs quickly. His hand is as thick and smooth as a baseball mitt. "Chip Sanborn. How are you?"

He nods. "Couldn't be better."

"That's great."

"How about yourself?"

"Oh, I'm fine."

The final word lingers in the air, and he pauses for a moment, waiting to see if she'll continue. When she doesn't, he asks, "So what're you up to these days?"

Kathryn glances at the woman sitting beside Chip, who is studiously perusing the in-flight magazine. "I'm a reporter," she says. "Freelance." It isn't exactly true; she was an arts editor for a small weekly paper in Charlottesville, but she quit that job three weeks ago. "What about you?"

"I'm running my dad's paint store. Actually, we're calling it a home decorating center now. I was just at a home show in Atlantic City. People are really into fixing up their houses these days. Everybody's getting married, having babies—you know, the whole nineties nesting thing."

"Yeah," she says, "I read about it."

"So how's your brother doing?"

All at once, Kathryn remembers who Chip Sanborn was: the star of the Bangor High basketball team. Her brother, Josh, was a freshman when she and Chip were seniors. Josh sat on the bench for three miserable years. "He's fine," she says. "Josh."

"Josh. Still playing b-ball?"

"Um, not much, I don't think. He's living in New York, working as a mortgage broker. I don't see him very often. His hours are crazy."

"Good for him," says Chip. "Smart kid."

Kathryn smiles. She's beginning to feel as if she's making polite conversation with an uncle. "Yeah, well . . . We'll be landing soon, I guess. I'd probably better . . ." She makes a motion of turning around.

"I heard you got married a while back," he says. "To a grad student or something."

She feels her face flush. "Um-hmm. What about you?"

"Oh, me and Donna've been married for—jeez, it's almost six years."

"Wow," she says.

"You know Donna," he says, leaning forward. "Donna Murphy. She was in our class."

A memory flashes through Kathryn's head: a snowy Friday in 1986, a sweaty gymnasium, seconds to spare; Chip, star of the team, scoring the winning basket—*swish!*—against Bangor's rival, South Portland. Donna, the shortest one on the cheerleading squad, the one who always stands at the top of the human pyramid at pep rallies, rushes onto the court in front of the roaring crowd and smothers him with maroon-and-white pompons as he twirls her in the air. "Yes," Kathryn says. "How is she?"

"Oh, she's doing great. Has her hands full with our two little boys. Here, I've got a couple of pictures." He reaches into his back pocket, takes out his wallet, and flips it open for Kathryn to see.

Both kids in the photo have Chip's frank gaze and Donna's shiny blond hair. "They're adorable," Kathryn murmurs dutifully. All at once she's filled with dread at the idea of returning to Bangor. Here is Chip, self-satisfied, robust, with a stable marriage, two kids, and a prosperous business, treating her, she imagines, with a smug, pitying kindness—the way you might treat a starry-eyed adventurer who sets off in search of fame and fortune and comes home empty-handed. *We always knew you'd be back, and look!* his expression seems to say. *Here you are! What a shame, what a pity—and yet, how thoroughly predictable. . . .*

"So where're you and—I'm sorry, what's your husband's name?"

"Actually, Chip," she says, taking a deep breath, "I'm not married anymore."

"Oh," he says. "Jeez. I'm sorry."

"Don't be. I'm not."

"When did it happen?"

"About twelve hours ago."

"Oh, jeez," he says, reaching out and touching her shoulder. The woman beside him glances up, then looks back down at her magazine. His words fade, and Kathryn can feel the humming vibration of the slowing plane through her seat.

KATHRYN STEPS OFF the small plane and down the narrow steps onto the tarmac. The air is pleasant and warm, almost hot, and smells of the pines at the edge of the runway. Chip, just behind her, offers to lift one of her bulky carry-ons.

"I think I've got it," she says. She smiles, so as not to seem impolite.

"So," he says as they walk toward the terminal. "You going to the reunion?"

"Reunion?"

"Our ten-year reunion. I thought that might be why you were coming home."

"Oh—no." She feels that familiar dread rising up in her stomach. "I didn't even know about it."

"Didn't Daphne Cousins send you something in the mail?"

"I don't think so. But I've been kind of hard to reach."

"Well, it's not until the end of this month. You've got some time to think about it." He fumbles in his jacket with one hand and pulls out a business card, then slips it in her handbag. "If you want to go, I've got the info. Just give me a call."

"Okay. Thanks."

She can feel Chip looking over at her for a moment. Then he says, "I can understand why you might not want to go. Jennifer disappearing like that on graduation night kind of changes the way you think about high school, doesn't it? I know it does for me."

"Yeah," Kathryn says. She looks at him curiously. Does he mean it, or is it just something to say? He and Jennifer barely knew each other; they probably exchanged ten words during four years of high school.

He shakes his head. "It's just so . . . weird, you know? Poof. Gone." He balls his hand and then opens it, like a magician making a hand-kerchief vanish. "But heck," he continues, rallying, "it'd be a shame to let it ruin our reunion. Right? Right?"

"Right," she murmurs.

"It should be quite a party."

She nods. "Okay. Well. I'll think about it."

As they enter the building, Kathryn squints in the darkness. She can make out shadowy forms bobbing around, a sparse crowd. "Kath?" she hears from somewhere in the back.

"Mom?"

"Kathryn!" All at once she feels her mother's cool fingers touching her cheeks, pulling her into a quick embrace and then pushing her out to arm's length. "You look tired, sweetheart."

"I am tired," she says, dropping her bags. "But thanks for pointing it out."

"Oh darling, you're so *sensitive*." She smiles. "After all you've been through, is what I meant."

"Well, you look good." It's true. Her mother has just turned fifty-two, but she looks younger. Her short, highlighted hair is swept stylishly away from her face, which is tan and glowing. She's wearing jeans and white Reeboks, a deep green long-sleeved cotton shirt, and small gold hoops in her ears. "Matte lipstick, Mother—I'm impressed. Very 'in.' "

"Oh, you like it? The girl at the Clinique counter forced it on me." She fingers a strand of Kathryn's newly tinted hair. "Is red the 'in' color these days?"

"I don't know. Just thought I'd try something different."

"As long as you're making changes in your life."

"That was my thinking."

Her mother bends down over the bags. "Let me carry one of these." Kathryn urges her up. "I've got them. They're light."

"Now, look, I can handle it. Didn't I tell you I've been working out?" She stands up straight, hefting one bag like a barbell. "You're right—it is light."

"Hello, Mrs. Campbell!" Chip's outstretched hand emerges from behind Kathryn's shoulder.

Her mother reaches out and clasps it. "Let me see if I get this right: Skip Sanborn."

"Good memory," he says, "but it's Chip. You almost had it."

She beams. "Chip! Of course! So nice to see you. You know, I see signs for Sanborn Home Decorating all over the place these days."

"That's part of the new ad campaign I've been working on," he says, tilting his head modestly.

"I'm going over to wait for the rest of my bags," Kathryn mumbles, and tries to slip away. Her mother reaches out and holds her arm. "Darling, you remember Skip—Chip Sanborn. He has a decorating store. . . ." She squeezes Kathryn's arm lightly, an old code for "behave," and turns back to Chip. "It sounds like you're making a lot of changes over there."

"We sure are. And are you still doing interior design?"

"A little bit. Mostly real estate, these days."

He fishes around in his jacket and pulls out another card. "Well, I'll tell you what. Why don't you come on over to the store when you have a moment and let me show you around?"

"I'd like that." She smiles widely, just long enough, and takes the card. "Your father must be awfully proud of you, Chip."

"I don't know about that, Mrs. Campbell. But I think he appreciates the help."

"I'll bet he does. And call me Sally."

"Sally it is."

After he leaves, as they're walking over to the baggage carousel, Kathryn's mother turns to her and says, "You could be a little more friendly, dear. People might think you're rude."

"We went to high school together, Mother," Kathryn says, lifting two suitcases off the conveyor belt and loading them onto a cart. "He knows I'm rude." She wheels the cart into the lobby, out the automatic glass doors, and onto the sidewalk. "And anyway, I'm not in the best frame of mind for encountering local success stories." She pauses for a moment. "If there was ever a sign not to go to my high school reunion, I guess that's it."

"Oh, I forgot to tell you—you got some kind of letter about that. We're over here." Her mother motions toward a sporty silver Saturn parked illegally several yards down. "Well, it's silly to burn your bridges. You never know when you might need Chip Sanborn. He could be a very good business contact."

"For *what*?"

Her mother stops and faces her, one hand on her hip. "For me, maybe. Did you think of that?"

Kathryn shakes her head. "In fact, I did not think of that."

Her mother turns toward the car and unlocks the trunk. "I know it's hard for you to believe, Kathryn, but you and all your little friends are grown-ups now."

"No we're not, Mom," she says, heaving the bags in. "We just act like grown-ups every now and then to fool you."

"But that's what being grown-up is all about." Her mother pauses, a serene smile on her face. "Gosh, it's nice to have you home."

"Are you serious? We've been bickering since I got off the plane."

"This isn't bickering. This is classic mother-daughter communication. I've been reading up on it." She goes around to the driver's side and unlocks the door. "You have to learn to think of us as representatives of our generations instead of personalizing everything," she calls across the top of the car. "Now listen, honey. I've got a few little errands to do on the way home. They'll just take a minute, okay?"

What can she say? "Okay."

Her mother smiles brightly. "Good. Then we'll be taking the scenic route."

Bangor is a quiet place, a town of about thirty-five thousand people, the second-largest metropolitan area north of Portland. Even at midday, in the middle of the week in the middle of town, there is a quiet that blankets everything: the two-story, clapboard houses, the city bus making its slow, empty rounds, the low-lying malls that have multiplied like barnacles on the rough edges of town.

"So here we are," Kathryn's mother says lightly as they drive along, "mother and daughter, both of us divorced. Do you think it might be hereditary?"

Kathryn looks out at the flat, treeless expanse surrounding the airport. On one side of the long road that leads to the interstate lie several strip malls—low, boxy buildings with brand-name storefronts and fast-food islands in their parking lots. A few stores are new; others, their windows dark and empty, look recently abandoned. Their blankness makes her inexplicably sad.

It was twenty years ago, when Kathryn was eight, that she saw this town for the first time. She was riding in the cab of a sixty-foot-long moving van, sitting up on her knees to see over the dashboard. Her parents were following in the car behind; halfway through the interminable four-hour stretch of wilderness that led from Boston to Bangor, she convinced her father to let her ride with the two movers, her father's cousin, Patrick, and a coarse longshoreman named Gus, for the rest of the trip.

"Middle of fuckin' nowhere" was Gus's only comment as they began passing exits for the town. He stubbed a cigarette into the ashtray for emphasis.

"Long as there's a bar somewhere, it's okay with me," Patrick said.

"Oh, sure, there's a bar here. Has to be. Nothing else to do in a place like this but drink."

Gus lit another cigarette and Kathryn looked out at the few motels scattered along the highway like birds on a telephone wire. Every few miles they passed houses clustered around an overpass. The town of Bangor seemed to be mostly trees, the houses just a little oasis in a desert of forest. There weren't many cars on the road in either direction. The place looked unnaturally clean, as if someone had taken a scrubber and soaped it up, rinsed it down.

Kathryn's grandmother, who was born and raised in Bangor, had told her stories about the town—about what it was like before it had an airport, back when the train still came up from Portland, stopping along the way to pick up passengers and produce and dry goods. Heading south, the train carried potatoes from Fort Kent, blueberries from Cherryfield, raw lumber from the Maine woods. As a child her grandmother had sat in her bedroom window and watched the black smoke rise from the valley, closing her eyes to hear the slow-chugging train as it passed, the low haunt of the whistle.

"You crying?" Patrick asked Kathryn, peering at her closely.

She wiped her eyes. "I—It's just the smoke."

"Put your goddamn ciggy out, Gus, you're making the poor girl sick," Patrick said.

Gus looked at her sideways, then ground the butt into the dashboard and dropped it on the floor. "Can't take it, maybe she shouldn't be riding up here."

"Oh, relax. We're almost there, ya bully."

Kathryn sat very still between them, looking out at the gray road stretching ahead into oblivion, the gray sky, shoebox houses hunched forlornly against the hills, separated from the highway by chain-link fencing. She was sure they were going to the end of civilization. Her eyes began to water again, and she tried to choke back the tears.

"What grade you in?" Patrick asked kindly.

"Third."

"So you'll be going to a new school. Could be fun."

She shrugged. "I guess so."

"Ever been here before?"

"To visit my grandparents." She wiped her nose with the back of her hand. "But that was different."

He nods. "You knew you'd be leaving."

"Yeah," she said miserably.

He squinted out the side window. "I grew up in a place like this. It's not so bad. And it's not true you can't leave," he said, looking down at her. "You can, but you have to be headstrong to do it. Then again, you might come to like it. There's a lot to be said for living in a small town."

"Like what?" Gus said.

"People know you. There's such a thing called *neighbors*, Gus—ever heard of 'em? Take my word for it, they're a whole different breed than the vagrants and pimps that congregate on your street. When's the last time anyone brought you a tuna casserole?"

"I hate tuna casserole."

Patrick smiled down at Kathryn. "Well, then. It's a good thing old Gus here ain't moving to Bangor, Maine, now, isn't it?"

———

THEY STOP AT a light, and Kathryn's mother reaches over and squeezes her knee. "What's going on in that head of yours?"

She tries to pull her thoughts together. "It's funny being back."

"But you were just here a year ago."

"Not like this. Cowed and humiliated."

"Oh, Kathryn." Her mother laughs. "You're so dramatic. You should've pursued a career on the stage."

"I should've pursued a career, period."

Her mother purses her lips and looks at Kathryn sideways, cocking her head like a bird. Then she reaches out and touches her daughter's hand, where the gold ring shines on her finger. "You're still wearing this."

Kathryn retracts her hand.

"Don't you want to put it away?"

"One of these days."

"Closure is very important, sweetheart."

"All right, Mom. I'll get rid of it when I'm ready."

Her mother pauses, running her hands around the rim of the steering wheel. "You have to get on with it, Kathryn," she says finally. "Put that part of your life behind you. I know it's difficult, but—"

"I hear you," she says sharply.

The light turns green, and they drive along in silence. Kathryn watches the neighborhoods drift by, clusters of small white houses built in the thirties and forties shaded by leafy green trees, hanging low and full in the summer heat.

"You must be tired," her mother says in a clipped voice.

"Look, Mom, I'm sorry. I didn't mean to snap."

Her mother shrugs, a peacemaking gesture. "I was pressuring you."

"No, it's me. I'm just not handling this very well."

"There's no reason you should be," her mother says. She smiles. "I am glad you're home."

"Me, too," Kathryn says. She's not sure she is, but she says it anyway.

KATHRYN'S MOTHER STILL lives in the house that Kathryn grew up in, a white colonial with black shutters in a section of town called Little City, a residential neighborhood of oaks and maples surrounding a large rectangular island of green, well-kept park. The most impressive houses in Little City are great white confections with elegant slate roofs and full-length windows that line a broad street sloping down toward the river. The Campbell house, several blocks over, is modest in comparison. When Kathryn was growing up, their neighbors were young families and retired couples who puttered together in their flower gardens on summer mornings and sat on clean-swept porches all afternoon, alternately dozing and keeping a lookout for trouble. Not that there was any; the closest Taft Street came to excitement was when two men moved into a house together and built a deck, visible from the street, where they sunbathed in Speedos and massaged each other with tanning oil.

Like most houses in the neighborhood, the Campbells' was built in the twenties. It has a deep wooden porch, large living and dining room windows, and an original cedar-and-red-brick fireplace. When the Campbells first moved to Bangor from Boston, Kathryn would sit on the wooden porch swing in midafternoon and close her eyes, breathing in the clean pine scent of the hedges separating their property from the next-door neighbors', listening to the muted hum and swish of cars going by on Center Street, a block away. Sometimes her mother would come out on the porch and sit down on the swing with her, rocking back and forth with her foot. After a while she'd say, "You know, Kath, this is exactly how I grew up. Sitting on a porch swing, waiting for something to happen. Just sitting and waiting. Exactly like this."

Kathryn has heard all the stories, all the family lore. Her grandfather, John Lefebvre, a French Canadian, migrated to Maine in 1928 because he'd been told that anybody who works hard in America can become a success. As it turned out, in his case the hard work consisted of marrying Kathryn's grandmother, Alice, the caustic daughter of a wealthy Bangor banker, and becoming an apprentice to her father, who eventually passed on all of his knowledge and money to his son-in-law. Until his death in 1970, John Lefebvre never missed a day of work. Every day for forty years, he left the house at precisely eight-fifteen in the morning for the bank building on Main Street and returned at exactly five-forty-five in the afternoon, wearing a black fedora and a mustache that faded from black to white but never changed shape.

For fifteen years, from the late thirties to the early fifties, Kathryn's grandmother wrote a column for the *Bangor Daily News* called "Opinions," most of which were hers. She wrote about everything from books to fashion to politics, occasionally outraging an upstanding citizen, which amused and excited her. "Oh, look!" she'd say, brandishing a letter. "Delightful! Somebody else has got an opinion, too!" Her acid wit was put to constructive use in her column, but it was often, unfortunately, turned on her daughter Sally, an only child, burning her and making her wary. "Your mother is a nice girl, but she needs to learn to stand up for herself," Alice confided to Kathryn tartly one time, after she'd compared her daughter's hairstyle to a certain breed of dog and Sally had left the room in tears.

When Kathryn's mother was eighteen she left for Boston College, where she met Kathryn's father, Mike, a scholarship student. He lived in Irish South Boston in a fifth-floor walk-up; his father worked on the docks, unloading fish and dry goods in the grimy darkness of early morning while most of the city slept. Mike aspired to be an accountant, and he took classes during the day and toiled on the docks at night. When he came to pick up Sally for dates, his work clothes would often be in the backseat of the car, smelling of the sea. That smell, and the exhaustion on his face mixed with grim determination, convinced her that he possessed something she needed: a kind of certainty, an uncomplicated desire for what she took for granted. So she dropped out of college six months shy of graduating and married him.

They settled in Boston, Kathryn was born, and when John Lefebvre died—of a heart attack on the way to the office, so the story went, his black fedora wedged on his head and his white shirt buttoned to the top—Alice, up in Bangor, began making noises about being all alone. It was Mike, finally, who convinced Kathryn's mother that they should move to Maine. Boston, he said, was full of accountants. In Bangor he could afford the big house he'd always dreamed of: white, with black shutters and a red front door.

"DID YOU TELL your father you were coming home?" her mother asks Kathryn at dinner, several hours after the flight. They are seated at their usual places at the walnut table in the kitchen, Kathryn in the middle and her mother at one end. A mat set at her brother Josh's customary place holds a sweating bottle of white wine and the dinner her mother has prepared in advance, a curried chicken salad and cold artichokes.

"Yes," Kathryn says. She had called him several months ago to let him know about her breakup with Paul and that she'd be in Maine this summer, though she didn't tell him exactly when. Her father had never taken to Paul; the first time he met him, a month before their wedding, he told Kathryn he thought Paul was pretentious. "That boy didn't deserve you," he said bluntly when she told him she was filing for divorce. "Now you can get on with your life."

Kathryn has never been close to her father, even before he left her mother for his secretary and moved to a neighboring town. He wasn't around much when she was growing up. Her mother always said it was his work—he was trying to build a business, she said, putting in long hours to support the family—but months before he announced he was leaving, Kathryn suspected something. When he finally told them about Margaret, Kathryn mainly felt relief. At least now they knew for sure.

"Don't you need to let him know you're here?" her mother says.

"I'll give him a ring tomorrow. How's Grandma Alice?" she asks.

"Oh, pretty good, considering," her mother says. She squeezes a lemon wedge over her artichoke. "They're friendly to her over there, which drives her crazy, but other than that she seems fairly content."

"Does she know I'm in town?"

"Sure she knows."

"Maybe I'll drop by and see her tomorrow morning."

"Whenever you feel like it," she says. "There's no rush. She's not going anywhere."

"But I *want* to see her."

Her mother shrugs. "Okay, then see her."

Kathryn feels the air between them cool, and all at once an irritation toward her mother rises in her. She can't remember a time when her mother and Grandma Alice weren't engaged in some kind of petty squabble. When Kathryn was in high school she used to get involved, mediating between them, ferrying messages back and forth across the gulf of misunderstandings and wounded feelings, but after a while she realized it made little difference. She has always liked Grandma Alice; she finds her funny and clever and dry. Her mother's small grudges annoy her.

"What's going on with you two now?" Kathryn says.

"Oh, nothing really. I won't bore you with it. Although I do think she gets crabbier as she gets older." She flashes Kathryn a glance. "Now that I think about it, I guess it's a good idea for you to stop by. It might take some of the pressure off me."

"I'll just show you up, for being a bad daughter," Kathryn says.

"Ah," her mother says with a wry smile, "but I still win. For being a good mother, and raising you."

LATER THAT EVENING, after they've finished the dishes and her mother has gone upstairs to read, Kathryn sits on the front porch by herself with the lights off, listening to the rustling of the thick-leafed maples that line the sidewalk. She wonders, as she does every time she comes home, what has become of her remaining friends from high school: Will, Brian, Rachel, and Jack. In high school she would never have imagined they'd go years without speaking. But Jennifer's disappearance changed everything. It was like a chemical explosion: a sudden flash, a terrible trauma, and then the insidious, debilitating poison of fallout.

At first, in the weeks after it happened, the group had been closer than ever, up early every morning to join search teams and copy flyers and cover the phones. But as summer passed without any word, only Jennifer's brother, Will, was able to maintain the intensity. And the guilt and shame the rest of them felt for not sticking around, for going on with their lives, for not finding her, made it impossible to look each other in the eye. At some point, Kathryn thinks now, though they wouldn't admit it out loud, each of them had given up on her, and in doing so they broke their implied promise of loyalty and constancy; they betrayed the group.

And then something else began to happen: They started to wonder, quietly, behind each other's backs, whether one of them knew something he or she wasn't saying about the disappearance. They looked into each other's eyes for clues and quickly looked away, each aware of what the others were doing. At the very least, one of them might be keeping a secret. Who was it? What did that one know?

As the years passed, it became harder and harder to see each other. There could be no closure as long as Jennifer was missing; any conversation they had seemed meaningless unless it was about her, but there was nothing to say. So they stopped talking. When they ran into each other, their behavior was false and perfunctory, like lovers whose affair has ended badly. They had shared too much; they knew each other too well, which made the exchange of pleasantries irrelevant and anything else painful.

They never spoke about the rift. They let it happen, and felt powerless to stop it. They stopped confiding in each other and found different friends. And slowly, over time, they changed, or grew apart: Kathryn stayed in Virginia after college and got married, Will came out of the closet and moved to Boston, Brian settled in Portland, Rachel got caught up in her graduate work at the University of Maine, Jack threw himself into his job at the *Bangor Daily News*. In the end, letting go of each other was a relief, an escape from the fear and suspicion and increasing hopelessness, a deep dive into anonymity.

Sitting on the porch, Kathryn watches an older woman and her dog making their way down the street, two shadowy figures under the street-lamps. The dog zigzags back and forth, its tail wagging, sniffing the trees on either side. As the woman nears, Kathryn can see it's a neighbor, someone she vaguely recognizes.

She stops in front of the house. "Is that you, Kathryn?" the neighbor asks.

"Yes."

"Well, what do you know! It's Mrs. Adams."

"Oh, hello," Kathryn says, getting up. Mrs. Adams was the librarian at Mary Snow, her elementary school.

"Home for a visit?"

"Maybe longer. I'm not exactly sure."

"Really? That's wonderful. You and your husband thinking of moving up here?"

She hesitates. "No."

"Oh." Mrs. Adams's voice fades, and the dog continues down the street. "You know," she says after a moment, "my husband died last year." Kathryn starts to say she's sorry, but the old woman waves her hand dismissively. "It's all right. I'm learning to live without him. It's not easy, but that's what you do, isn't it? You just go on."

"Do you?" Kathryn asks absurdly. She seems so sure.

"Oh, yes. Takes time, is all. You'll see."

"I believe you," Kathryn says, the same thing she used to say when her mother said there were no monsters under the bed. *I believe you*—wanting the words and her certainty to make it true.

Despite the pleasant coolness and the quiet, Kathryn sleeps fitfully her first night home. She wakes with a start from a nightmare—falling or being pushed off a ledge into darkness—and looks at the clock: 10:00 A.M.

Her mother, she knows, has been up for hours.

Lying in bed, Kathryn can hear her downstairs on the phone, telling someone about a piece of property on Union Street, a little house just perfect for newlyweds or retirees. Kathryn stretches, wondering what that means. Too small, presumably, for children; too large for one person. But why too large? How could a small house be too large? She must be talking to one half of a couple, Kathryn decides, probably an older couple, about to retire, and she's flattering them with the reference to newlyweds—new lives, hopeful and in love. Kathryn throws back the covers. She hears her mother hang up the phone.

The late-morning air is threaded through with warmth. At the open window the white cotton curtains slide in and out, a slow dance. Kathryn watches for a while, looking beyond to the broad, flat leaves of the maple, deep midsummer green, whispering and shushing each other. The whole room seems suddenly alive. When she was little, her walls were covered with daisies, four fields of them stretching back, and in the early morning she would imagine that the stalks were in motion, swaying all around her, swaying with the curtains and the maple leaves, while she lay on her meadow of bed, perfectly safe, perfectly still.

After a few minutes Kathryn gets up, throws on some shorts, and starts to go downstairs. In front of Josh's room, she pauses. The door is slightly ajar. She pushes it with one hand and looks inside. The room is just as it was when Josh left for college seven years ago: the sky-blue walls plastered with a huge poster of Magic Johnson leaping through the air, another of the Fine Young Cannibals, a maroon-and-gold Boston College banner, a hand-lettered pep-rally poster that says GO RAMS! ALL THE WAY TO THE PLAYOFFS! An ancient Macintosh computer with a tiny screen sits on his neatly arranged desk.

For a while after their father walked out on them, Josh and Kathryn had spent a lot of time together. They stayed close to home, ostensibly reading and watching TV, but really keeping an eye on their mother as she tried to piece together a life for the three of them after the divorce. But eventually the strain of that became too much. "I'm sick of worrying about her," Josh told Kathryn. "I can't live this way." He became methodical and disciplined; he started going to the library to do his homework after school and, though not a natural athlete, threw himself into sports. Kathryn felt the same, but her anxiety manifested itself differently. She spent hours at Jennifer's house, began smoking pot, went to keg parties down nameless dirt roads when her mother thought she was spending the night with a friend—anything to avoid coming home to that quiet house soaked in their mother's sadness.

The difference in ages between Kathryn and Josh was like dog years in high school; the three grades that separated them might as well have been decades. When Kathryn left home, the divide only widened. Josh grew more conservative as he got older, joining the Young Republicans in college and eventually becoming president of the club. Meanwhile, Kathryn was living in a group house in Washington, D.C., subsisting on tofu stir-frys and working for one left-wing cause after another. When Josh moved to New York and became a mortgage broker and she returned to Charlottesville for graduate school in English, the distance between them seemed too great to bridge.

It had been years now since one of them picked up the phone to call the other without a birthday or national holiday as an excuse. Kathryn didn't even tell Josh about her divorce—she knew her mother would do it, and she wasn't in the mood to explain her personal life to this brother she hardly knew anymore. She was sure that Josh—who dated only model types and lived in a modern high-rise on the Upper East Side and once said he found what he called her "starving artist shtick" utterly incomprehensible—would be less than understanding about what she was going through. But one night about a month ago she came home to a phone message from him that caught her by surprise. "I just heard," he said. "I'm sorry. I may not be there, but I'm here for you. I mean that." They played phone tag for a while and that was the end of it, but it was nice to know that he cared enough to call.

Kathryn straightens a picture on the wall—a cheaply framed photo of the Bangor High basketball team, with Josh's head half obscured by somebody taller—and leaves the room, pulling the door shut behind her. Then she makes her way downstairs to the kitchen, where she pours herself a cup of coffee from the Thermos her mother has filled. Sitting at the round breakfast table, she leafs through the *Bangor Daily News*. The paper is a microcosm of the town: old-fashioned Yankee conservatism, homegrown rural pragmatism, liberal intellectualism (reflecting the influence of the state university in Orono, ten miles up the road), and a dash of hippie utopianism, which dwindled in the eighties but now seems stronger than ever, under the guise of New Age. Thumbing through the pages, Kathryn notices that the paper has jazzed up its headings, adding computer graphics and color, changing the Women's Page to a more inclusive Style section.

"Good morning," her mother says cheerfully. She's come in from the back wearing thick gardening gloves, a dirty apron, and an acid-green visor.

"You're out there early." Kathryn closes the paper.

"It's not so early anymore," she says, glancing at the clock. "But I've been in the garden off and on since six-thirty. It's age."

Kathryn grins. "You're not *that* old."

"I think it has something to do with menopause. I get up earlier every year." Her mother peels off her gloves and takes off the visor, then fluffs her hair. "Whoo. It's really warming up." She goes over to the counter and pours herself some coffee. "Been up long?"

"Not really. I had these awful dreams. How's the garden?" Picking up a pen, Kathryn begins drawing daisy chains around the headlines on the front page.

"Oh, I'll tell you, Kath, I get the most satisfaction from it." She sits down and takes little sips of her coffee. "The irises are flourishing, and even the clematis is beginning to bloom. Last month I dug in some horse manure, and it's made a big difference. You have to come out back and let me give you a tour."

"Sure," she says. For some reason her mother's forced cheeriness, especially in the morning, often has the effect of making her grumpy and monosyllabic.

Her mother sighs with exaggerated contentment. "You know what? Honestly? I don't know if you've come to this realization yet, but being single is really all right. You have so much time to do what you want. Marriage can be so limiting."

"Umm." Kathryn adds stems and leaves to some of the larger daisies.

"In fact, I may never get married again. Who knows? When I divorced your father, I was just starting to figure out what I wanted. Like, remember how your dad always wanted vanilla-bean ice cream in those big square containers, never any other flavor, just boring vanilla bean? Well, I didn't realize until he left that I don't even like vanilla bean. Quite frankly, I detest it." She shakes her head. "Can you imagine, all those years of putting up with vanilla bean when I could've been eating a flavor I liked?"

Kathryn looks up. A headache is starting to take shape behind her ears. "You didn't have to eat it, Mom," she says stubbornly. "You could've bought your own ice cream."

"But that's just the point," her mother says, leaning forward. "I didn't know that I deserved to have what I wanted. And you know why? Because I thought your father was right about everything." She sits back. "Boy, was I wrong!"

"So what's your favorite flavor now?"

"I don't have a favorite flavor," she says breezily. "I pick and choose. I switch around."

Kathryn nods, coloring in the daisy petals. Now they're black-eyed Susans.

"Hey," her mother says. "I forgot to tell you. Linda Pelletier and her husband, Ralph What's-his-name, moved to Florida a couple of months ago, and their house is on the market."

Kathryn puts down the pen. Linda Pelletier is Will and Jennifer's mother. "What?"

"I think they just got sick of being here. Too much water under the bridge. Anyway, they're gone now, and I'm showing their house. In fact, I need to go over there in a little while to air the place out. Do you want to come?"

"I can't believe they just *left*," Kathryn mumbles.

"Oh, honey, you can't blame them. All the memories and everything, it must have been torture. I'm sure we have no idea."

Kathryn knows the house well—a large, ramshackle Victorian on Lamott Street. Growing up, she spent countless hours at the Pelletiers'; the house was as familiar to her as her own. After her parents divorced, when she was twelve, and her family dissolved into enemy camps, she often sought refuge there. It was so different from her house, where there were strict rules about homework and television and junk food and chores. The twins' mother never seemed to care what they did, as long as they weren't too loud and didn't cause trouble.

For a while, from the outside at least, the Pelletiers had seemed like the perfect all-American family. The twins' father, Pete, was a Rotarian who played first base in the local men's softball league; their mother was a former Miss Penobscot County. Even as babies, Will and Jennifer were unusually beautiful and good-natured, winning the Best Baby contest at the Maine State Fair when they were two. But Kathryn had witnessed the fights behind closed doors, the mother's secretiveness, the father's drinking. She was spending the night when the news came that Pete had been killed in a car crash. Everything seemed to unravel after that. By the time Jennifer disappeared, the family had already broken apart.

"What do they want for the house?" Kathryn asks her mother now.

"One seventy-five."

"Isn't that a lot?"

"Actually, it's not outrageous for that street. I'll sell it before the summer's out." Her mother stands up and puts her hands on her hips. "I love this job, Kath. I'm damn good at it."

"It sure sounds like it." She smiles, amused at her mother's bravado.

Her mother smiles back. "I'm going to run upstairs and change," she says. She gives Kathryn a once-over. "You might want to, too."

TURNING ONTO A wide, well-kept street of enormous old residences set back from the road, Kathryn's mother slows in front of a white corner house with a turret. The grass is long and the shutters are closed, but flowers in pots along the walkway bloom as if they've been recently planted.

"Pete Pelletier put his heart into this place," Kathryn's mother says as she pulls into the driveway. "That's why it's in such good shape, even after ten years without much care. He rebuilt the foundation and installed a new boiler and fixed the roof." She puts the car in park and takes the key out of the ignition. "After he died, Linda used the money to put in a new kitchen, but she didn't do much else. It's just as well that she's selling it now, before it falls into serious disrepair." Opening her door and getting out, she motions for Kathryn to follow.

Kathryn knows all about Will and Jennifer's father—his tragic, thwarted life and early death. It had been his dream to become an attorney, but when Linda found out she was pregnant the summer after they graduated from Bangor High, and they got married and had twins, it was all he could do to get through college. When he became an insurance agent and started doing pretty well, he brought up law school again, but Linda discouraged him. "You're making a lot of money now," she reasoned. "If you go back to school we'll never see you. Don't you think you owe it to the kids to be around while they're growing up?"

So he stopped talking about law school and instead, when he and Linda were twenty-four and the twins were six, bought the dilapidated Victorian on a tree-lined street—a fixer-upper with a lot of potential, the real-estate agent opined as they signed the contract. The house and the family became his project. Evenings and weekends when Kathryn was over he'd be up on the roof, painting the kitchen, wallpapering the hall, fixing screen doors, and adding shelves and closets. He led Will's Boy Scout troop, took the kids on nature hikes, built a tree house in the backyard. Linda got a closetful of clothes, and they all went to Disneyland on vacation. But there was something about Pete that none of them could reach. He read the paper avidly and was hooked on all the local trials. Sometimes he went down to the courthouse to watch the trial lawyers at work in their sharp blue suits with their snap-front briefcases and eager assistants. Instead of bedtime stories, he told his children about the landmark cases of the century, the Scopes monkey debate, the Rosenberg fiasco, the Nuremberg trials. He knew many of the prosecutorial arguments by heart.

The twins' mother did as little work around the house as possible. She hadn't wanted to buy it in the first place; she'd wanted something new. She wasn't handy, she said, and besides, she had asthma; all that paint and dust filled up her lungs. "Can you hear him in there, banging away?" she'd ask Kathryn, dragging on a cigarette. "That noise is giving me a headache."

It's funny, Kathryn thinks now, that Linda didn't move after Pete was killed, given how she felt about the house. And even stranger that when she remarried, her new husband just moved in. Pete's death had been ruled an accident, but the rumor around town had been that it was a suicide—a desperate act by a man who had just found out his wife was having an affair and planned to leave him. Ironically, as it turned out, his death merely hastened the process—Linda Pelletier quietly married her lover just four months later.

Linda Pelletier had always been different from the other mothers—restless, unpredictable, moody. Often when Kathryn came by she'd be sitting on the front porch with a couple of teenage girls from the neighborhood, smoking cigarettes. She was still young herself; she'd been eighteen when she gave birth to the twins prematurely, and she considered herself a teenager well into her twenties. Other mothers in pastel sweatsuits and no-nonsense perms walked sedately by with their kids in strollers, waving at Linda as she sat painting her nails on the porch. Linda would be the first one in the neighborhood out sunbathing after a long, cold winter, the weak sun shining down on her and snow melting on the ground, a bottle of coconut tanning oil at her side.

When Linda was young, her hair had been as white-blond as her childrens'; now she tinted it that shade. She retained her cheerleader's figure by dancing in the living room with the music turned up full blast. She seemed happiest when she was dancing; she'd put in a cassette of Michael Jackson or John Cougar and get into a Danskin leotard and jerk around frenetically with her eyes closed to the thumping beat of the bass. When they were little, Jennifer and Will had danced with her, but as they grew older they became aware of how little she seemed to notice them while she was dancing, how little she seemed to care. So they pulled back. After a while, it was hard for them even to watch her.

The dancing never lasted long. At some point Linda would collapse on the couch, gasping for breath, and Will or Jennifer would run into the kitchen to rummage for one of the inhalers she kept around the house. All the while that they were growing up, the twins knew their mother wasn't well. The severe asthma she'd had as a child had left her with badly damaged lungs and a weak constitution, which the cigarettes didn't help. She took naps most afternoons; some days she didn't get out of bed at all. Often she didn't have the energy to make dinner, so as soon as they could reach the stove top standing on a stool, Will and Jennifer began doing it themselves—Hamburger Helper and Chef Boy-ardee and frozen pot pies. They'd bring trays of food up to their mother's bedroom, where as often as not she'd turn her face to the wall, motioning for them to take the food away.

Linda Pelletier idolized Will; she called him her little man. When she was sick and in bed she'd call weakly for him—"Will? Will?"—her voice trailing down the stairs to where he and Jennifer and Kathryn would be doing homework at the kitchen table.

"You'd better go up there," Jennifer would say.

"I don't want to."

"You have to."

"I don't want to," he'd say fiercely.

"Go to Mommy, little man," Jennifer said, scornful and jealous.

Will would drag his feet up the stairs to the room where his mother lay. Sitting there in silence with Jennifer, Kathryn almost believed she could hear Linda's labored breathing, the catch in her breath that meant her lungs were full of fluid.

Will and Jennifer both inherited the condition from their mother, and were in and out of the hospital as infants. By the time they reached middle school, Will seemed to have outgrown it completely, and Jennifer was fine as long as she carried an inhaler (though, loath to use it as a ploy for pity as her mother did, she kept it a secret from most people at school). Still, Kathryn could remember times when Jennifer had been so sick that the fear in the air was palpable. Soon after they became friends, in the fourth grade, Kathryn had come over with a get-well plate of cookies and the twins' mother let her go up to Jennifer's room to say hello. As she climbed the stairs, she could hear the hiss of the humidifier and Jennifer's loud, jagged breathing. Standing at the door of the darkened bedroom, heavy with steam, Kathryn watched Jennifer's father smear Vicks VapoRub over her narrow, fluttering ribs. When Jennifer turned and caught her eye, she whispered, "Don't tell anybody." It was a moment Kathryn would never forget.

KATHRYN AND HER mother make their way up the path, under a huge, splaying elm that shades the side porch and half of the yard. "This tree has gotten so big," Kathryn murmurs. Looking up into the branches, she sees a scar made by a rope swing she remembers from years ago.

Her mother takes a ring of keys, like an oversized charm bracelet, out of her bag. "I'll have to get them to trim some branches before we show the place. It cuts out light."

"I like the shade," Kathryn says. "It makes the house so private."

"Light is a major selling point," her mother says.

"Did you talk to Linda before she left?" Kathryn asks, changing the subject.

"Not much. Just logistics. I'll be going through Will for any negotiations."

"Really?" she says, surprised. "Where is he?"

"I thought you'd know that," her mother says, glancing back at her. "He's still in Boston, practicing law. Some gay-rights stuff, from what I've heard." Jangling the keys, she tries one after another in the lock in the massive door.

"Have you spoken to him?"

"Not yet. I have his number, though. If you want it."

"Okay," Kathryn says, keeping her voice neutral. She's not sure that she does.

The door opens inward, and they step into the dark hallway. "Here we are," her mother says. She pulls back the shutters and opens the windows. Light filtering through the trees touches the carpet. "Come on," she says grandly, like the lady of the house. "I'll show you around."

"I think I know the way," Kathryn says. Leaving her mother behind opening shutters, she wanders through the empty rooms.

All traces of the Pelletiers are gone, save the faint outlines of pictures and mirrors on faded wallpaper. The house seems less grand than Kathryn remembers, though she knows from her mother's real estate training course that unfurnished rooms always appear smaller. She walks through the living room, with its dark wood floors and bay window, to the olive-green dining room to the blindingly white kitchen. This is the one room that Linda Pelletier designed from top to bottom, and her vision is evident in each gleaming detail: the gold drawer pulls, the shiny linoleum, the starburst crystal light fixture hanging over a phantom table. Kathryn runs her hand along the Formica countertop, remembering how obsessive Linda had been about keeping it clean. She was constantly brushing off crumbs, spraying Fantastik and rubbing it in circles, scolding the twins to put their dishes in the dishwasher. "I think she'd be happy if we didn't eat here at all," Will had groused to Kathryn one time as his mother wiped around him.

Walking up the stairs to the second floor, looking out the long windows at the patchy grass and unruly hedges in the broad expanse of yard, Kathryn thinks about how many times she's done this—let herself into the house and then made her way unnoticed up to Jennifer's room. At the door, though, Kathryn always knocked. Jennifer was very private, and anyway she usually locked her door.

Kathryn had always loved hanging out at the Pelletiers'. She and the twins played cards and Monopoly and Scrabble and watched *Little House on the Prairie* on the small red black-and-white in Jennifer's room, or sat on the back porch doing the crossword and the anagram and reading the funnies out loud to each other. They made batches of brownies and ate all the batter. It was in the Pelletiers' attic that Kathryn smoked her first cigarette, and then her first joint.

With Will and Jennifer, Kathryn had often felt like the single friend of a sophisticated married couple who keep her around to amuse them. Part of it was that they were both so striking: white-blond hair as fine as corn silk, light-blue eyes, small regular features. In the summer their skin was smoothly tan, like wet white sand. Kathryn, who was freckled and pale and had hair the color of a murky puddle, somehow felt enhanced by association—which was strange, she realized; usually around such attractive people she felt diminished. But Will and Jennifer seemed to care so little about their appearance. Like old money, their looks were just a given.

The twins were smart and subversive and cool, with a ready wit and a mischievous glint in their eyes. When Kathryn was with them, she felt sharper and stronger, emboldened by their glamorous insouciance. With the two of them she did things she wouldn't have dreamed of doing alone: sneaking out of the house when she was supposed to be asleep, convincing a gullible bouncer at the Bounty that she'd left her ID at home, skipping a day of school with a transparent excuse and going to Bar Harbor.

In high school the twins had been effortlessly popular. Will was humble and friendly but also sure of himself, and, through some combination of confidence and obliviousness, unconcerned with what people thought. Though less outgoing than her brother, Jennifer could be equally charming. She mocked her imagined awkwardness, cultivating a sense of herself that was so much at odds with who she was that it was impossible to take seriously, but had the effect, intentional or not, of evaporating envy.

Although they looked alike, the twins were in many ways opposites. They seemed to share different halves of the same personality. Will liked to be with people, and Jennifer, shy by comparison and somewhat melancholy, preferred to spend long stretches of time alone. Kathryn guessed it was this character trait that made her closer to Jennifer: They spent long, quiet afternoons together talking; they found comfort in their shared solitude. They told each other intimate secrets—not about the facts of their lives, Kathryn realized later, but about how they felt about them. Kathryn knew, for example, how hurt Jennifer was that her mother seemed to favor Will; Jennifer knew all about Kathryn's father's betrayal. Even at the time, these moments together seemed rare and special; the intimacy felt to Kathryn like a gift. It seemed that these secrets they shared with each other were the most important ones they had.

But sometime during senior year, Jennifer began holding back. There was never any discussion about it; Kathryn just felt her withdrawing by degrees. It was so subtle that for a while Kathryn told herself she must be imagining it. Jennifer wasn't becoming more diffident or remote; Kathryn was just clinging to this friendship out of a fear of the unknown—of graduating from high school, leaving home, going away to college. She didn't want to admit to herself that Jennifer might be pulling away, so she pretended it wasn't happening. Later she recognized this as a self-protective impulse; she'd learned from painful experience during her parents' divorce that knowing too much could be worse than not knowing anything. So she was willfully ignorant, and this ignorance haunted her when Jennifer disappeared and no one seemed to have the slightest idea why.

Now, stepping into Jennifer's room, Kathryn looks around at the peeling pink wallpaper with its faint floral pattern, the grungy hot-pink carpeting, the row of skeletal coat hangers in the otherwise empty closet. The last time Kathryn had been in this house was a week before she left for college. She remembers it well: Will pale and tense, with dark hollows under his eyes, his mother chain-smoking on the front porch, clutching cigarette after cigarette with nervous fingers. For over two months Will had been in charge of the volunteers who were trying to find Jennifer, and they'd turned up exactly nothing. Kathryn fumbled through a good-bye, but she didn't know what to say, and he, distracted, barely noticed. It had gotten so that whenever she tried to talk to him, she felt false, and she hated herself. It wasn't that she had stopped caring—it was that her caring felt so inadequate. It couldn't bring Jennifer back, and it couldn't dull Will's pain. So after the shock, the disbelief, the heart-clamping two and a half months of waiting to hear, Kathryn went away to a new life, relieved to be leaving. Will stayed behind, organizing search parties, tacking up posters, writing legislators and congresspeople, asking for something, anything, in the way of help.

When she telephoned from college, Will's voice was tired and defeated. He rarely called her; he said it always seemed as if he was interrupting something. And it got harder and harder for her to call him. She'd sit on her bed in her sterile dorm room, listening to his listless voice as she watched her roommate get ready to go out to a party, the sounds of guys playing hackeysack drifting up from the courtyard below. It felt as if her life had been split in two. After a while she stopped calling and began sending postcards instead, and then, eventually, she stopped writing, too, not knowing what effect it had on him, feeling only the monumental numbness that had crept in like a fog and settled over all of them when Jennifer disappeared.

"I think that's enough," Kathryn's mother calls up the stairs. "There's a cross-breeze. Where are you?"

"I'm in here," she says. "Just a moment." She starts to cry, and then she stops herself. Jennifer is gone. Words can't express the enormity of the loss. No story can contain it. Her absence is a presence, ghostly and haunting, touching all who knew her. It is impossible that she disappeared, inconceivable that she will never return. She is at once nowhere and everywhere, a constant shadow, elusory and insubstantial, her life an unkept promise, a half-remembered dream.

Kathryn's grandmother is seated in a wheelchair in the main living room of the Oak Bluff Retirement Home when Kathryn arrives.

"Grandma Alice?" Kathryn calls across the room, and the old woman looks up, the glare from the overhead light reflecting in her glasses. She is wearing a blue-striped dress, flesh-colored support hose, and dainty powder-blue nylon slippers, her thin legs splayed slightly on the metal footrests. Her wispy gray hair is haloed around her head.

"Kathryn," she says in a shrill voice, holding up a folded newspaper. "Just in time. What's a five-letter word for 'streetwalker'?"

"Streetwalker?" Kathryn says, coming toward her. "Whore, I guess."

"W-H-O-R-E." Her grandmother bends over the crossword, carefully filling in the blanks with a pencil. She looks up. "I had 'hussy.' This seems to fit better. But it is a rather ghastly word, isn't it?"

"Who makes up these crosswords, anyway?"

"I don't know. Perhaps I should fire off a letter to the paper about it."
She sets the crossword in her lap. "Of course, I write a letter about once a
week for some reason or other. I can just imagine the dread in that office
every time an envelope with my shaky handwriting comes in."

"You keep them on their toes, Grandma."

"And they need it, too. Who else but someone like me has the time
to mess with them?" She looks up at Kathryn, squinting into the fluorescent light. "You're looking a little tired, my dear."

She sighs. "I know. Mom's already pointed that out."

"So I don't need to mention the hair," she says. "Red's not really
your color, you know."

"Well, that makes two things that you and Mom agree on."

"That's because it's not opinion, dear; it's fact." Grandma Alice leans
forward. "The divorce is final?"

"Yep. I'm a single woman now, Grandma, just like you."

She sticks out her chin. "Too bad. I always liked Paul. But I suppose
what I liked about him was probably what made him a bad husband."

"Oh, really?" Kathryn moves behind her wheelchair. "Want to go out
on the porch?"

"In, out, whatever." She folds her hands in her lap and Kathryn
wheels her outside. "He was quite a flirt, wasn't he?"

"Did he flirt with you, Grandma?"

She cranes her neck to look up at Kathryn, and grins. "Outrageously."

Kathryn wheels her over to a spot in the shade near several old
women sitting in wicker chairs, fanning themselves.

One of them nods. "Hello, Alice."

"Hello, Mary, Joan," she says.

"Lovely day, isn't it?"

"A little hot for my taste," Joan says, making a face.

"Is this your granddaughter here?" Mary asks.

"Yes, it is. Say hello, Kathryn."

This is an old joke between them. "Hello, Kathryn," Kathryn says.

Grandma Alice looks up and smiles, and then pinches her arm, hard, on the inside. "We just came over to say hello. We're going over here." She points to an empty corner of the porch.

When they're safely out of earshot, Kathryn says, "I can't believe you *pinched* me, Grandma."

"Did I ask to be set over there? Gawd. Those two will talk your ear off."

Kathryn sits down in a white chair opposite her. "So, do you have any friends here, or are you rude to everyone?"

She narrows her eyes. "I'm not rude. It's just my personality." Sitting up straight, she primly smooths her blouse. "And yes, I do have friends. Selectively."

"So you're not lonely, then."

"Of course I'm lonely sometimes," she says. "Everyone who's alone gets lonely—it's inevitable. But I'd rather be lonely than have to chitchat with frivolous old ladies." She gives Kathryn a shrewd look. "Of course, it's much harder when you're accustomed to companionship. You're pretty lonely these days, I'd wager."

"I don't know," Kathryn says. "I don't know what I'm feeling. I'm just kind of numb."

"Well, that's all right."

"No it isn't." She leans back and closes her eyes, the heels of her hands against her temples. "It's humiliating. Paul has a life."

"And so do you."

"No I don't. I'm alive. I'm breathing. That's the most you can say for me."

"Here we go, Kathryn feeling sorry for herself. . . ."

"Grandma, I'm just facing reality. I came home because I didn't know what else to do."

"And what's wrong with that? You've been through a mess. You need some time to relax."

"I don't want to relax. I want to get on with my life."

"For God's sake, girl, take the pressure off," she says crisply. "Life is long. There's nothing you have to get done in such a hurry."

"I feel as if I'm drifting."

"So drift." She lifts her thin, knobby hands from her lap and waves them back and forth in the air. "You've been moving in one direction, and now you need to go in another. You've got to take some time to figure out which way to go."

"Oh, Grandma," Kathryn says.

"Besides, I need you around for a while. Put some distance between me and your mother."

Kathryn reaches over and squeezes her hand. "She tries."

"She tries, I know. She tries. All that trying makes me tired. Promise me one thing: Promise me that when it gets to the point where you have to try so hard, you'll just leave me alone. Okay?"

She starts to protest. "But she means—"

"Promise?"

"I promise," Kathryn says.

After leaving her grandmother with her crossword puzzle, Kathryn sits in the car in the parking lot, twisting the ring on her finger. *There's nothing you have to get done in such a hurry.* She imagines Paul tonight, playing bass guitar with his band at a small club in Charlottesville as he does most Saturdays, a little cluster of groupies swaying together up front. Her life with him seems suddenly hazy and far away.

KATHRYN HAD MET Paul at the University of Virginia, where both of them were enrolled in the English master's program. She was twenty-five, he was twenty-seven. She'd been writing a newsletter for a women's health organization in Washington, D.C., a low-paying and tedious job, and had come to the conclusion that maybe she should consider teaching instead. He'd spent the previous two years living in Africa, learning Swahili and contracting intestinal diseases. The first time she saw him, with his curious Indian elf shoes, dark hair, and piercing brown eyes, she thought he must be foreign, but when he opened his mouth she heard the elocution of a New England prep-school graduate.

"Of course," he'd replied thoughtfully to a small, reedy professor's assertion that E. M. Forster's work expressed a dialectic uncertainty about identity versus nature. "But shouldn't we be interrogating these on a grid of social analysis rather than wallowing in solipsistic interpretations of the text?"

"Yeah," Kathryn murmured, thinking aloud. Paul, Professor Digby, and the rest of the class turned to look.

"Was there something you wanted to add, Kathryn?" the professor inquired.

She looked down at her notebook, blank except for a shopping list and a few mazelike doodles, and shrugged. "I just agree. That's all."

After class Paul caught up with her in the hall. "Thanks for speaking up in there. I'm so sick of these old-school professors who won't engage current theory."

"Mmm," she said.

"So," he said, loping along beside her, "do you really agree with me, or were you just annoyed at Digby?"

She stopped. "I pretty much agree with you. Though I'm not sure it has much to do with what he was talking about."

"I know. I just wanted to bring it up. So few professors at this place are really grappling with the imperialist, almost fascistic hold of Western so-called literature over—"

"You know what?" Kathryn broke in. "I'm late to meet someone. I've got to run."

"Oh. Sure."

"I love your shoes," she said. "Well, see you later."

By the third week of school, Kathryn had begun to loathe the English department. She hated the thick burned coffee in the makeshift student lounge, the sign-ups for reading groups on arcane subjects, the desperate tone of the grad-student newsletter, the tense, pale faces of second-years waiting to find out if they'd made the cut. By the end of the first month she decided that she wasn't going to stick around to find out.

"I'm getting the master's and getting out of here," she told Paul. They had begun meeting after class and walking across the Lawn to the College Inn, a student hangout, for coffee. "All I'm really interested in is the reading, anyway. I'm no good at the criticism part."

"So you don't want to teach."

"I don't want to teach enough to put up with all the bullshit." They walked up the white marble steps of the rotunda. It was late afternoon on a hot day; leafy branches drooped over the wide marble porches extending from either side of the dome. "And besides, I'm sick of being poor and undervalued and anxious all the time. What kind of a life is that?"

"But it won't always be this way," he said. He sat on a bench overlooking the grounds and started playing with a large, yellowing leaf.

"Oh, no, not always. The next step is to fight to get a spot in the Ph.D. lineup, then to finish an overly cautious and politically correct dissertation, then to get a job at a mediocre college—somewhere in the continental United States, if you're lucky—then the whole tenure nightmare, then departmental bickering and backstabbing . . ."

"You do make it sound pleasant," he said.

Kathryn sat against the wall, her legs up on the bench. "Well, what about you? What do you like so much about it?"

He started to tear the leaf into little pieces. "I can't imagine doing anything else."

Though they had little in common, Kathryn and Paul got along well together for a time. She appreciated his passion for his work—he was so definite, so confident in his opinions. Surely some of that would rub off on her! And though he would never admit it to anyone but her, he secretly admired her disdain for the program, her unwillingness to play the game. It helped him keep perspective when the pressure got too much. They were constantly arguing and making up, which Kathryn mistook for a good sign. After all, her parents had never fought, never so much as raised their voices, and look at what happened to them.

Paul's parents, WASPs from Main Line Philadelphia, were cordial but stiff with Kathryn, and her parents didn't know what to make of Paul. "Are you sure he's not gay?" her mother whispered worriedly after meeting him for the first time. "He wears those odd shoes. And remember, you thought Will was straight, too." "I think I'd know by now," Kathryn said, laughing, but the question kept her up at night. He could be; how would she know? When she finally asked him, he took the question more seriously than she would have liked. "I've given it a lot of thought," he said, "and I can honestly say that no, I don't think I am."

By now, despite her misgivings, Kathryn had grown to love him. When he took her hiking at Rockfish Gap and presented her with his grandmother's engagement ring, she didn't hesitate to say yes. They were married a year to the day after they met, in a tiny stone chapel on the edge of campus, in the middle of a rainstorm. Kathryn wore a long white vintage dress and pearls; he wore a tuxedo he owned and a bow tie made of kente cloth. At the front of the church on the right sat Paul's nuclear family; Kathryn's mother and brother, Josh, sat at the front on the left, and her father and stepmother sat in the middle. A scraggly bunch of their grad-school friends, bearded and bespectacled and pale, filled the middle pews. Rolling thunder drowned out their vows.

After the ceremony they raced across the wet lawn through pouring rain with tux coats over their heads toward the cars. Josh rode to the restaurant with Paul's siblings, Maura and George.

Paul and Kathryn, following behind them in Paul's ten-year-old Saab, watched Maura pull out a joint and hand it to Josh over the seat. "They're smoking pot," Kathryn said, incredulous.

Paul nodded.

"I can't believe it."

"They're celebrating, Kat." He turned to look at her, and she noticed that his eyes were glazed and red.

"Oh, my God," she said. "You're high."

He shrugged and put his hand on her knee. She pulled away. "Oh, c'mon, Kat. Lighten up," he said.

Kathryn dropped out of the program six months later, after abandoning a master's thesis on the topic of "[Gyn]Ecological [W]Rites of Spring: Edna Pontellier's Rude *Awakening*." Paul made the cut three months later and headed off into the thickets of the Ph.D. program, exploring D. H. Lawrence and Zola and their depiction of miners as working-class heroes. His working title, he joked, was "Mining the Great Minds' Mines."

As Paul's research took him deeper beneath the surface, Kathryn found herself gliding contentedly along the top. She'd been writing occasional articles for the *News-Sentinel*, a weekly newspaper run out of a tiny office in the basement of a warehouse, and when she quit the program they asked her to edit the arts page full-time. The job didn't pay much, but it was enough to live comfortably on and start paying off her student loans. Her life quickly settled into a pleasant routine. She went to exhibits and openings, poetry readings, play performances. She bought fresh vegetables at the farmer's market on Wednesdays and warm bread at the gourmet food and wine shop on Market Street in the afternoons. As she got to know the town beyond the university, she found that much of the population consisted of grad-school dropouts like herself who had come to Charlottesville for an education and never left. Looking around, she saw overqualified writers and artists and historians and architects and educated faculty spouses competing for the same menial jobs, and suddenly she realized what people were talking about when they said they stayed in this scenic college town for the lifestyle—they wanted to be around people like themselves, hardcover-book-reading, museum-going, white-wine-drinking underachievers. Playful yet pragmatic, liberal yet sensible, they reveled in the pleasant weather and the beauty of the place, they had exquisite dinner parties and took occasional trips to local mountain inns. They recycled (paper, plastic, and aluminum), they petitioned for carpaccio at the local supermarket, and they subscribed to *The Washington Post*.

For the next two years life was good. Life was comfortable. And it began to terrify Kathryn. She saw herself at fifty, living in a house on Altamont Circle or perhaps out in Keswick, publishing seasonal poetry in the literary supplement of *The Daily Progress* and serving cocktails and grilled shrimp to the backstabbers in her husband's department who were scheming to deny him the chairmanship. She felt a desperate urge to escape. It was as if she had arrived in hell and found it to be a pleasant, comfortable, even interesting place. The only way you knew you were in hell was that it slowly began to dawn on you that you were never going anywhere, never doing anything. You were never getting out.

Paul, meanwhile, had become friendly with three hard-edged women from the English department, and several undernourished men. He played guitar in an all-male rock band that called itself Sons and Lovers, and soon developed a little following. People would call the apartment and, when Kathryn happened to answer, hang up. "It's your groupies again," she'd say. "Or one of the three harpies."

"Don't call them that."

"They're depressing. You only like them because they have crushes on you."

"Sounds like you're jealous."

She narrowed her eyes. "Should I be?"

"Oh, please, Kat," he said. "God. You know, ever since you quit the program, you've been nothing but nasty about it."

"I have not," she said, her voice rising to an unnatural pitch.

"If you have such disgust for what I do, then why did you marry me?"

"Because I liked your shoes. And because you promised you'd finish in three years."

He lifted his chin, an old prep-school gesture, and said coldly, "Let me explain something to you. Writing a dissertation is not like writing a six-hundred-word story for the arts section of a lame-ass weekly newspaper, with its bullet points and catchy little hooks and Monday-afternoon deadlines. This is my fucking profession. This is my life. And if you don't like it . . ."

"If I don't like it, what?"

"You can go to hell," he said.

"I'm already in hell! This is hell!" she shouted, laughing maniacally.

"Well, you know what Eliot said," Paul said dryly. "Or maybe you don't. 'What is hell? Hell is oneself, hell is alone, the other figures in it merely projections.'"

The marriage lasted another six months. Paul confessed to having slept with one of the harpies ("She bolstered me," he said. "She helped me find a piece of myself I'd lost"), and Kathryn confessed to being bored to tears with the minutiae of his academic research. Neither of them had much in the way of assets, so the break was fairly clean. The only sticking point was their dog, a pug named Frieda they'd bought in their first year of marriage from a Turkish rug dealer on the downtown mall.

"I should keep her," Paul said. "After all, you're the one leaving me."

"Only because I'm leaving," Kathryn said. "You wanted the divorce."

"You suggested it."

"Oh, come on, Paul. You were the one having the affair."

"Let's not go into all this again," he said. "I think we should think about what's best for Frieda. I can provide her with stability. You don't even know where you're going."

"Yes I do—I'm going to Maine."

He snorted. "You think your life here is hellish, wait till you spend some time in Bangor. You'll be out of there by the end of the summer."

Kathryn relinquished the dog. They didn't fight over wedding presents; Paul kept the ones from his side of the family, his friends, and she kept the ones from hers. The day before she was to fly out of Charlottesville for good, she packed her meager belongings into boxes and drove into the countryside to the UPS command center to drop them off. As she stood in the front office, watching her brown boxes ascend the ramp on little rollers and disappear over the top, Kathryn felt a great weight lift from her. She didn't care if she ever saw the packages again—in fact, part of her wished that she'd given a false address. It would be fitting, she thought, for the boxes to be stuck in limbo, riding around in those big brown trucks until somebody figured out that there was no destination. She was, for the first time in a long time, free of baggage. She felt as light as air.

The next day, after sleeping late again, Kathryn decides on an impulse to drive out and see her father. He lives in Hampden, ten miles from Bangor, in a modern home with a swimming pool on twelve acres of land. A partner in one of Bangor's largest accounting firms, he drives a forest-green Miata and a Jeep Wagoneer and keeps bottled water and fresh-squeezed juices in the refrigerator. When Kathryn was in high school, every time she went to visit him there'd be music on the sound system wafting out to the driveway and back behind the house to the pool—the kind of music that she and her friends listened to, REO Speedwagon and Jefferson Starship and the Bangles. Hearing it as she walked up to the door always made her wince.

Kathryn used to wish she had one of those fathers who was around at night and on weekends, who'd help her with her homework or toss a ball with her in the park. Even before he moved out, her father wasn't like that. He never quite seemed to be part of their family. He was vacant with them; he kissed her mother on the top of the head when he came home from work, holding her, literally, at arm's length. Kathryn and Josh pulled back and watched. When he left the house in the morning, they watched him dither about when he'd be home; they saw the look on their mother's face when he called to say that, yet again, he'd be working late.

Margaret Fournier had been Kathryn's father's secretary. She was also, on Saturdays, a gymnastics instructor at the Y. Most of the girls in Kathryn's middle school had, at one time or another, taken gymnastics with Miss Fournier in the cold, cavernous gymnasium at the West Side YWCA. They were in awe of her—in her brightly colored leotards, her hair pulled back in a bun, Miss Fournier looked like a star. The first time Kathryn saw her in street clothes, ill-fitting jeans and a baggy acrylic sweater, drawing on a cigarette as she waited for the bus, she was shocked at how she looked: scrawny, mean-faced, cheap. Kathryn remembered this image when her father came to tell them he was leaving.

It took her mother years to get over the hurt. "Did you know about it?" she'd ask Kathryn or Josh, trapping them in the hall as they left for school. "Could you tell?"

They'd shrug and squirm away, embarrassed at the naked pain in her eyes. When their father called the house wanting to speak to Josh or Kathryn and their mother answered the phone, her voice, calling their names, would take on a tense, high-pitched quality. They'd pick up the receiver without looking at her and answer their father's questions like prisoners under duress. Their mother became intensely busy; she volunteered at the hospital and was elected president of the PTA. Before the divorce was finalized, she binged on shopping; Kathryn would come home to find boxes of shoes piled up in the hall, transparent makeup bags filled with tubes and vials on the table. She redecorated the living room and had the yard landscaped, charging it all to her husband's credit cards.

One night at dinner she told Kathryn and Josh that she had decided to become an interior decorator. "So I'll be taking night classes," she said. "And I'll need you two to do your part around here."

After that, everything changed. When their father left, their mother had continued to run the house pretty much as she always had. She fixed the kids a hot breakfast before school, picked them up on time when they had to get to piano lessons or track practice, and put dinner on the table at six. But now that she was a student, too, the old family structure crumbled. They ate cold cereal standing at the sink, and Kathryn and Josh arranged rides to after-school activities and learned to do their own laundry. Kathryn started cooking dinner, strange and creative combinations of whatever she could find in the fridge. On the evenings when her mother was home, the three of them did homework together at the kitchen table.

Now that she was out and about, their mother became known as one of the cool moms, the type who wore brightly colored turtlenecks tucked into Guess jeans and flirted with the coaches at their kids' baseball games. She always looked stylish and put-together—a lot more put-together than her kids did. She often complained, half jokingly, that she was the kind of mom who should've been rewarded with cheerful, straightforward children who organized bake sales and home-coming rallies, instead of the bookish, reticent ones she got. "I don't understand you," she'd say when she found Kathryn lurking in her bedroom on sunny afternoons. "Have you looked outside? It's a beautiful day!"

"I'm reading, Mom."

"Don't you want some exercise?"

"Maybe later."

"Are your bicycle tires pumped up?"

Kathryn would sigh exaggeratedly, a finger marking the place in her book. "Don't know."

"I'll check," her mother would say brightly. "It's a nice day for a bike ride. Maybe I'll go, too."

Josh became very protective of their mother. He even refused to visit his father and Margaret, but Kathryn dutifully went when they called. When she visited them in their stark new house with its vaulted ceilings and hot tub on the deck, she felt like a nun in a bordello. She disapproved of everything.

"For chrissakes, Katy, lighten up a little," her father would laugh at her cloudy expression. "Did you bring a swimsuit? No? Maybe you can fit into one of Maggie's."

Margaret was wary around her, careful to be polite. She made perfectly balanced dinners out of gourmet cookbooks, substituting juices, she explained, for the salt and fat. Kathryn became a spy, searching for clues about what it was that made her father happy, what he had found with Margaret that he couldn't get at home. Margaret, she discovered, was trying very hard. The shelves of her nightstand were full of titles like *Wine Made Easy*, *A Beginner's Guide to Classical Music*, and *Understanding Opera*; home-decorating magazines with pages pinched down were arranged by month in the kitchen. Jars of vitamins lined the kitchen counter. Under the sink in the master bathroom Kathryn found a variety of douches—Lemon Fresh, Summer Sunshine, Floral Breeze. In Margaret's dresser were lacy negligees, silk teddies, sheer French-cut underwear and a see-through black merry widow. Kathryn fingered the pieces slowly and then shut the drawer, imagining Margaret on top of her father in that outfit, moving her lithe gymnast's body, completing the fantasy he'd constructed for himself out here in the countryside, far from the ruins of his life with them.

Margaret had stopped teaching gymnastics, but she still knew the names of Kathryn's friends. "How's Jennifer?" she'd ask, taking a long drag on a cigarette as they sat sunning by the pool. "Still practicing on the parallel bars?"

"She's okay," Kathryn said. "How come you smoke so much, if you're so into vitamins and stuff?"

Margaret would look at her over the rim of her mirrored sunglasses. "It's an addiction, Katy. I'm trying to stop."

"Don't call me Katy, if you don't mind."

"Oh, I'm sorry. Doesn't your father call you that?"

"Yeah, but no one else."

"Well, okay, *Kathryn*," Margaret said, stubbing the butt into an ash-tray. "Anyway, smoking keeps me thin. Your father likes me that way." She smiled conspiratorially.

Kathryn frowned. "Huh. He's really going to like you in twenty years, with a tube sticking out of your throat so you can talk."

"God," Margaret said, settling back into her chair, "you're a load of fun to have around."

When Kathryn returned home after these visits, her mother would circle her warily, sniffing for clues. Kathryn tried to ignore her, answering her probing questions with simple, vague responses: *Yes, um hmm, I don't think so, I don't know.* More and more often, she found herself retreating into a world where her parents couldn't go. She didn't want to be complicit in their small digs and jabs; she hated feeling as if she had to explain or defend one to the other when they were both so invested in their own versions of what happened. If she let herself, she could be swallowed up in her mother's unhappiness or lulled by her father's denial. She didn't want to be bitter, but she also didn't want to pretend that everything was all right. It was safer to keep her distance.

Later, Josh would corner her in her bedroom to get the dirt. "Did Margaret look like a bimbo? Was Dad a total lech?"

"There was douche in the bathroom under the sink. All kinds of it," she reported.

"What's douche?"

"Oh, for God's sake, find out for yourself," she said. "I'm not going to explain it to you."

"What's this about douche under the sink?" their mother asked Kathryn a few days later as they sat in the kitchen doing homework.

Josh winced, and Kathryn looked at him with disgust. "Moron."

"I still don't know what it means," he shouted.

"It's a feminine wash," their mother said. "That's all you need to know right now."

"A feminine *what*?"

"I was snooping," Kathryn said.

"What else did you find?"

"Nothing really. Fancy underwear. That's about it."

"Umm. So—does your father seem happy?"

"I don't know." She danced as far away from the question as she could. "It seems like it. But . . ."

"But what?"

Kathryn looked into her mother's steady, anxious eyes, knowing that the truth was too diffuse to convey. Her father seemed to think he was happy; he held up his acquisitions like trophies; he acted as if his life now was all he'd ever wanted, all he'd ever wished for. "I don't think he knows what it means to be happy," she said suddenly, and she realized that it was true.

AFTER PARKING HER mother's car in the driveway beside the Miata, Kathryn crunches up the fine gravel walkway to the front door. She rings the bell and hears chimes echoing in the cavernous house, but no one answers. She turns the knob; the door is locked. Finally she ventures around to the back, where she finds her father and Margaret, wearing shorts and T-shirts, trimming hedges.

They look at her as if she's an apparition.

"Katy!" her father says, and carefully lays down his shears. "I'm all sweaty, but . . ." He reaches out and circles her shoulders in a stiff mime of intimacy. "Did we know you were coming?"

"No, sorry," she says. "I just got in a couple of days ago. Hi, Margaret."

Margaret stands holding the Weed Whacker as if she isn't sure what to do. "Well, this is a surprise."

"I can leave and come back another time."

"No, no," she says, without much conviction.

"You're looking good. Isn't she looking good, Maggie?" her father says, a little too heartily.

Kathryn can feel Margaret's appraising eyes. "Sure," she says.

"You look like you've lost weight. Have you lost weight?" her father says.

"I don't know. Maybe."

"Hey, I just remembered, Katy," he says. "I've got something for you inside. I was going to send it to you, but now that you're here . . . Where's that article I cut out of the paper, Maggie?"

"You stuck it on the fridge. I'll get it." She puts down the apparatus and takes off her gloves.

"Why don't we all just go inside for a moment, get something to drink?" he says. "Come on, Katy. How are things going?"

"Fine," she says. "How about you?"

"Fine, just fine," he says as they follow Margaret to the sliding doors and go inside. "How was the flight?"

"It was fine, Dad."

Margaret goes into the kitchen and comes back with a flimsy piece of newspaper and hands it to him. He passes it to Kathryn. She glances it over. It's a classified ad: Upward Bound instructors needed to teach disadvantaged kids during summer term at the university. She looks up. "Thanks, Dad, but I'm not really interested in teaching right now."

"I thought you might be interested in earning some money."

"I don't even know how long I'm staying here."

"Haven't you gotten rid of that apartment in Virginia?"

"Yeah, but I could still move back there—or anywhere. I don't know what my plans are yet."

"I see." He taps his fingers on the table. "Is Paul still in Charlottesville?"

She nods.

"Still working on that dissertation?"

"Um-hmm."

"I'm just wondering what you're doing for money these days. It's not coming from Paul, I assume."

"No. I didn't take any money from him. There wasn't all that much, anyway. I have a little saved up, which should last me a while. A little while, at least."

"Who wants a Poland Spring?" Margaret asks, clasping her hands together.

"I'll have one," he says. "Katy?" She shakes her head. "Listen, honey," he says to her, "you need to be thinking about your future. That's all I'm saying."

"I *have* thought about it," she says stubbornly. She feels like a child.

He shakes his head. "I don't think so. And you know, I'm not going to bail you out. I just don't believe in it. I don't want you to expect it."

"Have I ever?" She looks at him for a moment, standing there in his Nike shorts and buttercup-yellow tennis shirt, tanned and fit, a band of white skin around his wrist where his Rolex belongs. "I think maybe I should be going."

"Aw, Katy," he says, reaching forward awkwardly and clasping her shoulders. "I just want what's best for you. You know that, don't you? And I want you to feel good about yourself. Can you blame me for that?"

"Of course not. But I just got divorced, Dad. I need some time to work it through."

He shakes his head emphatically. "I can tell you right now, time is the last thing you need. You need to get busy."

Margaret, appearing with a tray of bottled water and ice in a bucket, wrinkles her nose at Kathryn and smiles. "Listen to your father, Katy," she says. "He's always right on the mark about stuff like this."

ON THE WAY home, Kathryn pulls off the highway and puts the car in park on a wide gravel shoulder. She closes her eyes and leans back against the headrest, breathing deeply and rubbing her temples with her fingers. Her father, she has to admit, is right to be concerned. Most people her age do seem to be more settled. She hears about their buying houses, having children, and holding down jobs, and she wonders if she will ever feel that she is capable of a normal life. How do people avoid getting mired in indecision, considering the potential for disaster, the probability that things will go wrong? Or is doubt a self-fulfilling prophecy? Do the people who proceed with optimism and good faith create their own reality? Does shutting out fear keep disaster at bay?

To enjoy your life, she thinks, you must ignore so much, discount the possibility of tragedy, deny the evil that shadows hope. That seems impossible to her. But it is sobering to contemplate that this bleak awareness might define her future—that she can't trust others, so she won't make herself vulnerable, so she is destined to move through a random series of superficial relationships. There may be less to lose that way, but it is, she knows, a lesser life.

She has forgotten so much. She has willed herself to forget. She has forgotten what it is like to feel, and she isn't sure she wants to remember. Like water from a well that takes a while to run clear, pain would come first, and she's not sure she has the faith to wait for something better.

A car honks, and she opens her eyes. Looking around, she realizes that car after car is slowing beside her, trying to determine if she needs help.

KATHRYN DOESN'T WANT to go home, but she doesn't know what else to do. She passes the Broadway exit and then, instead of continuing north indefinitely, gets off at the Bangor Mall. When she was growing up here, the mall was a shopping oasis in acres of farmland, but now it's surrounded by complexes and megastores. The farmland is virtually gone.

Heading down the long entrance road to the mall, Kathryn approaches the loop that surrounds it. She's always been confused by the array of tributaries and side exits that intersect the loop, and at the fork she hesitates. She's not sure what she's doing here or what she wants to find, so she doesn't know which way to go. Like a homing pigeon she veers left with the traffic, past the back entrance of Sears, and turns into the parking lot at Porteous, the place she always used to park in high school—the only store for a hundred miles where you could find Clinique cosmetics.

The mall was a second home to her then. On gray winter days when there was nothing to do, she and Jennifer would drive to the mall and roam around aimlessly, in and out of the Gap and Spencer Gifts, getting a Blizzard from the Dairy Queen booth, stopping at the pet store to see the hyperactive puppies in their stacked cages. They knew the mall as well as they knew the high school—where the cool kids hung out, where the hidden bathrooms were, which days certain stores got their shipments. They went to the mall to lose themselves, but also they went there to be found. Everyone ended up there eventually; it was the unifying center of a centerless town.

Thinking back now, Kathryn realizes that these were some of the best times she and Jennifer had together—giggling, sharing secret jokes, sitting at the fountain near the entrance and assessing the high school guys who sauntered past grinning at them, affecting nonchalance. She felt closer to Jennifer then than she'd ever been with anyone. "It's like having another twin, being friends with you," Jennifer told her. "God forbid," Kathryn said, but she was secretly thrilled to have a sister, a twin, to no longer feel separate and alone.

Now, walking past the jewelry shops screaming "50% off" and the empty shoe stores, Kathyrn can see that the mall is no longer the center of Bangor's shopping universe. There are too many new establishments out there on the periphery, too many superstores offering cheaper prices and a better selection. Years ago her parents and their friends lamented the coming of the mall and the slow death of the downtown, but they had no idea how things would evolve—that one day the mall itself would come to seem quaint and old-fashioned, a modest relic of a simpler time.

At Cosmos Pizza Kathryn gets a Diet Coke with lots of ice in a giant paper cup and sips it slowly through a straw as she makes her way down the promenade, stopping every now and then to look in a store window. She pretends to be checking out the merchandise, but she's actually watching the salesclerks, most of them high-school kids who, through bad luck or bad planning, got stuck in Bangor for the summer. As she watches them snap their gum, surreptitiously yanking on their clothing as they check their reflections in the mirrored columns, she is struck by how young they seem, how unsure and self-conscious. Was she that way? When she was in high school she had felt so old.

Thinking back, the elements of her life were so simple then. She got up early on cold mornings, showered quickly in a steam-filled bathroom, layered herself with warm clothing, shoveled something sugary into her mouth on her way out the door, and headed off to school with an L. L. Bean backpack full of books, half-finished papers, and notebooks covered with doodles. For a long time it seemed that there were infinite amounts of time to spend. After an hour or two of some after-school activity and an hour or two of homework (which could always be finished secretly in the bathroom late at night, or in the early-morning hours before school, or even, in a pinch, in the cafeteria at lunch), the rest of the day stretched ahead like a long, flat road. There were usually some household chores to do, and then dinner, and then the freedom of the evening, unasked for and unappreciated, would be frittered away.

There was a time when Kathryn would spend whole evenings on the phone with Jennifer, methodically removing the shell-colored nail polish from her toes and repainting them, each one a different color, as they went over the day's minute details, obsessing over a glance, a close call, a mortifying moment at her locker. She spent entire afternoons in her bedroom doing nothing, as she explained when her mother asked what she was up to: "*Nothing, Mom.*" "Don't be evasive with me, Kathryn," her mother said. But it wasn't evasion, it was the truth; she was doing no one thing—not reading, not cleaning, not using her time efficiently, not planning ahead.

In high school Kathryn and her friends had existed in a netherworld between the bad kids and the good kids, the ones who skipped school and got in serious trouble and the ones who became class monitor and teacher's pet. They were courteous but irreverent, skeptical about ritual but usually game enough to participate in school-related functions like pep rallies and fund-raising drives. As class president, Will was the one most involved in activities; his presence at various events actually mattered. The others were happy to go along, as long as it was generally understood and agreed that none of it had to be taken too seriously. There were things that mattered, to be sure; it was just that few of these things were part of their lives at Bangor High.

Like most of her friends, Kathryn felt that the adults in her life existed around her, setting limits, asking questions, prying. Kathryn moved through each day as if around an obstacle course, ducking inopportune questions, ignoring unwanted advice, sliding in just under curfew. She couldn't imagine how she might communicate with these people, even if she wanted to. Her parents talked about responsibility and limits and planning for the future. They wanted her to save time, to be aware of time, to use her time wisely. This concept was meaningless to her. Why worry about time when there was so much of it, when it was as plentiful as air? She wanted to squander time, to use up great gobs of it. As far as she was concerned, everything happened too slowly.

High school always seemed to Kathryn like a way station for real life, a place where nothing meaningful could happen and there was no point in even trying. She took school seriously; she fretted over tests and made decent grades, but she never quite believed that anything she learned in high school would spill over into Real Life—that mythical time in the future, after college, when she would be an adult in the world. Of course, she was as terrified of leaving home as she was at the prospect of being left behind. She procrastinated filling out college applications until the last possible week, scrambling to ask for recommendations, dashing off the personal essay. It seemed to her like a school assignment, an exercise; it was impossible to imagine that it might actually be her ticket out.

Being a teenager was like being a member of a large, disparate tribe with its own language, a patois invented from the necessity of deceit. The kids hid things from teachers and parents and each other, and sometimes, without even knowing it, from themselves. High school was all about deception. Otherwise, how would any of them have survived it? If Kathryn had told her parents the truth about her life, they would never have let her out of the house. As it was, they were suspicious, setting curfews and quizzing her about her friends, extracting meaningless pledges and promises, checking up when possible. Kathryn quickly learned to recite the catechism they wanted to hear: *I'm the good girl, the conscience of the group, the one with common sense. I would never do drugs / have sex in someone's car / sit between two friends, unbelted, in the back of a hatchback that's passing a truck at ninety miles an hour up a hill on a two-lane road. I would never take the kinds of chances that could get me killed, because I know how precious my life is to you, how shattered you would be to lose me.*

She let them believe this, and they let themselves trust her—and as long as nothing terrible happened, they could all convince themselves that Kathryn deserved that trust.

WALKING AROUND THE mall now, Kathryn's feet are beginning to drag. The mall always makes her tired; she wonders if there's something in the air-conditioning that zaps people's energy and keeps them there longer, like drugged captives. Finally she summons her energy and makes her way to the car, then drives the five hundred yards to the cineplex across the street. Scanning a list of titles and playing times, she finds an action-adventure movie starring Mel Gibson that's starting in eight minutes. She buys popcorn and another Diet Coke and settles into a seat in the empty theater. When the previews begin, she leans back, soaking up the bright images and sounds in front of her like a sun-worshipper at the beach.

The movie is fast-moving and visceral, and for two hours she thinks of nothing but the drama onscreen. When the lights come up, it takes her a moment to orient herself, and then she does: she's in a deserted movie theater at three o'clock in the afternoon on a Tuesday. In her hometown, living with her mother. With nine hundred dollars to her name, a student loan to repay, and no job to speak of, driving her mother's car. On the way out of the theater she slips into another movie that's just starting, but it's about a guy who loses his wife and his job and decides to drink himself to death, and she's pretty sure she's not in the frame of mind to see it.

"So, my darling," Kathryn's mother says several days later when she finds her sitting at the kitchen table in boxer shorts and a Women's Studies T-shirt, reading the paper. "Do you know what time it is?"

Kathryn glances at the clock. "Eleven forty-five."

Her mother looks at her.

"What? Did the time change?"

"It's eleven forty-five," her mother says. "The morning's almost gone."

Kathryn looks at her over the top of the paper.

"You've been here almost a week now, Kathryn, and I wasn't going to say anything, but I just can't stand by any longer without telling you what I think."

Kathryn lowers the paper and folds it slowly, avoiding her mother's eyes. "Fine. Go ahead."

"Well . . ." She takes Kathryn's empty mug off the table. "More coffee?"

"No, thanks."

"I think I'll have some." She goes over to the counter, takes down a Maine Black Bears mug, and fills it from the pot. "This is what I have observed," she says, opening two packets of Equal with her teeth and pouring them in. "You stay up late watching talk shows—"

"Does the noise bother you?"

"That's not my point. And then you sleep late every morning. You wander down here around eleven or eleven-thirty, and then it's afternoon before you're dressed, and half the day is gone."

"Um-hmm."

"Don't you think there's a problem here? Look." Her mother comes over and sits in the chair beside her, setting her mug on the table. Kathryn inches her chair away. "It's no secret that you're depressed."

All at once a flock of emotions, seemingly from nowhere, wings its way through Kathryn's brain.

"And I think you're hiding."

"From what?"

"Yourself. Your expectations of yourself."

"Oh, Mom—" Kathryn starts, but her mother cuts her off.

"Listen, I know what's going on. When your father left me, the jerk, I—"

"This is hardly the same thing. Paul and I agreed, mutually—"

"Bull-oney. Nobody ever agrees mutually," she says. "Something happens, one person pulls away, and the other one gets self-protective and pulls back too. And Paul was having an affair, wasn't he?"

"Yes, but that was just a symptom."

"Whatever. All I know is that divorce does terrible things to your sense of self. Your esteem."

Kathryn lets out a short laugh. "Have you been buying those self-help books again, Mom?"

"That kind of cynicism is just what I'm talking about."

"Oh, for God's sake."

"Face it. You're listless." Her mother slowly wags her head. "Being in denial is not going to help."

"Look, Mom, I appreciate your concern, but I wish you'd just leave me alone, okay?"

"No," she says, leaning closer, "I will not leave you alone."

"Why are you treating me like a child?"

"Because you're acting like one."

Kathryn covers her face with her hands. "Do me a favor. Please get off my back. Just for a little while. Please."

"All I want is for you to be—"

"I know, I know—"

"Don't you interrupt me!" Her mother's voice is fierce.

Kathryn takes a deep breath.

"I am sorry about what you've been through," her mother says angrily. "I'd have given anything for the last few years to have worked out differently for you. I know it hasn't been easy. But this is just no good. You've got to work through it. You are twenty-eight years old, Kathryn. I run into girls from your class all the time, and they're having babies and teaching school and buying houses and planning for retirement and generally acting like adults. But you don't seem to want to make any hard decisions."

"You don't call getting divorced a hard decision?"

"I call it inevitable. That marriage was doomed from the start. You weren't in love with him, you just kind of fell into the relationship because it seemed like a good idea at the time. In fact, so far, it seems to me, inertia has been the driving force of your adult life. You fell into a job in Washington that you kind of liked, then you went to graduate school, which you didn't finish; you got yourself married and settled in Charlottesville, which you kind of liked, got a job that you kind of liked ... and then, when things didn't work out, you abandoned it all and came back to where you started—with no clear idea of what you want, no plans, no goals for the future."

Kathryn looks at her mother steadily, and her mother looks back.

"I think this goes way back, Kathryn," she says finally. "I think this has to do with Jennifer. And I think it's time for you to start working it out."

INERTIA, KATHRYN THINKS, lying on her bed that afternoon, staring up at the ceiling. What a strange word. Who'd have thought her mother would come up with it? She likes the sound of it—*inertia*—a far-off echo, a secret, a lulling whisper in her head. She hasn't tried to name this disconnection she's been feeling; she hasn't dared to pin it down. Having a word, and such a word, to describe it is somehow comforting. She likes that it characterizes actions, not feelings; it covers her without defining her. It's safe.

For the first time in a long time, she thinks back to that night by the Kenduskeag. After Jennifer left, she and Will had made their way down to the river, just the two of them, leaving everyone else behind. "Will you remember this?" he said. "Will you remember me?"

She wonders sometimes what would have become of them if nothing had happened, if they'd all simply gone off to college as they expected to after that last summer in Maine. Maybe she and Will would have continued to see each other whenever they could for a while, and then the phone calls and the visits would have dwindled, and finally she'd have found out from a friend at Princeton that he was gay—or maybe he'd have told her himself. Jennifer would have gone to Colby, as she'd planned, and Kathryn to Virginia, and the two of them would've stayed friends, coming back together in the summers between school years, sleeping on the floor of each other's dorm room on occasional weekends. But then they'd have gotten caught up in their separate lives and separate friends and forget to call, and eventually they'd have been standing on the shores of each other's lives, squinting hard into the distance to see to the other side.

Instead, things fell apart. Jennifer's sudden absence destroyed the fabric that had held everyone together. The police were secretive, then hesitant, and finally admitted there'd been no leads. Kathryn moved through college in a kind of daze, forming friendships cautiously when at all, making respectable grades, avoiding loud parties, keeping herself organized and managing her time efficiently. Everybody who knew about Jennifer's disappearance remarked on how well Kathryn was doing, how quickly she had "bounced back"—as if what she did and how she appeared had any relation to how she felt.

For a long time the guilt was enormous. She felt guilty when she laughed, when she made a new friend, when she momentarily forgot. She'd be walking down the street in the middle of the day and the sun would be shining and a child would laugh and she'd be wondering what to make for dinner, where she might find some thin-stalked asparagus, whether she had a lemon in the fridge, when something would trigger a memory—a glimpse of blond hair, a low, throaty laugh, a dim recollection of Jennifer at fourteen encountering asparagus for the first time, leaving behind a small mound of fringed tips. At times like this Kathryn would stop short, her thoughts dissolving like an Etch-a-Sketch, her stomach caving in on itself like a hill of sand.

During her sophomore year she spent a semester in London. She read eighteenth-century British poetry and took to wearing black from Marks & Spencer. In the late afternoon, around teatime, she would leave her cramped, ugly flat and walk through the damp streets, smelling the rain that was never far away, looking at the grim, pale faces of Londoners too long on the dole. Yet she felt perfectly at home. She began losing weight, first because the food at the college was so bad and then because she learned to savor the feeling. She was shrinking, disappearing.

She began smoking cigarettes to stave off hunger, and wore black eyeliner and layers of clothes because being thin made her cold. Her London friends noticed the change, but thought it was cool; they joked about how fresh-faced Kathryn Campbell had been transformed. Her unhealthy glow was like a lighthouse beacon, drawing castaways. But she wasn't capable of offering shelter; she had a hard enough time giving solace to herself. Instead she willed men toward her and then, before daylight, left them. It helped, she knew, to be so light. Somehow it was easier to leave and feel no remorse when your mind was dizzy with hunger and the weight of your body left no imprint on the bed.

When she returned to the States at the end of May, her mother and brother barely recognized her. She slipped off the plane, dressed in tatters and pale as the moon. Her mother stepped back in horror; her brother stepped forward, impressed. "Wow, Kath," Josh said appreciatively as she came toward them, "you look like a freak."

Her mother put her arms around her and squeezed, and all of Kathryn's muscles tensed. "You're a bag of bones," her mother whispered. "Hugging you is like hugging a tired old woman." She held Kathryn's face in her hands, and Kathryn looked away. "What have you done? What have you done to yourself?"

Kathryn shrugged, her bony shoulders moving up and down in a sigh.

"You're a different person," her mother said.

"Jet lag," she murmured.

Kathryn slept for three days in the room she'd grown up in, with the shades drawn and the door closed. Every few hours her mother came in to check on her, pull up the sheets, touch her forehead with cool, soft hands. In her dreams she saw the same images over and over, a series of snapshots fading in and out: footprints disappearing into the grass, an open window, an outstretched hand, miles of highway, a shallow grave. These pictures became a kind of visual mantra. She didn't know why she had seized on them, but in an odd way they comforted her. They helped her face the fear that was gnawing at her inside.

On the evening of the third day, as her mother and brother were sitting down to dinner, Kathryn appeared in the kitchen wearing nothing but a long T-shirt and underwear, and announced that she was hungry.

Her mother leapt up to fix a plate, and Josh leaned over and pushed Kathryn's long hair away from her face. "About time," he said. "I was beginning to think you'd gone missing, too."

The next morning, a warm, sunny day, Kathryn drives out to see Rosie Hall, a friend of her mother's and her sometime therapist, who practices in a little cluster of beige-colored prefab buildings in an industrial development on the edge of town. Kathryn was doubtful when her mother suggested she call Rosie, and she's even more doubtful now, looking around the empty waiting room—a cramped space with two folding chairs, a country-style woven rug, and a cheap wooden table holding a lamp, a collection of magazines spread out in a fan, and a dying spider plant.

On the phone the secretary had said, "Lucky you, we can squeeze you in today! Rosie has to pick up her son Jeff from baseball practice at five, so you'd better come a little before four." Kathryn's been waiting ten minutes, sitting in one of the metal chairs, leafing through a three-month-old *Personal Quest*, and there's no sign of Rosie.

"Nice day out there, huh?" the secretary says from behind a short divider.

Kathryn looks up. "Yeah."

She shakes her head and goes back to typing. "But I guess you can feel lousy in all kinds of weather."

Kathryn looks up again to see if she's joking, and the secretary gives her a sympathetic smile. Kathryn glances at her watch.

"She'll be out in a minute," the secretary says. "She wants to make sure everybody gets their money's worth."

As if on cue, the office door opens and a tall, shy-seeming man with a prominent Adam's apple, a faded flannel shirt, and heavy work boots emerges. "Thanks, Rosie," he calls back. "See ya next week." He nods to the secretary. "Doris."

"Be seeing ya, Lance. Take care." Doris waves him out the door and turns to Kathryn. "You can go in now."

Standing up, Kathryn puts the magazine back in its place in the fan and steps through the door. She finds herself in a large, empty room with no windows, beige carpeting on the floor and walls, and a wide lozenge of humming fluorescent light on the ceiling. Big square pillows and foam-stuffed baseball bats are scattered around the floor. On the wall a hand-printed poster declares, in green block letters, ROSIE'S TER-RIBLE, HORRIBLE, NO-GOOD, VERY BAD DAY ROOM, with names signed in different colors around it: Amy, Angie, Dick, Gretchen, Mike, Sue. Another poster, a faded cartoon of a turkey, says DON'T LET THE TURKEYS GET YOU DOWN.

"This is where we do group." A short, softly rounded woman with large pink-tinted glasses and curly brown hair appears in the doorway to the next room.

"Why are the walls carpeted?"

She picks up a foam bat and swings it, hard, at the wall. It bounces off. "So nobody gets hurt." She smiles. "You must be Kathryn. Come on in." Kathryn follows her into a dim little office containing three old, overstuffed chairs, a cluttered desk and straight chair, and a bookcase filled with books, most of which, it seems to her at a glance, are self-help. "Sit wherever you like," Rosie says.

Kathryn looks around. One chair, large and lumpy and low to the ground, has broad arms and a floral print; another is a rocker, with a stuffed leather seat; and the third, covered in red chintz, is a wingback. She feels like Goldilocks. "Is this a test?"

"I don't know. Could be, I guess!"

Kathryn narrows her eyes at her. Reaching out tentatively, she squeezes the arm of the wingback. "I'll take this one." She sits down and sinks low in the loose stuffing, struggling to sit upright. Finally she wrenches herself up.

"Not quite right?" asks Rosie.

Kathryn motions toward the lumpy floral.

"That's people's favorite," she says. "I guess it's kinda womblike or something. Why don't you take your shoes off and make yourself comfortable?"

Kathryn slips off her shoes and sits in the low chair, tucking her legs under for ballast. Rosie takes a pad and pen from her desk and pulls the straight chair up close. Kathryn shrinks back into the cushions.

"So," Rosie says, chuckling, "you chose the floral. What do you think that means?"

"Hmm," Kathryn says. "I think it means that Baby Bear is going to come home and find me in his bed."

Rosie shakes her head and writes something down on the pad.

"What are you writing?"

She looks up. "I wrote humor-slash-evasion."

"Oh, come on," Kathryn says, "did you really expect me to take that question seriously? Okay, I'll take it seriously. I chose the floral because rocking chairs make me nervous and the wingback has no springs. And I notice, by the way, that you're in the straight chair."

"Why do rocking chairs make you nervous?"

Kathryn looks at her watch.

"Are you feeling that this is a waste of time?"

She stands up and begins backing away. "Look. I—I think maybe this was a bad idea. I'm obviously not in the right frame of mind, so maybe we should just—"

Rosie puts the pad on her lap and sits forward. "Kathryn," she says calmly, "your mom's paying for the hour. Why don't you just sit back down—for goodness' sake, you can sit on the floor if you want to—and relax, and we'll see how it goes."

She shakes her head skeptically. "I don't know."

"Here's what we'll do," Rosie says. "We'll start over. We'll start now. You've just come in the door, you're choosing the chair you want, and we have a whole hour ahead of us to talk about what's going on in your mind."

"Don't you have to pick your son up at baseball practice?"

"Oh, it won't kill him to sit on his fanny for a few minutes," she says. "Now. What are you doing back in Bangor?"

"SO." ROSIE LEANS forward, propping one arm on the other, her hand on her chin. "Let me see if I've got this straight. Your marriage is finished, but you're not sure you ever got it off the ground to begin with. You don't know what you want to do with your life and feel incapable of finding out. You're living with your mother at a time when everyone your age seems to be getting on with their lives. And your ten-year high-school reunion is coming up in a couple of weeks."

"Pretty grim, huh?" Kathryn says.

Rosie taps her fingers on her chin. "It's a lot to deal with, that's for sure." She pulls a day calendar off her desk. "How is Tuesdays, four o'clock?"

"What do you mean? You mean permanently?"

She laughs. "Lord, no. I'm not one of those analyst types who think it has to take years to see results. I was thinking more like a month or two."

"I don't know," Kathryn says. "I'm not sure how long I'll be here. I might just stay a couple of weeks. I don't know how long my mother and I can stand living together."

"Have you considered getting an apartment?"

"No. I don't want to . . . settle."

"You mean compromise, or settle down?"

She thinks about this for a moment. "Both, I guess."

"Well, it's pretty clear that you need to deal with this stuff. You can do it with me, or you can do it with someone else, but you need to do it."

Kathryn makes a face. "I'm not sure I want to."

"What are you afraid of?"

"There's just so . . . much. I don't know what good it'll do to go digging around. And it feels self-indulgent to babble on about my stupid problems when really I'm fine, and things are fine, and it's not like my home was destroyed by a hurricane or a flood or an earthquake or anything—"

"Actually, that's a pretty good analogy. In many ways your life has been torn apart—and now, slowly, you have to figure out how to put the pieces back together." She scribbles a note on her pad and looks up. "So how about next Tuesday? And then we can take it from there."

"Tuesday? I'm not sure. I might be doing something, I can't remember."

Rosie smiles and hands Kathryn her card. "Here. You call me in the next day or two and let me know. I'll have Doris pencil you in in the meantime. So call us either way."

Slipping the card in her bag, Kathryn stands to leave. On the way out, Rosie says, "I just want to say one thing. Your mother and I are friends. I'm not going to pretend we're not. But what goes on in here has nothing to do with my relationships outside this office."

The phone rings behind them, and the receptionist picks it up. "Rosie?" she says, covering the mouthpiece with her hand, "it's Margaret Campbell. Should I have her call you back?"

Kathryn gapes at Doris. "*Margaret?*"

"Phone calls are confidential, Doris, remember?" Rosie scolds, giving her an exasperated look. "Take a message." Turning to Kathryn, she says, "Doris seems to think we're running a beauty salon in here. Look, I'm not going to lie to you. Both Margaret and your mother come to me."

"Oh, God," Kathryn says, putting her hands up.

Rosie stops and puts her hand on Kathryn's arm. "You know what a small town this is. But I've lived here for forty-three years, my whole life. I don't have any problem keeping things separate."

"I don't see how that can be true."

Smiling, Rosie says, "Somebody once defined genius as the ability to hold two conflicting ideas in your head at the same time. I'm not saying I'm a genius, but I do believe I'm capable of that." She pats Kathryn's shoulder. "Anyway, it's up to you. I can understand if you feel uncomfortable."

Walking down the steps into the sunlight, still bright in the late-afternoon sky, Kathryn has to stop to catch her breath. It all feels too familiar; things are closing in. And yet somehow, on the surface, she feels strangely, almost clinically, detached. Even the sad little details of the past year she recounted to Rosie seem curiously unconnected to any real emotion she might have. What *am* I feeling? she wonders, getting into her mother's car and reaching under the seat for the keys. It's been so long since she's asked herself that question that she doesn't have the slightest idea how to answer.

AT A STOPLIGHT Kathryn pulls up beside a minivan driven by a harried-looking young mother. In the back, a row of car seats and several tow-headed children are shaded by a screen attached to the window with suction cups. Toys and bottles and boxes of crackers orbit around them.

The chaos of it, the drudgery, the endless mess; the idea of becoming a mother is as foreign to Kathryn as the idea of becoming, say, a mortician—and about as appealing. She knows babies are hard work; she did enough baby-sitting in high school to temper any romantic illusions she might have had. And it's hard to imagine feeling ready to nurture someone else when she can barely manage her own life.

And yet. As she looks over at the children, their faces upturned and eager, their chubby starfish hands, she has to admit she feels a twinge of melancholy. The end of her marriage signified many things: a rending of vows, a crumbling of intention, an admission of defeat. But it also represented the death of hope, of potential. It ended her dreams about the kind of person she was and the kind of life she and Paul would lead together. Somewhere deep down she is unutterably sad about the babies they will never have, the ghost children they imagined late at night as they lay in bed in the dark together: one boy and one girl, three boys, two girls, all with Paul's dark eyes and her fair skin. Sometimes, still, she thinks of these children, as silent and otherworldly as angels, hovering just out of reach.

As the light turns green, Kathryn pulls ahead, watching in her rearview mirror as the woman in the minivan shouts over her shoulder and tosses a stuffed animal into the backseat, trying to keep from swerving into oncoming traffic.

"WE GOT A postcard from Josh in the mail today," Kathryn's mother says when she gets home. She holds the glossy card up with two fingers. "He's in Nepal. Says he's sorry he can't make it to Maine while you're here, but this is all the time he can get off work."

Kathryn takes the card, a *National Geographic*–style shot of the snow-capped Himalayas. She turns it over and scans it. "Wish you could see this place . . . incredible hiking trails . . . unbelievable views," she says aloud. She looks at her mother. "You hoped he'd be coming home, didn't you?"

She shrugs dismissively, but Kathryn can tell she's hurt. "He's a grown man," she says. "I can't expect him to use up what little vacation time he has on me. But I did think he might, knowing you were here."

"Mom," Kathryn says gently, "Josh and I haven't been close in years."

"I keep hoping that'll change," her mother says, smiling sadly. For a moment she seems lost in thought. Then she clasps her hands together. "So how'd it go?" she asks. "I'm about to pour myself a glass of wine. Care to join me?"

"Sure," Kathryn says. "It was interesting."

Her mother opens the fridge and pulls out a bottle. "White okay?"

Kathryn nods. Her mother takes down two stemmed glasses and gets a tray of ice out of the freezer. "No ice in mine," Kathryn says.

"I shouldn't either—I know it's not too classy. But it's jug wine. Why stop there?" She half-fills the glasses and motions toward the sliding glass door. "Let's go out in the garden. I feel like celebrating. I may have sold a house today."

"May have?"

"They're still deciding, but I think I've got them." With her glass in one hand and the bottle in the other, she leads the way out the door and down the steps to the white wicker chairs sitting under a tree in the back. She sets the bottle on a little wicker table. "So what do you mean, 'interesting'?" she says, taking a long sip of wine.

Kathryn shrugs. She doesn't want to talk about it. She can feel herself closing up, like a drawbridge.

"Did you talk about Jennifer at all?"

"No." She takes a deep breath. "Margaret called while I was there," she says, subterfuging.

"Oh, really?" Her mother's expression stays the same, but her eyebrows lift. She has another gulp of wine. "Why didn't you talk about Jennifer?"

"It just didn't seem right. It seemed like too much."

Her mother leans forward and tops up her glass.

"And anyway, I'm not sure I feel comfortable with her," Kathryn says, trying to change the subject again. "It seems really bizarre, everybody going to the same therapist. I don't see how she can keep everything separate. The friendship, the therapy thing, seeing you and Margaret and me—"

"I didn't know she was seeing Margaret."

Kathryn looks at her mother, biting the lip of her glass, and suddenly she's sorry she mentioned Margaret at all. She knew when she said it that her mother might be hurt; after all these years, Margaret's name still has that kind of power. When Kathryn was in high school and fighting with her mother, the meanest thing she could say was "Margaret never yells at me!" or "Margaret said I could." Eyes gleaming, flushed neck betraying her anger and pain, her mother would say, "Why don't you just go live with your father and *Margaret*, then?"

"Well," Kathryn says now, "anyway, Doris says hi." She forces a laugh. "That woman needs to go to secretary school."

Her mother nods slowly.

For a few minutes they sit together in silence. Then Kathryn says, "Mom . . ."

"What?"

"I have an idea. I want to take you to dinner. Somewhere fun, somewhere we can sit outside. My treat."

"Your treat?" she says, bemused. "How do you think Rosie would analyze this?"

"She'd probably say I was trying to get in touch with my inner child by nurturing the Great Mother."

"Daughters who feed their mothers and the mothers who let them."

"Hey, pretty good."

"I've been in that office quite a bit," she says, collecting the wine bottle and glasses and standing up. "I know all the slogans. Now, where are you taking me? I'm starving."

AFTER A LEISURELY dinner at Mama Baldacci's, a cozy Italian restaurant with red-checked tablecloths and meatballs the size of tennis balls, they return home and Kathryn's mother heads upstairs to take a bath. Kathryn sits out on the porch swing, pushing it back and forth with her foot. She thinks about how Rosie said that her life has been torn apart and she has to rebuild it. Frowning in the darkness, she tries to figure out what it is that she doesn't agree with, what it is that rings false to her. There's a drama to it she knows she hasn't lived. There was never a cataclysmic moment in which things might have been, however briefly, etched in relief against memory, against things to come—a moment which, by its sheer magnitude, defined her history and her future. Instead, Kathryn thinks, she has disintegrated slowly over a number of years. By the time of her divorce she was already less than a whole person, shadowing through her life without much in the way of will or ambition. It is true that she doesn't know what she wants, but it's more than that: She doesn't, any longer, possess a want. She feels somehow lighter than she should, lighter in the mind, a solid will slowly turned to sand.

Kathryn thinks about all the stories she could tell Rosie over the next month or two, stories that might intrigue her and provide clues to Kathryn's depression—if that's what it is—but would essentially leave her alone. She thinks about what remains unspoken: Jennifer, Will, the last night by the river, the constant turning over, like the worrying of beads, the question of what happened to her best friend the night she disappeared. It is a question as relentless as it is haunting, the only constant in the past decade of her life. *Where did she go? Where did she go?*— the rhythm of it like the chugging of a train through a deep and far-off valley. It is a question that embraces mystery, with one embalmed response: *Nobody knows.* Yet there is an echo, fainter but more urgent, that haunts her: *Somebody has to know. Somebody, somewhere, knows what happened.*

Kathryn can go days without thinking about it—weeks, even. She finds she has an amazing capacity to forget. Sometimes she feels as if she is skating along the surface of her life, her past the dark, roiling water underneath. When the ice cracks—and it does, it has—she moves a little faster, cutting deeper with the blade, working back to safer ground.

Turning off the porch light, Kathryn heads upstairs to her room. On an impulse she goes into her closet and takes down a box marked "College Papers"—she seems to remember having written about this once, long ago. It was her first year at UVA, as she recalls, in a composition course. The grad student teaching the class wanted the students to express themselves; he didn't care much about form. He was always giving them assignments like "Describe a meal you love" and "Help a blind person visualize the color blue."

Kathryn finds the course folder and leafs through it until she gets to the paper. Then she sits on her bed and reads it:

Kathryn Campbell
Composition I/Instructor: J. Trainer
October 14, 1986
The University of Virginia
Assignment: Write about something you've lost

Ever since Jennifer disappeared, I feel as if I've been wandering in a foreign country without a map. When I try, I can recall a blur of details about what happened after she left us that night by the river—Will's strained voice on the phone the next morning, telling me that Jennifer hadn't slept in her bed; the stiff formality of the thick-belted policeman in the driveway, with Mrs. Pelletier behind him on the porch, wrapped in Jennifer's letter sweater; searching with Jack and Brian and the other volunteers through the spongy underbrush near the Kenduskeag—but mostly I don't try. Remembering the details doesn't seem to help.

When Jennifer disappeared some kind of time was permanently suspended. We don't know if she's dead, so we can't bury her

—no casket, no wreath of flowers, no eulogy, no funeral, no mourning. When I read about the relatives of soldiers in Vietnam still missing after fifteen years, people who believe that there might be a chance the person is alive, who cling to each fragile lead as if it might yield the answer, I think I understand. I loved Jennifer like I love my own family: imperfectly, carelessly, with an irrational certainty that while I might grow up, go away, move on, she will always be just where I need her, just the same.

A year before she disappeared, Jennifer got a passport. She always dreamed of traveling to foreign lands. I imagine that the telephone call will come in the middle of the night: Someone has seen her. She's in London, selling jewelry on the street. In Paris, with some brooding French poet. Or a postcard arrives: She just wants to let us know she's fine and living on a fishing boat in New Zealand. Climbing the Swiss Alps. Lying on a beach in St. Croix.

In my nightmares, I conjure other scenarios: They've found her body in the tall grass by the edge of Green Lake. They've found her in a shallow grave in the Maine woods. In the town dump. In a basement apple room.

In the four months since she left us, I think I've thought of everything.

Jennifer is my best friend, and now she will always be my best friend, because she exists for me now only as she was. There is a part of me that will probably never age, that will stay suspended, poised, eighteen years old and holding my breath, until we find out what happened.

At the bottom of the page, the instructor has written, *"Kathryn—Fiction? Nonfiction? Who is Jennifer, and why should we care? We could use more details: The narrator talks about how s/he feels after his/her best friend disappears, but what does s/he miss about her specifically? Why was she such a significant person to him/her? Also, the narrator seems pretty de-*

tached. Have you researched this? Is it a typical response? (See Kübler-Ross's study about the stages of grief if you plan to expand this into a short story.)

The imagery and analysis are good, though the 'details' the narrator doesn't want to remember are ultimately what will make the story interesting. √. —J. Trainer"

Kathryn smiles at the grade. It was unusual for her not to get a check-plus—she usually managed to get the tone just right. How fitting, she thinks, that in this one instance she wasn't able to pull it off.

"Well, look at this," Kathryn's mother says at breakfast. Kathryn has gotten up early to make banana-walnut pancakes, an old before-school favorite, in an attempt to extend the goodwill between them a little further. Her mother is sipping coffee and leafing through the paper. Her voice is chirpy; breakfast, Kathryn knows, is her favorite meal of the day. Kathryn flips three lopsided pancakes on the griddle and puts them in the toaster oven to stay warm. "Jack Ledbetter has been promoted to assistant news editor of the paper."

"Really?" Kathryn sticks a glass jar of maple syrup in a pan of water and puts it on the stove to warm.

"I see his byline all the time," her mother says. "Here it is now. Let's see: It's a profile of a lobsterman. 'Harley Gerow eats lobster for breakfast, lunch and dinner, but he can't stand clams.' That's the first line. Catchy, isn't it?"

Kathryn looks over at her. "You want to stir up some juice?"

She folds the paper and goes to the freezer. "I just thought you might be interested." She takes out a small, orange, frost-covered cylinder and kneads it with her fingers to soften it. "Didn't you two use to be friends?"

"Sure, in high school. We lost touch after that."

"What happened?"

"Nothing happened. We just lost touch. You can't stay friends with everybody you ever met in your life."

"Wasn't he down at the river with you all that night?"

Kathryn looks at the bubbling pancakes and weighs them with the spatula to see if they're done.

"What do you mean, missing?" Jack had said when she called the next morning.

"She didn't sleep in her bed."

"I don't understand."

"She didn't sleep in her bed," she said again, impatient, repeating to him what Will had said to her, as if somehow the words might be enough to contain their meaning.

Kathryn's mother looks at her intently. "You haven't stayed in touch with any of them, have you?"

She turns away. "No."

"Which one of us is going to be famous?" Brian said as they sat around the campfire. "Who's going to be the alcoholic? Which one of you girls will ditch your husband for me when we come back for our ten-year reunion? Who's dying young?"

The pancakes are overcooked. Kathryn flips them, three rigid brown disks, and tosses them into the trash. Her mother squeezes the solid chunk of concentrate into a pitcher. She pours water into the juice can to measure it, and then into the pitcher, stirring the mixture with a whisk. "Well, anyway," she says, "I was thinking: Why don't you give Jack a call and see if there's an article you might be able to work on?"

"You mean for the paper?"

"Sure, why not?"

"Oh, Mom." Kathryn takes two plates from the cabinet above the sink and balances them above her hip as she rummages through the silverware drawer. "I don't think I want to write anything just now."

"But Kathryn, you're so good at it." She carries the pitcher of juice and two glasses to the table. "You want ice?"

"No, thanks. And I'm not that good. I'm adequate. And anyway—"

"That clipping you sent me about the French circus, now, that was really inspired. Don't try to tell me otherwise."

"Mom—"

"Where this lack of self-esteem comes from, I don't know," her mother says, exasperation in her voice. She opens the freezer and loads ice into her glass, three hard clinks. "I mean, I go out, I take people to see a house, and I know I'm going to sell it because I tell myself I can. That's all it is, Kathryn, is believing in yourself."

"Mom. Stop. I don't want to write articles about lobsters for the *Bangor Daily News*."

"Oh, I see," she says, "I get it now. You're too good for the *Bangor Daily News*."

"That's not what I'm saying."

"Then what are you saying?"

"I'm saying that it would be silly to make plans. I don't know how long I'm going to be around."

"Let's be realistic," her mother says. "You don't seem to know what you want to do, and you don't have anywhere to go. I'd say you're going to be here awhile."

"Oh, my God," Kathryn mumbles, despair rising up in her at the thought. "Maybe I should just leave, today, now, go to Boston and try to piece together a life for myself there. . . ."

Her mother looks at her, then pours two glasses of juice, holding the handle of the sweating pitcher in one hand, supporting it carefully with the other. She sets the pitcher down. "Why are you so terrified at the thought of living here?"

"Which one of us will end up on the Left Bank?" Brian said. "Who's

going to Santa Fe? And who's going to be stuck here in Bangor, with a snowmobile and a monster-sized television and brochures for cruise-line vacations tacked up on a bulletin board in the kitchen?"

"Because it would feel . . . cowardly."

"But that's silly. Lots of people live in Bangor their whole lives, and they're perfectly happy about it. Look, you don't have to make any hard and fast decision right now. You can stay here until you get your feet on the ground. And, you know, Frank Harnish has offered me the use of one of his cars while you're home, so you'll have your own transportation and not feel dependent on me."

"Who's Frank Harnish?"

"Oh, just a friend," her mother says, "a dear, dear man who runs a car dealership out on Valley Road. But anyway, the point is, you have options."

Kathryn can tell by her mother's studied-casual tone and the way her hand flutters to her throat that she's been keeping this from her. "So what's the story?" she demands. "Are you seeing this guy?"

"*Qu'est-ce que c'est* 'seeing'?" Her mother gives a little laugh and waves her hand dismissively. "We have dinner together every now and then. No big deal."

"You've never told me about him, but you've told him about me?"

"Just the basic facts."

"Failed marriage, failed career, living at home with Mom—those facts?"

"Basically. Hey, we're getting a little yellow Saturn out of it."

"You're amazing," Kathryn says, shaking her head. For a moment the room is quiet except for the gurgling of the coffee machine. "Don't you remember when we first moved here," Kathryn says, "and we used to sit on the front porch together and you said the quiet could drive you out of your mind? Can't you remember what that felt like?"

"Gosh, I was awfully dramatic," her mother says dryly. "I can see where you get it from."

"I just don't want to end up here before I've even started."

"Look, Kathryn," she says. "I don't understand what it is you have to prove to yourself or God knows who else. You're here now, you've got free housing for a while and some time on your hands, so I'm just suggesting you do something productive."

Kathryn gets up and pours two mugs of coffee, stirring milk into hers and Equal into her mother's.

"All I'm talking about is writing a little article for the local paper. I'm not suggesting you buy a house, for God's sake." Kathryn brings her a mug, and she holds it with both hands. "I just want you to be happy with yourself," she says. "To feel valued for your skills. To do something meaningful while you're here."

"You want to be able to brag about me."

"Maybe a little of that, too," her mother says, lifting her shoulders in a coy you've-found-me-out shrug. "So will you talk to Jack? For my sake?"

"Oh, Mother."

"Just this one thing. It's all I ask."

Kathryn props her elbow on the table and puts her head in her hand. "All right," she says. "All right all right all right."

THE OFFICES OF the *Bangor Daily News* are on the fringe of town, beyond the cluster of turn-of-the-century downtown storefronts, beyond even the litter of fast-food restaurants and gas stations on outer Main Street. The building sits beside the sprawling Bangor Auditorium, where a range of stars, from Reba McIntyre to Def Lepard to Billy Joel, come to perform, the last stop on many a Northeastern tour. Behind the auditorium is a racetrack populated with tired horses and bleary-eyed patrons clutching liquor bottles in paper bags. In front of the auditorium, five hundred yards from the *News* building, stands a thirty-one-foot fiberglass statue of the legendary lumberjack Paul Bunyan. He's wearing a red-and-black checked shirt and massive hiking boots, with an ax thrown over his shoulder and a hearty grin on his bearded face—a cartoon embodiment of the pioneer spirit.

When Kathryn had called a few hours earlier to see if Jack could meet with her, he didn't seem surprised. "I've been thinking about you," he said. "And I've been thinking a lot about Jennifer. I guess it's only natural, with the reunion coming up. It's hard not to think about what your life was like back then."

"I know," she said. "Me, too."

"I'm glad you got in touch," he said.

Kathryn parks on Main Street beside the flat-topped, red-brick *News* building. Leaving the car unlocked as she always does (a longtime habit of growing up in a small town), she enters the building and climbs a set of stairs to the front desk. When she asks for Jack Ledbetter, the woman behind the counter directs her up another set of stairs to the second floor. Kathryn emerges, panting a bit, in the newsroom, a wide-open brown-carpeted space filled with desk clusters separated by low dividers. A computer terminal sits on each desk. Glass-fronted offices ring the walls.

From out of one of these offices comes Jack, striding toward her with his arms outstretched. He *looks* like a reporter, Kathryn thinks, with his unruly hair, striped shirt half tucked in, loosened rep tie, and faded chinos. A grown-up boy.

"Well, look at you," he says, wrapping his arms around her. "Haven't changed a bit, except the hair. I like it."

"You're a good liar, Jack," she says, her voice muffled in his shoulder. "I always liked that about you. And you really *haven't* changed."

"I'm not lying."

"Ever since I got here, people have been telling me I look tired."

"What? No you don't." He pulls back and looks at her. "Okay, a little. But it's been a rough summer, hasn't it?"

"A rough year."

"A rough ten years, but we can talk about that later," he says, smiling.

"Anyway, you'll be fine; you're back in Bangor now. You can slow down the pace a little." Taking her by the hand, he leads her back to his office, past the reporters tapping at keyboards and the clerks looking at them furtively over the dividers.

"So are you the grand pooh-bah?" she whispers.

"No. I'm just the petty ruler of a little fiefdom. The pooh-bah lives in the big palace." He gestures toward a corner office, where a beefy, balding guy in a white shirt and tie is sitting behind a desk. The guy glances up, and Jack flattens his hand in a mock salute. A clerk, watching them as they walk past, smiles and shakes her head.

Jack goes into his office and sits behind his desk, motioning for Kathryn to sit in the chair opposite. She looks around. The walls are covered with clippings and cheaply engraved plaques, prizes for reporting and a river rafting certificate. Through the scrim of dirt over the window, she can see a green sliver of park and Paul Bunyan's indomitable profile. "A window office," she says. "Pretty fancy. By the way, my mom said to tell you congratulations on the promotion."

"Well, thank her for me. But the only thing I should be congratulated for is successful scheming. I rustled up an offer from a Massachusetts paper, so the *BDN* had no choice."

"Smart."

"Very smart. And now I have a window office, a whole bunch of people to boss around, and all the free doughnuts I can eat. Life could be worse."

"You know, I've been following that three-part series you're doing on deforestation," she says. "It's really good."

"Wait'll you see the investigative report we're doing on the blueberry industry." He leans forward conspiratorially. "It's a dangerous business, Kath, but somebody's got to expose these people."

She laughs, remembering that it was this kind of self-deprecating humor that had made Jack so popular in high school. He didn't intimidate anybody, as Rachel could; he didn't, like Brian, confuse people with his offbeat sense of humor. When Jack entered a room, whether he knew anybody or not, he'd soon be spinning stories, drawing people toward him. Somehow, he always managed to sidle up to people and befriend them before they could even think of turning away.

"So," he says, leaning back in his chair and putting his sneakered feet up on the desk. "I was over at Sanborn Home Decorating the other day, picking up some paint chips for my new office—"

"And you just happened to run into Skip Sanborn."

"Chip. But, yeah." He grins. "And he told me some pretty interesting things about you. He says you're a hotshot freelance journalist."

She squirms in her seat. "Not exactly. More like unemployed. I quit my job in Charlottesville a month ago, around the time I quit my marriage."

"I was sorry to hear about that."

She shrugs.

"But I guess it's probably better to know early if it's not going to work out, huh?"

"Yeah," she says, gliding over it, "I'm glad it's over. But what about you? What've you been up to?"

"This job keeps me busy."

"You're not married yet."

"Nooo."

"I always imagined you'd get married early, for some reason."

"Why?"

"I don't know. You were so close to Rachel . . ."

"Rachel and I weren't—"

"No, I know." She smiles. Is it her imagination, or did he suddenly get a little defensive? "I just meant that you seemed to have such a nice rapport with her. You were one of those rare guys in high school who genuinely seemed to like the opposite sex. Not just—you know. But really . . ." She shrugs.

His face relaxes into a grin. "Well, that's probably true," he says. "I just wish I had time for anything these days but work. Speaking of which," he says, leaning forward, "didn't you say on the phone that you had something to discuss with me?"

She sits up straight. "Well, if you can call it that. Actually, it's about— Well, as you've heard, I've been doing some writing in Charlottesville. . . . As a matter of fact, I brought a few pieces with me; they're mostly silly, but I thought you might like to—"

"I'd love to," he says. Then, before she can stammer on, "Would you like to write something for us?"

She sits back, surprised. "Yes."

"Good. I've actually got something in mind."

"You do?"

"Maybe. I've been thinking about it since you called." He squints, looking directly at her, as if trying to decide what to say. "I always thought you were a wonderful writer, Kath. The literary magazine was excellent our senior year."

"Oh. Thanks," she says, warming to his words and then reddening slightly at her reaction to this ten-year-old praise. The literary magazine, *Ramifications*, had been her baby; she started it and served as editor for two years in a row. When they were seniors, it won two statewide awards. "But that was a long time ago."

"I'm sure you've only gotten better. And I think this story would be perfect for you." He pauses. "You know our class reunion is this summer."

She grimaces. "I don't really want to do a piece about our class—"

"No. That's not what I'm suggesting." He unearths a telephone from a pile of papers and punches in a few numbers. "Cheryl, would you bring me that file you got from the library this morning?" He turns back to Kathryn. "I was looking at an old story the other day, and I came across all those news clippings about Jennifer. That was ten years ago, can you believe it?" He shakes his head slowly. "Anyway, most of them were from 1986, some from 1987, one from 1988. Then the story just went away."

"If there's no news, I guess there's no story."

"Well, yes and no. I think there is a story. And I'd like you to do it."

She inhales sharply. "God, Jack, I don't know."

He leans forward on his forearms and speaks quietly, coaxing her toward him with the urgency in his voice. "Listen: Jennifer disappears on the night of her high-school graduation. She just vanishes. No clues, no note, no physical evidence, nothing. Nobody ever sees or hears from her again. Now it's a decade later, the class of eighty-six is back for its tenth reunion, and her best friend, a reporter, decides to undertake her own investigation. Were there ever any suspects? Is the case closed?"

"But, Jack—"

"No, listen, Kath. This is an important story. I want you to go talk to Will, talk to Mrs. Pelletier, talk to Jennifer's teachers, the police, all of us who were with her by the river that night. Trace her steps after she left us. You probably won't find out anything new—but maybe, just maybe, you will. Either way, it's a story."

"But don't you think this might be a little exploitative?"

"No, I don't. Look, it's not like she died. She disappeared. What does that mean? How does somebody just vanish into thin air? It's unresolved, Kath, and if you want to get noble about it then you can think about the fact that you're opening up a case they gave up on way too soon. Remember how every year on the anniversary of the day it happened Mrs. Pelletier used to run an ad offering money for any information? And after four or five years the money figure went away? It was obvious they were giving up. They still ran the ad for a while, but it was just a memorial—and then, three or four years ago, it stopped altogether. Doesn't that seem creepy to you? Why hasn't anybody pursued it any further? How could we have allowed that?"

"Well, if you feel this way, why haven't *you* investigated it?"

He rocks back in his chair. "By the time I got here after college, the story was considered dead. I mentioned a few ideas to the crime reporter who covered it, but he wasn't interested." Gesturing with his chin toward the newsroom, he says, "Office politics. I didn't want to step on anybody's toes."

"So what's changed?"

"That crime reporter left, for one thing. Got an offer the *BDN* couldn't match." He grins. "The boss never liked him anyway."

A woman raps on the glass outside Jack's office, and he motions for her to come in. She hands him a folder.

"Thanks, Cheryl." She nods and leaves his office. "Also," he says, turning back to Kathryn, "now there's a hook—and that hook is you." He hands her the folder across the desk. "Here, you can start with this. It's just a few clippings and a time line, but it should refresh your memory. You can use our library to find the rest."

She takes the folder from him, and it falls open on her lap. "Snapshot of a family struck by tragedy." That's the caption under the grainy photograph in the Xeroxed clipping, dated July 15, 1986, on the top of the pile. There is Jennifer, her face guarded and secretive, standing on the steps of her home, with Will and their mother. Mrs. Pelletier's arm is draped around Will's shoulders, but Jennifer is standing slightly to the side. She isn't touching anybody.

"Think about it," Jack says.

"I'll think about it." She shuts the folder and stands to leave.

"Of course," he says, rising, "if you don't want to do this, I need someone to cover Egg Day at Broadway Park."

She smiles. "You drive a hard bargain, Mr. Ledbetter."

"Listen to this little ditty from the Egg Day promotional packet," he says, walking her out. " 'Humpty Dumpty had a bad summer, Humpty Dumpty's spring was a bummer, Humpty's winter was no good at all, but—' "

"Humpty Dumpty had a great fall," she says, shaking her head. "That's really awful, Jack."

"The choice is yours. Just let me know."

"HOW'D IT GO?" Kathryn's mother asks brightly when she gets home. She's come out into the garden to say hello.

"It was nice. He was sweet."

Her mother looks up from where she's digging in the dirt. "So . . ."

Kathryn can feel the weight of her mother's expectation on her shoulders, and she deliberately shrugs it off. "So nothing."

"You're not going to do something for the paper?"

"Maybe. I'm not sure yet."

"Oh, Kathryn." She sighs. "You are obstinate. Just like your father."

Kathryn crouches down, her arms crossed over her knees. "You can be pretty obstinate yourself."

Her mother wipes her forehead with the back of her white cotton glove, as big and rounded as a clown's. "Good thing, with a daughter like you to contend with."

"I believe the chicken came first, Mom," Kathryn says.

PART TWO

MEMORY

After four cups of coffee Kathryn's body is tingling. She might as well have injected the caffeine into her veins. She can't think straight, can't concentrate. Her senses sharpen: She hears a dump truck grinding down the street several blocks over; a child wails, an old lawn mower coughs into gear. The house is still. She wanders through the downstairs, chilly in the thin morning light, inspecting the familiar watercolor hanging in the living room and the Chinese plates on the dining-room wall. Little has changed since she lived here. It's strange to her now that she ever did—it feels so much to her like her mother's home.

Kathryn drifts upstairs, her eyes adjusting to the gloomy hall, and goes into her mother's bedroom. She opens the closet and sifts through the clothes, idly searching for pieces she doesn't recognize. This skirt is new, this blouse. A moss-green cardigan still has its tag, an orange price sticker revealing its bargain-basement provenance. When she was growing up, her mother bought clothes on clearance or not at all. It was more than the money: Once you had the necessities, her mother believed, anything else was frivolous. You didn't really need a moss-green cardigan, so if you bought it, it had to be an especially good deal. As a result, Kathryn had a closetful of clothing that was a half-size off, or slightly the wrong color, or made of a fabric that stretched or sagged. When she went to college and was earning her own money working in the dining hall, she began paying full price for small luxuries: black suede boots, a leather jacket, a pair of velvet jeans. Spending the money was a druglike high, but it didn't last long. After college, with a mountain of bills and three maxed-out credit cards, Kathryn had no choice but to return to her mother's careful ways.

Kathryn opens a window in the stuffy room, putting her hand to the screen to gauge how warm it is outside. The day is overcast, with a tarnished edge to the silver sky. The air is cool. She can hear the wind whistling sharply as it moves between the trees. She had forgotten how quickly the weather can change, how cold Maine can get in the summer. Standing there in her shorts and UVA T-shirt, she realizes that she's covered in goose bumps. She reaches into her mother's closet, tugs the green cardigan off its hanger, and slips it on, yanking off the tag and slipping it into the patch pocket on the front of the sweater, in case her mother wants to take it back.

Last night, when she and her mother were sitting down to dinner, Jack had called to see if she wanted to go out to the Sea Dog for a drink. "I can't tonight," she said into the phone, turning toward the wall as she used to do in high school to avoid her mother's inquisitive gaze.

"So?" her mother said as soon as she hung up.

"It was Jack."

"You could go. Don't feel you have to stay here because of me."

"I don't, Mom. I'm not in the mood to go out tonight." Kathryn sat down and spread her napkin on her lap.

"Maybe you should," her mother said, cutting squares into the vegetarian lasagna Kathryn had made that afternoon. "It might be good for you."

"What is this, peer pressure?"

"Jack Ledbetter is very nice. And he knows everybody in town. It wouldn't hurt to be seen with him." She motioned to Kathryn to hand her her plate.

"Wouldn't hurt what?" Kathryn asked. "Who am I supposed to be impressing?"

"That's not what I mean. I mean, for your career. Don't you need to be establishing contacts?"

Kathryn laughed. "That's really lame, and you know it. You just want me to go on a date."

"He was asking you on a date?"

She rolled her eyes. "We're not talking about this."

Her mother served herself a piece and propped the spatula in the serving dish. "Well, that's a little presumptuous, then, don't you think? Calling you at the last minute?" She took a bite of lasagna. "Umm, good. What is that, chicken?"

"Eggplant."

"I think you did the right thing, playing hard to get."

Kathryn poured herself a glass of wine, hesitating at the midway point and then filling it to the top. "Mom, I'm not playing anything," she said, taking a big swallow. "I just didn't feel like going out tonight. And it's not a date. Let's nip that idea in the bud."

Chewing thoughtfully, her mother said, "He's kind of cute, I think, in a rumpled, underpaid way."

"Did I say we're not talking about this?"

"Those big green eyes. And that hair—it probably used to be red when he was little, don't you think? There's still a little red in it."

"Mom," Kathryn said firmly. "How was your day?"

Now, looking at herself in the mirror over her mother's dresser, Kathryn wonders idly if Jack *was* asking her out. She tries to remember what he was like in high school, why she had never really thought about going out with him then. He was always there, part of the group, his shoulder brushing hers at football games as he passed her a soda or a slice of pizza. He was in the last row of class, laughing with Rachel. He was walking down the hall with cheerleaders, flirting with them at their lockers, dropping them off at class.

He was funny and charming with her, but never more. Even if he had been interested, Kathryn thinks, his friendship with Rachel would have taken precedence. It was as if he was afraid of hurting Rachel, of betraying her somehow. Kathryn always suspected that was why Jack never had a serious girlfriend in high school. Or maybe it was simply that he didn't need one; he had enough else going on, and he didn't want to complicate his life. At any rate, at some point, without ever discussing it, both of them must simply have dismissed the idea that there might be something between them. So they went through the motions of friendship without ever really connecting, without risking revelation, without hope of anything deeper than the occasional dialogue about chemistry class, or arranging rides to the movies, or how the foreboding sky suggested a possible day off from school. More often, their voices joined an ongoing conversation; their personalities melded into the group.

After getting dressed in jeans and the green cardigan, Kathryn hunts for a notebook and a pen. Her mother has left the car keys for the Saturn on a bulletin board in the kitchen that has always served as a message center, along with a note: "Frank brought the car over this morning. I'm assuming your driver's license is O.K.! I'm having drinks with Frank tonight (payback!) so don't expect me home before 7 or so. If something comes up for you, don't worry about calling—I'll figure it out. XX MOM." Kathryn sighs at the bulletin board and lifts the keys off the hook. Looking out the kitchen window, she sees a sporty, bright-yellow car in the driveway with dealer plates.

The inside of the car smells like a carpet showroom. Everything is beige. In the glove compartment Kathryn finds the registration and the owner's manual, still sealed in its plastic bag. Except for a ski trip to Utah when she and Paul rented a car, Kathryn can't remember the last time she drove a new one. The car she and Paul had in Charlottesville, the one he kept, was eight years old when they bought it, with ninety-two thousand miles, a fringe of rust around the bottom, and a strange clunking noise they never bothered to investigate.

Driving down Main Street, Kathryn feels as if she is vacuum-sealed in a biosphere. She turns on the air conditioner, just to see if it works, and cold air blasts out of the vents. At a stoplight she figures out that the strange black slit in the radio is in fact a CD player, and she discovers three CDs under the dash: *Victoria's Secret's Classical Music for Lovers*, *Wayne Newton Live in Concert*, and *Yanni at the Acropolis*. She opts for the radio. By the time she reaches the *News* building, she doesn't want to get out. The climate is perfect, she's just heard two songs by Cheap Trick on the classic-rock station, and she's found a spillproof cup container at the touch of a button. She could stay in this car all day. She's tempted to pull out of the parking lot and keep going, all the way down Route 1 to Winterport and beyond, maybe to another state. Hell, why not Mexico? But the next song is REO Speedwagon, and, well, she's here. She gets out of the car.

Inside, in the newsroom, a couple of reporters are sitting at their desks sipping coffee and staring groggily at computer terminals. One glances up and nods as she comes in. This pleases her, even though she knows he probably doesn't recognize her and he's just being polite. It makes her feel like one of them—a reporter on assignment. She can see Jack at the far end of the room in his glass-walled office, talking on the phone. His feet are up on the edge of his desk and he's bouncing in his spring-coiled seat, tossing a beanbag in the air.

As she walks toward him she is suddenly nervous. He's busy, and she isn't; he's wearing a tie, and she's in jeans. He's been here for hours (she can see the evidence, paper coffee cups lined up on his desk), and she's just strolling in. This article is probably the least important thing on his agenda—he assigned it to her as a novelty, probably because he felt sorry for her—and it's the only thing on her mind. Plus, there's that business of the invitation to go out the night before hanging between them. Does he feel as awkward about it as she does?

"I can come back," she stage-whispers at the door to his office, but he gestures emphatically for her to sit down.

"Yeah. Right. Okay," he says into the phone, lifting his feet off his desk and sitting up in his chair. When he looks at her, she can see the stubble on his chin and circles under his eyes. "So let me know when you've got something down, and we can go from there. Right. Friday. I need it by three. Hasta la vista, baby." He replaces the receiver and stares at the blinking red lights on the handset. Then he looks up at her. "Hello," he says.

"Hello."

"You look rested."

"You look like you had a rough night." She smiles.

"Yeah, it's probably just as well you didn't go with us. Somebody's intern had the crazy idea to do tequila shots." He rubs his head. "I'm getting too old for that stuff."

"Oh," she says, "it was an office thing." She's surprised to find she feels a pang of disappointment.

"Yeah, I thought you might want to meet some of the others. They're a good bunch."

As always, Kathryn is struck by Jack's casual generosity, his impulse to bring people together. He was like that in high school, organizing Friday-night video evenings and arranging rides to parties. He had more friends than anyone she knew. But she remembers Rachel snapping at him once, in front of a large group, "I needed to talk to you. I didn't want this to be a huge thing with everybody else," and all of them standing there uncomfortably while Jack tried to explain that he didn't realize, he didn't understand, he thought it would be fun with more people, and he thought she'd think so, too. Looking at his bloodshot eyes across the desk, Kathryn promises herself that she won't make any more assumptions about his motives. "I'm sorry about begging off," she says. "Next time, okay?"

"Okay. And no interns, I promise." He hits the desk with both palms to signal a change in the conversation. "So what about the Jennifer story? Are you on board?"

Kathryn shifts in her chair and glances down at her blank notebook. She hasn't followed any of the half-dozen paths Jack suggested, from contacting the police department to reading old clippings to interviewing family and friends. She isn't sure where to start, and she's also somehow afraid of being seen as taking advantage of their misery. After all, she knows Jennifer's family, knows the pain they've been through and how raw it still is. It was an ordeal for them to have to talk to the police and the press as much as they did at the time; they certainly won't want to rehash the whole thing now. "Well, I've done some asking around," Kathryn says, "and it's the funniest thing. Nobody seems to know where she is."

"Really," says Jack.

"That's right."

"You're quite a sleuth."

"It's still speculation at this point," she says. "I'll let you know when I can get something more solid. In the meantime, I need you to point me in a couple of directions."

"At the same time?"

"Yes, I need a good spin on this story."

They both grimace at the lame wordplay, and he puts his face in his hands. "I can't keep up with you. I can't keep up with me. I need a cup of coffee."

THE LIBRARY AT the *News* is staffed by a heavy woman with a nimbus of salt-and-pepper hair wearing a batik-print skirt and a loose purple tunic.

"Joanne, Kathryn is doing a special assignment for us and needs to get into the archives," Jack tells her. "Can you set her up?"

Joanne nods, giving Kathryn a once-over. "What does she need?" she asks Jack.

"It's a missing-persons case," Kathryn says. "The girl's name was—is—Jennifer Pelletier. She disappeared in June of 1986."

"Oh, sure, I remember it. Unsolved, right?"

"Right."

"You got a lead?"

"Well—" Kathryn starts.

"She's covering some different angles," Jack says.

Joanne gives Kathryn a skeptical look. "I thought they worked that case up and down and sideways. Hard to see what different angles you could find after all this time."

Jack glances at the big clock above her head. "Hey, I've got a meeting in a couple of minutes," he says. "I appreciate your help on this, Joanne." To Kathryn he says, "Let me know if there's anything I can do." He lightly squeezes her arm and then lifts his hand in a wave. "Talk to you soon."

Kathryn looks after him as he leaves. She's slightly stunned by the smoothness of his departure, the friendly squeeze and empty promise of it. The squeeze conveys both empathy and distance; it lets her know that Jack has brought her as far as he is going to, and she'll have to go the distance alone. Though it seems like an intimate gesture, there is nothing personal about it.

"So what are we after?" Joanne demands.

"I need to see any story related to this case, and maybe even before. Is it possible to find unrelated pieces that might have mentioned her name?"

"We don't have a search database going back that far. But I'd bet her mother has a scrapbook. You could ask her."

Kathryn tries to remember if Jennifer or her mother had kept such a thing. Neither of them seemed the type.

"We do have all the articles on the disappearance, of course," Joanne continues. "I'll need to track down the microfiche. What's the date on that?"

"June thirteenth, 1986," Kathryn says automatically. "A Friday." The date is as fixed in her brain as her own birthday.

"Is that the date that it happened, or the date the first article appeared?"

"Friday the thirteenth, huh? The date it happened. I guess the first article would have appeared on Monday, the . . . sixteenth."

When Joanne goes off to find the articles, Kathryn sits at a table and begins to compile a list of people to talk to: Jennifer's mother, her brother, Will. Rachel, Brian, Jack. The detective who worked on the case, the reporter who covered it. Abby Elson, a friend of Jennifer's none of the rest of them knew very well. Chip Sanborn? Kathryn writes his name and then crosses it off the list. She wonders which teachers might have anything to say. Miss Hallowell was Jennifer's English teacher, but she'd moved to Portland a few years after they graduated. Like Jennifer, she had once, as a Bangor High student, starred in the school play, and she saw this as a special bond between them. Miss Hallowell had been distraught at the news of Jennifer's disappearance; she joined the search parties, organized a phone hotline, and cried a lot in public. Kathryn puts her name down with a question mark. Mr. Richardson, the flamboyant drama teacher who smoked cigarettes with his students behind the school, had featured Jennifer in several of his productions; he might have something to say. And then there was Mr. Hunter, the social-studies teacher who also ran the orienteering club. Kathryn and Jennifer had been in his class senior year, and Jennifer did orienteering. Mr. Hunter was young and charismatic, one of the few teachers at the school who was adept at jumping over the great divide between teenagers and adults.

"Well, here's what we got," Joanne says, handing Kathryn a manila folder. "You can use one of those projectors over there." She motions toward a row of old-fashioned-looking light boxes with darkened screens. "I'll be here if you need anything else." She turns around and busies herself at her desk.

"Thank you," Kathryn says.

Joanne nods. "Those stories have been picked over by everybody and his brother, but who knows, maybe you'll find something nobody else could." She shrugs doubtfully.

Kathryn puts her bag on the first table she comes to and switches on the machine. Opening her folder, she sees that the four sheets of film are labeled neatly in chronological order, beginning with the Monday after Jennifer's disappearance, June 16. She takes the top sheet and puts it on the light table, moving the magnifying glass above it until the first article is projected onto the screen. BANGOR HONOR STUDENT MISSING, the headline announces. It's by a staff reporter named John Bourne. "After graduating with honors from Bangor High School on Friday afternoon, Jennifer Ann Pelletier and her family celebrated over dinner at Pilot's Grill. Then, like many new graduates, she met up with her friends for what her twin brother, William, 18, says was a 'casual, relaxed get-together' down by the Kenduskeag. Around 11:30 P.M., according to witnesses, she said she was tired and wanted to walk home," Kathryn reads. The article continues:

No one has seen or heard from her since.

The Bangor Police Department is taking the disappearance seriously, and is asking the public's help in locating Pelletier. According to Detective Ed Gaffney, she is 5 feet 5 inches in height, and weighs 117 pounds. She has shoulder-length blond hair and blue eyes. The night she disappeared she was wearing Levi jeans, a white cotton shirt, a black cotton sweater, a black and silver belt, black shoes, and silver earrings and bracelets.

Pelletier exhibited no unusual signs of behavior or mood in the weeks before her disappearance, according to friends and family members. "She was excited about graduating, and kind of sad about it, too, like all of us," her brother said. "But she was her normal self."

Described as a popular, well-liked student, Pelletier was active in drama and sports in high school, with a leading role in the school play, "Grease," this spring. She lettered in cross-country last fall. She was also a member of the National Honor Society and the orienteering club, and she volunteered regularly at Westgate Manor, a local nursing home.

Game wardens using dogs searched the area for Pelletier on Sunday. A ground search, organized by her family, was conducted by volunteers, "with no results," Gaffney said. Local shelters were also checked.

Anyone with information about the missing girl is asked to contact the Bangor Police Department at 555-7370.

There are dozens of articles in the summer and fall of 1986, Kathryn can see, skimming the sheets of film. The headlines tell the story: SEARCH FOR BHS STUDENT INTENSIFIES, NEW EVIDENCE FOUND IN DISAPPEARANCE, POLICE MOVE TO QUELL RUMORS IN CASE OF MISSING STUDENT, THEORIES ABOUND RE: BANGOR GIRL'S DISAPPEARANCE. After a while, because there's so little news, the stories focus on Jennifer's state of mind. In GIRL'S DISAPPEARANCE REMAINS A MYSTERY, John Bourne writes, "For all of her 18 years, Jennifer Pelletier has lived in Bangor, and she knows it like the back of her hand. When she was a child she was obsessed with maps of the city, and she'd spend hours studying them, her mother, Linda Pelletier, recalls. 'Jennifer knows every shortcut and side street in this town,' she says. 'She would never just get lost here.' She did so well in orienteering at Bangor High School that the club leader, social-studies teacher Richard Hunter, says 'it's as if she has a built-in compass.'"

By 1987, the headlines have become more desperate: GIRL'S DISAPPEARANCE STILL A MYSTERY, POLICE "ACTIVELY INVESTIGATING" CASE, MOTHER SEEKS AID, RESIDENTS OFFER REWARD IN CASE OF MISSING GIRL. As the years go by, they achieve a tone of resignation: NEW NEWS ON

PELLETIER CASE ONLY RUMORS, AN UNSOLVED MYSTERY, GONE BUT NOT FORGOTTEN. Finally, eight years after her disappearance, WILL JENNIFER PELLETIER EVER BE FOUND?

Along with the articles on the case, most of them written by John Bourne, the microfiche records a series of advertisements placed in the classifieds by "The Loving Family of Jennifer Pelletier." The first one, dated July 4, 1986, reads, "This is one of your favorite holidays, Jennifer—a time of celebration and joy. Wherever you are, and whoever you're with, we want you to know how badly we miss you and how much we love you. Please come home!" Another, a few months later, implores, "Whoever has information about my daughter, I beg you to let us know! You aren't helping her or yourself by keeping quiet. We will find out what happened to her, it's only a matter of time. Do the right thing—come forward."

The lack of a response to this plea reverberates in Kathryn's ears. No one came forward. If anyone knew, they never told.

She switches off the light and sits back in her seat. All these articles building toward a resolution that never comes. Optimism and energy turn to warning and fear, and then, inevitably, new stories take precedence and interest wanes. Nobody cares what happened to Jennifer Pelletier anymore; it's yesterday's news. They did the best they could, they tried their damnedest to find her, and nothing ever turned up. The case may still be open, but the book is closed.

So maybe that's how it should be, Kathryn thinks. Here's Jennifer's life, on four sheets of microfiche, and maybe that's enough. "She's either dead or she doesn't want to be found," Paul used to say when she worried over the details late at night. "Either way, there's not a hell of a lot you can do about it. Let her go, Kathryn. Give it up. She's gone."

"You're right," she'd murmur, but she didn't believe it. Jennifer might be dead, or she might be hiding, but she wasn't gone to Kathryn. She'd never be gone. The fact that she vanished on a special night in a familiar place only made the impact of it more intense, seared in Kathryn's memory from the moment she walked out into the darkness.

Kathryn gets up from the table, slides the film sheets back in the folder, and takes it to Joanne at the front desk. "Could I get copies of these?"

"Sure." Joanne glances at the clock. "But I won't have them ready for an hour."

"I can come back."

The woman nods. "So you knew this girl, huh?" she says abruptly, looking sideways at Kathryn.

"Yes, she was a friend of mine. And Jack's. We were all in the same class at Bangor High." Then, sensing something odd in Joanne's reaction, she says, "Did you know her?"

Joanne wrinkles her nose. "Not directly. I heard some things."

"About the disappearance?"

"No." She looks down, straightening things on her desk. "If I did, I could've gotten some reward money. No, she went out with my nephew, Tim Peavey."

"I remember Tim," Kathryn says. "He was a football player, right? And baseball?"

"Carnation All-American."

"When did he go out with Jennifer?" she asks, puzzled, trying to think back.

"It wasn't long," Joanne says. "She wasn't very nice to him."

It's coming back to her now. It was the summer before their junior year, and as far as Kathryn knows, Jennifer dated him only once or twice. She used to say that he was dogging her, wouldn't leave her alone. He was always pushing notes, covered with hearts and great big I LOVE YOU's, through the vent in her locker. "I don't know if they were exactly *going out*," Kathryn says, trying to be tactful.

"Listen, honey," Joanne says, looking Kathryn in the eye. "She went out with him and then she dumped him, and it hurt him pretty bad.

Everybody thought she was a little angel, but she was far from that. Once you got to know her—"

"I did," Kathryn says abruptly. "I did know her."

Joanne purses her lips in a little smirk. "Then you know."

Kathryn starts to respond and then thinks better of it, tacitly giving Joanne the last word. She is suddenly tired, bone tired, as if she's been losing blood without realizing it. "Well, listen, I'll be back in a while to pick up that stuff. Thanks for your help."

"Sure," Joanne says with a smile. She seems cheerier for having gotten that off her chest.

Outside the air is warmer now, though clouds still mottle the sky. Kathryn gets into the Saturn and it's as if she's an astronaut in a spaceship—all she has to do is buckle in and shoot for the skies. She likes the feeling. She turns the key in the ignition and Foreigner blasts from the speakers: *Hot blooded, check it and see, I got a fever of a hundred and three. . . .* " She turns onto Main Street and follows it back into town, past the struggling independent bookstores, a preppy clothing outlet showcasing Izod shirts and argyle socks, several ethnic restaurants. Instead of turning left onto Harlow Street toward home, as she'd planned, she continues through the traffic light and up the hill on State Street, past pawnshops and drugstores and the 7-Eleven, until the houses become larger and grander. They're mostly doctors' estates; Eastern Maine Medical Center sprawls for half a mile on the right side of the road, a modern monolith on the banks of the Penobscot.

At the end of Main Street, on the border between Bangor and Veazie, Kathryn turns left up a winding hill, passing the mental-health institute and half a dozen car dealerships, the cars on each lot shimmering in the sun like a phalanx of beetles. She can see the sign for the Bangor Mall in the distance.

Once you got to know her, Joanne said. What does she know? She never even met her. But Kathryn has to admit that there's an element of truth in what she was saying. Jennifer could be sulky and unpredictable. And she could be thoughtlessly inconsiderate, asking for favors and giving arbitrarily in return, opening up to people and then just as quickly closing off again.

Kathryn remembers one Christmas, when they were fourteen, that Jennifer received a beautiful pair of ice skates, creamy white leather with shiny silver blades and pink laces. Her mother had ordered them out of a catalogue at White's Sporting Goods store. Kathryn's run-of-the-mill pair from Standard Shoes, bought in an end-of-season sale the previous spring, looked tacky in comparison.

The day after Christmas was clear and cold. There had been a snowstorm on Christmas Eve, and though plows had come through the neighborhood twice, the streets were still coated with a layer of packed ice. At eight-thirty that morning, groggy with sleep, Kathryn opened the front door to find Jennifer standing there with her new skates on, clutching the doorframe with one pink-gloved hand. "Hey, Kath," she said. "I'm on my way over to the park. Will said there's ice over the whole baseball field. Want to come?"

Kathryn looked down at the skates, and then at Jennifer's pink socks, white jeans, white jacket, and pink-and-white scarf. Her blond hair was pulled back into a pink ponytail holder. "I just woke up," Kathryn said.

"I can wait."

"Don't you have boots? It's three blocks over there. Road salt can't be good for those."

Picking her feet up one after the other, like a pony, Jennifer said, "Aren't they beautiful? But I feel like an idiot, like I'm trying to be Dorothy Hamill or something. You're the one who can skate."

"You can skate," Kathryn said, without much conviction.

"No, not really. But you know what my mom says: If you can't *be* good, at least look good." She grimaced and stuck out her tongue. "So come on."

"I'm not feeling so hot today," Kathryn said. "And my skates are butt-ugly."

"Yeah, but you're good. It doesn't matter what they look like," Jennifer said, yanking playfully on Kathryn's arm. "C'mon, c'mon, c'mon."

And so Kathryn went. She put on her skates and guided Jennifer to the park. When they got there she spent an hour trying to teach Jennifer to skate backward, and then, when Jennifer fell and hurt her knee, she held her steady as they hobbled back home.

Jennifer was always getting people to do things for her—skating lessons, homework, a later curfew, a second chance. But she didn't expect these favors for free. What she gave back was as undefinable as it was unspoken, and it was only years later, after Jennifer was gone, that Kathryn began to understand why she had so willingly accepted the mercurial nature of Jennifer's friendship, why all of them gave so much to her and expected so little. It wasn't that she was funny, or creative, or even particularly empathetic, though at times she could be any of these things. The fact was, each of them had been in love with her in some way, in love with the idea of her, the ideal she represented: her physical beauty, her poise, her audacity. She didn't seem to feel the need to explain herself, to rush to fill a silence, to justify the choices she made, the way the rest of them did. Ultimately, though, Kathryn thought, this may have been her undoing. Because when Jennifer did express fear or hurt or vulnerability, they may have believed her, but deep down they never really took it seriously. She was saying these things, they thought, to show that she was normal. To be like them.

So the lady at the *News* is right about Jennifer, and she's wrong, Kathryn thinks, and it doesn't matter. It doesn't matter how nice Jennifer was, and how many people loved her, and how many she hurt or alienated or fooled. She's gone; that time is long past.

Glancing at her watch, Kathryn sees that it's been forty-five minutes, so she heads back to the *News* to pick up the copies. Joanne isn't around, but there's a folder on the front desk of the library with Kathryn's name scrawled on the front. She slips the folder into her bag and goes out to the newsroom. She can see Jack in his office with his shirtsleeves rolled up, talking on the phone. He's gesturing animatedly with one hand and scribbling on a pad with the other. She dawdles, fiddling with her bag, waiting to see if he'll hang up, but after a moment it becomes clear that he'll be on for a while, so she slips out without his seeing her.

At the front desk she asks about John Bourne, the reporter whose name is on most of the stories about the disappearance.

"Oh, he's been gone for some time now," the birdlike receptionist says. "It's probably been five years."

"Do you know where he is?"

"I think he went to some paper in Detroit." She calls over her shoulder: "Helen! Do you know where Johnny Bourne ended up?"

"Hmm," says a woman with large red glasses, sitting in a cubicle. "*Detroit Morning News*, I believe. Let me check." She turns the knob on her Rolodex and starts flipping through cards. "Yep, here it is," she says. "Or was. This is three years old."

"Fine," Kathryn says, "whatever you've got."

The woman gives her the number, and Kathryn scrawls it on her notebook. She feels satisfied with herself all at once, the way you might after a strenuous workout or an exam you've actually studied for. She has accomplished something for a change, and however small, however preliminary, it's a start.

On the way home Kathryn stops at Shaw's to pick up some mussels, lettuce, and fresh bread for dinner. It's only four-thirty; her mother won't be home until seven. Maybe she'll even make a cobbler—peach, her mother's favorite—as a surprise. She hasn't shopped like this, with another person in mind, since she was married. Weighing the peaches in her hand, inspecting them for ripeness and bruises, she feels strangely content. There are mussels in her basket, white wine is chilling in the fridge, she has a task to occupy her for the next few hours, and something to talk about when her mother comes home. Maybe it really is this simple, she thinks; maybe all I've needed is a worthwhile task and someone to cook for.

As she's standing in line with her cart, the woman beside her says, "Kathryn, right?"

"Ye-es," Kathryn says, looking at the woman's unruly brown hair and soft laugh lines, trying to place her.

"Jan Starley. Used to be Forrest. We were in the same English class," the woman says. She points to the toddler standing at the front of her cart like the captain of a ship. "And this little guy is Taylor. Say hi to the nice lady, Taylor."

"Don't say hi," Taylor says, turning his face away.

"Sorry." Jan rolls her eyes. "He's at that age."

"He's really cute," Kathryn says. He looks over at her from under a shock of shiny black hair, and when he sees her noticing, he grins and crouches down.

"He knows it, too. Careful, don't step on the Froot Loops," Jan warns him. She brushes the curly hair out of her eyes and leans her forearms on the cart. "So how've you been?"

"Fine," Kathryn says, "how about you?"

"Oh, gettin' by." She squints at Kathryn as if she's trying to remember something. "Gosh, I haven't seen you since—well, it must have been sometime that summer. After school ended. Everything was so . . ." she says, and pauses.

"I know," Kathryn says.

Jan tousles Taylor's hair. "I can't believe nothing ever came of that. She just . . . disappeared, didn't she?"

"It looks that way." It's strange, but somehow it's easy to talk about Jennifer like this, as if she were nothing more to Kathryn than a mutual acquaintance or an item in the paper.

"Well, maybe she'll turn up. It happens, doesn't it? She's probably on a beach somewhere in California."

"I wanna pretzel," Taylor demands, and Jan pulls open a bag and gives him one. "Broken," he says, making a face. She hands him the whole bag.

"Probably just wanted to make a clean break," she continues. "Hey, who knows, maybe she'll show up at the reunion. That'd make a good story, wouldn't it?"

"It would," Kathryn says. "It'd make a great story."

She pays for the food and makes her way to the parking lot, where the shiny yellow Saturn stands out like a traffic light: *Caution, slow down, proceed at your own risk.*

Days pass. Despite her good intentions, Kathryn can't seem to get going. She reads the paper front to back every morning, even the business section and the sports pages. She's beginning to recognize the names of local industry leaders and high-school sports stars; she knows that Dan Rivlin is expected to quarterback for Bangor High in the fall, though he broke his ankle last March in a snowboarding accident and they're worried it might slow him down. There's at least one story every day or two about boats lost at sea and lovers' quarrels that end in violence, and the paper covers them faithfully, in sordid detail, until the boat is found or the case comes to trial. Kathryn knows the trivial facts of each one.

Sometime in midmorning she takes a long shower, shaving her legs and using conditioning treatments on her hair. She pretends she's at a spa. She tries a mud mask she finds in her mother's medicine cabinet and leaves it on until her face, in the mirror, looks papery and wrinkled, as if she were a hundred years old. She gives herself a pedicure with her mother's pumice stone and Lancôme Barely Buff nail polish. In the afternoon she sits in front of the television with the remote in her hand, flipping back and forth between Oprah and Ricki Lake. At five o'clock she pours herself a glass of wine.

Tuesday morning she calls to cancel her appointment with Rosie, claiming that she's got a head cold or something, maybe the flu. "I'm sorry to hear that, dear," Doris says, her voice full of concern. "You want to reschedule?"

"I'll call you in a few days, when I'm feeling better," Kathryn rasps.

"You take care of yourself," Doris says. "Tea and honey. And stay in bed!"

"What's going on?" Jack says when he calls near the end of the week. She's watching Regis and Kathie Lee—now on mute—but she doesn't tell him that.

"Not much." She rouses herself, trying to sound chipper and efficient. "I've been reading through all those clippings and the police reports." It's sort of true; yesterday she opened the folder and riffled through the pages, but after skimming an article she felt a little nauseated and put it aside.

"Anything you didn't expect?"

"Not yet," she says. "I'll let you know."

"Hey, I spoke to Rachel yesterday. I was surprised to hear that she hasn't heard from you about the article."

"I've been really busy. I was just going to—"

"Look." Jack's voice is low and knowing. "I'm going to be honest with you, Kathryn. I'm thinking of assigning this piece to someone else."

Kathryn feels her stomach drop. "What?"

"I need someone who's really going to go after the story," he says. "I can understand why that might be hard for you, and I'm thinking I probably made a mistake asking you to do it." He sighs. "Look, there's a lot to this story, a lot of research and people to interview. I need someone who's going to make it happen. I don't have the time to be on top of it."

"But I'm doing it," she protests. She sits up straight on the couch and the remote falls to the floor, blasting Regis singing a show tune at full volume. Down on her hands and knees, Kathryn scrambles after the remote, finally clicking off the TV. "Sorry," she mutters. "Anyway, I'm totally on top of it, Jack. I'm just—"

"I need an article by next Friday," he says bluntly. "That's just over a week from now. Fifteen hundred words. It's scheduled to run on Saturday, the day of the reunion."

"I can do that."

"All right, then. I want you to talk to as many people as you can before then, and I want you to explain to our readers why the hell nothing has ever been found."

"Okay. I'm not sure how much—"

"Or I can assign this to a staff reporter. It doesn't really matter to me, Kathryn. I just want the story done."

She takes a deep breath. "Okay. I'll do it."

"I'm thinking this might be a series, three or four pieces," he says. "How does that sound to you?"

"Fine."

"Good," he says. "Well, good luck. I'll give you a call in the next day or two to see how it's going."

"You don't have to check up on me," she says. "I'll get the story in on time. I promise."

"When do you want to interview me?"

She calculates quickly—she should probably talk to a few people first, just to have something to show for herself. "How about . . . Sunday?"

She can hear him flipping pages. "Is Governor's Restaurant okay? Four o'clock?"

"Sure."

"See you then," he says.

After she hangs up the phone, she sits on the couch for a moment, looking at her shadowy reflection in the gray TV screen. She has a sick feeling in her gut, one she's had too many times over the last few years.

All those papers that weren't handed in on time, the neglected friendships, missed work deadlines, unfinished master's thesis, appointments made and broken. She recognizes the tone in Jack's voice, disappointment and exasperation mingled with pity, and it frightens her. She realizes with a little shock that she hasn't cared this much in a long time—not when she was quitting the English program, not when her marriage was beginning to fall apart, not even when she returned to her small bedroom in her mother's house and realized that its parameters represented the scope and measure of her ambition.

In some strange way it has been liberating to be the kind of person others couldn't rely on. The people in her life came to expect little of her; they just learned not to ask. But they also gave less themselves, and eventually whatever rocky soil her relationships were built on crumbled away. She doesn't want that anymore. She doesn't want Jack to think of her that way. She's scared, all of a sudden—of failing him, of failing herself. And somewhere deep down she knows she's also afraid of failing Jennifer, whose disappearance, she is beginning to understand, eroded whatever sense she may once have had about who she is. Jennifer's absence is a rebuke and a challenge, and Kathryn knows that until she confronts it she will probably be lost as well.

"Could I speak to John Bourne?"

"Hold, please." There's a click, and suddenly Kathryn is listening to a Detroit weather report. This is the third time she's been transferred and put on hold, and the second time she's heard the forecast. Partly sunny, with variable clouds and a chance of precipitation later in the day. She taps her pen on the notebook cover impatiently. Doesn't the guy have voice mail? "Just a moment, I'll transfer you," a woman says, and Kathryn is on hold again. Then, finally, a man's voice is on the line. "Johnny Bourne," he says pleasantly. "What can I do for you?"

Kathryn sits up straight and opens her notebook. "Oh—hello," she says. "I'm Kathryn Campbell, with—ah—the *Bangor Daily News*. I spoke to you a few times years ago when you were covering the Jennifer Pelletier case. I don't know if you remember it—the girl who disappeared."

"Of course I remember," he says. "I'm not sure I remember you, though, to be honest. Were you one of her friends?"

"Yes, that's right," she says. "And now I'm with the *News*, and we're doing a follow-up on the story. So I wonder if I could ask you a few questions."

"Did they find her?" he asks quickly.

"No. It's just—well, it's been ten years, and—"

"Jesus, it has, hasn't it?"

"Yeah. And most people have pretty much forgotten about it. So we wanted to do a piece on what happened back then, and what's been going on since. I'm planning to reinterview some people—"

He laughs shortly. "Have you started yet?"

"No."

"Well, all I can say is, good luck."

"What do you mean?"

He sucks air through his teeth. "It was a tough story. Frustrating. I kept thinking, Something's got to break, somebody's got to know more than they're telling. I went over my transcripts again and again, trying to find a clue, or a contradiction—anything that might give me more to go on."

"I just read the articles," she says. "You did a good job with what you had."

"Well, thanks. But it's no fun to write those kinds of pieces unless they lead to something. It's frustrating as hell. That case still bothers me. I guess it always will, at least until she turns up under somebody's front porch one day."

"So you think she's dead."

"Oh, probably. But your guess is as good as mine. I said all I knew in those articles."

"Really?" she says, disappointed. "I was wondering if there might be anything else—anything you couldn't use because you didn't have substantiation."

"I usually found a way to use what I had," he says. "But in the end I just didn't know that much."

"Do you think the police were keeping things from you?"

"I don't think the police knew jack shit. Pardon my French."

"It's okay, I'm bilingual," she says, and he laughs. She can feel her reporter's skills coming back to her—the ability to put a subject at ease, to win his trust, get him to open up. It makes her more comfortable, too.

"The cops just ran out of leads," he continues. "Not that they had many to start with. Gaffney, that son of a bitch—"

She scans her notes. "The detective."

"Right. He had the instincts of an ostrich. Anytime it seemed like they might be getting close to something, he put his head in the dirt."

"Like what?"

He's silent for a moment. Then he says, "There was a lot of stuff that didn't add up. Like, where was she on Tuesday night the week before she disappeared? She was home or out with friends every other night that week, but nobody saw her after eight P.M. on Tuesday."

"Maybe she went to bed early," Kathryn says.

"Maybe. But her brother said there was no answer when he knocked on her door at ten. And the door was locked."

"Jennifer was pretty private. She usually locked her door."

"Well, that's why I didn't put it in an article. And when I tried to follow up with her brother, Bill—"

"Will."

"Bill, Will, it's been a while. Anyway, he and his mother acted like I was invading their privacy or something. So I mentioned it to Gaffney, and he just blew it off."

Kathryn makes a note to ask Will about it. "What else?"

"Oh, nothing concrete. Cumulatively, though, there was a lot of weird stuff. The father's death, probably suicide. The girl's quasi suicide attempt. The mother remarrying, what, three months later? The way the girl treated some of the guys she went out with."

"So you know about that. The football player."

"Yeah, and someone else. Brian somebody."

Kathryn is startled. "Brian White?"

"Something about the prom. She got him to ask her, so he says, and then she blew him off. Not a big deal, really, just one more detail that didn't quite make sense."

She dimly remembers the incident—some mess she'd repressed that, at the time, had threatened to break up the group. Brian had been the one, in the end, to let it go. Jennifer acted as if it had never happened. "You didn't write about that either," Kathryn says.

"You're right. I didn't. Again, it didn't really add up to anything." He sighs, and Kathryn can tell that the conversation is winding down. "Sorry I couldn't be more helpful. Just one piece of advice: Don't waste too much of your life on this story. Wherever that girl is, I think she's long gone."

When the phone call ends, Kathryn hangs on to the receiver for a minute, absently rubbing it against her cheek. *Don't waste too much of your life on this story.* It was lightly said, a flippant warning, but it turned her cold. Because that's just it, she thinks—I already have wasted too much of my life on this story. I've been waiting for her to come back for the past ten years, waiting for the past to catch up with me so I can begin my future. I need some kind of answer. It doesn't have to be the whole truth, she thinks, whatever that is, or was. Just something I can live with.

The phone starts to beep and she replaces it on the hook. Outside, the light is thin and white, the air is cool. Another morning gone, another afternoon. She curls up on the couch and rubs her hands up and down her arms, letting herself drift into dreamless sleep.

The police station is a neat brick building set on a hill near downtown Bangor. Kathryn parks her car in one of three spots reserved for visitors, near a row of white Fords and Chevys with the blue Bangor Police Department seal on the side. On a tall pole in a patch of grass near the entrance, the state flag and the American flag flutter limply in the breeze.

At ten o'clock on a Friday morning the station house is quiet. Two men are standing at the front desk filling out forms; four uniformed officers, three men and a woman, are drinking coffee and talking. Another is tapping away at a computer keyboard, whistling "Take Me Out to the Ball Game." Kathryn watches them as she waits for the form-fillers to finish their business. She looks around the large, nondescript room with its banks of filing cabinets and citizen safety posters. A large wall clock covered with a metal grille ticks away the minutes, and three ceiling fans whir overhead.

"What can I do for you?" the desk sergeant asks when it's finally Kathryn's turn.

"I'm looking for somebody," she says. "A detective, I believe. Ed Gaffney." She holds up the sheaf of newspaper articles she's carrying as proof of her intent. "He oversaw an investigation about ten years ago— the disappearance of a girl named Jennifer Pelletier."

"Ay-uh, I remember it." The sergeant nods. "Never solved."

"Right. Well, I'm doing a follow-up story for the *News*."

"Something turn up?"

"No. Not yet."

He nods again, more slowly this time. "Well, Gaffney's here," he says. "I don't know if he'll talk to you. He got pretty sick of the reporters covering this case the first time around."

"I only have a couple of questions," she says. "Tell him it'll be five minutes. I promise."

He points at her, his hand cocked like a gun. "Two things you learn in this job," he says. "Never turn your back on a suspect, and never trust a reporter. Especially when they give you their word." He walks across the room to a glass-enclosed office and shuts the door.

Kathryn watches the two men in the office—the wiry desk sergeant and the potbellied, dark-haired officer behind the desk. Gaffney is wearing black aviator glasses, like a celebrity on a talk show, and, though the others look as if they haven't been outside all summer, he sports a deep tan. Now that Kathryn sees him, she recognizes him from the investigation. He wasn't the one who interviewed her—it had been some female officer with a gruff manner and a barbershop haircut. But he was on the news a lot back then, commenting solemnly at press conferences on their habitual lack of progress.

Gaffney rises slowly, hitches up his pants, and adjusts his belt. Then he nods his chin toward Kathryn and the desk sergeant comes out to get her.

"So," Gaffney says when she's standing across from him, "I understand we've got a new reporter on this old case. Don't they have anything better for you to do?"

"I'm Kathryn Campbell," she says, holding out her hand. "I appreciate your talking to me."

"Is that what I'm doing?" His eyes narrow, and he puts his hands on his belt. She lets hers drop to her side. "Kathryn Campbell," he muses. "That name sounds familiar."

"Maybe from the case," she admits. "I was a friend of—"

"No, wait a minute. You related to Sally Campbell, by any chance?"

"Um, yes," she says, startled. "She's my mother."

He stands there, staring at her, and then he breaks into a grin. "Well, son of a gun. She's a good woman, your mother."

Kathryn smiles uncertainly. "How do you know her?"

"You ask your mom," he says. "Tell 'er Gaff says hi."

" 'Gaff'?"

"She'll know," he says. "Now. What can I do for you?"

TWO HOURS LATER, Kathryn has a copy of the missing-persons report in her hand, which Jennifer's mother had filled out a day and a half after Jennifer vanished. Sitting in the Bagel Shop, chewing on a bialy, Kathryn runs down the list:

Description: Medium-length light blond hair, 5'5", 117 pounds, light blue eyes.

Distinguishing features: A mole near her heart, a scar on her right arm, and another across her right knee.

What were they wearing? Blue jeans, white cotton shirt, silver belt, black boots, black sweater, amethyst ring (I think).

Access to a vehicle? Not that I know of.

Possible destinations? Unknown. But her passport is missing (I don't know how long—we couldn't find it in her room yesterday).

Has the person gone missing before? Not longer than a night.

Frame of mind before they left? Fine. A little distracted, maybe. No indication that she wanted to leave or had plans to leave.

Will you go pick them up if they're found? Of course.

At the bottom, Jennifer's mother has scrawled, "Jennifer is not the runaway type. Please help us find her before something terrible happens. We'll do anything we can to get her back.—Linda Pelletier."

Consulting a burgeoning case file, Detective Gaffney went over the details of the case with Kathryn in his office. Jennifer's mother first called the police at 3:00 P.M. on Saturday after trying to track her daughter down herself. At 4:30 P.M. an officer went to the house, where he talked to Mrs. Pelletier and Will for forty-five minutes. He filled out a report and wrote at the bottom, "Last seen Friday around midnight. Probably at somebody's camp or in Bar Harbor. Mother very concerned, but concedes daughter isn't always reliable. Agrees to wait until morning to send out APB."

Sunday morning, according to a follow-up report, the police sent out a statewide all-points bulletin with Jennifer's vital statistics and short interviews with family and friends about her state of mind. Kathryn finds her own quote, which echoes the others: "She wouldn't just run away—she isn't like that." And then, as if to prove it, "She is excited about being a counselor at Camp Keonah in two weeks." Several people mentioned that she had appeared distracted lately, and that it wasn't the easiest year, but things seemed to be getting better. At the bottom of the report, Detective Gaffney had typed, "8/25/85 Father died in single-car accident—possible suicide. 9/25/85 J.P. rushed to ER to have stomach pumped—possible suicide attempt. Mother remarried 11/16/85. No further incidents. Active in drama club, sports, good student, popular. Plans to attend Colby in Sept."

That afternoon, the police took a K-9 unit to the site on the river where Jennifer was last seen. The dogs were given a piece of her clothing and set loose. Jennifer had said she was going home, but her scent told a different story. The dogs followed her trail for several miles, turning left on Outer Kenduskeag instead of right toward her home as everyone expected. But when the dogs reached Griffin Road they got confused, two of them heading north, the other one running in circles around the intersection, and police had to abandon the effort. After that, a five-person team set out on foot along the route, looking for a sign of struggle or a scrap of fabric. In the underbrush near Kenduskeag they found a hammered-pewter barrette that Will later identified as his sister's; she often clipped it to a belt loop on her jeans. In the report Gaffney speculated that she may have been keeping to the side of the road to avoid notice.

The next day the first article appeared in the paper. Divers were sent into the Kenduskeag; a small boat traveled slowly up and down the river as two officers with binoculars scanned the shoreline and examined rock formations protruding from the water. By late morning a citizens' patrol that Will had organized fanned out across a mile-wide expanse, moving slowly through the trees and long grass and the housing developments around Husson College. When they reached the Griffin Road intersection they split into three groups, two following the road in each direction, one moving straight ahead on Kenduskeag Avenue and the area surrounding it, a flat, marshy field and a small wood.

Late that afternoon, on the road going north, someone picked up a gum wrapper, berry-flavored Carefree, Jennifer's favorite kind. That and the barrette were the only clues they found, through weeks and months of searching. They set up a hotline and followed up all the leads phoned in, no matter how tenuous or absurd they seemed, but nothing panned out. Jennifer had vanished, it seemed, into a car going north, a car that detectives concluded must have picked her up on Griffin Road sometime between 12:30 A.M. and around 5:00 A.M., when traffic got heavier and someone would probably have seen her.

When the story went out on the wires the next day, people began to report having spotted her as far north as Quebec. There were dozens of sightings of an eighteen-year-old girl with white-blond hair—at rest stops, all-night diners, after-hours clubs. But, as Gaffney told Kathryn, hundreds of people say they've seen the Loch Ness Monster, too. It may exist, but there's never been any conclusive proof. And until there is, the case is no closer to being solved than it ever was. "A mystery like this is a powerful thing," he said. "It gets under your skin. You keep thinking you're going to figure it out; the girl's going to turn up, you're going to find that piece of the puzzle that shows you the whole picture. And then, when you don't . . ." His voice trailed off. "Nobody wants a case like this. It eats at you for the rest of your life."

Intent on the papers in front of her, Kathryn is startled when a Bagel Shop employee addresses her. The girl is wearing a kerchief over her dark, frizzy hair and balancing a tray of dirty mugs on her hip. "Done with that?" she says, gesturing toward Kathryn's half-eaten roll and cold coffee.

"Uh, sure," Kathryn says. She looks around and notices the noontime crowd filling up the tables. "I guess I'll get some lunch," she says apologetically. The girl nods and moves away, and Kathryn goes up to the counter to order a bowl of matzo-ball pea soup—a comforting if peculiar combination she remembers from high school. She used to order this soup on winter days when her mother brought her downtown to the Grasshopper Shop across the street for a rare mother-daughter spending spree. Laden with bags of 100-percent-cotton shirts from Guatemala and leggings from Esprit, they'd stagger into the Bagel Shop for a ritual lunch. They both pretended the shopping was a bribe, but Kathryn secretly liked these lunches as much as her mother did. The only thing was, her mother always insisted on ordering the most traditional Jewish food possible—pickled herring, gefilte fish, chopped liver. "When in Rome . . ." she'd say brightly, and then spend an hour pushing the food around on her plate.

Settling back into her booth with the brimming bowl of soup, Kathryn leafs through the pages from Jennifer's folder that Gaffney let her copy. The file was open, and it would be until she turned up, but Gaffney said he wanted to keep some of the information from the general public, like the interview with Jennifer's mother. He allowed Kathryn to read it at the station, but not to take it with her and not to allude to it in any articles. The folder also contained pages from Jennifer's senior-year diary, a document remarkable mostly for its lack of distinguishing detail. "Tuesday, November 14," one typical entry read. "Went to school early with Will, finished chem report. Read 20 pages of Catch-22 for English. After school went to Dairy Queen with K.C."—at the sight of her name, Kathryn's stomach tightens—"Made plans for the wknd. Orienteering. Wiped. An early night."

Orienteering. It was a club Jennifer belonged to—or a sport; Kathryn couldn't remember the distinction. Mr. Hunter had started it the spring of their junior year. It grew out of a segment of gym class where they were sent into the wooded acres around the school with compasses and hand-drawn maps and taught how to navigate their way out. Most of the kids got lost on purpose and used the time to smoke or fool around or head off to the parking lot to gossip for an hour in an unlocked car, but a small core of people really got into it. They studied it like a foreign language, figuring out how to read the position of the sun in the sky, the shadows of the trees, bent stalks, matted grasses, the minute gradations of a quivering compass, the inscrutable crosshatchings of a poorly photocopied contour map. The whole exercise held little interest for Kathryn, but Jennifer was captivated. When Mr. Hunter convened an after-school group, she was one of the first to sign up. "It's an amazing concept," Jennifer enthused. "It's what the Indians have been doing for thousands of years. Once you learn to find your way out of the wilderness on your own, you'll never be lost." She went on about how to identify desire lines, the foot trails people create through unmarked territory. "How can you not want to know this stuff?"

"When am I going to need it?" Kathryn said, rolling her eyes. "You may not have noticed, Jen, but we live in towns these days. With paved roads and sidewalks and these newfangled things called street signs. I'm not planning on getting lost in the woods anytime soon."

"What about hiking?"

"Wherever I want to go hiking, I can promise you, somebody has already been. And there are clearly marked paths and rest stops and other hikers to say hello to along the way. Wandering out into a forest or up some obscure rock face is not my idea of a good time."

Jennifer grinned. "You're a wimp. And I feel sorry for you if something ever happens and you actually need those skills to survive."

"Like what?" Kathryn said, imagining a camping trip gone wrong.

"Like, I don't know. World War Three."

"What are you talking about?"

"It could happen," Jennifer said. "And I'm going to be ready for it, and you're not."

Kathryn looked at her for a long moment. "Where are you getting these crazy ideas?"

Jennifer pulled back. She didn't answer. Finally she said, "All I'm saying is, this stuff could be useful to know."

Kathryn nodded and they dropped the subject. After that, Jennifer didn't talk much about it, except to say that she'd been hiking near one northern lake or another and saw a moose, or watched the ice break up on a warm day.

In class, Kathryn kept an eye on Mr. Hunter to see if she could detect a strain of freakish nationalism, but he gave nothing away. Whenever she asked him a direct question—about the citizens' right to bear arms, about nuclear stockpiling or the function of government, he always turned the question around: "What do *you* believe?" When she pressed him, he said, "My opinion is irrelevant. It's more important for you to figure out what *you* think."

"Oh, he's just playing teacher," Will said when she told him. "You know how Hunter does that. I'm glad Jen is so interested in something."

"A little too interested."

"Nah, it's just something to do," Will said. "If I were a shrink I'd say it's probably a way for her to have some control in her life. Finding her own way out of the woods and all that. We all have our thing. You, for instance, are unnaturally obsessed with the literary magazine. I'll bet you dream in four-page spreads." He laughed, and she had to admit there was some truth to that.

Leafing through the photocopied pages of Jennifer's journal as her soup gets cold, Kathryn notices that the references Jennifer makes to orienteering become more cryptic, and more frequent, as the year progresses. "OT practice at the university, 2 hrs," she writes in October. By March, the entries have become "OT P.M.," or "OT A.M.," twice a week. How often did the group meet? Kathryn had thought it was only on Wednesdays. She makes a note to ask Jennifer's sycophantic friend Abby Elson, who joined the club in the spring of their senior year.

Kathryn pushes the soup aside and gathers up the papers she's spread out on the table. There are a lot of people to talk to, and she's not sure where to start. "Don't expect anyone to be happy to see you," Gaffney told her. "It's been a long time, and people have come to terms with this in their own ways. You can't make someone talk. Anyway, these people have already said what they have to say. It's unlikely you'll uncover any evidence that's policeworthy. But—" he shrugged and pushed his sunglasses back on his nose—"it could happen, I suppose. You knew the girl. She might've said one thing to one person and one thing to another, and nobody figured out how to put the pieces together. Who knows, you might already have some information you don't even realize you've got."

"So you don't think she was kidnapped by some random lunatic," Kathryn said.

"She could've been," he acknowledged. "But it's unlikely. As long as I've been on the force in Bangor we've never had a stranger-to-stranger abduction."

It chills Kathryn to think that she might know something, that she might have known all along. "The first thing you look for is motive," Gaffney said, but that's just the problem—she doesn't understand her own motives, much less anyone else's. Her father always said, "The world is very simple, Katy," and she wanted to believe him, even after he left them and the simple fact of their family was exposed as a lie. His leaving was so complicated a betrayal that she could only handle thinking about it in the most elemental of ways: Her mother was good, her father was bad, they didn't need him, Margaret was a slut. This impulse to see the world in black and white affected everything she did. In high school she had considered Jennifer her best friend, but did she ever really try to understand her? She didn't know what Jennifer thought about her father's death, and when Jennifer ended up in the hospital herself, Kathryn was only too willing to believe that it wasn't serious.

It was a month to the day after her father died that Jennifer swallowed the pills—fifteen Halcion capsules she stole from her mother's medicine cabinet and downed in one big gulp. Will had come home from a football game to find her on her knees in the bathroom, puking her guts out, sobbing into the toilet bowl, and he heaved her into the car and drove her to St. Joseph's, where they pumped her stomach and made her stay a few days in the psych ward for observation.

The doctor said it was a classic cry for help—too little time alone and too few pills to do serious damage. It was what they all wanted to hear; it was inconceivable to think otherwise. But the first time Kathryn saw Jennifer after it happened, she knew that explanation was too simple. "I did want to die, in a way," Jennifer whispered, her face drawn and blank. "I guess in a way I didn't."

"And that's why you're still here," Kathryn said gamely. They had told her to be upbeat.

"I'm still here because I planned it wrong." She almost smiled. "Now I know: more pills—more time."

Kathryn felt a band of fear constrict her chest. She squeezed Jennifer's arm. "Don't even think of leaving me in this place."

"You'd be fine."

"Jesus, don't talk that way."

Jennifer looked at her for a long moment. Then she turned away. "I'm just tired."

"If there's anything I can do . . . We're all here for you, Jen," Kathryn said, a little desperately, trying to strike the right chord. "Will is freaking out. We all are. We all just . . . We care about you so much. You believe that, don't you?"

She nodded absently, distractedly, as if she didn't.

"Your mother is out there crying. She hasn't stopped for two days."

Jennifer shrugged.

"By the way, we haven't told anyone," Kathryn says. "As far as anyone at school knows, you've been out with the flu."

"I don't care if the whole fucking town knows." She turned her empty eyes toward Kathryn. "I just really don't care."

When Jennifer came back to school, everyone acted as if nothing had happened. And from the outside, things looked fine. She was polite to the teachers, friendly with the other kids. Kathryn knew that once a week she went to see a shrink at the hospital, but Jennifer never talked about it, and Kathryn never asked. It was easy to believe what the doctor said, that taking the pills was an adolescent impulse, an extreme, one-time reaction to her father's death.

But Kathryn saw that something inside her had changed. Jennifer became evasive and moody. She couldn't be counted on to show up even if she said she would; she disappeared for hours without explanation; she began spending more and more time alone. She rarely called Kathryn anymore, though she seemed happy enough when Kathryn called her, and she didn't seem to want to make plans. She applied to college halfheartedly, at her mother's insistence, and when she got into Colby early admission, she withdrew her name from the other places she'd applied, put the acceptance letter in a box under the bed, and didn't talk about it again.

When, after Jennifer disappeared, the reporter covering the case asked if she had been disturbed or upset, Kathryn didn't mention the suicide attempt. Nine months had passed; it was ancient history. It was almost as if it never took place. But somebody did tell the reporter; there was a paragraph in one story about how distraught Jennifer had been over her father's death, and how, in a particularly low moment, and quite understandably, she halfheartedly attempted to take her own life—an attempt that failed because it was never intended to succeed in the first place. Since then, the reporter said, things had seemed to improve for her. Her suicide attempt was only a sad footnote in the case; it didn't explain anything.

Still, when Kathryn reflects on that year, she wonders whether they all downplayed the significance of it because they feared the truth: that maybe she was a lot more serious about it than anyone wanted to acknowledge, that it wasn't halfhearted at all, that Jennifer wanted to die. Jennifer was expert at hiding what she really felt—she always had been. It made her a good actress and a complicated friend. And so, Kathryn thinks, maybe they were all complicitous in her deception, taking her at face value, wanting to believe that how she acted was how she felt. And meanwhile she slipped through their fingers and out of their lives, leaving only questions and puzzles behind.

ON THE WAY to her car Kathryn passes the Grasshopper Shop and decides to go in. She browses in the racks for a few minutes, finding an Indian-print skirt on sale for half price. It's a style she hasn't worn since college, but, suddenly nostalgic, she buys it anyway. She's tempted by a pair of blue suede clogs, but they're not on sale, and though her mother is pretty much supporting her for the moment, she knows the money in her bank account won't last long. I have to start writing these pieces and get a little income, she thinks—not that it will be much money, just a few hundred dollars for the first piece, Jack had said, and then, if things go well, he would see about more. But the more she gets into the story, the more the idea of writing about Jennifer's disappearance makes her anxious. She wonders if she's exploiting this, exploiting Jennifer, for her own gain. Is she just stirring up trouble to take her mind off her own problems? The question bothers her, and she tries to push it out of her mind. She starts to leave the store and then, impulsively, goes back and buys the clogs.

Crouching on the floor, she takes off one of her sneakers and slips on the wooden shoes. "There's no place like home," she says to the salesgirl, and she clicks the clunky heels together three times. The girl feigns a smile and turns to another customer, and Kathryn sighs to herself. I'm turning into one of those strange and slightly desperate women I used to make fun of when I was her age, she thinks, the kind who tell inside jokes that nobody gets and try to seem younger and hipper than they are. She looks down at the clogs, velvety blue, and brushes the suede in one direction. Her feet are like snails, nestled and safe in their shells. She puts her old sneakers in the empty shoebox and leaves it on the floor, a little present for the girl behind the counter.

ON THE WAY home, Kathryn swings by the real-estate agency where her mother shares an office when she's not out showing houses. The building is a tidy two-story colonial with window boxes of red geraniums and well-trimmed shrubs; it looks like a Disney version of a new house. Inside, it's decorated like somebody's idea of what house buyers might aspire to: fake Orientals, Waverly swags, gleaming Bombay Company furniture.

The receptionist at the front desk is new. She insists on taking Kathryn's name and getting an okay from her mother before letting her past the foyer.

"God, it's like getting in to see the president," Kathryn grumbles, sinking into a chair in her mother's office.

Her mother puts down the document she's been reading. "Hello, sweetheart," she says pleasantly. "What brings you here?"

"I was just passing by. And oh, I have a message for you: 'Gaff says hi.'"

Her mother leans back in her chair. "I had a feeling you'd run into him sooner or later."

"So, Mom," Kathryn says with a teasing smile, "what's the story?"

She places her fingertips on the desk, like two little tents. "What did he say about me?"

"Nothing. He said to ask you. So what did you do to him to make him so nice to me?"

"Oh, for goodness' sake," her mother says, shaking her head, "your mind is in the gutter." She cranes her neck over the desk and looks at Kathryn's shoes. "What on earth have you got on your feet?"

"Don't change the subject," Kathryn says.

"I haven't seen a pair of clogs in fifteen years."

"Well, you're obviously not up on the latest trends. These are all the rage these days."

"I didn't realize my daughter was so cutting-edge."

"I guess you haven't seen my navel ring."

Her mother rolls her eyes, and Kathryn smiles. She likes seeing her mother at work, with her flying-toasters screensaver, her blinking telephone and framed print of historic Bangor on the wall. "So," she says. "Was it a full-fledged affair, or just a one-night stand?"

Sighing, her mother says, "Ed is a sweet, sweet man. We spent some time together a few years ago."

"Was it serious?"

"Not really. We're too different. But I have to say, he is one of the gentlest, most sensitive men I've ever met."

Kathryn thinks for a moment, trying to reconcile the buttoned-up detective she met—with his two-way radio, pistol, handcuffs, and keys hanging off his belt like a giant charm bracelet—with the man her mother is describing.

"By the way," her mother says, clasping her hands together, "there's something I want to talk to you about. Frank has asked me to go to his camp next weekend. How would you feel about that?"

"You mean, morally?"

"Honestly, Kathryn."

"I mean, I like the Saturn and all, but don't do this for me," Kathryn says.

Her mother shakes her head.

"I'm just kidding, Mom. But hey, this is getting serious, isn't it?"

She half-shrugs, pretending to arrange things on her desk.

"When am I going to meet this guy?"

"One step at a time," her mother says.

"So—are you in love with him?"

"Ah, I think I'm going to take the Fifth on that."

"Oh, come on," she prods.

"Kathryn, stop. I haven't had to report to anyone in a long time. I'm not used to being so . . . enmeshed."

Slightly stung by her mother's words, Kathryn says, "Well, I'm sorry. You don't have to tell me anything you don't want to."

Her mother draws a deep breath and lets it out slowly. She leans forward with both forearms on the desk. "Look," she says. "You and I have been leading pretty separate lives. You haven't particularly wanted to know what's been going on with me, and I haven't needed to tell you. When things with Paul got tough, you stopped calling altogether, until you decided you wanted to come home." Kathryn starts to protest, but her mother holds up her hand. "Let me finish. I was happy for you to come home. I am glad I can provide some kind of haven for you now. But you can't expect that all of a sudden I'm going to tell you everything about my life, when you weren't interested in it for so long." She sits back. "Things are different. I'm different. A lot has happened to me over the past few years. And I want to share that with you, but it's going to take some time. Also," she adds, "I'm just really busy these days. I'm afraid I can't be around for you in the way you might have expected me to be."

"I didn't expect anything," Kathryn mumbles, but it isn't true. She did somehow expect that things would be the way they were when she was home for visits, and her mother had made time for her. She hadn't realized how much things have changed over the years; dropping in for only a few days at a time, she had imagined that what her mother did at holidays—drop everything to attend to her and Josh—was the way it would be. Her mother always used to be the one pushing for a close relationship; Kathryn was always the one pulling away. Now, suddenly, she realizes what it feels like to be the one with more time and more interest. It's unsettling; everything is upside down.

Her mother glances at her watch. "You know what? I'd love to finish this conversation, because I think it's a healthy thing for us to do, but I've got a three-o'clock." She smiles apologetically, but the smile is fleeting, and Kathryn knows her mind is already on other things. "And, sweetie," she says as Kathryn gets up, "if you have time, would you swing by the cleaners and pick up my linen blazer? I completely forgot about it this morning, and I need it for a meeting tomorrow." She digs through her purse, and, finding the pink receipt, slips it into Kathryn's hand. "I'll try to be home early. Do you have plans tonight?"

Kathryn shakes her head.

"Isn't there anyone in town you want to see?" she ventures. "What about that nice girl Rachel? You know she's teaching at Orono on some prestigious fellowship—I guess she won some big award for her dissertation and got it published. And I hear she has a cute little house. I'm sure she'd love to hear from you."

"Yeah, maybe I'll give her a call," Kathryn says, easing the conversation to a close. She needs to talk to Rachel anyway, but she's dreading it. Whatever connection they once had has long been broken, and the string of accomplishments and cute little house that Kathryn, too, has heard about don't make it any easier.

"I'm very proud of you, Kathryn," her mother says, cocking her head like a bird.

"For what?"

"For getting out of that marriage and doing what you need to do to nurture yourself. For taking time to heal. I really admire you for that."

Kathryn starts to respond—she knows her mother is partly in earnest, partly smoothing things over, and partly giving her a pep talk—but she lets it go. "Thanks, Mom," she says, squeezing her hand. "I'm proud of you, too."

WHEN KATHRYN GETS home, the answering machine is blinking. She pushes the button. "Hi, Mrs. Campbell, hi, Kathryn. It's Jack. Ledbetter. Kathryn, I know it's not Sunday yet, but I'm wondering how the interviewing is going. I thought maybe we could talk about it, if you—you know—think that might be helpful." He clears his throat. "Like maybe tonight, if you don't have anything going on. I was thinking maybe we could—" The machine emits a long beep, and then the next message says, "Five-thirty at the Sea Dog. I'll be the one wearing a baseball cap." He laughs, and Kathryn knows why—half the guys there will probably be wearing baseball caps. "I hope you're coming. I hate drinking alone."

When Kathryn gets to the Sea Dog, a dimly lit, fern-filled microbrewery on the bank of the Penobscot, Jack is nowhere to be seen. She sits outside on the deck under a green-and-white striped umbrella and watches the activity on the river and at the tables nearby. Next to her, a man and a very pregnant woman are holding hands. "How about Leonardo? That's a strong name," Kathryn overhears the woman say.

The man shakes his head. "I'm holding out for Buck."

There's a loud whoop from the other end of the deck, seven or eight college guys raising their pint glasses in a toast.

"I'll have what they're having," Kathryn tells the cute, ponytailed waiter. Is she flirting with him? She isn't sure.

He smirks. "I don't think it's what they're having—it's how much. You want a pitcher?"

"I'll start with a pint," she says. "What are your specials?"

"Blueberry lager is the feature this week."

She makes a face.

"Okay, then. How about an India pale ale? Smooth, not too rich, full-bodied."

She squints up at him. "Sounds nice."

"One pale ale coming up." He turns on his heel and goes inside.

She leans back in her chair, closing her eyes, feeling the late-afternoon sun on her eyelids. Since when was Bangor such a happening place, with fancy beers and handsome waiters? A shadow passes in front of her eyes and she opens them to see Jack standing there. "Sorry I'm late," he says, flopping into a deck chair. "Office bullshit."

"I don't mind," she says. "I was enjoying the view."

He grins. "With your eyes shut?"

"Metaphorically," she says.

He shrugs off his light jacket. His movements are artless, unstudied; he seems not to notice that anyone might be paying attention. Watching him, she thinks of Paul, who was always so aware of how he was being perceived and what was going on around him. "You're not wearing that, are you?" he said more than once as they got ready to go out. He always dressed carefully; his leather jacket was thicker than most, imported from Italy; his shirts were washable linen and three-hundred-count cotton. At restaurants he liked to sit with his back against the wall so he could observe the room. One time, Kathryn remembers, when she was telling him about something that had upset her, he held up one finger, and she paused, thinking he had something important to say. Instead he leaned forward, tilting his head to the left, and she realized he was eavesdropping on another couple's conversation.

Reaching across the table for the menu, Jack scans it quickly, shutting it a moment later with a decisive flap. He looks up and smiles at her. "So," he says, "really, have you been waiting long?"

"Years," she says.

The waiter materializes out of nowhere with Kathryn's beer and takes Jack's order. "How is it?" he asks Kathryn as she takes a sip.

"You're right. Nice body," she says.

"Thought you'd like it," he says, smiling down at her.

Jack gives him a once-over as he leaves. "No offense, Kathryn, but isn't he a little young?" he whispers.

"A little young for what?" she asks innocently.

They sit in silence for a moment, looking out at the river. A flat-bottomed houseboat drifts by, with a young boy and an old man out on the deck. The boy waves at the restaurant crowd, and a few scattered people wave back. He holds up a big fish, and several people clap. The old man helps him put the fish in the bucket.

"People are so damn nice here," Kathryn says.

"No, they're not."

"Mmm. But isn't it lovely to think so?"

Jack shifts in his chair. "To you, maybe. To me it sounds patronizing."

"What do you mean?" she says, her voice rising defensively.

"I think it's a way of distancing yourself from this place. If you can say that everybody here is one way or another, you don't really have to engage it."

"That's ridiculous."

"Oh, really." He scratches his chin. "How long have you been here, almost three weeks? And have you been in touch with anyone from the group yet?"

"Not yet," she says. "But I'm going to, soon, for this article."

"You wouldn't otherwise?"

"I'm sure I would sooner or later," she says, though she isn't sure at all.

"When's the last time you saw Rachel?"

Kathryn tries to think. She and Rachel had never really been close, though they hung out in the group together a lot senior year. Kathryn had always been a bit intimidated by Rachel—she was so cagey and secretive, and she seemed to know more than she was telling. It was hard to fathom what she was thinking behind her dark, impassive stare.

"She's a guy's girl," Jennifer said once. "It's that inscrutable poet thing. They love it that they can't figure her out."

"It's been a while," Kathryn admits. "What about you?"

"Oh, we had dinner last week. Did you know her doctoral dissertation was published by some major university press this spring? And she's up for tenure next year."

"I did know," Kathryn murmurs. "That's great." She had received an invitation several months back to a publication party in Rachel's honor; she sent a bowl from a Virginia pottery maker along with a note offering excuses about why she couldn't come. She didn't tell the real reason: that Rachel's life—her directedness, the ease with which she seemed to achieve what she wanted—seemed a rebuke of her own. "Rachel was always destined to have a brilliant career."

"Yeah," Jack says. "I'm really happy for her."

"To tell you the truth, I used to think you two might end up together. In high school you were practically joined at the hip."

He squints into the middle distance—at the porch rail, maybe, or the lettering on someone's T-shirt. "Nah," he says. "It wasn't like that between us. We were just . . . friends."

Sensing his hesitation, she presses him. "Always?"

"Mostly always, yeah."

"*Mostly* always . . ." she says expectantly.

He nods. "We fooled around once. It was a mistake."

"When?"

"Graduation night."

"You're kidding." She sits up in surprise.

"Nope. We just . . ." He shrugs almost helplessly. "After the group broke up, we went over to the water tower for a few hours. Anyway, it was a stupid thing to do. She liked Brian, and I didn't know what I wanted. And then, when we found out a few hours later that Jennifer never made it home, we were really freaked. We pretty much pretended it never happened."

She listens, studying his eyes. "Have you ever talked about it?"

He shakes his head. "After that night something changed between us. We couldn't quite look each other in the eye. It shouldn't have happened anyway, and then the memory of it got wrapped up in what happened to Jennifer. It took a long time to rebuild the friendship, and even then it was never as easy as it was before."

"So you don't see much of each other these days."

"No," he admits. "I think part of it is just growing up. She's busy; I'm busy."

"Is she seeing anyone now?"

He shrugs. "I don't ask those kinds of questions."

She takes a sip of her beer. "Anything else you want to tell me? Did you and Rachel concoct some diabolical lovers' plan to get rid of Jennifer?"

"Hmm," he says. "That's an interesting idea. And what would our motive be?"

"Maybe you did it for kicks. You were acting out some obsessive little fantasy that night and you carried it too far."

"Do I seem obsessive to you?"

She smiles lightly. "That nice guy Ted Bundy didn't seem obsessive either."

"Well, it would be an interesting twist," he says. "Newspaper editor assigns article on murder he committed. It could be a novel."

"Or a made-for-TV movie. And why do you say it's a murder? I'm not assuming anything."

"You think maybe I'm keeping her in a dungeon?"

"Okay, Jack." She holds her hands up. "Let's just get off this idea that you did it for a minute. She could be anywhere. She could have run away."

"She could have," he says. He sits up and looks around. "Where the hell is my beer? Your boy toy is slacking off." Flagging down another waiter, he orders again.

When his beer arrives, Kathryn says, "So Rachel is living in Orono. Where is everybody else?"

"You really don't know?"

She shakes her head.

"That surprises me. I always thought of you as the glue of the group."

"You did?" she says. "I always thought it was you. Or Jennifer."

"I wasn't organized enough to do the legwork that would've required. And Jennifer was the queen bee. You were the one who brought us all together."

"I was?" She tries to remember. It had just seemed natural, the way they gravitated toward each other freshman year, but now that she thinks about it she probably was the one who made it happen. Through her, two separate clusters of people came together: Brian and Rachel and Jack had been friends at Fifth Street Middle School; Kathryn and the twins had attended Garland Street. The first semester of ninth grade, Kathryn and Brian were lab partners in a biology class. Kathryn introduced him to Will and Jennifer, though, as it turned out, Brian already knew Jennifer from an after-school theater group they'd both belonged to the previous year. And Brian brought them all to meet his friends Rachel and Jack.

"You Fifth Streeters were so different from us," Kathryn says. "It's a miracle we became friends at all."

She's joking, but there's some truth in it. Garland Street Middle School was a tougher place than the more homogeneous Fifth Street. Garland Street kids came to the high school talking about grain alcohol and blow jobs and heavy-metal bands. Fifth Street kids were more sheltered and more straitlaced, and they tended to stick together like nervous sheep around a pack of wolves. Eventually some of the more adventurous Fifth Street kids ventured over to the dark side and were corrupted, poisoning the entire group. It was a natural process, but exposure to Garland Street hastened it. Even when the class seemed fully integrated, senior year, prejudices lingered. Down deep, the Garland Street kids still found the Fifth Streeters a little callow and naive, and the Fifth Streeters thought the Garland Streeters were slightly seedy and even dangerous.

"It's true," Jack is saying. "If something bizarre had to happen to one of us, it's no surprise it was one of you Garland Street weirdos."

"Ah, the prejudice lingers."

"Hey, I'm not prejudiced. Some of my closest friends are Garland Streeters. Can't we all get along?" He lifts his pint glass in a toast and takes a long drink. "Here's to multicultural harmony."

After a few months at Bangor High, the six of them began hanging out together. At lunchtime they found each other in shifts, drifting together with an ease born of familiarity, like pigeons on a stoop. Will was always first; his art class, right across the hall from the cafeteria, ended early. Rachel and Jack usually came together, Rachel with plastic containers of home-prepared foods: organic granola, carrots, hummus, and sprouts; Jack with individually packaged multi-pack-sized Three Musketeers bars and M&M's, the wrappers rustling in his pockets as he walked. Brian ambled in by himself, usually with a thick paperback he was in the middle of reading. Kathryn and Jennifer rushed in late, scrounging food from those who'd come early.

Once they all became friends, it was true, Kathryn had done what she could to keep them together. She made sure that plans were disseminated; she worked hard to ease feuds and jealousies and misunderstandings. The group was more important to her than anything else in high school, and, without even realizing it, she arranged her life around it. She didn't have many boyfriends, and the ones she did have tended to be from away, guys she'd met at summer camp or through friends who lived in other towns. She liked their passionate letters and yearning phone calls, the surprise packages that arrived in the mail filled with hand-lettered cassettes and sweatshirts printed with other schools' mascots, the delicious intensity of delayed gratification. She didn't want to date anyone from Bangor High who might interfere in her everyday life. For one thing, he'd have to get by the group.

Later, after Jennifer had been missing for a while and the group had broken apart in clumps, Kathryn tried to figure out why it had mattered so much to her, why the loss of it was so devastating. What it came down to was something quite simple: She felt like herself in the group; she was comfortable. This comfort derived in part from feeling that the things she said and did mattered—she made her friends laugh, they listened to her. She felt safe in a way she'd never felt anywhere else. In the group all of them were able to subvert their high-school personas. Kathryn, literary-magazine editor and aspiring reporter, could admit that she was addicted to *The National Enquirer*; Rachel, ethereal and brainy, who wouldn't touch cafeteria food and grew her own sprouts on the kitchen windowsill at home, revealed a silly sense of humor and a secret passion for Pop Tarts. Jack, the affable pop-culture fanatic, preferred Beethoven to rock music. Though he claimed to be uninterested in sports, Brian knew the batting average of every member of the Red Sox. And Jennifer, who labored through English class and struggled to finish assignments, who complained that she had nothing to say and wouldn't know how to express herself if she did, admitted that she faithfully kept a journal every day. She had since she was ten. The journals, one for each year, a page for each day, were lined up on a high shelf in her room, dates written on the cracked bindings in Magic Marker, stuffed with grade reports and arts-page clippings with her photo from the school play in grainy black and white.

What about Will? Kathryn wonders now. What secret did he reveal? "It's funny that Will never told us he was gay," she muses.

"I don't think he figured it out until later," Jack says. He takes a long sip of his beer, and puts his glass down on the table. "Listen," he says. He shifts uncomfortably in his chair. "I've been putting off telling you this, but I think you should know. Will is HIV-positive."

She stares at him. "You're kidding."

He shakes his head.

"When did he find out?"

"About a year ago."

"Oh, Jesus," she says.

"He's doing well," Jack says. "The protease inhibitors are making a big difference, and his T-cell count is fine. He hasn't been sick or anything, not since the beginning."

"When did he tell you?"

"I saw him a few months ago in Boston. Really, Kathryn, he's doing fine."

"God, I feel terrible," Kathryn says, putting her head in her hands. "I kept up with him through college, but then . . ."

"Look, he understands. It was that way for all of us," Jack says. He smiles, softening the impact of the moment. "Anyway, you'll see him at the reunion. You can talk to him then."

"Ohh," she sighs, more a sound than a word. She feels as if she's been hit in the chest.

By this time it's happy hour and the deck is packed. In the entrance to the deck there's a bottleneck of people carrying plates of chicken wings and nachos in and out. They sit in silence for a few minutes, staring out at the crowd.

"Look over there," Jack whispers, motioning toward a group of women several tables over. Their table is covered with wrapping paper and baby clothes, and blue and pink balloons are tied to the back of a chair.

Like so many people in Bangor, the women look familiar, but Kathryn can't place them. "Who are they?"

"They were in our class. Fifth Streeters. Kristi Wilson, Dawn Sommers, Heidi Murkoff and Susan Kominsky. Most of them are married now. Looks like Heidi's got a bun in the oven."

In high school, Kathryn remembers, Jack knew everyone. It always amazed her, walking down the hall with him, how many people he connected with. And he had a knack for names. It wasn't just other students—he also knew the names of the cafeteria ladies and enough about them to make conversation as he pushed his orange plastic tray along the lunch line. Between classes he got to know the janitors; he brought the principal's secretary a Whitman's Sampler on her birthday, and he always had a joke for the vice-principal. Jack's teachers loved him, the cafeteria ladies gave him seconds, and the school secretary excused his tardiness. The janitors let him into school on Saturdays when he'd forgotten his books. Jack was adept at the parting quip, but he also had greater skills at his disposal. Brian called it "high-beaming"— the ability to compress sincerity into a two-sentence exchange.

Kathryn scrutinizes the table of women. Several are wearing unflattering cotton A-line tops. "She's not the only pregnant one," she says. "I think Kristi was in my English class."

"You want to go over and say hi?"

She grips the handles of her chair and, still seated, moves it around so that her back is to the group. "I don't think so," she says.

Jack laughs. "Well, aren't you sociable?"

"This is exactly why I'm not going to the reunion," she mutters. "First, I'm a loser, and second, I can't remember anybody's name."

"Well, I can't help you with the first one, but as far as the name thing goes, they'll all be wearing huge 'Hello, my name is Donna' tags."

"Okay. But what if I don't want to remember anybody's name?"

"That's another issue. But I'm afraid you have no choice. I'm sending you there on assignment."

"What?" she says sharply.

"You have to go. It's part of the story. Girl disappears, best friend back in town for reunion, etc. The reunion part is crucial. And—uh-oh, don't look now, but—"

"Jack! I thought it was you sitting over here!"

"Hey, Dawn, how's it going? You remember Kathryn Campbell." He kicks her leg under the table, and Kathryn turns around.

"Kath," Dawn says, holding out a small, cool hand for her to grasp. "God, I haven't seen you since . . ."

"Probably high school," Kathryn says.

Dawn makes a motion like she's trying to get a helmet off her head. "I like the red."

"What?"

"Your hair. It's so . . . festive."

"Oh," Kathryn says, self-consciously tucking a strand behind her ear. She's pretty sure it's not a compliment. "You're looking very . . . healthy," she says, trying to deflect.

Dawn puts a hand under her protruding belly. "Only eight weeks to go," she says proudly. She motions back toward her table. "Heidi's due at exactly the same time. Isn't that amazing?"

"Yeah, that's great, congratulations," Kathryn says. She looks over at Heidi, who lifts her fingers in a caterpillarlike wave. Kathryn waves back.

"So you're in town for the reunion?" Dawn asks.

Kathryn looks at Jack, and he nods. She nods, too.

"It should be interesting," Dawn says. "I saw Pete Michaud the other day. I couldn't believe it—he's totally bald. And Marcie Daniels, remember her? She was on the squad with Kristi and me. Anyway, she's gained like fifty pounds, it's so sad. And Janis McAlary, I heard a rumor, I don't know if it's true, that she's living in Portland with a woman. You know, I always wondered about her."

And hey, did you hear about Kath Campbell? She dropped out of school and got a divorce and a bad dye job and moved back in with her mother. . . .

"So what've you been up to?" Dawn is asking. She glances at the ring on Kathryn's left hand. "Married, I see. Kids?"

"Oh, well, no." Kathryn covers the hand with her other. "No kids. And I'm not married—not anymore. It's pretty recent," she adds.

"I'm so sorry," Dawn breathes.

"Actually, she's in town to do a piece for the paper," Jack says, sitting forward.

"Oh! What about?"

"The Jennifer Pelletier case."

Dawn's eyes grow large and round. "Did something—"

"Nothing new. It's just a follow-up. But it's been a while since anyone took a good look at it, and we thought it was time."

"Absolutely," Dawn says, nodding. "We all—I mean, it's unbelievable, isn't it? People don't just drop off the face of the earth." She shudders. "And they never found the slightest clue, did they?"

"Not yet," Jack says. "We're working on it." He smiles at Kathryn, and she smiles at Dawn.

"Well, good luck," Dawn says. She nods over her shoulder. "I should get back. By the way, everybody says hi."

"Hi, everybody," Jack says loudly, half standing and waving a big wave. Kathryn waves, too, and the three women wave back.

"See you at the reunion," Dawn says. "If I can find a tent big enough to wear." She laughs and pretends to waddle back to the table.

When she's gone, Jack says, "See? That wasn't so bad."

"Which part?"

Jack sighs. "You know what you remind me of? Those old ladies who lock their doors and stay inside all day, feeling sorry for themselves. And if anybody comes along and knocks on the door, they open it just a little"—he acts it out—"but keep the chain on. *'Hello?'*" he says in a quavery, suspicious voice. "*'What do you want? Go away.'*" He pretends to slam the door.

"Do I really?" she says, slightly wounded.

"You're just so damn self-protective," he says. "Come on, Kathryn, lighten up. Everybody has problems. One of Dawn's brothers died last year in a car accident, did you know that? And she always wanted to go to medical school, but she had to take care of her mother, who has Parkinson's."

Kathryn blushes. "I didn't know."

"No reason you should. The point is, everybody has a story. Yours isn't the only one."

"God, Jack," she says. "You must think I'm a total narcissist."

"I'm assuming it's a phase," he says. He looks at her for a moment.

"Now, listen, whaddaya say we order some food? We missed the free wings, and I'm starving."

She smiles, looking into his gray-green eyes, and he smiles back. He seems so certain, and she feels so uncertain about everything. "All right," she says. "I'd like that."

WHEN SHE GETS home that night, her mother is sitting in the red wingback in the living room in her bathrobe, flipping through *Country Interiors*.

"What are you doing up?" Kathryn asks. She looks at her watch; it's 12:30 A.M.

"I couldn't sleep," her mother says. She yawns and stretches her arms over her head, and the magazine slides to the floor. "So," she says casually, "where have you been?"

"I was out with Jack."

"Oh, really."

"Didn't you see the note I left on the table?" she says, trying to ignore her mother's insinuating tone.

"You said you were having drinks."

"We did have drinks. Then we had dinner."

"And then?"

Kathryn rolls her eyes. "God, Mom! I feel like I'm in high school."

Her mother stands up and smooths her bathrobe, tightens the belt. "Well, to tell you the truth, Kathryn, I was a little worried. It's late to be out driving around. Especially if you were drinking."

"I wasn't *drinking*. I had a few drinks. Over six hours. And you don't need to be worried about me; I'm an adult."

"Adult or not, you're living under my roof."

Kathryn stands very still, counting to ten under her breath.

"And besides," her mother adds, "I was curious about how it went. Six hours is a pretty long date."

"It wasn't a date."

"Well, whatever it was. Six hours is a long time for anything."

Kathryn is tempted to tell her mother to leave her alone, that she's tired and has a headache and wants to go to bed, but something in her mother's voice changes her mind. She's probably been sitting in that chair for hours, Kathryn thinks, keeping an eye on the clock and pretending to read magazines. It reminds her less of high school than of college, when she and her roommates would wait up for each other to report the evening's events. Unlike some of her friends, she's never had that kind of relationship with her mother; their exchanges have been more fraught. She has always felt the pressure, real or imagined, of her mother's agenda: that Kathryn not scare her, not let her down, not marry someone unsuitable and end up divorced, as she did. But now the worst has happened. Her mother's fears have been realized, and somehow, oddly, it may have taken the pressure off both of them.

Kathryn puts down her bag and sinks onto the couch. "Will Pelletier is HIV-positive."

"Oh, Kathryn," her mother says.

Tears well up in Kathryn's eyes, and her mother comes over and sits beside her on the couch, putting her arms around her. "Baby," she murmurs, kissing her head, and Kathryn feels herself relax into her mother's warm embrace.

Rachel lives in a small cottage in Orono, near the University of Maine campus. The front yard blooms with roses—pink roses spreading up the front walk, white roses climbing a trellis around the gingerbread-hut front door, yellow roses with orange-tipped thorns beside a white fence. The roses will survive for only a few months in the fickle Maine weather. It is so like Rachel, Kathryn thinks as she pulls into the driveway, to lavish time and attention on such fleeting beauty.

Rachel had been different from most of the kids at Bangor High. Her parents were Russian Jews, professors at the university, and they lived in a drafty modern solar-powered house with floor-to-ceiling bookshelves and overlapping Indian rugs. In high school it was Rachel's ambition to be a poet; she read Sylvia Plath and Emily Dickinson and e. e. cummings, and scrawled her own poems in a large hardbound notebook that her father had picked up for her in England, carrying it everywhere in her Guatemalan bag.

When she was fourteen she asked her parents to send her away to boarding school. No one understood her in Bangor; school was boring, the teachers were bland. Without more stimulation, she insisted, she would wither and die like a raisin in the sun.

Her father said, "So you're suffering here."

"Yes, I am," Rachel said solemnly.

"You don't belong, you're an outsider."

"Exactly."

"Well, then, this may be the most important time in your life!" her mother exclaimed. "What more could a poet ask, than to be unappreciated and misunderstood?"

Rachel never tried to fit in with most of the other kids, in their ragg sweaters and penny loafers and copycat hairstyles. Her fine, dark hair was cropped short against the delicate bones of her face, and she dressed in velvet dresses from thrift shops with long underwear and hiking boots and dangling jewelry. Kathryn had always envied Rachel's resolute self-assurance, her daring in dressing outlandishly, the way she'd go to movies or coffee shops and sit serenely by herself without the slightest concern about what anyone else might think. Kathryn was more insecure, always looking around for someone she knew, self-conscious about sitting alone.

The wooden gate is slightly ajar. Kathryn walks up the short stone path to the house and raps the brass knocker. The door opens and Rachel appears, smiling, wearing a floral peach dress and a necklace of seed pearls.

"Oh, Kath!" she says, coming up and hugging her from underneath, her arms going around Kathryn's shoulders. "It's wonderful to see you."

"You, too," Kathryn murmurs. She pulls back awkwardly. "Look at you—you haven't changed." It's true; Rachel's dark hair is still in a pixie, and she's as slender as she was in high school, with pale, dewy skin.

Lightly touching Kathryn's shoulder, Rachel looks into her eyes. "You have. You look . . . wiser."

She resists the impulse to laugh, or cry. "You mean older."

"Like you've learned something over the years."

"I wish that were true," Kathryn says, shaking her head.

Rachel goes into the kitchen to put a kettle on for iced tea—a characteristically elaborate and old-fashioned gesture, Kathryn thinks—and Kathryn settles on a couch in the living room. Opening her bag, she takes out a tape recorder, notebook, and pens. She looks around the room at the Victorian furniture and white cotton curtains and books stacked in piles as high as coffee tables. On the mantelpiece over the fireplace are several photographs of Rachel in exotic places—on the Spanish Steps, on a gondola in Venice, holding up a beer stein in a brightly lit café—with people Kathryn doesn't recognize. There are a few pictures of Rachel's cheerful, bespectacled parents, and one of a dark-haired man in a Bangor Rams T-shirt, standing in a clearing. Kathryn looks closer. "Hey, isn't this Mr. Hunter from the high school?" she asks.

"Oh, yes," Rachel says, coming into the room. She's carrying a tray with a teapot, two tall glasses full of ice, a small bowl of lemon wedges, and a plate of English digestive biscuits. "We've gone on a few treks together up north. Is Celestial Seasonings okay? I don't keep caffeine in the house."

"Sure," Kathryn says, clearing a space on the coffee table for the tray. "You didn't do orienteering in high school."

She laughs. "No. It was Jennifer's thing, you know? But it's a great way to get exercise. I'm sorry I didn't take it up sooner."

Kathryn nods. "So how'd you hook back up with him?"

Rachel lifts the lid of the teapot and jiggles the bags a few times. Replacing the lid, she pours the tea into two glasses. The ice splinters and cracks. "I didn't really know him back then. I never took his class. But we happened to both be doing a five-K run for, I don't know, the United Way or something a few years ago, and we started talking, and he told me about orienteering and, well . . ." She shrugs. "I've only done it a few times, but I love it."

Kathryn takes a cool glass, wet with condensation, and wraps her hands around it. "What do you love about it?"

Rachel squeezes a lemon wedge into her glass and stirs her tea with a long, tarnished spoon. "Well, you know Jennifer and I both ran cross-country—and there are similarities. Orienteering is a running sport. But unlike cross-country, you run with a map and compass and choose your own way. There's always the possibility that you'll get lost—and for me, that adds to the excitement of it." She takes a sip of tea and places the glass back on the tray. "Actually, technically what I do is called wayfaring: recreational, noncompetitive orienteering. I'm more interested in the running and the art of navigation than in winning a competition, not that there are opportunities around here for adults to compete anyway. Rick—Mr. Hunter—learned about it from friends in Massachusetts who belong to the New England Orienteering Club. Sometimes he goes down there for competitions, but I prefer to do it just for fun."

"You seem to know a lot about it," Kathryn observes.

"I guess I've gotten hooked."

"So, just out of curiosity, are you and Mr. Hunter . . . ?"

"Rick," Rachel says, and smiles. "No, no, no." She shakes her head dismissively. Then she bites into a biscuit, as if to end the discussion. "I was sorry to hear about you and—is it Paul?" she says.

"Yeah. Thanks."

"But I guess it's better to do it now than later, when kids might be involved."

"Yeah," Kathryn agrees.

As they sit in silence, sipping tea, Kathryn thinks back on all the evenings they spent together as part of the group, the secrets they told, the jokes they shared. In a strange way, Rachel knows her as well as anyone does. But they never did the hard work together of forging a separate friendship, and when Jennifer disappeared and then they went to different colleges, the ties that bound them to one another slowly dissolved. She looks at Rachel's face, her clean profile and dancing eyes.

This is the face of a friend, she thinks, and I don't have many. "This is nice," she says suddenly. "I hope we can see each other more."

Rachel leans back, stretching her arms over her head. "And without a tape recorder next time," she says.

"TALK TO ME like a stranger," Kathryn says. They've finished their tea and put the tray on the floor, and Kathryn is filling out a label. She peels the narrow strip off its backing and affixes it to a cassette. "Some of the questions I ask may be annoying or intrusive, and some you'll think I know the answer to already—and I might. But don't assume anything."

Rachel nods.

Kathryn inserts the cassette into the player and pushes the record button. Rachel moves forward in her chair, and they both watch the black tape thread onto the empty spool.

"This is an interview with Rachel Feynman at her home in Orono, Maine, on July nineteenth, 1996. I'm going to jump right in," Kathryn tells her. "How well do you feel you knew Jennifer Pelletier?"

Rachel takes a deep breath and looks out the window at the rose-bushes, the blue sky beyond. "It's weird," she says. "I consider—I considered—I still have trouble talking about her in the past tense, you know? Even after all this time." She returns her gaze to Kathryn. "I keep thinking she's going to show up with some kind of rational explanation for why she's been gone. Anyway, I considered her one of my closest friends, but after she disappeared and people started asking questions about her, I realized that I actually didn't know her very well at all."

"What do you mean?"

"I don't know. She was quiet, not reclusive or anything, but there was a level of reserve; you knew not to push things past a certain point. Will always seemed more open, though now I wonder. I mean, who knew he was gay? Sometimes I think I must've had my head in the sand all through high school—or maybe we were just lying to each other the whole time."

"Do you think we were?"

She pauses. "I think we all had secrets. Some of us knew things about others in the group not everyone knew. That's only natural, I guess. You and Jennifer were closer to each other than you were to me, so I'm sure you know a lot more about her than I do."

"Well, I've found I can't assume anything," Kathryn says. "I'm not sure I know any more than you."

Sitting back, Rachel says, "Well, you and Jennifer were so close—I have to admit I felt a little left out. But then again, I was closer to Jack, and maybe that bothered you. I always wondered if you might have had a little crush on him. Because when he asked me to the prom, even though we were just friends, I remember I felt this weird vibe from you. I don't know, maybe I was imagining it, but I wondered if you were hoping he'd ask you. Then when you went with Will, I thought I was wrong, and maybe you two had a thing going. Little did I know he was gay." She laughs.

"Me either," Kathryn says. Then, prompting, "And Jennifer went with Brian."

"Right."

"That was kind of surprising to me. I thought he was going to ask you."

"I—hmm," Rachel says. "Do we have to get all this on tape? I don't really see how it's relevant."

"Just background."

"It just seems trivial—who had a crush on whom, and all that."

You brought it up, Kathryn thinks, but she keeps it to herself. "What do you think I should be asking?"

"I would think you'd be asking more about Jennifer's state of mind on the night she disappeared, if she seemed upset or whatever. If I noticed anything out of the ordinary."

"All right," Kathryn agrees. "So what did you notice?"

"Well, I've thought about this a lot. I'm sure we all have. She seemed strange to me that night—kind of removed and distant."

"More than usual?"

"Yes. I think so. Though the fact that she just disappeared makes everything seem strange in retrospect. Even the color of the sky, and the way it was so empty. No stars. And there was a full moon, wasn't there?"

"It was a crescent moon, I think," Kathryn says.

"Really? I could have sworn it was full." She gives her a wry smile. "It's funny that we both remember the moon, but remember it differently. I'm sure you'll find that with these interviews. We all have different perspectives."

Kathryn settles back against the pillows on the couch. "So how did Jennifer seem strange to you?"

"When we drove up—I was with Jack and Brian and Will—the two of you were on the hood of that old red car you used to have. You sat up right away and came over, but Jennifer just stayed there. At first I thought she was asleep or passed out, but she wasn't. She was just lying there, staring up at the sky. Then I got paranoid and thought maybe she was avoiding me or something. We'd kind of had it out the night before. But you know about that."

"Vaguely," Kathryn says, remembering. "Something to do with Brian, right?"

"Mostly. But . . . I wasn't going to talk about this."

"Just tell me a little about the argument."

"Well, it wasn't really an argument. We didn't raise our voices or anything. It was more like a discussion, where two people get together to tell their sides of a story."

"So what was it about?"

Rachel is silent for a moment, biting her bottom lip. Then she says, "Again, I'm not sure this is relevant. But basically, it was about Brian, on the surface, at least. I knew she wasn't interested in him as a boyfriend, and I knew she knew I was. So it was weird to me that she went to the prom with him. I mean, he asked her, and of course she can do what she wants. But I guess I thought that out of respect for my feelings she would have said no. Given that she had no interest in him," she adds.

"Are you sure about that? That she had no interest?"

"Yes. She made it absolutely clear. I mean, I can understand her wanting to go and needing a date, since obviously she couldn't go with the person she wanted to go with. But she could have had anyone—it didn't have to be Brian. Not that he would have asked me if she had said no, but even if he hadn't, at least I wouldn't have had to deal with the embarrassment of both of them knowing how I felt and feeling sorry for me."

"So why did she go with him?"

"I don't think she really thought about it. Or maybe she did—and decided that her need to have a good time outweighed my possible discomfort. Who knows? She was peculiar that way. That's what I mean about feeling like I never really knew her. I could rarely tell what she was thinking, or even what she was feeling. It was as if she had a loose wire somewhere. Something about her was . . ." She pauses, searching for the word. "Disconnected."

"How did things end up between you?"

"Well, in our discussion that night she said she was sorry, that if she had realized how much it would upset me for her to go with Brian, she would have reconsidered. I said it didn't upset me—it unsettled me. More about my relationship with her than my relationship with Brian. I said it was about trust. And then she said something that struck me as bizarre. 'Trust isn't a word I know,' she said. 'It isn't in my vocabulary. I don't believe in it.' I just stared at her. I didn't know what to say."

Kathryn makes a note on her pad. "I want to go back to something for a second," she says, tapping her pen against her teeth. "What did you mean when you said she couldn't go with the person she wanted to go with?"

Rachel looks at her doubtfully. "Do you really want this on tape?"

"Do you want me to turn it off?"

"It's up to you. I did promise, after all. You must have, too."

"I'm not sure . . ." Kathryn says, confused.

"Not to tell. I mean, obviously. You and I have never discussed it, and if anyone did, it would be the two of us."

Kathryn shakes her head. The objects in the room seems suddenly to have come into sharp focus, and the air is still. "I don't know what you're talking about."

"How could . . . ?" Rachel's voice trails off. She stares at Kathryn in silence for a long moment. Finally she says, "Hmm. I think we'd better turn that thing off."

They both reach for the button, and Rachel pushes it first.

"Tell me," Kathryn demands.

"I'm sorry, Kath. I need to think about this."

"Think about what?"

Rachel stands up and crosses her arms in front of her chest. She goes to the window and adjusts the flimsy curtains, looking outside. "I just need to think."

"What is this all about?"

"I thought you knew," she murmurs. "I thought we both did."

Kathryn shakes her head impatiently.

Absently pushing her hair off her face, Rachel turns back around. "This is very . . . awkward."

"I don't understand."

She smiles weakly. "Really, Kath, this is irrelevant."

"Then why can't you tell me?"

Rachel holds her hand out at arm's length and waves it back and forth. "I'm sorry. I've said too much already."

"Listen, Rachel," Kathryn says, trying to be reasonable. "Jennifer's gone. If you know anything—"

"I don't," she says quickly. "I don't."

Kathryn glances outside; the color has drained from the sky, and the rosebushes are swaying to one side in the wind, petals falling on the grass like confetti.

Looking down at her watch, Rachel says, "You know what? I actually need to do some stuff. I'm teaching summer school, and I have a seminar tomorrow morning I haven't even started grading papers for."

"Sure. Okay." Kathryn sighs. She gets up. Opening her bag, she gathers the tape recorder and cassettes and notebook and dumps them in. At the door she hesitates. "Call me when you change your mind," she says.

"Kath Campbell!" Brian says. "How the hell are you?" It sounds like he's talking to her through a tin can.

"Just a sec," she tells him as she clicks through channels on her mother's cordless phone, trying to improve the reception. "I'm fine," she says when the echo is gone. "Is this an okay time to talk?"

"Yeah, it's good."

"How is Portland?"

"I love it. Thinking of moving north?"

"Yeah, well, I'm in Bangor right now, actually," she says. She leans back in the rocker, putting her foot up on a Moroccan hassock her mother brought back from a cruise several years ago. "Staying with my mom for a few weeks."

"Up for the reunion."

"Yeah, kind of. Reunion, divorce."

"Ouch. Sorry to hear that."

God, she thinks, I wish I could make a general announcement.

"That's okay, it's for the best," she says quickly. "How about you? Any drama in your life these days?"

"Not much. Still working for Geary's Ale, running their distribution now. And I'm engaged."

"Congratulations! That's drama."

"Yeah, she's great. A Biddeford girl. You'll meet her at the reunion. Maybe we can get together beforehand, try some new Geary's flavors."

"I don't know about this fruit concept, Brian," she says. "Blueberry beer is a little wacky for me."

"Oh, that's last year's news. The new thing is fish. We're introducing a wild trout that'll knock your socks off."

Kathryn laughs. She had forgotten how strange and quirky Brian is, how obliviously good-natured. In high school he didn't seem to notice when people couldn't get his obscure jokes or pop-culture references; he was happy just to amuse himself. His mind was like flypaper, collecting bits of trivia and arcane facts, and you were lucky if you clued into half of what he was saying.

Brian is nothing like the rest of his family. His father, Cubby White, has been the head coach of the Bangor High football team for twenty years. His two older brothers were star players, but Brian never showed any interest in football. He was smaller and slighter than they were, and wore John Lennon glasses. He also seemed to lack any kind of competitive drive. While his brothers were fighting over everything from Risk to girls, Brian was quietly building model airplanes in his bedroom, working his way through Sherlock Holmes, and writing and illustrating his own comic books.

For years, Brian and his father didn't get along—Brian was always aware of being an embarrassment to him, of having let him down. But eventually they reached a kind of truce. Brian would go to pep rallies and football games as a show of family unity and school spirit, but he wouldn't be expected to cheer. Cubby would give up on trying to make Brian into something he wasn't. This didn't always work—Brian managed to find a way to disappear in the fourth quarter when the score was tied and his father had more important things to think about, and Cubby couldn't help himself, sometimes he just had to say what was on his mind—but it worked often enough. Brian made it through high school that way.

"So I got your message last night," he tells Kathryn. "This is a good thing you're doing."

"I don't know," she says, "It's probably futile. It's been so long, I can't imagine I'll turn up anything new."

"It's worthwhile, no matter what. It fucked us all up for long enough, the least we can do is face it head on."

"It fucked you up?" she says with surprise.

"Nah, I take that back," he says. "It fucked you guys up. Didn't affect me at all."

She considers this for a moment. "Rachel seems okay. Jack seems fine."

"Oh, come on. Jack is a workaholic, Rachel hasn't had a female friend since high school. And that's just on the surface."

"What about you?"

"Well, college was a blur." He laughs, an edge in his voice. "I still wake up in a cold sweat, I just don't self-medicate as much as I used to. But I lost a few years. Like keys. I don't remember where I put them. I keep meaning to have replacements made."

"Do you think Jennifer's disappearance is the cause of that?"

"Yeah, I do," he says. "It rocked my world pretty bad." He sighs. "Have you talked to Will?"

"Not yet."

"I guess he's doing pretty well, considering."

"That's what Jack says."

"When did you find out?"

"Just a couple of days ago."

"I'm surprised you didn't know sooner. It's been a year."

A finger of shame runs down her back. "I've been so out of it, Brian," she murmurs.

"Well, now you're right in the middle of it," he says. "So let's go. I'm afraid I won't be much help, but I'll do what I can."

"Okay." She thinks for a moment. "Have you talked to Will lately?"

"Sure. He'll be up for the reunion. And really, he seems to be doing fine."

"All right," she says, taking a deep breath. "All right, here we go." She picks up her notebook and flips it open.

"I CAN'T REMEMBER much about Jennifer, to tell you the truth," Brian says. "When I think of her, what comes to mind first is her yearbook photograph—she's wearing a striped shirt and hoop earrings—and her nutty quote."

"Do you remember what it was?"

"Yeah. It stuck in my brain, because it's from this cheesy song by John Waite called 'Missing You,' and I always wondered why she didn't just go the Kahlil Gibran route like everybody else. I think the exact quote is, 'There's a message in the wild / And I'm sending you the signal tonight.' "

"Oh, yeah," Kathryn says, thinking back. "Missing You" was a popular song when they were in high school, and for a while it had been Jennifer's favorite. She called it her anthem. Kathryn remembers driving Jennifer to school in her old Toyota, singing along with the radio at the top of their lungs: *"I ain't missing you at all since you've been gone— away / I ain't missing you, no matter what my friends say . . ."*

There had been a strident note in Jennifer's voice when she sang along that made Kathryn uneasy. Jennifer would shut her eyes and ball her fists and bite down on certain words—*"at ALL, no matter WHAT MY FRIENDS SAY"*—with evident emotion. But when Kathryn tried to get her to explain what she was feeling, she shrugged it off. "It's just a song, Kath," she'd say, "It doesn't mean anything."

"It's tempting to find some meaning in it, but go figure—I have no idea what it means, or if it means anything at all," Brian is saying. "But it kind of sums up for me how little I knew her. I guess I just didn't 'get' her."

"What didn't you get?" Kathryn asks.

"A lot. I was pretty clueless. Like that whole prom thing. Somehow I had this crazy idea that she was interested in me. I mean, she'd been flirting with me for weeks before I asked her. Well, maybe not flirting—but she was suddenly friendly in a way she'd never been, and I guess I misinterpreted. So I rent the tux and the limo, get a wrist corsage the size of a cabbage, take her out to the Greenhouse for dinner—the whole shebang. And she's like a different person. Totally cold. Man, that night sucked. And it wasn't so much the money, though it took a month of working my ass off at Broadway Video to pay for it. It was more that I couldn't believe what an idiot I'd been to think she might actually like me."

"Did you ever talk about it with her afterward?"

"A few days later she called and asked me to meet her at McDonald's, so of course I went. When I got there she was sitting at a corner table behind this huge fake plant, crying her eyes out. She didn't even really acknowledge me, she just started going on about how sorry she was and how fucked up she was and how she wanted to explain but couldn't, and how her life sucked and she'd screwed everything up and now Rachel hated her and I probably hated her and most of all she hated herself. What could I say? I just sat there and tried to make sense of it. I didn't know what the hell she was talking about. So I made some lame-ass move like patting her on the hand, and that was when she bolted. She knocked over her soda and didn't look back. So I got down on the floor with wads of McDonald's napkins, and by the time I looked up, her car was gone."

"*Did* you hate her?" Kathryn asks.

"I actually felt sorry for her," he says. "Even that night at the prom, when she was an unbelievable bitch, I knew down deep that it really didn't have anything to do with me. I thought maybe it had something to do with her father. Nobody really close to me has died, so I don't know what it's like, but your dad offing himself in a public park—that has to screw you up pretty bad."

"Did she ever talk about that with you?"

"No," he says.

"What about Rachel?"

"What about her?"

"Do you think she was angry at Jennifer?"

"I don't know. I know she was pissed at me."

"She thought you were going to ask her," Kathryn says.

"I guess so. Don't get me wrong, I thought Rachel was cool. But I never liked her like that. We were just friends—I thought she knew that."

"Do you think that's how Jennifer thought of you? As 'just friends'?"

"Probably. I guess so. But the thing is, I'm usually a pretty good judge of whether someone likes me or not. I don't tend to set myself up for disappointment. And for a few weeks, at least, Jennifer acted like she did."

"Did either of you feel guilty about Rachel?"

"We never talked about it," Brian says. "And I told myself that I had nothing to feel guilty about; I never told Rachel I'd go with her or anything like that. But I know, deep down, that I was a shit. Because to be honest, if Jennifer hadn't come along, I probably would have asked Rachel. And I would have had a much better time, too."

"Brian, did you ever figure out why Jennifer asked you?"

"I've thought about this a lot, because she could've gone with any-body. I decided it was because she wasn't interested in anyone, and she wanted to go with a friend—which meant me or Jack, since going with Will might have freaked people out. And she never seemed quite at ease around Jack, for some reason. So that left me. I just wish I'd figured that out before I got my hopes up." He sighs loudly. "God, it's weird to think about high school after all this time. There's so much about those years that I've forgotten. I don't know why that is, except that when Jennifer just vanished into thin air it kind of obliterated everything else."

"What do you think happened to her?"

"I don't know," he says. "I've always had this nagging feeling that if she wanted to be found, she'd come back."

"So you think she ran away."

"I know she was unhappy. I know she was hiding things."

"Like what?"

"Little things, but still . . ." He pauses for a moment. "Like one time during class when I snuck out behind the school for a cigarette, I ran into her coming back in. From nowhere. She was totally startled and strange. Another time we were walking up the ramp and she dropped her notebook and pages went flying and she freaked. She wouldn't let me help her pick them up; she kept saying she could do it herself, and that I should go on ahead. When I tried to help her anyway, she grabbed the pages out of my hand and told me to 'fucking stay out of it.' Stuff like that."

"If you had to guess, where would you say she is?"

"Her passport was missing, right? I'd say Australia, or New Zealand. Somewhere far away—somewhere warm."

"But do you really think she'd do that to Will?"

"Maybe Will knows where she is," Brian says. "Who knows? Maybe he's been there."

"No, he was devastated," Kathryn says. "He organized the search party."

"If she did go somewhere, she wouldn't have let him know for a while. But think about it: Maybe one day at college, maybe his sophomore year, Will gets a phone call out of the blue and it's her, letting him know she's alive. It wouldn't surprise me. Look, I just think she's out there somewhere. And I think if you keep looking long enough, you're going to find her. She didn't walk off the face of the earth. Somebody has to know where she is."

WHEN THE PHONE call is over, Kathryn goes up to her room to find her high-school yearbook. Sitting on her bed, she slowly turns the pages, looking for clues in Jennifer's various poses. In her senior portrait Jennifer might be any pretty high school girl, though now to Kathryn her smile seems unnatural, frozen in place. She sits on bended knee wearing a sleeveless maroon uniform, number twelve, in a picture of the cross-country team. In another photo she stands in the back row of a group of serious-looking National Honor Society students. Under the banner headline SUPERLATIVES, she and Jack are grinning and tapping their foreheads under a hand-drawn thought balloon that says "Most Likely to Be Remembered." In a photo montage of the school play, she's wearing first a high ponytail and a poodle skirt and then a cascade of curls and a leather jacket, above the caption "You're the One That I Want!"

Brian is right, Kathryn thinks. None of us really knew her. She fooled us all into thinking this was who she was. Or maybe we saw what we wanted to see. Is it only in retrospect that her smile seems dutiful? Is her life mysterious only because she left a mystery behind?

For four years of high school she and Jennifer had seen each other every day; they spent more time together than with their own families. For a long time it seemed that they told each other everything. It was thrilling to know each other so intimately, to build a library together of secrets and memories. Kathryn knew that Jennifer had four cavities and a brown mole on her chest, and that she wore St. Eve cotton high-cut bikinis and Warner's stretch-knit front-clasp bras. She could remember all of Jennifer's haircuts, from the fifth-grade wedge to the short-lived bob to the layered disaster the summer after ninth grade, and she suffered with her through the overbleached highlights that resulted from an experiment with peroxide and a bottle of Realemon. But after a while this familiarity became wearing. They knew too much to excite or impress each other. They began noticing patterns in each other's behavior and commenting on them: *But you always do this. That is so like you. That kind of guy always breaks your heart.*

Every now and then Kathryn would discover that Jennifer had kept something from her, and her confidence in the friendship would be shaken. When confronted, Jennifer always apologized, citing absent-mindedness, blaming it on her crazy week or PMS. But Kathryn knew it was more than that. At some point, Jennifer had started holding back. At first it was just small things—a new pair of shoes that appeared without discussion, an unremarked-upon encounter with the guy from chemistry class who they both thought was cute. Over time, though, larger, more important details slipped by. Kathryn didn't know that Jennifer was going to the prom with Brian until Rachel called her, furious. She never knew that Jennifer was interested in, or possibly seeing, someone else. What other things didn't she know? How serious were Jennifer's lies and omissions?

There were always reasons for Jennifer's evasiveness, reasons that made sense. Her home life was awful—far worse than Kathryn's, where even though she had to endure her parents' bitter divorce, she still knew each of them loved her and cared about her. Jennifer's mother was grasping and needy and, at the same time, disengaged; her father worked long hours at the office and drank too much when he came home. So Kathryn didn't press her to be more open. She thought she understood. After a while she came to accept the fact that there was something unknowable about Jennifer; it was as if her core was wrapped in a thin layer of ice. In a strange way Jennifer's inscrutability was almost alluring to Kathryn; it gave her access to a different level of emotion, an intoxicating unhappiness, fathomless in its depth and complexity. So Kathryn, who laid herself bare with every expression, who could no more hide what she was feeling than she could shed her skin, wanted both to become more like Jennifer and to shatter the glassy surface that kept them apart.

Now, looking at the pictures in the yearbook, she wishes she had asked more questions, demanded more answers. She should have forced Jennifer to talk. But Jennifer didn't want to talk. And how would Kathryn have forced her to, anyway—tied her down and tortured her? There was probably a way Kathryn could have been more receptive, more tuned in to what her friend wanted or needed, but she didn't know what that was. After all these years, she thinks, I still don't.

Later that afternoon, in the middle of a thunderstorm, Kathryn drives to Governor's, a diner on a commercial strip littered with fast-food restaurants and car-lube shops. She dashes inside and is ushered to a red vinyl booth; within seconds, an enormous laminated menu and a glass of water materialize before her. Overhead, an electric toy train chugs around on a track. Pictures of all of Maine's governors, with the current one in the middle, line the back wall. Waitresses laden with food rush around as if they're in a relay.

The sky outside is separated into milky curds. Rain falls in sheets, drumming the asphalt and the cars and the road signs, making everything shiny. Though it's only four o'clock, the cars on the road have their lights on. Kathryn loves this feeling of being warm and dry in a cheerful, busy place when it's miserable outside. She takes out her tape recorder and cassettes and notebook and piles them on the table, and then opens the menu, examining the dizzying array of options.

By the time Jack arrives, late as usual, the waitress is already coming toward them with a burger and fries. "Sorry," Kathryn tells him, "I was starving."

The waitress sets the food in front of Kathryn and shakes out her hands. "Whew, heavy. Enjoy it. What about you?" she says to Jack.

"Just some tea, thanks. Earl Grey."

"We got Lipton."

"Fine, whatever."

When the waitress leaves, Jack leans forward and says, "Isn't it great to be home? Where else in the world would the heaviness of the food be considered a bonus?"

Kathryn smiles, a little nervously. She knows he's trying to break the ice. This is their formal "meeting," as opposed to the informal one at the Sea Dog two days ago, and Kathryn has been feeling jumpy and insecure all day about the work she's done on the story since he threatened to take her off it.

She spent the morning transcribing the tapes of her conversations with Rachel and Brian, and they seem frustratingly incomplete. She wishes she'd asked different questions, or at least more of them. So many of the things they discussed seem trivial: who liked whom, who was jealous of whom. And she could kick herself for not having pushed Rachel further, gotten her to tell what she knew. Kathryn knows that in backing off she broke the first rule of reporting, that you don't want to give your source too much time to think. If you have to go back for more information, they're almost always less willing to give it.

The waitress returns with Jack's tea, the red paper tag hanging over the side of the cup. He bobs it up and down several times before taking the bag out, placing it in the bowl of a spoon and wrapping the string around it to wring it out into his cup. "It's gotta be strong," he explains when he notices Kathryn watching this process. "On days like this all I want to do is stay in bed."

"You and Rachel both do the tea thing," she observes. "Most people I know drink coffee."

"Yeah, but she's a purist," he says. "I need the caffeine." He looks over at her burger. "Hey, that looks pretty good. I'm hungrier than I thought."

After he flags down the waitress again, he sits back against the red vinyl. "So let's get started," he says. "I've been thinking about Jennifer all day, trying to figure out what I might know or what I might have seen in her that might shed any light on this at all. At the time it seemed so impossible that anything like this could happen, I think I was in shock. And I have to admit, I kept some things to myself. I told myself that if somebody just asked me the right question, I'd tell everything I knew, but nobody ever did."

"But you're a reporter, Jack," Kathryn says. She turns on the tape recorder and pushes it toward him. "Wouldn't you have wanted to make sure they had the whole story?"

"I wasn't a reporter then, just a freaked-out potential suspect," he says. "And anyway I didn't want my own feelings about Jennifer to get in the way."

"What do you mean?"

He lifts the cup of tea to his lips and blows on it, then takes a sip. Setting the cup down, he says, "Here's the thing about Jennifer and me. I'm going to be completely honest, Kathryn, so I'm sorry if this sounds harsh. But I don't think we liked each other very much. We hung out together in the group, of course, and we were always polite to each other. But I didn't trust her. I thought she was unbelievably self-absorbed. I thought I could see through her, and I know she sensed that. So we kind of avoided each other, at the same time that we saw each other every day."

"Was that awkward?"

"Not really. It's amazing what you can get used to."

"When did this start? Did something happen?"

The waitress arrives with Jack's burger and sets it in front of him, and he takes a moment to put ketchup on the fries and mustard on the bun. Then he takes a bite. "This is huge," he mutters. "It's like eating an entire cow." He wipes his mouth with a napkin. "Yeah, there was one thing. But it wasn't what she did, so much, that bothered me. I could understand that. It was how she did it, and why."

"You mean the thing with Brian?"

"No."

She smiles uncertainly. "Then I'm not sure I know what you're talking about."

"You probably don't."

"Okay." She puts her forehead in her hands and then bends her head, running her fingers through her hair.

"Listen, Kathryn," he says gently. "There were things she didn't want to think about, much less talk about—even with her best friend. Maybe she thought if she didn't think about them, then they weren't real."

Kathryn shifts in her seat. "I'm surprised you feel you have such a strong grasp of who she was."

He sighs. "I'm just trying to face some things I couldn't—or wouldn't—at the time. I think we were all that way. We didn't want to spoil the picture of that beautiful lost girl on the front page of the paper. Star of the school play, National Honor Society, all that bullshit. Volunteer work at the nursing home. The photo they ran made her look like a blond angel. Disappearing like that only heightened the sense people had of her as vulnerable. And she was, I guess. I mean, obviously—where the hell is she? But something about her didn't add up. I don't think she was such an angel. Yes, she'd been through a lot, but I don't think that's any excuse for what she did to Brian that night at the prom—and how she treated Rachel." He shakes his head. "I have the feeling that something else was going on. That she had this"—he hesitates, groping for words—"other life. Does that make any sense to you?"

"I don't know," Kathryn says. "When I talked to Rachel, it seemed like . . ." Her voice trails off. "She knew something. She wouldn't tell me much." A memory, shadowy and sharklike, moves through her brain.

"What do you want to know? I tell you everything," Jennifer had said

one afternoon as they were lying in her scrubby backyard on cheap reclining lawn chairs, trying to get a tan before the prom.

"You've gotten mighty secretive lately," Kathryn said, trying to keep her voice light, "and I've had just about enough."

"There's nothing," Jennifer insisted. "My life is an open book."

"Don't be coy with me, missy. That might work with some people."

"What do you want to hear?"

"Everything."

"Ev-ery-thing," Jennifer said slowly, wrinkling her nose. She closed her eyes and tilted her chin toward the sun. "That's a pretty tall order. I wouldn't even know where to start."

Kathryn sat up and looked at her. "Cut the bullshit. What are you keeping from me?"

Jennifer laughed. "Oh, Kath," she said, "you're taking things way too seriously. I'm just teasing you."

"I don't think so."

Sighing exaggeratedly, Jennifer sat up and adjusted her bikini top to keep it in place. "Okay, you really want to know? I'm sleeping with Dr. Smalley. I scooch down to the principal's office between classes and we fuck on his desk."

"Ugh, Jen. Don't even joke."

"I knew you couldn't handle it," she said with a shrug.

"I've always felt guilty that I didn't tell anyone about this," Jack is saying. "I probably should have brought it up with the police during the investigation. But it seemed irrelevant—only hurtful to Will and the rest of the family, and maybe to Jennifer, too, wherever she was. I didn't see how telling it would shed light on anything." He takes a bite of his burger and puts it down. "But I've thought about this for a long time, and I think I was wrong. So I'm going to tell you now." There is a brief silence. "It's about what happened to her father. How much do you know?"

"Well, it was pretty clear that it wasn't an accident."

"Yeah," he says. "The insurance adjusters are probably the only ones who believed it was."

"I know that their mother was having an affair and planned to leave him."

"Did Jennifer ever talk to you about all of that?"

"Yeah. Mostly about how much she hated her mother for being so selfish—and feeling like she couldn't ever say anything because her mother was so sick and frail half the time. After her father died, her mother went to bed and wouldn't get up, and Jennifer was convinced it was an act. She didn't trust anything her mother did, not after finding that letter from Ralph Cunliff that made it clear there was something going on between them. They were talking about running away together."

"So you know, then. That Jennifer found the letter."

Kathryn nods. "She read it to me over the phone. She'd been going through her mother's bag, looking for cigarettes or something, and the letter was in an inside pocket." She thinks back, trying to remember the moment of that call. Josh had answered the phone. He raised his eyebrows at her as he handed it over. "It's Jen," he mouthed. "She sounds *wacked*." When Kathryn put the phone to her ear, she could hear Jennifer's jagged breathing through her clogged nose, the raspy sounds of uncontrolled crying. "Jesus Christ, she's such a fucking slut," she sobbed when Kathryn said hello. "She's just fucking unbelievable. I don't even know why this surprises me. She never gave a shit about him or anybody else except herself; it's not like this is out of character or anything. I can't fucking believe I didn't see it. Cunt."

The word startled Kathryn; she'd never heard Jennifer use it before. But she wasn't surprised at the story. She understood without being told whom Jennifer was talking about; her mother was the only person who evinced such rage.

"I hate her, I hate her, I HATE HER!" Jennifer said, her voice rising in a shriek. "She doesn't give a shit what she does to this family! She doesn't give a flying fuck!"

Josh made a face—ooh, I'm scared—across the table at Kathryn, and she threw an orange at him. He caught it and grinned.

"She's not getting away with this." Jennifer was sobbing. "There's no fucking way."

"What are you going to do?" Kathryn asked.

For a moment all she could hear was Jennifer's labored breathing. Then she said, "I don't know. Something."

Kathryn heard a note in her voice she didn't recognize, an intensity that made her afraid. "You want to come over, Jen? You could stay here tonight—or a couple of nights, if you want."

"Thanks, but I can't," she said abruptly, stifling a sob. "I have to talk to Will."

"Does he know about all this?"

"Who the fuck knows what he knows. It's unbelievable, the way he sticks up for her." She blew her nose, and Kathryn held the receiver away from her ear. "This time she's really done it. Even Will has to see what a piece of work she is."

"Does she know you know?"

"She's out. I don't even want to think about where."

"Come over," Kathryn pleaded. "*Dallas* is on tonight. You'll feel better."

Jennifer wasn't crying now. Her voice was steady and cold. "I'll talk to you later," she said. "Please—obviously—keep this to yourself."

"Of course."

"I—" She cleared her throat. "Thanks for being here for me."

"Oh, Jen," Kathryn said, wanting desperately to connect somehow, to break through the formality she could feel crystallizing like ice between them, "where else would I be?"

Now, with Jack, Kathryn turns the salt shaker upside down and watches a tiny white mound grow on the Formica. With her finger she pushes stray granules back into the pile. "As far as I know, she didn't say anything to her mother," she tells him. "At least not right away. Will said they should wait, figure out how they were going to handle it before the whole thing blew up in their faces. But then it blew up any-way."

"When their dad killed himself."

There is a pause. Kathryn bites her lip. Jack pours milk into his tea and stirs it.

"Jennifer told him, didn't she?" Kathryn asks.

"Yep." He nods.

"How do you know?"

He lifts the cup to his mouth with both hands and takes a sip. "Will told me."

Kathryn takes a deep breath and lets it out slowly.

"It would be easy to believe that Jennifer just snapped—after all, she and Will agreed they were going to wait awhile before they did any-thing," Jack says. "But she didn't wait; she called him that day at work, told him everything she knew. Will said it was almost like she was as angry at her father for being oblivious about it as she was at her mother for doing it. She wanted to push it in his face. She thought maybe thinking other people knew about it would finally make him mad enough to do something—make their mother accountable somehow, I don't know. Anyway, it was a terrible miscalculation. He didn't even confront their mother, for chrissakes. He just made sure his insurance papers were in order and his desk was neat at work and there weren't too many loose ends she'd have to deal with. He paid all the bills that afternoon. And then as soon as it got dark he drove his car to Little City park and sat there drinking Dewar's out of the bottle and getting his nerve up."

"Did Will tell you all this?"

Jack's mouth twitches into a smile. "No. There were three eyewit-nesses, according to the police. A dropout named Jim Oulette was sitting on a swing in the playground smoking a joint and listening to his Walk-man. Two little girls on Linden Street were having a sleepover in a pup tent, looking at the stars with a pair of binoculars. They all saw him sitting there in his car, drinking something out of a paper bag, and they all heard him rev the engine at midnight and accelerate across the middle of the park, straight into that giant oak at the far corner."

"Jesus." She shakes her head.

"I only found out the details later, when I'd been working at the *News* for a few months and I got access to a reporter's private file on the story. Of course, they didn't print any of that. It was officially labeled an accident. So the wife got the insurance money and the kids were taken care of. I'm sure that's why they didn't push for an investigation. What was the point? The story was tragic enough."

"And Linda got her white Lincoln."

"And her new kitchen," Jack says with an ironic smile. "And her new husband."

The waitress comes over and stands by their table, scribbling on a pad. She rips off the sheet of paper and puts it between them, facedown. "More coffee, folks?"

Kathryn says, "Sure," and Jack says, "No, thanks," at the same time. He looks at his watch. "I'm supposed to meet a friend at the gym in fifteen minutes," he says apologetically. "But I can stay a little longer."

Kathryn looks up at the waitress. "I guess that's all, then."

"You can pay at the front," she says, already turning away. After she leaves, Kathryn starts getting her things together. She can feel Jack's eyes on her as she gathers her notebook and pens and rummages for her wallet. Then, gently, he says, "Are you surprised she didn't tell you?"

She looks down at her paper placemat printed with a goofy grinning cartoon governor and the dessert menu, and folds a scalloped edge with her finger. "No," she says. "I guess I knew, deep down. I knew there was more to that story. I was afraid to ask." She feels her chest constrict and she sits back, then suddenly covers her face with her hands.

"Hey," Jack says, leaning forward.

"It's so sad. All of it," she murmurs. "For her to tell him like that— and then to have to live with what he did. No wonder she swallowed all those pills. Now that I know, it makes a lot more sense."

He nods slowly.

"Do you think it has anything to do with her disappearance?" she asks.

"I think it has to, somehow. Don't you? Maybe only peripherally, but it's got to be a factor or a clue."

"But you don't think she ran away."

"I just can't see that," he says, shaking his head.

"So what do you think? That she went off and killed herself somewhere no one could ever find her? Or did her mother find out about it and murder her in a fit of rage?"

"I've thought about that," he says. "I could be wrong, but it doesn't make much sense to me. Why would she kill her daughter over this? If that woman was in love with her husband, she had a funny way of showing it. She's having an affair with some guy, her husband kills himself over it, and four months later she's engaged? That's a pretty short mourning period. I can't imagine she's too upset he's gone." He squints at the bill and reaches into his back pocket, pulling out a battered wallet. "This is on the paper," he says as they slide out of the booth. "It's the least we can do, since we're paying you jack."

"As it were."

"As it were." He grins.

At the front of the restaurant, she turns to face him. In the bright light of rainy midafternoon she can see fine lines around his eyes. All of a sudden she's aware of finding him attractive in a way she never did in high school, when he was lanky and awkward and had skin like a baby.

"So are you going to have this story for me by Thursday?" he asks.

"Yes."

He smiles and gently cuffs her shoulder, the way a bear might. "I knew you would."

"No, you didn't."

Laughing, he looks down. "Let me put it this way: I knew you could."

"I'll have the story," she says. She opens the door and looks back at him. Then she steps into the rain.

By the time Kathryn rouses herself from bed the next morning, at eight-thirty, her mother is already gone. She makes her way to the bathroom, pulling her T-shirt over her head as she goes, and turns on the shower, holding her hand under the spray as she adjusts the knobs. She squirts toothpaste on her toothbrush and then pees brushing her teeth. Rinsing her mouth, she looks at herself in the mirror over the sink. Her face is puffy and wan, and she seems to be breaking out on her chin. The red dye is growing out of her hair, and her roots are dark, darker than she remembers them being in the first place. In the strong morning light she sees a silver glint, and she reaches up and finds it, isolating it with searching fingers, and yanks it out. Opening the medicine cabinet, she shakes three aspirin into her hand and downs them with a cupped handful of water. Two of them lodge in her throat and start to dissolve, leaving a bitter, chalky taste that makes her gag.

Stepping into the shower, she turns her face toward the spray and closes her eyes. She doesn't want to think, doesn't want to remember, but because she's stone-cold sober and all alone, her mind won't stop churning. Ten years of restless uncertainty were better than this, she thinks. At least then she had a way of thinking about Jennifer that kept her memories neatly contained in a box. How well can you know somebody? You see them every day, perhaps for years, share things with them you've shared with no one else. And then one morning you wake up and realize you know nothing about them—that the person who seemed to open up to you was exposing only a shell. Because you were blind, or gullible, or because you didn't want to know, you missed all the signs and signals that might have pointed the way toward the truth. So now you're left with a gaping hole in your life, a bottomless mystery, and you don't have the slightest idea how to solve it, because your basic assumptions were false to begin with.

She's reminded of how she used to feel when she read Encyclopedia Brown stories in sixth grade. The main character always had to solve a mystery in his neighborhood; commonsense clues were embedded in each story, and he inevitably figured out the answer. Before it was revealed, however, the reader was given a chance to guess. The answer always made sense; it would be a small clue, an offhand remark or casual observation, but half the time she missed it. And always, she couldn't believe she hadn't gotten it by herself, hadn't seen it all along.

After her shower, sitting on her bedroom floor in a towel, Kathryn calls Rosie to schedule an appointment.

"Rosie's out," Doris chirps. "Little League," she explains. "But we have something for Thursday at ten. And oh, look at this! There's a cancellation for later today, three o'clock. Your choice."

"I'll take both of them," she says.

"Well, all righty," Doris says with surprise. "I'll put you down, hon. Glad you're feeling better."

When she hangs up the phone, Kathryn takes a deep breath and stretches out on the floor. She looks outside; it's a beautiful day, sunny and warm. The big green leaves of the elm in front of the house rustle and turn in the breeze. It's the perfect day for a run, she thinks. A run might be just what she needs.

Heading out Kenduskeag Avenue toward the airport, across the highway overpass and through a new housing development, Kathryn feels the muscles in her legs constrict in protest. She hasn't gone running since Charlottesville, and that was months ago, when she still had a job and a routine and some semblance of a marriage. She feels like stopping, but she doesn't dare. If she stops now, she might never start again; she might give up entirely and spend her days in her bedroom on Taft Street with the shades drawn, waiting for her mother to come home. She wonders if her mother is secretly as afraid as she is that she might not pull through this; that she might just sink into some kind of torpor from which she'll never emerge. She has a cramp in her side now, and it slows her a little, but she doesn't stop running until she's back on Taft Street, half a block from home.

IT IS CLEAR to Kathryn, when she finally broaches the subject of Jennifer, that Rosie has been expecting her to bring it up. "Ah, yes," she says, "the missing piece."

"There's so much I want to say to her," Kathryn says. "There's so much I want to ask."

"Like what?"

"Like—like—why she didn't feel that she could confide in me. Why she kept me in the dark. It's painful to admit," she says, her eyes filling with tears. She half laughs, trying to diffuse her own sadness.

"What do you want to say to her?" Rosie pulls a tissue out of the box and hands it over.

Kathryn wipes her nose and shakes her head to clear it. "I guess I want to say I'm sorry. For not being a better friend. I keep wanting to make it right between us." She thinks for a moment. "I want to tell her that I may not understand what's going on with her—I may not have a clue, but it doesn't matter. I'm here, and I'll be here when she needs me. I never told her that."

"Could she have heard you?" Rosie asks gently.

"I don't know." She pulls at the wadded-up tissue in her hand, tearing it to shreds.

Eventually Rosie starts to talk, and Kathryn, full of conflicting and unexplainable emotions, is content to listen. "Of course you feel guilty," Rosie says, leaning forward. "Of course you can't get past this. The simple fact of anyone vanishing into thin air is horrific enough, but in this case it was compounded by how it happened, and when. Her disappearance was the literal manifestation of the sense of loss you already felt that night. You were leaving high school, soon to be leaving home. The world you knew was disappearing. And ever since, I'd suggest, you've existed in this state of limbo between two worlds," she says, holding her hands out and cupping them as if she's balancing ostrich eggs, "unable to let go of the past, unwilling to embrace the future"—one hand falls and rises, and then the other—"afraid, always, that letting go would mean giving up."

"But wouldn't it?" Kathryn says.

Rosie cocks her head. "She'll always be a part of you, Kathryn."

"So how do I—what do I—" she asks helplessly, and Rosie says, "You do exactly what you're doing. That's all you can do."

When the session is over, Kathryn feels like a wet sheet on a clothesline, limp, wrung out, nearly transparent. Leaving Rosie's, she drives down to a small park by the Penobscot and sits on the bank watching the boats and the picnicking families. No one says a word to her; it's almost as if she is invisible, or the action in front of her is on a screen. She stretches out on the grass and closes her eyes, feeling the late-afternoon sun on her eyelids, drifting in her own separate space and time.

"I'm sorry, Kath," Linda Pelletier says briskly when she hears her request. Kathryn has tracked her down by phone at her new condo in Florida. "I've said everything there is to say to the police and the press already."

"But it's been years since anyone's written about this," Kathryn says. She twirls the phone cord between her fingers. "There might be a new way of looking at it, or a detail that never came to light."

Mrs. Pelletier sighs with undisguised irritation. "Really, I don't think so. People forget things after this much time. If anybody has anything new to say, they probably made it up."

"But don't you think it's worth a try?" Kathryn ventures, knowing as she does that she's stepping precipitously close to a line. "As long as she's still missing, shouldn't we do what we can to find her?"

Kathryn hears Mrs. Pelletier suck in her breath. "You have no idea what this has been like for me. You have no idea what I've been through."

"You're right," Kathryn says quickly. "I'm sorry. I know this has been a terrible ordeal." She leafs through the papers on the table in front of her. "But I have the interviews you gave right here, and there are a few questions the police didn't ask that I've been wondering about."

"Like what." It's a challenge, not a question.

"It would be helpful to know more about your husband's death and Jennifer's suicide attempt."

Mrs. Pelletier laughs dryly. "I've already said all I have to say about Pete's accident and Jennifer's reaction to it. There's no link, as far as I can tell, to any of this.

"Look." She sighs. "I understand why you're doing this. But we've been dealing with it day in and day out for ten years, and you're just coming in now—like somehow you're going to ask the magic question and somebody'll say, 'Gosh, that's right, I forgot! I saw her down at the bus station that night, buying a ticket to L.A.!' There's nothing more to find, Kath. And I've just had to accept that we might never find out what happened, unless she decides to wander home. Or unless somebody stumbles across—God forbid . . ." She stops, her voice choked with emotion.

"Do you think she ran away?"

"Frankly, I don't know anymore," she says after a moment. "I didn't use to think so. But who knows who's going to do what? She was my daughter, but I don't think I knew her. I thought I did, but . . ." Her voice trails off. "That's my regret," she says softly. "I do regret that. Maybe . . . but there's no way of knowing. Anyway, we're moving on with our lives. We need to put the pain of this behind us."

" 'We'—you mean you and Will?"

"No, I mean me and Ralph," she says, a quiver of tension in her voice. "This has been hell on Will. And then—his lifestyle choices and the consequences of that . . . I just think the strain of this has made him a different person. I wish I could help him, I really do. But he's got to help himself."

When the conversation is over, Kathryn opens the back door of the house and walks out into her mother's garden. Sitting down under the apple tree, she gazes up at the gnarled branches and the small, unripe fruit. She thinks of Mrs. Pelletier in the days after Jennifer vanished, her face drawn and scared. Without benefit of makeup, her eyes were rabbity, her lips chapped and white. She seemed not to know what to do; she stood on her porch wrapped in Jennifer's letter sweater, her eyes darting anxiously up and down the street as if she expected her daughter to come sauntering up any minute. In interviews on TV she was always pleading and sobbing, her mute, hulking husband at her side. Five weeks to the day after graduation she was hospitalized for exhaustion. When she was released from the hospital, she told the newspaper that her doctor had forbidden her to go back to search-party headquarters. Will had to keep it going on his own.

Kathryn's own mother had been disapproving. "You'd think she could pull herself together and try to be useful," she said, clucking her tongue at the television, where Linda Pelletier was huddled behind her son as he patiently answered questions on the local news. "If I were her, I'd be up day and night looking for my daughter." Kathryn didn't doubt it; she knew how tenacious her mother was. But sometimes, in a particularly indulgent moment, she let herself wonder how long it would last—how long before her mother would decide there was nothing more she could do and it was time to let it go, let her go. Her mother could be fickle; she threw herself into hobbies and projects and friendships and then, without warning, it seemed to Kathryn, abruptly gave up and moved on. It was a bleak thing to think about, how your mother would handle it if something happened to you, and it always put Kathryn in a bad mood. But it was just one of the many questions that Jennifer's disappearance had stirred up in her. It was part of the wound that wouldn't heal, and she picked at it like a scab.

The school secretary confirms that though Miss Hallowell quit teaching several years ago to sell beauty products and Mr. Richardson recently retired from teaching drama, Mr. Hunter is still at the high school, still teaching social studies. Kathryn leaves a message for him at the school, and later that day he returns her call. His voice on the phone is guarded; he seems not to remember who she is.

"Jennifer Pelletier's friend," Kathryn reminds him. "We were in your class together senior year."

"Oh, right. Miss Campbell. Brown hair," he says finally. "You went to Penn, right?"

"Virginia."

"That's right." He laughs; she's not sure why. She remembers this now, that he was always laughing at his students, always finding some private humor at their expense. It made Kathryn uncomfortable, but it also gave her a small, edgy thrill. The lure was that you might someday be in on the joke—that you might earn his trust enough for him to confide in you. "I know who you are. It's all coming back," he says. "Jennifer's shadow."

Kathryn knows he's needling her, but it stings nonetheless. "Oh. That's a pleasant way to be remembered."

He laughs again. "Well, I'm sure you've carved your own path since then."

"I haven't had much choice," she says dryly.

"No, I guess not," he says. "So what can I help you with?"

"I have a few questions," she says, and explains about the article.

When she finishes, he pauses for a moment before answering. Then he says, "I believe my statement is on record."

"I know. This isn't for the police."

"Well . . ."

Hearing the hesitation in his voice, she says quickly, "I guess this is as much a memorial as anything else."

"The problem is, I didn't really know her all that well."

"That's okay. I only have a few questions."

"Well . . . all right," he says. "Why don't you come by the high school sometime tomorrow morning? I have some stuff I need to do there anyway."

"Where can I find you?"

"Right where I was ten years ago," he says. "Room 201, up the ramp and to the left." He laughs again, that same dry sound. "They'll probably scatter my ashes up there someday."

BANGOR HIGH SCHOOL, built in 1961, sprawls on a flat-topped hill on the outskirts of town. A long, circular drive in front connects two ribbons of road, one in each direction, that circle back to Broadway. The school is bordered on two sides by grassy playing fields fringed with fir trees that stretch back into a wooded expanse, large enough for science-class forays and orienteering classes, but too sparse and circumscribed to get lost in. As Kathryn drives up to the front entrance the next morning, she thinks about these woods. Up until midyear, when accumulated snow made surreptitious entry difficult, kids would slip through the trees to smoke cigarettes or pot or engage in other unsanctioned activities. Every now and then one of these forays would coincide with a class excursion, and two half-dressed seniors would find themselves looking up into a huddle of leaf-gathering sophomores.

The school is virtually empty now, its ramps and hallways startlingly quiet. Kathryn hasn't been here in years—possibly not since she left it ten years ago—and she's amazed at how vivid her memories are, brought back in a sudden rush of sights and sounds. She remembers the lockers, metallic brown, that fell open when you found the combination and shut with a satisfying click; water fountains with too much pressure; hand-lettered Student Council election posters; snow tracked down long hallways; the squeak of chalk on a dusty board.

Her life back then was dictated by routine. At 7:59 lockers would click and clatter, rubber-soled boots squealing around corners, hall monitors clapping their hands: "Let's go, people!" School began promptly at eight. By 8:03 the classroom doors were shut and the hall was quiet. Announcements began. The vice-principal's voice crackled over the PA system: a lacrosse match, a bake sale, auditions for the talent show, rehearsals for the one-act plays. The school was unevenly heated; in some classes students were falling asleep, in others they'd be hunched over their desks, knees together, hands tucked under their arms like birds on a sill.

Because of the way the place was built—with wide ramps and hallways and open public spaces on the one hand, and narrow back stairwells and small secret rooms off empty corridors on the other—it was possible to conduct a very public life and a very private one at the same time. It took time to learn about these secret places, and the kids who did generally kept it to themselves. The teachers and administrators, for the most part, didn't want to know. And some of them secretly thought, Give the kids their hiding places. What harm can it do? There were a few incidents—one time a janitor stumbled on an unconscious student behind a stairwell with a bottle of malt liquor; it was rumored that a fifteen-year-old girl who dropped out of school had gotten pregnant in the back row of the darkened auditorium—but nothing tragic. Nobody had died, or disappeared.

By eleven o'clock the sounds and smells of school became a stew. In a senior English class the students would dutifully copy the themes from Macbeth that their teacher spelled out on the board—*greed, lust, jealousy, betrayal*—watching dust motes float in a slice of sunlight. Wafting from another part of the building, the smells of art class—acrylic paint and turpentine—mingled with the meaty aroma of Salisbury steak from the cafeteria and the faint scent of formaldehyde from biology, where rubbery frogs, splayed and pinned to a board, were being dissected.

The back of the day was broken by noon. Afternoon classes were never as focused as those in the morning; the kids knew it was a waiting game. There'd be more doodling, more flirtation, and by one-thirty school might as well be over. The seniors left early, trickling out to their cars or migrating to different parts of the building for play rehearsal or band practice or ROTC, and outside to play sports. At three o'clock a small army of teenagers replaced middle-aged women in hairnets at fast-food restaurants all over town. The best low-paying jobs came with hefty discounts or tips; landing a job at the Weathervane, where Monet pearls and pastel cotton sweaters could be had for 40 percent off, would set you up for the year.

In the main office now, Kathryn chats for a few minutes with the principal's secretary, a woman who had been the vice-principal's secretary when Kathryn was a student. Then she makes her way to Mr. Hunter's classroom, her footsteps echoing in the stillness like a ticking clock in an empty room.

He may not remember her, but Kathryn has no trouble remembering being his student. Mr. Hunter was one of the most charismatic teachers she ever had. He always acted as if he didn't care whether anyone showed up to his class; he pretended that teaching these morons annoyed him. He said he didn't expect his students to understand what he was talking about because they were ignorant, because they were philistines—but that anyone with half a brain should already know this stuff. He stood at the doorway at the beginning of class, ushering the students inside, corralling them with his voice: "Mr. Peterson! So nice of you to join us!" "Well, Miss Geary, are you planning to bring Mr. Wilson for a show-and-tell today, or are you going to leave him in the hall?" Students learned not to be late; anyone who showed up after the door was closed risked speculation about where they'd been, an analysis of their clothing, or having to give an impromptu lecture on the topic of the day.

Though he pretended to be cynical about social studies, it was clear that he was passionate about the subject. "Social studies is the world—*your* world," he'd say. "Look at today's paper. South Africa is divided over apartheid. There's a battle over abortion in Kansas. Junk-bond millionaires are ruling world financial markets. All of this has to do with you, and you know why that is?" He'd sit on his desk and appraise them coolly. "Because, whether you like it or not, you are part of this world, and it is part of you. The ways we interact and the things we learn and the ways we choose to share that knowledge are affected by and have an impact on what's happening in your *neighborhood*," he'd say, pounding a fist into his open hand for emphasis "what's happening in your *state*, in your *country*, and throughout the planet." Though the students affected nonchalance, they seldom exhibited the telltale signs of a restless class—passing notes or drawing in notebooks or crinkling candy wrappers. The air in Mr. Hunter's classroom felt crisp and clear. Much of the time the students were raising their hands to talk, reading essays aloud, debating euthanasia and the drinking age, taking turns being president and discussing how best to allot welfare money to the states.

"I'm wasting my mind with you people," he'd mutter under his breath, loud enough for them to hear. "I could be orienteering in Spain right now, teaching English to flamenco dancers."

"Then why aren't you?" one brazen student would venture to ask.

"Very good question," he'd say. "I suppose it's because I'm a little slow. I've been operating under the illusion that every now and then I'm actually doing some good—that I'm teaching you people something. Not all of you. Mr. Kellerman, for example, would rather be reading comics than participating in this discussion, but I understand that I'm not going to reach everybody. Still, I do like to think that some of you people are listening to me once in a while, that some of the stuff I'm putting out here might crowd its way into your brains. I know I'm probably delusional, but hey, it helps me get out of bed in the morning."

Mr. Hunter, then in his mid-twenties, was one of the younger teachers in the school. He was ruggedly handsome, with short, virtually black hair, dark eyebrows, and brown eyes. The bones in his face were strong and well defined, and when he smiled he had dimples. Most teachers dressed unimaginatively, the women in frumpy, stretch-cotton dresses and low-heeled shoes, the men in worsted-wool pants and nondescript ties and shirts. Mr. Hunter was different. He wore khakis, button-downs, colorful ties, and blazers, with patterned socks and black suede shoes. His eyes were large and expressive; with a subtle change of focus his entire demeanor would shift. He was thin and muscular, with the elegant carriage and intense gaze of a German shepherd. But there was something about him that could intimidate, a coldness behind the eyes, the way his smile could turn into a sneer without notice.

A certain kind of student was drawn to Mr. Hunter—the type who felt he spoke for them, who felt, as he said he did, that they were players in a phony game but players nonetheless. They weren't so alienated that they drugged up or dropped out, but despite their generally respectable grades, their tendency to join school clubs, their jean jackets and Gap T's and Bass shoes, they considered themselves different from the other kids in their class. Mr. Hunter cultivated these students through gesture and expression. Like birds in a flock, they recognized each other's characteristic markings: a like-minded restlessness; a bone-deep boredom, invisible to the naked eye; an appreciation of irony and a sense of their own destinies as unpredictable, and therefore different.

Kathryn remembers being one of these. Mr. Hunter would roll his eyes at her when she interviewed the hockey captain for the school paper; he shook his head and smiled as he passed her selling whoopie pies in the hall outside the cafeteria for the French Club school trip. She felt, somehow, that he knew her—though in a strangely impersonal way, as if he had quickly surmised the type of person she was and dealt with her on that basis. It was disconcerting and oddly flattering to be analyzed and categorized so openly. He always seemed to catch her at the most embarrassing moments—or was it that the moments only became embarrassing when he noticed?

Reaching the door to Hunter's classroom, Kathryn hesitates. Then she knocks, and he glances up. He still looks young, she thinks fleetingly, but he probably isn't mistaken for a student anymore, as he sometimes was ten years ago. He's sitting at his desk at the front of the class, filling out some kind of form. The blackboard behind him is blank and clean.

"Well," he says, a slight smile on his face, "it's a new you."

She knows right away it's the red hair he's talking about. He was always noticing things about his students other adults seemed oblivious to. "So, Mr. Pierce with your newly pierced ear, let's hear your take on affirmative action," he'd say, or "How is it possible, Miss Buckley, for one girl to own so many shetland sweaters? You are probably single-handedly boosting the economy of some small Scottish community."

Like everything else about Mr. Hunter, this attention was complicated—it was both unnerving and strangely flattering. As he well knew, most of them spent their days vacillating between wanting desperately to be noticed and wanting to sink into the floor, and he managed somehow to tap in to both desires simultaneously.

"People change," Kathryn says.

Mr. Hunter leans back in his chair. "Think so?"

"People grow up," she says. She doesn't know why she's taking the bait; it doesn't matter, she shouldn't engage it. But this was always the way it was in his class. He'd ensnare students in an argument they couldn't win—about human behavior, nature versus nurture, do-goodism versus pragmatism—and before they realized it they had become Exhibit A of a lecture, the example of muddy thinking that proved his point.

"They get bigger," he says. "Their skin wrinkles. They pay bills and hold down jobs. I don't know if they change." He sits forward and sweeps his arm across the rows of empty desks, a phantom class. "See, in my experience, the fourteen-year-olds who walk in here on the first day of school already possess the core of what they will become. They might as well be thirty years old."

She shakes her head. "I'm not the same person I was in high school."

"Oh? How have you changed, other than superficially?"

Again, she flinches. Is she being overly sensitive, or are his comments laced with barbs?

"You don't follow Jennifer around anymore," he says, prompting her.

"Just for the record, I don't think I followed her around in high school," she says, a little irritated.

He nods amiably. "Okay. And you don't now. So that's the same. But—actually you do. Don't you? It's been ten years, right? And here you are, following her around again."

She tells herself not to react, but she can't help the flush of heat that rises to her cheeks. "I am," she says. "You win."

"Nah, I didn't win. I trapped you," he says. "So let's start over. Welcome back to Bangor, Miss Campbell. How can I be of help?"

WHEN, FINALLY, HE talks about Jennifer, Mr. Hunter becomes thoughtful, his voice low and serious, stripped of its usual irony. "She was a pretty good student," he says. "Worked hard but didn't always think things through. When she focused she could be surprisingly original. She seemed older than her years in some ways, younger in others."

"Older, how?" Kathryn asks.

"She had an old soul," he says. "She had the soul of a seventy-five-year-old woman. Like she had enough distance to look at life objectively."

Kathryn nods, recognizing this as true. She remembers Jennifer's mother snapping, "For God's sake, Jen, lay off! You're not my moral monitor," and Jennifer muttering under her breath, "Then don't act like such a child." She did seem more mature sometimes, older than the rest of them: her mother, her brother, her friends.

"So how was she younger?" Kathryn asks.

He thinks for a moment, cupping his chin. "There was a petulance," he says slowly. "She was obstinate and willful sometimes when it wasn't appropriate. She always wanted her own way."

His assessment strikes Kathryn as peculiarly personal, somehow—more than she would have expected from a teacher, even one as perceptive as Mr. Hunter. "How well did you know her?" she asks.

"Not well," he says offhandedly. "How well did I know any of you?"

"You probably knew her better than most," Kathryn insists. "All that time after school."

"Right, orienteering," he concedes. "I knew her from that."

"Do you think you learned anything about her that might be useful for me to know?"

"Probably not." He seems deep in thought. Then he says, "She possessed something very rare, an internal compass. No matter where she was, how deep in the woods, she could always find a way out."

"Not always, apparently," Kathryn says.

"I suppose not," he assents.

"What do you think happened to her?"

"My hunch is that she lost her compass." He raises his shoulders in a shrug. "It might have been the night she disappeared, or it might have been a long time before. But somewhere along the way she got disoriented, and she made a judgment call she couldn't reverse."

"What does that mean?"

"I don't know. It's speculation. You asked me what I thought." He spreads his arms, and then his fingers, like a flower opening to the sun in time-lapse speed. "She struck me as lost in some way."

"So where is she?" Kathryn asks in a playful tone, as if the question is hypothetical.

"I think she's waiting for someone to find her." He pulls in his arms, and then points a finger at Kathryn. "How's your sense of direction?"

She gives him a wry smile. "It's getting better."

"Then maybe you're the one to do it," he says.

AFTER LEAVING THE school, Kathryn takes Interstate 95 where it jogs from the east side to the west side to run an errand for her mother. She passes over the Kenduskeag at the spot where, late one night during the winter of her senior year, two of her classmates, Ryan Vining and Troy LaGrange, missed a curve and smashed through the guardrail in a gold Corvette at a hundred miles an hour. They sheared the tops off a cluster of trees before slamming into an embankment. The car and their bodies were torn to pieces.

Even now, all these years later, whenever Kathryn reaches this turn in the road, she remembers the shock she felt on hearing the news. She and her mother drove to the spot the next morning and parked by the side of the road in a line of cars. Walking slowly through the battered, snow-dusted trees, they saw flashes of gold, a steering wheel, bloody patches and what might have been bits of flesh scattered through the underbrush. Other kids and their parents were there, too, silent or sobbing, their faces stunned and empty.

Kathryn had wanted to go to the spot to make herself believe it, but she found instead that being there only made the whole thing surreal. "Look up," her mother said softly, and she did, into a clear sky, a warming sun, a flutter of birds rising from the trees. "How can the sky be so blue today? It doesn't seem possible."

Kathryn was suddenly impatient with her mother, angry at her for being sentimental. "You think it should be raining?" she snapped. "Like in a TV movie?"

Her mother reached out and held her arm. "Don't talk to me like that."

"Then don't be so stupid," she said, knowing as she did that she was going too far. She slowed her breathing, waiting to see what her mother would do.

"This could have been you," her mother hissed, twisting her fingers into Kathryn's arm. "So don't you tell me how I should react. What do you think I'm afraid of those nights I stay up waiting? You kids are so goddamn thoughtless—" She dropped Kathryn's arm and covered her eyes with her hands. Then she turned abruptly and went up to the car.

Kathryn watched her mother get in, start the engine, and accelerate past the cars that were slowing to get a look at the accident. Then she walked home along the riverbank, alone.

PART THREE

REUNION

It's early evening when Kathryn arrives at Abby Elson's dilapidated apartment building on Union Street. The driveway is jammed with old cars, so Kathryn parks on the road in front and gets out carefully as traffic whizzes by. Scanning the crudely lettered names beside the buzzers at the front door and not finding Abby's name, she makes her way to the back, past an open Dumpster and a rusty motorcycle, and climbs an external flight of stairs to a second-floor landing.

Through the screen door, Kathryn can hear the whine of a radio. She presses her nose to the screen, trying to see into the gloom.

"Hey."

The voice startles her. "Hello?" She sees a glowing red dot in the darkness, and then Abby Elson is standing in front of her, scrawny and pale in faded jeans and a tight red shirt, trailing a cigarette in one hand.

"C'mon in," she says, holding the screen open. "Don't mind the shit everywhere."

Kathryn makes her way inside, stumbling over a gas can by the door and a shovel propped against the wall. "Sorry," she mutters, bending down to get the shovel as it clatters to the floor.

"Forget it, leave it. I been telling him to get that goddamn thing out of here for a week," Abby says, opening the refrigerator. "What can I get you? Want a beer? Oh, there's a Sprite in here, too."

"No, thanks, I'm fine," Kathryn says, but Abby has already tossed her the soda.

Sinking into a chair at the Formica kitchen table, Abby gestures across from her. "Have a seat."

In high school Abby had been a beauty, with long dark hair, doe eyes, and a tiny waist. She looked like a Disney heroine. She was always dating someone, usually the star athlete of whatever major sport was in season, especially if he, too, was a little unconventional. Her boyfriends tended to wear leather jackets and drive fast, souped-up cars.

Abby's mother had taken off when she was little, and Abby and her father and another sister who worked at Sizzler lived in a trailer park near the mall. Kathryn went there once, with Jennifer, and she was amazed at the economy of scale within those narrow walls. Everything fit: the queen-size bed, the full bath, the cheerful kitchen and comfy den, Abby's berthlike sleeping area set off by a screen. Compared to the drafty, rambling old houses Kathryn and Jennifer lived in, trailer life seemed liberating. Abby appeared to have no chores; she sat out front in a folding chair under the flimsy, flapping awning, painting her nails with frosted polish and waiting for her boyfriends to call.

Abby was Jennifer's friend. None of the rest of them knew her very well. "I just don't get it. What do you see in that girl?" Will would ask every now and then, an amused smile on his face.

"You're a snob," Jennifer would answer. "She happens to be very bright."

"She's had half the football team. She's not great for your reputation."

"I don't give a flying fuck about my reputation," she'd retort. "And if you're so shallow that you care that much what other people think, I truly feel sorry for you."

Kathryn hadn't cared so much about Abby's reputation, though it was a convenient excuse when she needed a reason to complain about her. As Jennifer began spending more time with Abby, senior year, Kathryn felt increasingly left out. It wasn't that Jennifer was spending less time with Kathryn; it was that she began to seem distracted and distant. The two of them would be walking to class together and Abby would appear, dropping a folded note into Jennifer's shirt pocket and winking as they passed. Or Kathryn would be over at Jennifer's and the phone would ring and Jennifer would disappear with it into the next room, talking in an excited whisper.

"Who was it?" Kathryn would ask when she emerged.

"Oh, just Abby."

"How is she?"

"She's fine," Jennifer would say, and that would be it. She never told Kathryn what they were talking about, and she never shared the notes. Kathryn began to feel like a wife who suspects her husband is having an affair but can't prove it. She looked everywhere for clues of Jennifer's betrayal. "Best friends?" Jennifer would coyly ask, winding her arm around Kathryn's back, sensing her mistrust.

"So you're writing an article," Abby says now. She takes a long drag on the cigarette.

Kathryn pops open the Sprite and it explodes, spraying the table and her tape recorder. Leaning her chair back on two legs, Abby reaches over to the counter and grabs a dirty rag. "Here," she says, tossing it over. Kathryn mops up the mess, wiping soda from between the cracks of the recorder.

"I just have a few questions," she says, setting the machine back on the table and pressing Start.

"Okeydokey."

As Abby talks, Kathryn looks around the small, dark apartment.

There's a gray-and-red uniform from T.J. Maxx hanging over a floral chair in the living room and a pair of hiking boots on the floor. An ashtray on the large-screen TV is full of butts; a motorcycle helmet sits on the couch like a severed cartoon head. "Jennifer was in my gym class second semester junior year, that's how we met," Abby is saying. "At first I thought she was an uptight blond bitch, but she turned out to be pretty cool. Pretty funny. Really knew which way was up. We didn't really get tight, though, until senior year, when I joined orienteering and we started spending a lot of time together. We were partners. You had to have a partner so there'd be someone who knew what time you left and what time you were supposed to be back. Your partner had your coordinates."

In the living room a cuckoo clock in the shape of Mickey Mouse is ticking loudly. It's exactly 6:30 P.M., and Minnie pops out of Mickey's mouth with a squeak. Kathryn jumps. "That thing drives me crazy," Abby says, rolling her eyes, "but Lane thinks it's funny. He ordered it on QVC one night when I was asleep."

"So what do you think she liked about it?" Kathryn asks.

"About what?"

"Orienteering."

"In what sense?"

"I don't know," Kathryn says. "What sense is there?"

"People did it for a lot of different reasons." Abby leans away from Kathryn, hooking her arm over the back of the chair. Her face is guarded. "To get away from their boring shit lives. To learn how to survive by their wits." She shrugs. "Because they grooved on nature."

"Why did you do it?"

She holds her cigarette out at arm's length, seeming to study it. "It started out as a way to avoid two weeks of detention for smoking, but then I got into it. I just needed some space, I guess. I didn't have much of that."

Kathryn remembers seeing Abby's family lined up in the bleachers at graduation, a whole row of them, holding up a sign that said WAY TO

GO, ABBY! and pumping their fists in the air when she picked up her diploma. She was the youngest of six children, most of whom were married or divorced, with children of their own, by the time she started high school.

"Why do you think Jennifer did it?" Kathryn presses her.

Abby puts her head down, and then she looks up at Kathryn and grins. "Why do you think?"

Kathryn starts to parrot what Jennifer had told her—that she loved knowing she could find her own way in the wild, that being so alone was almost spiritual—but something in Abby's voice makes her pause. "You might have a better idea," she says.

"But you two were 'best friends,' " Abby says mockingly. She taps ash from her cigarette into a chipped teacup on the table.

Kathryn looks at her. "I thought so." She swallows hard. "But you probably knew her better than I did."

Abby smiles. "You're probably right."

Kathryn flushes, a knot in her stomach.

Abby stubs out her cigarette, squishing it into the cup. "I'll be honest," she says. "I love knowing something you don't. It's hard to give that up."

"How do you know I don't know?"

"You wouldn't be here if you did."

Kathryn tries to piece together what she knows: Jennifer's L. L. Bean boots drying out in the hall; practice once, then twice a week; pizza parties at Mr. Hunter's cabin on Pushaw Lake; night sessions to test their skills in the dark. "Hey, Jen," Kathryn had said one afternoon, sitting on Jennifer's bed, idly playing with her compass, "this thing is broken."

"Oh, yeah, it just broke," Jennifer said, taking it away from her and putting it in a drawer. "I'm using Abby's for the moment."

"Then how can Abby find you?"

"What?"

"Isn't she supposed to have a compass, too?"

Jennifer furrowed her brow. "She's borrowing one from Mr. Hunter. He has a couple. It just happened," she repeated, irritation in her voice.

"How often did the team meet?" Kathryn asks Abby.

"Usually once a week, sometimes more."

"I was looking at her diary. Spring of senior year she had the team meeting twice a week."

"Uh-huh."

"So did you?"

They stare at each other for a moment, and then Abby stands up. "I think I've said all I'm going to."

"What do you mean?"

"That's all I'm going to say."

"Come on, Abby," Kathryn says. "I need your help."

Abby shrugs. "Sorry."

Kathryn clicks off the tape recorder. "Well, thanks for being so open."

"I don't get your questions, anyway," she says. "I don't see what they have to do with finding out where she is."

Outside, it's drizzling and the light is fading. When Kathryn gets to her car, there's a wet ticket under her windshield wiper. She takes it out and examines it, squinting under the weak fluorescent streetlight to see the damage: twenty dollars. She looks up and down the street; the sign that says NO PARKING ANY TIME is twisted and half obscured by a SHIT HAPPENS bumper sticker, but is nonetheless visible, if she'd been inclined to look.

She fumbles with her keys, opens the car door, and heaves herself into the seat, tossing the ticket in the back. "Fuck," she says, touching her forehead to the beige plastic steering wheel. "Fuck fuck fuck." The horn sounds loudly, and she yanks her head up fast.

Kathryn gets up early Wednesday morning, as the sun is rising. She puts on her running shoes and laces them up in the gloom of the kitchen before going out on the porch to stretch. The morning air is cool, even chilly. The street is quiet. A thick layer of dew, like lint from a dryer, coats the grass. The sky, watery and gray, has been touched by the sun only lightly, a benediction.

Down at the end of the block, Kathryn can see the paperboy on his bike, flinging rolled newspapers onto front porches. She remembers her own days as a paper carrier: the thrill of lofting those papers, lightening the bag as you sailed by each house, sometimes hitting the doormat—the target—square in the center. This was a trick you could get away with only in the summer, she remembers; winters buried the paper in snow, and spring and autumn risked rain.

After her interview with Abby, Kathryn had eaten a quiet dinner with her mother and gone to bed early. But she didn't get much sleep. She kept thinking about what Abby said about knowing Jennifer better than she did. Now, as she jogs slowly down the street, she realizes that the reason Abby's comment rankled so much is that it's probably true. For years, the only emotions Kathryn has let herself feel have been sorrow and fear about Jennifer's disappearance. But whatever it was that Kathryn once felt is now complicated and deepened by the ghosts she is stirring up. The fact is, if she can admit it, Jennifer exists for her now as surely as she did ten years ago—not as a tragic eighteen-year-old victim, but as a person with complexities and contradictions. And Kathryn is newly angry at her for keeping parts of her life separate, for trusting others with her secrets. She is angry and hurt and flushed with another emotion, one she can hardly believe and never would have imagined, after all these years: She is jealous. Jennifer is the center of attention again, as always; as they put it in grad-school jargon, *Jennifer determines the discourse.* Part of Kathryn is almost impatient: Come on, she wants to say, the jig is up. You've held out long enough; we're all bored now, ready for the game to end. You win. We care enough, after all this time. Now at least have the decency to tell us where you are.

Of course I didn't know her, Kathryn thinks, stopping in the middle of the street to catch her breath. I was working with partial information—trying to solve a puzzle with pieces missing, trying to answer a riddle with only half a clue.

"SO I HEAR you spoke to my mother." Will's voice on the phone is gentle, teasing; Kathryn can tell right away he's not upset about it, as she had feared.

"Will," she says. "Are you in town? I thought you were coming in tomorrow."

"I got the day off and figured what the hell. Maybe seeing you guys first will make the reunion less of a nightmare."

"You don't have to go," she says.

"Are you kidding? I'm class president, remember? I planned this shindig."

"Oh, yeah," she says. "Now I remember why I never ran for office."

"You never ran for office because your ego didn't require false adulation and praise."

"No, I never ran for office because I was afraid nobody would vote for me," she admits. "So is your mom totally pissed?"

"She's a little riled up," he says. "She'll get over it. She hates the press; she got burned pretty bad once and vowed she'd never talk to a reporter again."

"What happened?"

"*New England Monthly* did a feature story seven or eight years ago. They came up here, interviewed all kinds of people, followed her around for three days, wined and dined her at Pilot's Grill, got her to show them home movies and Jennifer's room. And then the article came out, and it basically pointed the finger at my mom and Ralph."

"Oh, I remember that story."

"Yeah, it sucked. So you can see why she's wary. Anyway, how are you?"

She has forgotten this about Will: that conversation with him is a torrent; it's easy to feel swept along in the rush. He can be disarmingly direct, but his frankness is an illusion. You come away knowing little about him but a lot about yourself.

"I'm fine," she says.

"I heard about the divorce," he says bluntly. "What a lousy bastard. He didn't deserve you."

"Who told you?"

He laughs. "Come on, Kathryn, who doesn't know?"

"Thanks, Will. That's comforting."

"Look, at least you don't have the black plague. If anybody at the reunion shakes my hand, I'll be surprised."

Caught by surprise, she inhales sharply. "Oh—"

"I know you know," he says. "I asked Jack to tell you. I would've done it myself, but I wasn't sure what to say. 'Hello, Kath, I haven't spoken to you in seven years, but I just wanted you to know I'm dying'?"

"You're not . . . dying," she says lamely.

"No. Well, I mean, we're all dying, right? And any one of us could get hit by a truck tomorrow. Yeah, I did a lot of that kind of justifying at first. And the cocktail I'm on seems to be working for now; I have no symptoms. But I'm not kidding myself. I have a lethal virus in my blood. It'll probably get me one of these days."

"I'm so sorry, Will."

"I know. Thanks. You know who's really sorry? The guy who gave it to me. Or he would be, if he knew." He laughs shortly, fending off sympathy. "It's a wacky world, isn't it, Kath?"

She bites her lip. Most Likely to Succeed, Will was voted in high school. The only one who got into Princeton. He was the golden boy, the one all the girls had crushes on—and, she realizes now, probably a number of the guys. Like Jennifer, he had blond hair, light eyes, a tall, lithe body. But he had something else, too, that Jennifer didn't: an encompassing charm, a willingness to play the game. It was probably part of figuring out his sexual identity: He could move easily among any of them, he would not let himself be narrowly defined.

Kathryn remembers the first time she realized she had a crush on him. It was at a high-school dance junior year; the whole group was there, and they were dancing in a ragged circle, pulling in other people, pairing off among themselves. They'd been drinking in the parking lot before the dance—one of Brian's older brothers had bought them a case of Budweiser—and after two beers Kathryn was drunk. A slow reggae song started playing, and the dance floor cleared. But Kathryn was caught in the low familiar beat, and she swayed to it with her eyes closed. All at once she felt someone's arm around her waist, and she looked up to see Will, smiling, moving his hips with hers to the music. *"I don't know what life will show me, but I know what I've seen,"* he crooned in her ear. She felt a thrill go through her—a thrill connected to covert glimpses in the hall between classes, faded notes on lined white paper passed in third period, a stolen kiss in an empty gymnasium. She felt young and shy.

The first time Will kissed her, they were sitting on her front porch in the dark. Jennifer had been out with them that night; they'd gone to *Footloose* and were singing the title track at the top of their lungs in the car on the way back. But at some point Jennifer grew quiet and asked to be dropped at home. Brian was out of town with his parents, and Rachel and Jack were at a party Kathryn and Will had no interest in, so they ended up on her porch, with its white columns and slatted railings, watching the glow on the side lawn from her mother's bedroom window.

"This is very fifties," Will said, leaning against the banister. "Sitting out here on the porch with your mother pacing around upstairs."

"Almost like a date," Kathryn said. They both laughed uncomfortably. "I wish she'd just go to sleep."

"She can't go to sleep. She's programmed with that mother gene that keeps her awake until you're safely in bed."

Kathryn played with the chain of the porch swing she was sitting on, idly moving the swing back and forth with her foot. "What in the world does she think is going to happen to me? I'm with you, for God's sake."

He tilted his head, his disheveled blond hair falling over one eye, feigned annoyance on his face. "What's that supposed to mean?"

Kathryn laughed. "She knows you're a nice guy."

He shook his head. "I'm sick of that shit. Just once I'd like someone to think I'm dangerous."

She smiled. "Well, you might have to do something dangerous, then."

He looked at her keenly. Then, all at once, he leaned forward and kissed her. Startled, she pulled away. "How dangerous is that?" he said. He pushed her long brown hair off her face and pulled her closer, kissing her again.

"So this piece you're writing for the *Bangor Daily News*," he says now. "Have you found out anything new?"

"I don't know yet," she says. "I still have to talk to some people. Like you."

"We can talk. I have to tell you, though, I don't have much faith in this process. I'm inclined to agree with my mother—to dig all this up again is painful, and probably a waste of time. We did so much . . . I don't know. I don't know, Kath," he says quietly, and she can tell that he's trying to keep his emotions in check. The whole time they were searching for Jennifer she saw him break down only once, and that was the day, several weeks after it happened, when divers found a body at the Bucksport dam. It turned out to be a vagrant from Old Town, but they didn't know that for several hours. Will's face, when they told him, was a terrible mixture of relief and fear, and when the police left, he tripped over a chair and then kicked it, savagely, across the room, splintering a back leg. He retreated to an upstairs room, but his loud sobbing reverberated through the house.

"You're probably right. There's not much point in doing this. But maybe it'll stir up something; maybe something got overlooked. It's worth a try, don't you think? Otherwise we're just giving up. Are you really ready to do that?" she asks.

"Listen," he says sharply. "I busted my ass longer than anybody. It's wrecked my fucking life. Don't tell me I'm—"

"I'm sorry, Will. I was out of line."

"Jesus, Kath." He sighs. "I know you're trying to help. Five years ago—three years ago, even—I would have welcomed this. But coming now, it just seems so disruptive, so late. We could have her declared legally dead now, did you know that? We won't, but we could." He's silent for a moment. "You know, when Jennifer was little, she used to get lost all the time. She'd go off into corners and closets, or behind boxes in the attic. Mom was always looking for her, calling after her, trying to get me to track her down. 'You know how her mind works,' she said. 'You'll find her faster than I can.' I did usually find her, but it was more because I knew the hiding places and the limited possibilities for escape than that I knew Jennifer so well." He pauses again, and Kathryn can hear him breathing. Then he says, almost inaudibly, "She is dead, I think."

THEY MEET THAT night down by the river. His hair has darkened over the years; his face is narrower, more chiseled. His eyes are tired. They sit on the bank in the darkness and listen to the water lapping the shore. Then, taking her hand, he leads her across the large slabs of rock that form a stepping-stone path.

"Remember this?" He stops and turns, and she walks into him. "We used to come out here when your mom thought we were at the movies."

"Back when I thought you were straight."

"And I didn't know what the hell I was."

They sit on the rock and watch the gurgling water, and he tells her stories she already knows, about his mother's affair and his father's suicide and Jennifer's role in all of it, about seeing Jennifer, wan and ghostly, in the hospital bed after she got her stomach pumped, about the next few months of silence and retreat. Jennifer began staying out late, leaving the house early in the morning—anything to avoid being at home. Their mother was distracted; she didn't notice as much as she should have, or if she did she didn't do much about it. Jennifer hated her stepfather; it was hard for her to be in the same room with him. It was easier for everybody when she was gone.

Will knew that Jennifer was secretly seeing someone. She spent a long time getting ready; she pounced on the phone on the first ring and took it into her room, locking the door. He could hear her making plans. But she wouldn't admit to it, wouldn't even admit that there was someone. "I just want to be by myself, for Christ's sake. Is there something wrong with that?" she'd snap when he pushed it. One time he followed her. He was several cars behind her on Broadway when she spotted him at a traffic light. She pulled into the Pizza Hut parking lot and sat there, smoking in her dark car, until he left.

"She was different after our dad died," he says, trailing his fingers in the water, picking up a handful of stones. "I didn't really recognize her after that. And I guess I pulled back, too. I couldn't stand that haunted look in her eyes. It was spooky how well she hid it from other people. At school she acted normal—better than normal; she even seemed happy. But you could see that blankness, if you knew how to look. Remember her senior picture? Her smile looked painted on, like a doll's."

"I was just noticing that," Kathryn says. "I'd never really seen it before."

"That's the kind of stuff I became obsessed with after . . ." His voice falters. He drops the stones in the water, and they make tiny individual splashes.

"What else?" Kathryn says gently. "What didn't you tell the police? What secrets did you keep?"

"There are so many kinds of secrets, aren't there?" he says with a faint smile. "How far back do you go? Do you start with the little things, like smelling whiskey on my dad when he dropped me off at school? Or picking up the phone and hearing my mother say 'I love you' to some man I've never met? What about the lies my parents told each other, the lies they told Jen and me, the lies we all learned to tell?

"I remember this one time when Jen and I were six and the paperboy—Jimmy Butera, I even remember his name; he must've been about fifteen—took us with him to catch a snake out in the field behind the Poseys'. That was what we thought anyway. He ended up pinning Jen down and making her take her clothes off."

"Jesus," Kathryn says.

"She started having an asthma attack—you know, coughing and choking—and I was trying to pull him off her. Finally the whole thing freaked Jimmy out, and he took off. After Jen calmed down, the two of us went home and told our mom, though he'd threatened to break our arms if we did. It didn't matter anyway; Mom was most concerned about the fact that Jimmy's father was president of one of the big banks downtown, the one Dad did business with. She didn't want to cause trouble over nothing, she said, and besides, boys will be boys and maybe we learned a lesson." He laughs sardonically. "We learned a lesson, all right. I think that was the last time Jennifer ever confided in her."

"God, that's awful," Kathryn says. "I never knew."

"Why would you?" He shrugs. "It wasn't important, just one more thing to hide. One more thing to be ashamed of." He laughs again, a hollow sound devoid of feeling.

"How could—why did—"

He looks at her, hard, for a minute. "I don't have any answers," he says. "And I'll tell you something. I've learned to live without them. I don't expect to know the whys of anything anymore." He smiles, the corners of his mouth trembling. "It's pretty good training for a defense attorney, actually. Comes in handy when there are things you don't want to know."

"But you want to know what happened to Jennifer, don't you? Wouldn't you give anything to find out?"

She watches him looking out at the darkness, at the slip of moon, the starless sky, the water flowing past and around them. "I spent a lot of time looking for her," he says finally. "Now maybe I just need to come to terms with it."

When they stand up to leave, he laces his fingers through hers and draws her close, kissing her softly on the forehead. Shutting her eyes against the light of the moon, she lets herself sway against him, and he pulls her closer, wrapping his arms around her shoulders. All at once her eyes are swimming and her head is light and she's crying, dripping hot tears onto his chest, brushing her face against his denim shirt.

LATE THAT NIGHT, when Kathryn gets home, she finds a note for her on the kitchen counter. "Paul called," it says in her mother's neat, grammar-school cursive. "Says he has something he needs to talk to you about. Wants you to hear it from him first. Too tired to wait up. Love, Mom. XXO."

Kathryn looks at the clock: It's 1:15 A.M. She picks up the phone and dials Paul's number. It rings four times before the machine picks up.

"Rena and Paul are otherwise engaged," a woman says in a girly singsong. "Leave a message and we'll deconstruct it when we get a chance." Kathryn pauses for a moment, then hangs up.

She's turning off lights, heading upstairs, when the phone rings in the kitchen. She runs back to get it. "Hello?" she says cautiously.

"Kat? Oh, it was you," Paul says. "Go back to sleep, it's okay," she hears him murmur to someone in the background. "Sorry," he tells Kathryn. "Star six-nine. I had to find out who it was. This weird guy in the department is kind of stalking Rena, so we treat all hang-ups like crank calls."

"So this is your news?" she asks.

"Oh. Um. Yeah." He laughs, a bit defensively. "I'm sorry to tell you this way, but I wanted to tell you myself before you heard it from someone else."

"Oh, you did, huh?"

"She transferred into the program a couple months ago. From Brown," he adds, as if that should somehow matter. The nerve, Kathryn thinks, trying to impress me with his new girlfriend's résumé.

"So how long have you two been shacking up?"

"Well," he says carefully. She knows the phrase *shacking up* irritates him. "Almost a week. Look." The unctuousness in his voice has evaporated. "It's late and I don't want to get into anything with you. But I didn't need to call. I was just trying to be considerate."

"I think I'd rather have heard it from someone else," she says.

Paul sighs.

"Excuse me if I don't offer congratulations," she says. "I hope Rena knows what she's in for."

"Rena has nothing to worry about," he says. "Rena is nothing like you."

She's silent for a moment. Then she says, "How's Frieda?"

"She has fleas. I got her a collar. Look, Kathryn," he says, "I didn't mean to say that. You provoked me."

She sighs. "I know."

"I'm sorry," he says. "I don't know what else to say."

When she hangs up the phone, Kathryn sits in the dark kitchen watching the blurry shapes around her morph into objects she recognizes—an Early American wall clock, the pine kitchen table, a ladderback chair—as her eyes adjust. After a few minutes she makes her way easily up the stairs and into her room without turning on any lights. The terrain is so familiar, she knows it by heart.

"I want to hear about Paul. You've barely said a word about him." It's Thursday morning at 10:05, and Rosie is settled in her overstuffed chair with a notebook in one hand and a pen in the other. She's wearing a floral dress so similar to the upholstery that it's hard to see where the chair ends and she begins.

"What do you want to know?"

"Well, for starters, why did you marry him?"

"Do we have to talk about him? I don't really want to."

"What do you want to talk about?"

"Umm . . . do you think I should dye my hair again? It's been almost a month." Kathryn laughs nervously at her feeble diversion.

Putting down her pen and crossing her arms, Rosie says, "Oh, you want to talk about roots, huh? Okay. Tell me about your father."

Kathryn makes a face. "Very funny."

"It's up to you," Rosie says briskly. "We can talk about your hair, if that's what you want." She squints at the top of Kathryn's head. "Yeah, you might want to touch it up. If you're happy with that shade."

"You don't like it?"

"I'm not sure it's the most flattering color. But what do I know? I'm a therapist, not a beautician." She shrugs. "As a therapist I'd make a different diagnosis."

"What do you mean?"

"When did you go red?"

"About four weeks ago, like I said."

"What's your normal color?"

"Field-mouse brown."

"Ever dye it before?"

"Nope."

Rosie nods slowly. "So you're starting over," she says.

"Well, obviously."

She picks up the pen and writes something in her notebook. "Or you're trying to hide," she says, without looking up.

Kathryn doesn't answer. She shifts in her chair.

"Which do you think it is?"

"Probably some combination." Kathryn looks out the one small window in the stuffy little room, at the gray sky and the gray gravel and the gray siding of another prefab building across the parking lot.

Rosie cocks her head. "Maybe you just don't want to be that mousy brown-haired person anymore. Maybe you're trying to figure out who you do want to be."

Kathryn looks at her, suddenly feeling spiteful. Do other therapists tell their patients how to analyze their experience? Her friend Gretchen, in Charlottesville, used to complain that her shrink never said more than three words the entire fifty minutes she was there. Isn't that standard procedure? And what's with the dress? Did she choose it on purpose to blend in with the chair?

"But I really think we need to talk about Paul, if you want to get anything done here," Rosie continues. "I think he's a major block to progress."

Paul. Kathryn grimaces. Is she really going to have to think about him? Whenever something triggers a memory—a word or an object, an expression, a fleeting glimpse of a dark-haired man—she turns her mind away. Her feelings are too sharp, too bright; it's like looking into the sun. She can't think clearly about him anyway. It's like that old joke about the blind man and the elephant; she can't seem to get a complete picture of what he is or who he is—he's just a collection of parts that don't seem to fit together. There was the Paul who brought her daisy chains and breakfast in bed, and the one who went through all her CDs without asking and sold the ones he didn't like. There was the don't-give-a-shit, pot-smoking laziness, and then the seismic ambition. She didn't ever feel as if she understood him, though she wanted to and she tried. For a long time she told herself that this was why she loved him—for his contradictions, for the fact that he was an enigma, always, somehow, a surprise.

"That's interesting," Rosie says. "That's just what you said about Jennifer."

Kathryn stops short. She hadn't even realized she was thinking aloud. "What?"

"You said that maybe part of what you liked about Jennifer was that you didn't understand her. She didn't quite add up."

"I said that?"

Rosie nods.

Kathryn considers this. "What more do you want to know about me?" she remembers Paul saying soon after they got married, his arms spread wide in exasperation. "I've told you everything!"

"No you haven't," she said. "I just want you to be more open. Tell me what you're feeling. Tell me what's going on in your head."

He thrust his hands at her as if pushing her away. "I don't want you in my head!" he shouted, slamming out of the room. "Stay the fuck out of it!"

When Jennifer disappeared, Kathryn had been angry at herself for not pushing harder. If only she had found the right way to ask, the appropriate tone, the magic question, maybe she would have learned something; maybe she could have helped. So when she met Paul and he was similarly evasive, she tried to pin him down. The very thing that had attracted her to him—the fact that she couldn't crack his code—eventually made her anxious and frightened, and her probing made him want to escape.

"Your father was emotionally unavailable, too, wasn't he?" Rosie says.

"Yeah." Kathryn shrugs, looking up at the white-spackled ceiling. "But so what? Isn't this just one of the four or five basic human dynamics, and I'm destined to play one position for the rest of my life against some predictable opponent? I'll always be whining for more, and they'll always be pushing me away. And our basic incompatibility will make a sustained relationship impossible, and I'll die unhappy and alone."

"Well, you've got it all planned out," Rosie says. She taps her pen against her teeth. "We can't choose our parents, and obviously they determine a great deal about who we are. But beyond our family, we choose the people in our lives for a reason. Patterns exist and dynamics exist because we haven't learned enough about who we are to stop them from playing out."

Kathryn glances at the digital clock radio on the bookshelf; it's 10:49 A.M. Is this the parting summation?

"You keep getting involved with a particular kind of person. Why?" Rosie asks. Replacing the cap on her pen, she lays it on the desk. "That's the question you need to be thinking about. And next time I hope we'll make a little more progress in that direction." She tosses her notebook onto the desk, and it slides across the smooth surface. "This is good work to be doing," she says, walking Kathryn out. "It's hard but important."

Of course it's important to you, Kathryn thinks; you're getting seventy dollars an hour. But a tiny part of herself has to admit that Rosie is probably right.

THERE'S NO ONE sitting on the porch of the nursing home when Kathryn arrives, and the parking lot is virtually empty. The afternoon sky is cloudy and bland.

"Where is everybody?" Kathryn asks when she gets to her grandmother's room. The old woman is sitting in a wheelchair by the bed, doing anagrams out of a book. Kathryn kisses her on her cheek, which is papery and soft and smells of talcum.

"Dead. I'm the only one who made it through the night," her grandmother says brightly.

"It wouldn't surprise me," Kathryn says. She holds up a paper cone of flowers. "What should I do with these?"

"It's 'quiet time.' They think we're in nursery school here," she snorts. "Gives the staff a chance to nap, is what I think." She flutters her fingers toward the bathroom. "There's a plastic pitcher in there. They don't trust us with glass."

Kathryn goes into the bathroom, finds a blue regulation hospital pitcher, and fills it with water. Coming back into the room, she asks, "So how are you, Grandma?"

"How I am is boring. And bored. So why don't you tell me something amusing?"

Kathryn smiles, unwrapping the funnel. "Mom is dating a car salesman."

"Hah."

"They might be in love."

"Good Lord," her grandmother says. "Tell me more."

Kathryn begins to disentangle the daisies from each other and snap off the ends, standing them in the pitcher one by one. "I don't know much," she says. "Mom's pretty tight-lipped about it. I haven't even met the guy. But he did loan me a car while I'm home."

"So you think he's grand."

"Basically."

Her grandmother nods. Then she looks down, studying Kathryn's feet. "Where in the world did you find those clodhoppers? They're frightful."

"They're clogs, Grandma. And they're really comfortable."

"So is my bathrobe, but I don't wear it out in public."

Kathryn holds up the pitcher. "What do you think of these?"

"Very nice," she says primly. "You know, Josh always brings me roses."

"When's the last time Josh came to see you?"

"It might have been yesterday, I remember it so well. A huge bouquet of yellow roses," she says, spreading her arms, as if to encompass them. "There must have been dozens. And baby's breath."

"Josh is a mortgage broker," Kathryn reminds her.

"And you're just broke." She laughs gleefully. "Oh, Kathryn, I need you around more often! I'd forgotten how witty I can be."

Kathryn gives her a patently fake smile. "Glad I can be of service." She turns and sets the flowers in the window.

Her grandmother claps her hands together. "So. Your mother has told me about the big investigation. Where are we with the story, Nancy Drew?"

"I have an article due tomorrow."

"How long?"

"Fifteen hundred words."

"Piece of cake."

"Easy for you to say." Kathryn crosses her arms, leans against the wall. "I've been talking to people all week, and I don't know much more than when I started."

"Is that a problem?"

"Of course."

"Why?"

Kathryn laughs, incredulous at the question. "Because," she says with exaggerated patience, "I have nothing to go on. I have nothing to say, nothing to build a story on."

"How many people have you interviewed?"

"Umm . . ." She counts them in her head: John Bourne, Gaffney, Jack, Rachel, Brian, Mrs. Pelletier, Mr. Hunter, Abby Elson, Will. "Nine."

"And none of them said anything interesting."

"No, they did. But I just don't know how I can—"

"What were you expecting, a confession?"

She half shrugs. "Well, it would be nice. It'd be a good lead."

Her grandmother frowns. "I didn't realize you were such a lazy reporter. Is that why you got fired from that paper in Virginia?"

"I didn't get fired," Kathryn says, annoyed. "I quit."

"Um-hmmph," she says skeptically. "So what are you going to do?"

"I don't know." She turns and looks out the window at the dishwater sky, the pine trees on the horizon rustling in the wind like a faraway army. "I'm thinking of calling Jack and asking for an extension."

"Pah." Her grandmother shakes her head in disgust. "In all my years as a reporter I never once missed a deadline."

"This is a little different, Grandma. I'm not writing about the Junior League."

Lifting her chin slowly, she looks Kathryn in the eye. "I am not going to dignify that with a response." The room is silent for a moment. Then she snaps, "That is the most insulting thing anyone has ever said to me. Take it back."

"I wasn't fired," Kathryn says petulantly.

"What?"

"I wasn't fired."

"All right, fine, then. You quit," she says, rolling her eyes.

"Okay. I take it back."

They stare at each other. Then her grandmother says, "I'm surprised at you, Kathryn. I didn't know you were such a big baby."

"Please, Grandma, don't insult me anymore. I'm starting to sympathize with Mom."

"And I'm starting to think you're more like her than I thought."

There's another long stretch of silence between them. Somewhere down the hall, a radio is playing. A telephone goes unanswered; Kathryn counts ten rings, eleven, twelve, before it stops. The room, she notices, smells of canned food and disinfectant.

"Well," her grandmother says finally. She clasps her hands in her lap. "I don't know if you are interested in my advice."

"I don't know, either," Kathryn says warily.

"For what it's worth, based on what you've told me, and my own— *admittedly limited*—experience, I believe you have more than enough material for a story." She pauses, waiting.

"Go on."

"To build a story is to master the art of illusion," her grandmother says. "There doesn't need to be a solid center; you just have to create the illusion of one. You have to trust your instincts."

"That's the problem," Kathryn says, sitting down on the bed. "I don't."

"You set the scene, divert the eye," her grandmother says. "Thoughts, feelings, everyday objects, offhand remarks: you take what you've got and craft around it." She makes an arc in the air with her hands, then lets them fall to her lap. "What do we want to know about this girl? We want to know what happened to her. What are the possibilities? That she was picked up by a stranger, or she wasn't." She begins counting the options on her fingers. "If she wasn't, maybe she fell into the river by accident. Or on purpose. Or she was picked up by someone she knew. Or she ran off. Every possibility invites a different set of questions: Why would someone pick her up? Why would she run off? Was she running toward something, or running away?"

"I don't know, I don't know," Kathryn frets.

"But it's all right not to know. Don't you see?" She reaches over and takes Kathryn's hand in her own cold, bony one and squeezes it tightly. "That's the story." She looks into Kathryn's eyes. "Do you understand what I'm saying?"

"I don't know," Kathryn mumbles, shaking her head.

"Of course you do," her grandmother says. She sits up straight in her wheelchair and smooths the blanket on her lap. "You just have to find a way in. When you have that, the story will reveal itself. It will tell you what you know. And what you know, my dear, may surprise you."

LATE INTO THE evening, sitting at the kitchen table, Kathryn listens to the tapes. The voices are more hesitant, more solemn, than she remembers. She hears things she doesn't recall having been said; she thinks of questions she should have asked. In the quiet, the disembodied voices tell one story, the silences another. Kathryn listens to the Morse code of pauses and unfinished thoughts and interruptions, and a pattern slowly begins to emerge. After all this time the pain seems fresh: what Jennifer did, what she didn't do, the trivial betrayals. They each seem to think that Jennifer somehow duped them into believing that they knew her, that they understood her, when, as it later became clear, they didn't know her at all. Jennifer's surface was a mirror, reflecting back to people the image they wanted to see; behind the glass, she did what she wanted.

But what Kathryn begins to understand, as she listens to the tapes, is that she and her friends are wrong to feel betrayed. Jennifer did allow them to know her, each in a different way. Some saw glimpses of her renegade spirit, others of her heavy heart. And maybe it wasn't that she was purposely deceiving them; maybe it was that she wanted so badly to be like everyone else, to be normal, that she felt she had to hide part of who she was to keep their friendship. Kathryn thinks about what Rachel told her Jennifer had said: *Trust isn't a word I know. It isn't in my vocabulary.* In the end, Kathryn thinks, Jennifer had too much to hide; she became too skilled at telling lies and keeping secrets. She was too adept at covering her tracks. It was inevitable that eventually she would become impossible to follow.

Opening the folder from the police station, Kathryn rereads the missing-persons reports, the all-points bulletin, the write-ups of interviews with family and friends. In the dry, official language of the police report what stands out most is how little evidence they had, how baffling and unexplainable the disappearance was. The small clues they had collapsed like a pile of ashes whenever anyone tried to build a case out of them.

Was she unhappy? Did she say or do anything unusual in the preceding six months? Had anything happened in the past year that might have had a profoundly negative effect on her? Was she secretive? Was she deceitful? Did anyone have reason to be angry at her?

The answer is yes, yes to everything—and yet somehow it still doesn't make sense, even after all the depositions and searches through the underbrush, even after analyzing her father's death and the suicide attempt and interviewing the mother she betrayed and the brother she lied to and the friends she treated so cavalierly. Something is missing—some vital piece. And until it is found, the story will never make sense; the pieces will add up to nothing, their accumulation as meaningless as a dead language. Without a key there can be no translation, just pages of unintelligible text.

In all my years on the force, Gaffney said, *I've never seen a stranger-to-stranger abduction.* It could have happened; anything's possible. But it probably didn't. Which meant that either she ran away or someone who knew her did her harm. How well do you know your neighbor? How well do you know yourself? In towns all over America, the lament when something terrible happens is the same: He would never do that, he's not the type. Nothing like this ever happens here. He seemed like such a nice guy, kept to himself, didn't bother anyone. And then, inevitably, people begin to see signs of deviance in the ordinary man's behavior. Well, he was a little strange. Killed squirrels with a BB gun, didn't cry at his mother's funeral, never had a girlfriend, couldn't hold down a job. But it always struck Kathryn that the details that surface after the fact could probably be culled from any life. We all have things to hide, things we're hiding from, habits and quirks and insecurities.

The facts of our lives can be so easily corralled into a story of good or evil, brilliance or insanity, conformity or aberrance. How can you know what anyone is capable of? How can you know it of yourself?

The same is true, of course, of the one to whom something happens. The first reaction is panic: She could be any of our children; she might be my daughter, my sister, my friend. The beautiful blond-haired girl in the yearbook photograph, with her shining eyes and soft striped blouse, her pop-song quote and wholesome activities, represented everything a parent could want, everything a teenage girl might long to be. But as time went on and details began to emerge, it was easy to particularize and distance what had happened to her. She was different. She took chances, kept secrets, had a life tainted by tragedy. She was out alone after midnight on a rural road. Her family life was sordid; her mother had affairs, her father committed suicide, her mother remarried under a cloud.

Kathryn puts down the folder and thinks for a minute. Then, impulsively, she picks up the phone.

"Do you know what time it is?" Rachel asks in a groggy voice.

"Yes, it's late. I'm sorry, Rachel. I just need one moment."

"Well—all right," she says after a pause.

Kathryn takes a deep breath. "Listen, I need to talk to you about our conversation the other day. Abby Elson mentioned something—"

"Abby?" There's a sharpness in her voice. "What did she say?"

"Not much," Kathryn admits. "But I have a feeling it's connected to what you were saying. Or weren't saying."

"Was there anything . . . specific?"

"No."

"Well . . ." Rachel's voice trails off. "Look, I told you. I'm just not sure what good it does to dredge this up."

"What good does it do to keep it secret?"

She doesn't answer.

"How do you know whoever it is wasn't involved in what happened?" Kathryn persists.

"I—for one thing, he didn't go anywhere. And for another, he told me he didn't know anything."

"Oh," Kathryn says with surprise. "So you talked to him about it."

Rachel sighs. "I should never have said anything to you about this."

Kathryn feels anger flash through her. "I can't believe you didn't tell anyone in the first place."

"Listen, Kath, if you're going to talk to me that way—"

"Rachel—"

"No, I'm sorry," she says, "I have to go. I'll see you at the reunion, okay?" There's a click, and the phone goes dead.

Early the next morning, sitting in the Bagel Shop with a cup of coffee and a sesame bagel with blueberry cream cheese, Kathryn pulls out a notebook and pen. She remembers what her editor at the *News-Sentinel* told her once, when she was stuck on a story: "Just jump in anywhere. Don't think. Write. Get those words on the page, and sooner or later the story will come."

For years, she writes, I have had a recurring dream. Standing on the deck of a cruise ship, I see someone fall overboard and I turn the other way, until the cries for help are swallowed by the sound of the waves and the ship's engine. When I turn back to look, I see only the placid ocean, stretching as far as the eye can see in every direction.

What is violated when someone disappears? A parent's trust, the safe borders of a small town—a town where people walk their dogs down dark streets at midnight, sleep in unlocked houses, pay for coffee on the honor system at the Gulf Station. Sleep is violated, the ease and elasticity of everyday interactions. Casual conversations with strangers. A neighbor's goodwill.

The town lost Jennifer. Not finding her was the same as losing her. The police, with their high-tech equipment, failed her. Her brother, her mother, the search party. The town.

Two men in yarmulkes are sitting at the next table, deep in animated discussion. Kathryn's been watching them for a while, slicing through the air with rigid hands, pounding on the table, before she realizes they're speaking a language she doesn't understand.

I've been feeling this way a lot lately, either not understanding what people are saying, even when it seems I should, or thinking that it makes perfect sense when it's unintelligible.

When I think back over those years and try to make sense of them to myself, whole areas are blotted out, like sunspots in my memory.

We used to play Truth or Dare in Jennifer's attic. "Dare," she always said. "I'd rather take a dare than tell the truth."

I didn't know her. I don't know anyone who did.

And then, finally, she finds a beginning:

I'm going to tell you the story of a girl who disappeared, in the hopes that you might make better sense of it than I can.

"Kath-ryn!" Her mother's voice swims in her head, winnows up toward the surface. "Are you awake?"

Kathryn opens her eyes, blinks a few times, squints at the clock: 7:15 A.M. "No," she mumbles, shutting her eyes and falling back on her pillow. She hears her mother pattering up the stairs, and then she feels a soft thwack on the bed. She looks up. Her mother is standing there wearing an old University of Virginia T-shirt and shorts, with an artificially bright smile on her face. "Page one," she says, gesturing toward the paper. "Pretty darn good. There's a picture and everything. Your grandma called, said she told you you'd find a way in. Whatever that means."

Kathryn struggles up onto one elbow, reaches for the paper. There's her story, just above the fold on the right-hand side. TEN YEARS LATER, A QUESTION STILL HAUNTS THE CLASS OF '86: WHAT HAPPENED TO JENNIFER PELLETIER? Under the headline is an old snapshot of Jennifer, which, with its eighties eye makeup and dangling earrings, now appears as dated as a photo from the fifties. The caption reads: "Missing since June 13, 1986."

Sitting on the bed, Kathryn's mother pats her legs under the thin cotton blanket. "I'm very proud of you, sweetheart," she says. "I have to admit, I wasn't sure you were going to pull this off."

"Thanks, Mom."

"But you did!" She squeezes her knee. "And it's very thought-provoking. The only thing I wonder is—did Linda or Will see this before you handed it in?"

"No, of course not."

"Hmm." Her mother nods, looking slightly troubled.

Ignoring her, Kathryn scans the first paragraph to see if anything has been cut.

"I'm sure they'll be fine about it," her mother continues. "It's just that—you know, some of this is quite personal."

Kathryn looks up. "That's the point."

"I know, dear." Kathryn goes back to reading the piece. "But there's personal and there's invasive," her mother says, "and I just think it's a very fine line. People's feelings are involved. Which is not to say that I don't think you've done an excellent job here, because I do. But I just wonder if you needed to be quite so . . . provocative about some things."

"I never said she was having an affair."

"And you never said Pete committed suicide, but the implication is there. I just wish you'd thought about the whole picture, is what I'm saying. Linda may have moved, but we still have some mutual friends, you know, and this could be a little awkward." She laughs nervously.

"Mom, you knew I was writing this," Kathryn says, sitting up and tossing the paper to the foot of the bed. "You talked me into it."

"Well, I know," her mother concedes. "I guess I had a different idea of what it would be."

In the next room the telephone rings, and then downstairs, in a faint echo. As long as Kathryn can remember, the phones have never been in sync. They look at each other while it rings again. "Are you going to answer that?" Kathryn asks.

"Let's let the machine get it." Her mother bites her lip, waiting for the click.

"Hello, is anybody there? It's a little early on a Saturday to be out, isn't it? Or late to be sleeping!" Kathryn's father chuckles, then clears his throat. "Well, Sally, as I'm sure you've guessed, I'm calling about Katy's article in the paper today. Front page, very impressive. I assume they pay well for that. Hope they know the value of talent when they see it."

Kathryn's mother is shaking her head with her lips pursed and her eyes closed, as if she's in pain. She can't stand it when he talks about money. Flinging back the covers, Kathryn bounds off the bed and runs into the next room. "Hello?" she says breathlessly into the phone.

"Hello?"

"Hi, Dad, it's me."

"What were you, asleep?"

"Talking to Mom."

"Well, I won't interrupt. I just wanted to congratulate you on a job well done."

"Thanks."

"I didn't realize that girl was so unstable," he says. "If I'd known, I never would have allowed you to spend so much time with her." He says it like he's kidding, but Kathryn can tell he means it. "So what do you think?" he demands. "Did she run off to join a cult?"

"Maybe," Kathryn says, not wanting to engage him. "What do you think?"

"I think it has something to do with the mystery boyfriend. Or possibly the brother. But you like him, right?"

"Yeah. Why would you think he's involved?"

"Oh, it could be some kind of gay thing. That's Margaret's theory."

"Really." Kathryn looks up; her mother is standing in the doorway. She rolls her eyes. "That's interesting. Well, I've got to go, Dad."

"Sure, okay," he says. "But just tell me one thing: Is this going to be a regular gig?"

"I think Jack wants a couple more pieces."

"What about after that?"

"I don't know."

"Think you can parlay this into some kind of job?"

"I don't know," she says again, resisting the pressure in his voice, trying to keep it light. "I don't know if I want to."

"Might be nice to have a steady paycheck."

"Yeah. Well, listen, Dad, thanks for calling."

"Sure. Oh, hey, Margaret says hi, too."

"Great."

"We're expecting you to solve this thing, Katy!" he says. "Don't leave us hanging!"

"Okay, Dad. Talk to you soon."

When she hangs up the phone, her mother says, "What a jerk."

"You didn't even hear anything," Kathryn says.

"I heard enough."

Kathryn doesn't answer. Her mother is still so bitter, it makes her resent them both—her father for acting like a jerk, and her mother for pointing it out.

Her mother looks at her watch. "I've got a showing later this morning, so I think I might do some errands while I've got an hour. I need mulch for the garden. Anything I can get for you?"

"Hmm." Kathryn pretends to think. "I could use a husband and a high-powered job, if you happen to run across any while you're out."

"Oh, that's right—your reunion is tonight, isn't it?"

"Ay-uh," she says in her best Maine accent.

"A little nervous?"

"Nah. I'm going there on assignment, like a reporter in Bosnia. It's not my war."

Her mother grins. "Keep telling yourself that. What are you wearing?"

"I was thinking flak jacket, combat boots. Maybe a bulletproof vest."

"You might want to bring a helmet," her mother suggests. "Just in case they aim for your head."

HER HEAD FEELS slick and oily, like a seal's. The conditioner smells of eucalyptus. "It's all natural," Lena, the Norwegian hairdresser, is saying. "Exactly what you need to repair this damage. We sell it up front for eleven ninety-five." Kathryn looks up to see Lena descending on her with a towel. "Let's see what we can do with you," Lena says, vigorously scrubbing her head.

Both of them scrutinize Kathryn's reflection in the mirror. Her face is pasty and her hair hangs down in wet red clumps, a thin skunk stripe of brown at the top. Next to Lena, who is tan and blond, she looks distinctly unwell. She wishes she'd at least worn makeup—lipstick, anything.

"You did this to yourself?" Lena asks, frowning at Kathryn's part.

"Yeah. You can tell, huh?"

"It's brassy." She peers closer. "And see this breakage here? And here?" she says, holding up the frayed ends.

Kathryn nods. "Can you fix it? My mother says you're a wizard at this."

Drying her hands on a towel, Lena shakes her head. "I can't turn a pigeon into a swan!" She laughs. "I saw that once on David Copperfield. He's amazing. And so good-looking." She purses her lips at Kathryn's reflection. "But maybe we can do something. What do you want?"

Kathryn looks at Lena, with her tanning-booth glow and shining white-blond hair, and suddenly she knows. "I want to look like you," she says.

AN HOUR AND a half later, when Kathryn gets to her car, there's a manila envelope with "KATHRYN CAMPBELL" written on it in capital letters propped on the front seat. She opens the envelope and pulls out a black Maxell cassette. She turns it over; it's unlabeled. She upends the envelope and a color photograph falls onto her lap. Picking it up, she looks at it closely. The picture is wrinkled and out of focus, and at first it's hard to tell what it is. In the foreground is a blurry hand, as if someone is trying to hide from the photographer. Behind the hand Kathryn can see a swing of blond hair, part of a cream-colored sweater, a sliver of faded jeans. The girl in the photo appears to be in some sort of clearing, surrounded by pine trees and some distant birches. No sky is visible.

It's Jennifer, of course. Kathryn recognizes the sweater and the hair. She turns the photo over; the back is blank.

Her hands are trembling, and her fingertips are cold. She picks up the cassette again, slips it into the tape slot, fumbles in her shoulder bag for her car keys, and turns the key in the ignition. After a moment, a girl's voice says, "What do you want me to say? Testing one, two, three." The girl giggles. "Don't just make me talk. Tell me what to say." Then the voice ends abruptly, and a song begins. The opening strains are familiar, but Kathryn can't quite place it until the ragged voice starts singing: *"Every time I think of you I always catch my breath / And I'm standing here, and you're miles away / And I'm wondering why you left . . . "*

It's that song from high school, the one Jennifer used to call her anthem, the one she used for her yearbook quote. Kathryn listens to it for a moment, then fast-forwards to the end of the song to see if there's anything else on the tape. Silence. She pushes the reverse button and stop-rewinds through the other side. It's blank.

At the police station, it takes Lieutenant Gaffney a moment to recognize Kathryn. "Well, I'll be darned," he says, when he finally does. "What are you trying to do, go undercover? You look like a different person."

She shrugs self-consciously. "I needed a change."

"Oh. Well, it's a change all right. I wouldn't have recognized you in a lineup." He listens to her story carefully, interrupting to ask questions, and pulls on latex gloves before he handles the photograph. "I'll send this to the lab to see if we can get anything off it. You touched it with your bare hands?"

"Yes," she admits. "Stupid. Sorry."

"I doubt there were any prints on it anyhow. Whoever left this stuff in your car was pretty careful. There's not much in the picture to pin it to a time or place." He holds the photo under a bright desk lamp, studying it carefully. "But I'd say this is probably contemporaneous with the disappearance," he says after a moment. "The photo's faded, and the clothing appears dated."

"I recognize the sweater. She wore it all the time senior year."

He squints at the photo, holding it up to his nose. "Looks like early spring. It's hard to tell with the pines, but that birch behind there doesn't have leaves yet." Tracing a faint line down the photo with his finger, he muses, "And the light is cold. There might even be snow on the ground. We'll get this blown up and see if we can get any clues as to where it is." He slips the photo back into the envelope and puts the envelope into a clear plastic bag. "Now let's hear that tape," he says. He leads her to the back of the station, into a small room with a so-phisticated recording system on one wall. When he puts the tape in and Jennifer starts talking, a strip of small red lights jump and flash.

"Tell me what to say."

Gaffney rewinds the tape.

"What do you want me to say? Testing one, two three." He rewinds again. *"Testing one, two, three."*

"Can you hear that tremor? She's nervous," he says. "Eager to please."

The tape rolls; Jennifer giggles. *"Don't just make me talk. Tell me what to say."*

"She looks up to this person," Gaffney says. "She's intimidated by him."

"You think it's a he?"

"I'm guessing. If it were a woman, or a girl, she'd probably have more of an edge in her voice. You know, like 'This is stupid.' I doubt she'd be this hesitant." Gaffney adjusts some knobs—turns up the treble, turns down the bass—and they listen to it again. This time, at a higher pitch, the voice sounds quavery. Kathryn can hear the anxiety in it. Flipping a switch, Gaffney mutes the voice, amplifies the background noise. A bird calls, another answers. A horn sounds twice.

"That's not a car," Gaffney says. He replays it at a lower speed. "It's not a truck either." He sits forward, his head cocked to one side, listening to it again. "That's a train," he says. "They're outside, near some tracks. And if this recording of her voice was made when the photograph was taken, they were in a wooded area somewhere." He adjusts the controls so that Jennifer's voice is audible again. "Yep," he says, "I'd say this was made a long time ago, and then transferred onto this tape. Hear how scratchy it is? Also, she sounds young, like a teenager."

When the song comes on, it fills the room.

"What do you think this is all about?" Gaffney asks.

"It was a big hit when we were in high school," Kathryn tells him. "For a while Jennifer was kind of obsessed with it. She used part of it for her yearbook quote."

They listen in silence for a moment. *"I spend my time thinking about you / And it's almost driving me wild . . ."*

"Did she associate this song with anybody in particular?"

"I don't think so." Kathryn tries to remember. "She must have had some kind of emotional connection to it, but it probably didn't mean much. We overreacted to pretty much everything."

Gaffney is holding up the flat of his hand, signaling her to stop talking. "Wait a minute. I want to hear that again," he says. He rewinds the tape, stops, runs it back a little more. *"There's a message in the wild and I'm sending you the signal tonight / You don't know how desperate I've become and it looks like I'm losing this fight . . ."*

The song plays to the end, and then there's an audible click. "Anything else on the tape?" Gaffney asks.

Kathryn shakes her head.

Holding his chin in his hand, he looks at her. "Somebody is trying to scare you," he says.

"Well, it's working." She laughs nervously.

"I guess that article you wrote smoked him out."

"So what do I do now?"

Gaffney leans back in his chair. "Well, number one, don't publish another story until you run it by me. You made some inferences I'm not sure it was wise for you to make. Remember, Miss Campbell," he says, hunching over the desk, "We don't know what we're dealing with here. This case is wide open. You could be putting yourself in danger by messing around in it." He sighs. "Try to think now. Is there anyone—anyone you know—who might have sent this to you?"

She looks up at the ceiling tiles above their head, gray and porous like the surface of the moon. "I really don't know."

"Well, be careful," Gaffney says. "We don't know what this person is capable of." He gets up, adjusting his belt with both hands. He isn't smiling, but Kathryn can tell he's pleased. "This could prove to be quite a break in the case," he says, walking her to the front desk, "but it has to be handled right. If anything out of the ordinary happens, anything at all, I want you to call me right away. Do you understand?"

"Yes," she says, "I understand."

At the door to the police station, Kathryn looks out at her car, parked fifty feet away. Then she glances up and down the street. A moon-faced woman is sitting in a pickup, tapping her fingers on the dash. Two boys walk by, a golden retriever trotting behind them. None of them so much as notices her. It's an ordinary Saturday, and people are going about their business as they normally do. She goes out to her car, unlocks the door, and gets in, locking it again before she starts the engine.

———

WHEN KATHRYN GETS home from the police station, in midafternoon, two lights are blinking on the answering machine.

"Hey, Kathryn, this is Jack," the first message says. "I'm trying to round up the gang for drinks at the Sea Dog before the party tonight. Your piece in the paper might've ruffled a few feathers, but I'm sure we can all put that aside for the evening and have a good time. For old times' sake, right? So five o'clock. Hope to see you then."

After the second beep, there's silence for a moment. Then a girl's voice is saying, "God, I feel stupid. I hate it when you make me do this." It's Jennifer again—Kathryn knows instantly. "Besides, what are you going to do with it?" In the background a low voice, barely audible, answers. "Just keep it for yourself?" The girl giggles. "Isn't that a little weird?" The message ends.

Kathryn stands over the machine, staring at it as if it might provide an explanation. She rewinds the message and listens to it again. *"What are you going to do with it? Just keep it for yourself?"* Panic, like quicksilver, runs through her veins. "Mom? MOM?" she calls, but then she remembers: Her mother has gone away for the night with Frank. "Think," she says aloud. She picks up the phone and calls 911, and after a few transfers she's talking to Gaffney. She plays the message for him, holding the receiver up to the tiny answering-machine speaker. As soon as it's finished she asks, "What should I do?"

"Well, first thing, bring the tape in," he says. "And then go to your reunion." There's excitement in his voice; she can hear it. "I know this is unsettling for you, Miss Campbell, but I have to tell you, it's a major development in the case. We've had more action today than we've had in the past ten years."

At 5:15 P.M. the Sea Dog is packed, and there's a line snaking out the front door. Kathryn walks past the PLEASE WAIT TO BE SEATED sign and wanders through the bar area, past the tables surrounding the small stage where a three-piece band is playing "Devil in a Blue Dress," and out onto the deck. It's a humid afternoon, and several women are fanning themselves with menus and complaining about the heat.

Kathryn already feels sticky, though she took a shower an hour ago. The outfit she's wearing—a cream-colored silk vest and brown-and-cream palazzo pants raided from her mother's closet—doesn't quite fit, and she keeps having to adjust her bra strap surreptitiously to keep it from showing. For the first time in months she's wearing shoes with narrow heels, a pair of her mother's strappy sandals, and she feels as if she's tottering on stilts. Her mother's Lancôme foundation, clearly intended for a different type of skin, feels like fingerpaint on her face.

Scanning the deck, Kathryn finally sees people she recognizes. Jack and Rachel are sitting alone at a table for six in a secluded corner, engaged in animated conversation. Kathryn threads her way over to them through the closely packed tables. "Hey, you guys," she says.

They glance up at her, and then their eyes go wide. After an awkward silence, Jack says, "Oh, my God." Rachel looks down, shaking her head. She takes a sip of what looks like iced tea and stares out at the water, avoiding Kathryn's eyes.

"What are you trying to do?" Jack says quietly, a funny smile on his face.

"What do you mean?"

"You look . . ." His voice falters. "You look just like her."

"What?"

"You look like Jennifer."

"*What?*"

Jack half laughs. "You just went blond for the hell of it?"

Kathryn steps back. Rachel still won't look up. "I—didn't . . ." A wave of shame washes over her, and she mumbles, "I'm sorry," and turns around, stumbling through the crowd and back into the restaurant, and then out the front to the dusty parking lot.

As she stands at the drivers' side of her car, pawing through her borrowed cream-colored leather bag for the keys, she feels a hand on her arm. She jumps.

"I didn't mean to startle you," Jack says. "But I don't want you to leave."

She finds the keys and tries to unlock the car, but her hands are shaking, and she drops the keys in the dirt. Jack bends down and scoops them up in his hand, making a fist around them. "Nope, you're not going," he says, holding the keys out of reach.

She halfheartedly attempts to grab them. "Just let me go."

"No."

"This was a bad idea." She leans against the car and shuts her eyes. When she opens them, Jack is looking at her curiously.

"Which part?"

She thinks for a moment. Her face feels hot and filmy. Pushing out her bottom lip, she blows air, making her bangs flutter. "Coming here. Going to the reunion. Writing that article. Coming home. Getting married. You name it."

"You forgot the hair." He smiles and pokes her gently in the ribs.

"Fuck you, Jack."

"Now, now—"

"I wasn't trying to— Forget it, I'm not even going to try. Give me my keys." She holds up her palm.

Clasping his hands behind his back, he says, "Listen. I'm sorry. It's just a little shocking to see you like this, because honest to God, Kathryn, you look like her, and it's hard to believe you didn't intend it. Not that it matters anyway—you can do whatever the hell you want. But you know, with the article and everything . . ."

Kathryn kicks at the dirt with her sandals, covering her newly polished toes with a fine brown powder. "I don't know why I did it," she mumbles. "I wasn't thinking."

He nods.

"What's up with Rachel?" she says, thinking about the expression of disgust on her face. It couldn't have been just the hair.

"She's kind of pissed at you. She'll get over it. She's mortified that all of Bangor knows she used to have a crush on Brian." He rolls his eyes. "So what. The story is strong. Provocative, gutsy. It's a really good piece of writing."

She smiles cautiously.

"I've been trying to reach you all day to tell you that, but you were never home."

"Well . . ." She debates whether to tell him now. She had planned to wait. "Some strange stuff happened," she says. "Someone left an envelope in my car with a picture of Jennifer and a tape of her voice and her favorite song from high school. And when I got home, her voice was on the machine."

"She called?" Jack says sharply.

Kathryn shakes her head. "I think it's old. A tape from a long time ago."

"What did you— Did you talk to—"

"I took everything to Gaffney at the police station. He's having it analyzed."

"It could be a prank."

"Yeah."

"Or it could be from her, right?"

"Gaffney doesn't think so. Someone was trying to get her to talk into a tape recorder, and she was sort of resisting. It doesn't seem like something she'd send."

"And the song?"

" 'Missing You,' by John Waite."

He makes a face of amused disgust. "Really?"

"She used it for her yearbook quote."

Leaning back against her car, he says, "Wow. I guess that article had an effect, didn't it?"

"I guess so."

"That's good."

"Right."

He looks at her intently. "You need to be careful."

She nods.

"I got you into this, didn't I?"

"Yep," she says.

"So do you hate me now?"

"Well, I'll tell you this," she says, tapping her foot against the front tire to get off the dirt. "If I disappear, I'm taking you with me."

He pretends to think about it. "I could be up for that," he says.

BY THE TIME they get back to the table on the deck, Will and Brian have arrived. "We saw you two deep-throating in the parking lot and decided to leave you alone," Brian says, standing up to give Kathryn a kiss on the cheek and shake Jack's hand. Brian looks a little different than she remembers; it takes her a moment to realize it's the glasses, gold-framed ovals. They've transformed his look from just plain nerdy to nerdy-hip. She sees him glance at her hair, but he doesn't say anything.

Will stands up, too, and reaches across the table to cuff Kathryn on the shoulder. "Hey, you. Quite a change."

"Yeah," she says.

"Suits you. I like it."

"Thanks."

Rachel gazes at Kathryn and then looks down.

Craning his neck to look around, Jack says, "Has anyone seen the goddamn waiter? He took my beer away."

"What are you doing here?" Kathryn asks Will. "I thought you were in charge of this thing tonight."

"I am, I'm in complete control," Will says. "Everything's all set to go."

"Aren't you supposed to be handing out name tags at the door or something?" Rachel asks.

Will slaps his forehead. "Name tags! Damn!" Then he laughs. "Remember Daphne Cousins? Class treasurer? She's way into all this stuff, so I'm letting her run with it." He glances at his watch. "I'll head over there in a while."

"Delegating always was one of your special skills," says Brian. "Remember that time I ended up washing your mother's car because you had a date with Laura Sanford? How did that happen?"

"Like everything else. I bribed you."

"How can you guys remember this stuff? I have a hard time remembering what I had for lunch," Jack says.

"Old grudges die hard," Brian says. "And—oh, yeah—we drank your beer, buddy. It was getting warm anyway."

Jack flags down a waiter and orders a Geary's. "Normally I'd order something decent," he tells the waiter, motioning toward Brian with his thumb, "but this guy works for Geary's, and I feel sorry for him."

"Don't do me any favors," Brian says. "We were just voted number one in New England in a blind taste test."

"Deaf, dumb, and blind," Will says.

They all laugh. "Why, I oughta . . ." Brian says, making a fist and pumping it in the air.

"Where's your little honey?" Jack asks Brian, settling back in his chair. "I thought we were going to meet her tonight."

"Couldn't do it," Brian says. "I was afraid if she met you guys before the wedding, she might call it off."

"Wise man," Will says.

The air is less humid now. A breeze ruffles the water, and waiters move around the deck with trays of lit votive candles, putting one on each table. For a moment all of them are silent. Rachel has her feet up on the railing and is looking out over the water, Jack is pouring his beer into a glass, Brian adjusts his glasses, taking them off and putting them on again. Will takes a sip of his root beer and puts it down. Just as the moment is stretching into awkwardness, he says, "I want to get this out in the open and be done with it." He looks at Kathryn. "I'm sure you all saw the story in the paper this morning. There was some sensitive stuff in there."

Out of the corner of her eye, Kathryn can see Rachel nodding.

"My mother hasn't seen it yet, but she probably won't be too happy about some of the things that came out," Will says. "Then again, she refused to be interviewed, so she doesn't have much of a right to complain."

"I didn't refuse," Rachel says in a bitter voice. "Hell, I invited her into my house. And then she fixates on petty high-school bullshit—" She stops, turning her face away and putting up her hand. "I promised myself I wasn't going to get into it tonight."

"No, this is good. Let's clear the air a little," Will says.

Kathryn starts to speak, but Jack touches her leg under the table. "Can I say something?" he asks mildly. "I assigned this piece because I really want to know where Jennifer is. I think we all do. I think it's very important," he says, looking at Rachel, "that we learn as much as possible about Jennifer's state of mind in the weeks and months before she disappeared. That may mean getting into some petty high-school bullshit."

"Oh, come on," Rachel snaps. "That stuff about the prom was completely irrelevant."

"I don't think so, Rachel," Kathryn says.

"Well, of course *you* don't."

Kathryn feels her face flush. "Jennifer used Brian, and she hurt you. It was totally out of character."

"I just don't think you need to dredge up every little squabble," Rachel says. "I don't see what good it does anyone."

"Well, if you'd tell me the name of the guy she was seeing, maybe I'd have something real to go on."

"Hold on, hold on," Will says.

Rachel ignores him, shakes her head. "You're just jealous she confided in me," she tells Kathryn.

"Maybe I am," Kathryn says. "So what? You're still holding back an important piece of information."

"Important to whom? The general public? I don't think so. It's all about the *story* now, isn't it? It's not really about Jennifer at all."

"Okay, time out," Will says, making a T with his hands. They both turn to look at him. "What do you know, Rachel?"

"Nothing." She folds her arms in disgust. "She's blown this way out of proportion."

"Blown what way out of proportion?"

Rolling her eyes, she says, "This is so ridiculous I can't believe I even have to engage it. I said one little off-the-cuff thing and suddenly it's this big deal. Well, listen," she says, reaching into the shoulder bag hanging over the back of her chair and pulling out her wallet, "I refuse to let this spoil my reunion." She finds a five-dollar bill and drops it on the table. Then she stands up. "I'm heading over there now. I'll see you guys later."

Jack reaches up and touches her arm. "Rachel, Rachel," he says lightly. "Jeez. Sit down."

She pulls away. "No."

"Is this how it's going to be all night, each of us getting insulted about something and storming off? C'mon, Rach. Sit down. Okay? Sit down."

She stands there for a moment, like a deer sniffing the wind. Then, reluctantly, she sits on the edge of her seat.

"Good. Okay," Jack says.

"I'm sorry, Jack, but I don't think you should have assigned this piece to her," Rachel says stiffly. "I don't think she has any distance."

"That's the idea. She isn't supposed to," he says.

"I think it's a mistake."

"Objection sustained," Will says, slapping his hand on the table. He looks at Kathryn sharply, as if to say *We'll talk about this later*, and changes the subject.

AT MILLER'S RESTAURANT, a red-painted one-story building on Outer Main Street, the sign out front that usually advertises steak and lobster specials says WELCOME CLASS OF '86! Kathryn pulls into the gravel parking lot in a convoy of cars. They scatter to find spaces, and when she parks and gets out, Jack is the first of the group she sees.

"Hang in there," he says as they walk to the entrance.

"She's tough."

"She's a good person, you know that. Just very private."

"I hate the way you stick up for her," Kathryn whispers.

He nudges her with his elbow. "She's right. You are jealous."

"I didn't deny it."

Inside the restaurant a hand-lettered sign points them to the left, where two vaguely familiar women and a bald man Kathryn doesn't recognize are presiding over a table of name tags and collecting money in a black tin box. Through the closed doors behind them, Jefferson Starship can be heard singing *"We built this city . . . "*

"Jack Ledbetter!" one of the women trills.

"Daphne, how's it going?" he says.

"Have you seen Will?" she asks, looking worriedly at the clock above the door. "He said he'd be here by six-thirty, and it's almost seven."

"He's right behind us. Daphne, you remember Kathryn Campbell . . . ?"

"Sure. Hello, Kath. How are you?"

"I'm fine, thanks, Daphne. How are you?"

"Good, good." Daphne raises her eyebrows. "Boy, you look different."

"You, too." It's true; Daphne's put on weight. Kathryn smiles.

"I saw your story in the paper this morning," Daphne says. "Quite a reminder."

"I hope it'll help turn something up."

"I hope so, too. I really do. It's just that . . ." Her voice trails off.

"What?" Kathryn asks.

"I just feel—well, I guess I shouldn't say anything." Daphne's eyes dart around at her companions at the table, who are looking elsewhere. Clearly, they've been talking about it. "And I hope they find her, I really do. I just feel it's a shame that our class reunions always have to be linked with this," she says. "Sorry. That's just how I feel."

Kathryn glances at Jack, who nods empathetically. "I know. It sucks," he says. "But it's important for us to keep it on the table. And look at it this way: It does put us on the map. Why else would anyone remember the class of 'eighty-six?"

"Well, I, for one," says Daphne, putting her hand to her chest, "have plenty of reasons. There's a lot more to our class than just this one weird thing that happened. But that's just how I feel." She glares at her friends. "I can't speak for anybody else."

Jack nods again, and everyone else stands around awkwardly. The bald guy smiles at Kathryn as if he's been waiting for a break and holds out a large sticker. "I found your name tag," he says. "I don't know if you remember me, Kath, but I'm Pete Michaud. I used to do magic tricks at assemblies."

"Oh, yeah!" She does remember; she loved those magic tricks—doves out of top hats, handkerchiefs out of his throat. She peels the paper backing off the name tag and puts it on her chest.

"That'll be twenty dollars, including the buffet," he says almost apologetically.

"So what are you up to these days?" she asks, bending over the table to write a check.

"Still performing. I have a couple of gigs around town. That's my card right there," he says, pointing at a stack on the table. "Course, I'm working at Wal-Mart to pay the rent. But I'm saving up to go to this magicians' expo in Vegas this fall. Should make a lot of contacts there."

"That's great," she says, tearing off the check and handing it to him. She takes a card. "If I ever need a magician . . ."

"You never know!" he says.

"I just had to speak my mind," Daphne breaks in. "No hard feelings."

"No hard feelings," Jack says with a big smile, taking Kathryn's elbow and steering her toward the banquet room. As they open the double doors, "Freeway of Love" comes blasting out.

The large room, with its red-patterned carpeting and red-vinyl-seated chairs, is decorated with crepe-paper ribbons and multicolored balloons. WELCOME CLASS OF '86! is spelled out across one wall in gilt cardboard letters, like a child's birthday decoration. There is no discernible theme. Several long tables, joined together and covered with white paper cloths, hold three punch bowls the size of aquariums and platters of what looks like cubed cheese. At the far end of the room, behind the empty dance floor, a disc jockey wearing mirrored sunglasses and an Ozzy Osborne T-shirt sits in the middle of a complicated sound system. The cash bar is mobbed with people.

"Okay, I'm here. Now can I leave?" Kathryn says.

"No way. We're gonna boogie all night," Jack says with a grin, swiveling his hips and pointing his fingers skyward.

"Then I need a drink."

They make their way over to the bar, Jack glad-handing people all the way. He's not even wearing a name tag, but everybody knows who he is.

"Ever thought of running for office?" Kathryn says as they wait for her vodka tonic.

"Nah. I'm a newspaper guy."

"It must get oppressive sometimes, being so known."

He looks at her with amusement. "You have turned into an old recluse, haven't you?"

"Oh, my God, it is you," a woman says, clutching Kathryn's arm. "I didn't recognize you at first. I'll have to get Chip over here!"

Kathryn looks at her name tag; it says Donna (Murphy) Sanborn. Then she follows Donna's gaze to several yards away, where Chip is slapping backs with a group of guys.

"We'll catch his eye in a minute," Donna says. She turns back to Kathryn. "He told me about your little chat on the plane." Her mouth falls into a pout. "Sorry to hear about your divorce."

"Thanks," Kathryn says. "Your husband was very sweet about it."

"He is a sweetie." Donna looks over at him fondly.

"And it sounds like his business is going great."

"Yep, it sure is. But he leaves his socks lying around everywhere, and he forgets to take out the trash. So he isn't perfect. But I love him anyway."

Kathryn feels a pang, envying the casual way Donna stakes her claim for him. Kathryn had never felt she could do that with Paul. Even when they'd been in love, it was never something they casually announced to people. Their bond always seemed too fragile, somehow, to withstand public scrutiny.

"Kath Campbell." All at once Chip is at her elbow with a big smile. "Long time no see."

"We were talking about you, honey. Were your ears burning?" Donna playfully pinches his waist. Pulling Kathryn closer, she says, "When you're ready to start dating again, let us know. Chip works with a couple of real cuties."

"I guess it's a little soon," Kathryn says, "but I appreciate the thought."

"By the way," says Donna, "that was a very moving piece you wrote. Jennifer was pretty screwed up, huh? I had no idea. I always thought she was Little Miss Perfect."

"Well, I guess if you scratched the surface of most of us—" Kathryn begins, bridling a little at Donna's blunt assessment.

"I'm going to be doing some business with your mom," Chip breaks in. "Did she tell you?"

"Not yet. But I haven't seen her much lately."

"She's a real dynamo, your mom."

"Yes, she is," Kathryn agrees. Smile and nod, smile and nod. She's lost Jack; he's off talking to someone else, a skinny guy wearing a Dysart's Truck Stop baseball cap. In the distance she can see Abby Elson talking to Tim Peavey, the guy who sent Jennifer all those love notes and thought he was her boyfriend. Kathryn catches her eye, and Abby looks away. Over at the hors d'oeuvre table, Brian is impaling a piece of cheese on a toothpick and Rachel's looking around for something edible. Will is nowhere to be seen; Daphne must have corralled him for table duty in the lobby.

"Well, whaddaya know, Kathryn Campbell," someone says, tapping her on the arm, and she turns to find Matt Rosen, the poetry editor of *Ramifications*, smiling at her with exaggerated surprise. Though his hair is shorter and he seems to be taller, he's dressed exactly as he was in high school, down to the oversized glasses, blue-striped button-down, and belt pulled one notch too tight.

"Hi, Matt," she says warmly. She and Matt had spent hours together after school, laying out pages and editing copy, and she's immediately at ease with his sly, intimate manner.

"I wouldn't have taken you for the marrying type," he says, grasping her hand with the ring on it.

"I must not be," she says with a rueful smile. "I'm divorced."

"Ah, then this is armor. Good strategy, with all these single guys milling around who used to have wild crushes on you."

"Really? Where?" she says, pretending to look around.

"Well, at least one." He grins and kisses her hand. "You're more stunning than ever. Divorce becomes you."

"You sure know how to flatter a girl," she says.

Matt heads off to buy her a refill. Chip and Donna have drifted away. Kathryn steps back, leaning a shoulder against the red flocked wallpaper, and looks around at her classmates. She sees a succession of people she'd just as soon not run into: a lacrosse player she had a one-night stand with; an odd guy whose freaky submissions to the literary magazine she'd summarily rejected; a girl she'd actually been pretty good friends with whom she hadn't thought about since graduation. Age and experience are recorded differently on each face—some are fleshier, some fit, some shockingly older, some virtually unchanged. There's Mindy Miller, Best Smile, with adult braces on her teeth to preserve her winning feature. There's Sean McCarthy, captain of the losing hockey team senior year, tan and buff, with a pretty little wife from somewhere else. Over by the deejay Kathryn sees three shy and awkward girls, best friends in high school, plainer and puffier now and uncomfortably dressed, furtively smoking cigarettes.

She has forgotten most of these faces, and she doesn't remember many names. But in a way, she thinks, scanning the crowd, these people know her better than anyone she's met since. They knew her every day, for years on end, before she figured out how to camouflage and reinvent herself, before she developed guile. In this world she'll always be Kath Campbell, lit-mag editor and best friend of Jen Pelletier, foot soldier in various sports and activities, with several forgettable short-term romances, a pitiable singing voice, and no memory for jokes. As an adult she can lie by omission, but in high school she tried it all—to see what she was good at, to know what to avoid.

With a little shock, she realizes how little it probably matters to these people what she's doing—or not doing—with her life. Everybody's been through something. She's heard that Karen Stevenson, who made fun of Kathryn's bargain-basement clothes in eighth grade, has an autistic child. Mark Farrington's sister was killed by a hit-and-run driver as she walked home from school. Barry Ballou was diagnosed with Hodgkin's and zapped with chemo; when his hair grew back, it was completely white. And on and on. Everybody has a story, and every story contains disappointment and heartache—if not yet, then to come. She remembers something a friend in Virginia told her once, when Kathryn was lamenting the sad state of her life. "People get it backwards," Renee had said. "They take good times for granted, expect that's the way life should be, which isn't the case at all. Life *is* the hard stuff—the deaths and tragedies and divorces. The rest is a fluke, an aberration. A lucky break."

"That's cheerful," Kathryn had remarked, but now it occurs to her that in a funny way it is. Why not assume the worst, and be pleasantly surprised? It can't be harder than being perpetually disappointed.

"Well, well, well," someone behind her says in a low voice. "More superficial changes."

She turns around. It's Mr. Hunter, with a curious smile.

"What are you doing here?" she asks.

"You're not content just to follow her. You want to become her."

She starts to respond defensively, then stops herself. She looks at him, at the challenge in his eyes, and something shifts in her mind. "Maybe so."

"It's convincing," he says. "I almost believe it." Appraising her slowly, he says, "The blond hair does bring out something different in you. I'm not sure what."

She sips her drink, watches him watching her.

"You seem bolder."

"I feel bolder."

"Oh?"

Her head is beginning to spin. Billy Ocean is singing "Caribbean Queen" in a seductive voice. *Watch it,* she thinks. "What are you doing here?" she asks again.

"I always go to these things. I take a perverse pleasure in watching my students age."

"Must make you feel old."

"No, quite the contrary. I'm like Dorian Gray." He laughs. "All of you get older. I just stay the same."

Scrutinizing the lines around his eyes, his sun-weathered skin, she says, "Don't fool yourself."

He smiles.

"No family. No ties," she ventures. "What's with that?"

Now he takes a drink, ice clicking against his teeth as he upends the plastic cup. "You don't know my story," he says.

"I know a little. You've never been married. You live alone on a lake outside of town. You've taught at the high school since you left college."

"Grad school," he says.

"Okay," she says. "Still. Didn't you ever want to do anything different?"

He looks up at the ceiling, festooned with ribbons, and purses his lips. "I don't think I want to be having this discussion with you. I'm imagining a different conversation."

"About what?"

"Let's talk about you."

"What do you want to know?"

"What are you really looking for?"

"What do you mean?" she says, her heart beating quickly. She's losing the advantage; she can feel it.

He laughs. "Come on. You know what I mean."

"No, really."

"This is not about finding Jennifer Pelletier."

She looks at him, trying to see what he's after, but his eyes are blank, reflecting pools. "What is it, then?" she asks finally, knowing as she does that she's playing his game, hating herself for wanting to hear his answer.

Leaning closer, he says, "I think it's about you, Kathryn. A diversion. A little attention." He shrugs. "You've lost a lot of things recently, haven't you? Your marriage, your job—"

"How do you know this stuff about me?" she snaps.

He smiles, a wide smile with lots of teeth. "Come on, remember where you are. Before long in this town everybody knows everything."

"Then why doesn't anybody know where Jennifer is?"

"I'm sure somebody does."

"You're sure?"

"It's only logical." He shrugs. "Nobody just disappears."

At this moment Rachel walks past and Hunter looks over at her. Kathryn sees a smile pass between them, a slow, private moment.

"How well do you know Rachel?" Kathryn asks him innocently when she's gone.

He shrugs. "How well do I know any of you?"

His words are vaguely familiar, but she isn't sure why. And then she remembers: It's the same thing he said in response to her question about Jennifer that day at the high school. Taking a long swallow, she drains her cup. "I'd guess you know some better than others."

"How well do I know you?"

"You don't," she says. "And what you think you know, you're wrong about. You don't know anything about my motives."

He raises his eyebrows in a skeptical gesture and tilts his head. "I'll say one thing, Kathryn. You're more interesting than I thought." Reaching out and taking her cup, he says, "You need a new drink."

"Someone's getting me one," she says. "Anyway, I need to get back to my friends."

"Your 'friends'?" He smiles. "Is that what you call them?"

"I really have to go."

"Just one more thing," he says. "I've been thinking about your being in my class, and why I had trouble remembering who you were. I think it's because Jennifer's presence overwhelmed you. You were never fully formed around her." He looks at her intently. "You're better off without her. You know that, don't you?"

Kathryn stares at him. She doesn't know what to say.

"Go," he says, spreading his arms wide in an extravagant flourish. "We'll meet again, I'm sure."

LATER, AFTER THEY'VE lined up for a buffet dinner of chicken Cordon Bleu and Will has given a short speech welcoming everybody and thanking at least half of them, and the lights have dimmed for an encore presentation of the senior-class video that was shown at their prom, featuring Eddie Valhalla dressed up like a Bangor Ram and the cafeteria ladies singing "Shout" and other highlights and high jinks of the Class of '86 in all its youthful glory, the room begins to clear. Ice melts in scattered cups; plates of half-eaten food litter the round tables, their crepe-paper tablecloths hanging soiled and crumpled like forgotten promises. The carnation centerpieces have been ravaged for buttonhole boutonnieres and makeshift corsages.

"What was *that* all about?" Brian says, stretching, laughing, looking around at the others. The five of them are sitting at a table, picking at a plate of strawberries Rachel managed to snag before the buffet disappeared.

"Chicken and ham," Rachel says, making a face. "Haven't they ever heard of vegetarians? I'm starving."

"I saw you eating those cheese cubes," says Will. "Isn't that enough protein for you?" He shakes his head in mock exasperation. "I work my butt off for you people, and all I get are complaints."

"Well, the deejay was great," Jack says dryly. "Those golden hits of the eighties really brought it back. I think I relived all four years of high school. Promise me we can try something different next time? Even John Tesh would be an improvement."

Brian sits up. "Hey, man, I like John Tesh."

"I saw you hangin' with Mr. Hunter," Will says to Kathryn. "It's too late for grade-grubbing, you know."

Kathryn's eyes meet Rachel's, and then Rachel looks away.

"What did he want?" Jack asks.

"Want?" Sensing a sharpness in his voice, Kathryn gives him a questioning look. "He was just goading me."

"I never liked that guy," Brian says. "I never understood how Jennifer could stand to spend so much time with him."

"It was the club," Will says. "She was way into that back-to-nature stuff."

All at once, with a cold certainty, Kathryn knows. She looks at Rachel. "He's the one. Right?"

"What?" Rachel mumbles.

"The one you wouldn't name. The guy Jennifer was seeing. I don't know why I didn't think of it."

All of them turn to look at Rachel. She doesn't reply. Behind them, the deejay is packing up his equipment. "Karma Chameleon" is blaring from the speakers.

"Is it true?" Will asks.

"I don't know," Rachel says, averting her eyes.

"Jesus fucking Christ," Will says, bounding out of his chair, knocking it over. "Cut the bullshit, Rachel."

"Yes," she says quickly, almost defiantly.

"Yes, what?"

"Yes, Jennifer was having some kind of thing with him. It wasn't that big a deal."

"When?" Will demands.

"Spring of senior year."

"How long have you known this?" Jack asks.

"Look," she says, leaning forward in a conciliatory way. "She asked me not to tell anyone, and I promised." She lets out a heavy sigh. "I found out by accident; I ran into them together one evening when I was going for a run out by Pushaw Lake. So Jennifer kind of had to tell me." She flashes Kathryn a look. "And then, after she disappeared, I didn't see much point in bringing it up. I thought it would make her look bad, divert attention from the real story. I didn't want to complicate the investigation."

"So you withheld information," Will says.

"I didn't think it was anything anyone needed to know about. It was private, between them. I knew that if anyone found out he'd probably lose his job. And people would assume things that weren't true."

"Like what?"

"Like—I don't know. That he might be somehow involved in what happened."

"And how do you know he wasn't?" Brian asks. The light overhead is reflecting in his lenses, and his eyes are hard to read.

Rachel blinks. "I just—I don't believe he was."

"You didn't even tell *me*," Jack says.

She swallows. "I promised I wouldn't tell anybody."

For a moment all of them are silent, taking it in. Will picks up his chair and stands with his arms pressing down on the back of it, as if he's gripping someone's shoulders. "I think I'm going to have a talk with the police," he says finally.

"Oh, come on. That's ridiculous," Rachel says. "This is exactly what Rick was afraid of—that it would all be blown out of proportion."

" 'Rick'?"

"Hunter," she says.

Will lets out a dry, mirthless laugh. "When did you and 'Rick' get so familiar?"

"We've been . . . I've taken up orienteering."

He shakes his head. "So that's how it starts, huh?"

Kathryn touches Will's arm. "Before you contact anybody, I'd like to talk to him again."

Will glances at Jack, who lifts his fingers and shrugs his shoulders.

"I don't know, Kathryn," Will says.

"I'll be careful."

"Careful?" Rachel laughs incredulously. "You guys are way off base on this."

"No," Will snaps. "You're the one who's off base. Protecting that oily piece of shit—"

"I wasn't protecting him. I was protecting Jennifer."

"Yeah, right."

"What is that supposed to mean?" Rachel says.

"Come on," Will says. "You didn't even like Jennifer. She stole Brian out from under your nose—"

"Hey, that's not—" Brian protests.

"Oh, so we're back to this," says Rachel.

"Yes, Rachel," Will says, "it's all about *this*. High school. That's what it's about."

Rachel stands up and looks around at the group. "Well, I'm sorry, I'm not going to be a part of it. You all need to turn him into a scapegoat because Jennifer's still missing and there has to be a logical reason for it—there has to be someone to blame. Well, maybe you're not going to find a reason. Maybe you're just going to have to accept the fact that she's gone, and she's not coming back." She turns to Will. "Anyway, don't you think you should be focusing your energy on your own life right now?"

Will looks at her in disbelief. "Rachel, you are so full of shit," he says.

She grabs her bag off the table, and Jack rises in his chair. "Listen," he says in a low, reasonable tone. "I hope we can trust you to keep quiet about this for now."

"Don't worry," she says. "I wouldn't want to get in the way of all this amateur sleuthing. Besides, Rick can take care of himself. He has nothing to hide."

Jack nods, chin forward, a conciliatory gesture.

"Well," Rachel says bitterly, "happy tenth, everybody." She turns to leave, and Jack touches her arm. "Whoa, slow down," he says, but she flinches away, and he doesn't try to stop her. They all watch her go, banging through the double doors to the lobby.

ON THE WAY out to their cars, Jack says, "So, what are we all doing now?"

Kathryn's head is pounding and she feels slightly sick from the greasy food and vodka tonics and all the recent drama. "Life in the Fast Lane," the song that was playing as they left, is echoing in her ears. "Haven't you had enough for one evening?"

"I'm going to bed," Will says tersely.

"And I have to drive back to Portland," says Brian. "I'm going sailing tomorrow morning at ten."

"That was smart planning," Jack says.

Brian shrugs. "Cindy's dad. You don't say no." He acts put out, but Kathryn can tell he's pleased about it.

"What about you?" Jack asks Kathryn, nudging her shoulder.

She smiles. "I need my beauty sleep."

"You look pretty fine to me."

"Always the charmer," Brian says, rolling his eyes.

"I feel lousy," Kathryn says. "Too much vodka, I guess."

"A coffee would help," says Jack.

She shakes her head. "Sorry."

"Damn, you guys are boring," Jack says.

"Face it, man," Brian says. "We're getting old."

When Will and Brian have gone on ahead, Jack asks, "Are you okay going home by yourself?"

"I'll be all right," Kathryn says. "Thanks."

He nudges her again. "Be careful."

It isn't until Kathryn is on the way home that she begins to feel a little afraid. She looks in the backseat, locks the doors, glances in her rearview mirror to see if anyone is behind her. As she drives through the downtown, the streets are deserted. The traffic lights are blinking, some red, some yellow. Three men are milling around outside the bus station; there's no bus in sight. The storefronts are dark and sad-looking, as if they were abandoned long ago, in a different era. The bank clock says it's 11:41.

She pulls into her mother's driveway and sits there for a few minutes with the motor running, looking up at the dark house. Then, almost without thinking about it, she puts the car in reverse and circles back out onto the quiet street, the wheels squealing slightly as she drives away. She cuts through Little City, slowing through stop signs, taking her foot off the brake as she coasts down the long sinuous stretch of Kenduskeag Avenue, gathering speed as she approaches the bottom of the hill. Taking an abrupt right on Harlow Street, she crosses the river, a gurgling shimmer in the darkness, made barely visible by the dim glow of streetlights. She makes her way up another rise, paralleling the river until the road takes a sharp turn left past a cemetery, and crosses Ohio Street at the top.

Driving at night has the feel of an adventure, a reckless journey into uncharted space. On the dark side streets, up steep inclines and around narrow corners, she can only see as far as the headlights; everything she passes is swallowed up behind. The streets are eerily quiet; the houses she passes are dark blank squares, virtually invisible except for the occasional metallic light of a TV screen.

She wants to drive fast on these roads, to push her foot on the pedal all the way to the floor. There's something about the stillness that makes her want to get wild, scream at the top of her lungs, disappear in a puff of green smoke like the Wicked Witch of the West. She remembers this feeling from high school, when any kind of altered state seemed preferable to the state she was in. The method didn't matter—a fast car, a scary movie, alcohol, sex, drugs—the effect she was after was the same. She wanted to be somewhere, anywhere but where she was. She wanted to surprise herself.

A LITTLE WHILE later Kathryn pulls up in front of Jack's building and sits in the car for a moment before turning it off. Glancing up at the old Harlow Street School building, her eyes go to the second-floor corner, where Jack has told her his apartment is. The windows are dark except for a small glow from somewhere inside. She takes a deep breath and gets out, locking the car behind her.

At the entrance to the building, Kathryn hesitates. Jack may have urged her to go out tonight, but he didn't exactly invite her over. He probably would never have imagined that she'd just drop by—not without calling first, and certainly not this late. She hadn't imagined it, either. She has learned from experience that most people don't like to be dropped in on unannounced. In high school, after she learned to drive, she had made the mistake of assuming that her father's house was also her home, and she showed up there a few times without asking in advance. The first time she didn't even knock; she went straight to the fridge to get a soda. She was sitting at the glass-topped kitchen table drinking Diet Slice out of a can and flipping though a fitness magazine when Margaret rounded the corner with a juice glass, saw Kathryn, and screamed, dropping the heavy glass on the Italian tile floor. It shattered, cracking one of the tiles. The next few times Kathryn had knocked, but it didn't seem to make much difference. Her father and Margaret were always ill at ease, as if she'd caught them doing something illicit. One time it was pretty clear that they'd been having sex; her father came out of the bedroom buttoning his shirt, and Margaret stayed behind the door the entire time Kathryn was there. After that she stopped going out to see them so often, and she usually made appointments in advance when she did. As a result, her visits became carefully orchestrated affairs: three chicken breasts marinating on the counter, place mats and cutlery neatly laid out on the dining-room table, a family movie from the video store sitting in its plastic case on top of the TV.

Kathryn may not have planned on coming to Jack's apartment tonight, but now that she's here she realizes she's been thinking about it for a while. Calling him first seemed too premeditated, and it also risked the possibility that he might hesitate or even say no. She knows that the risk she's taking now is worse—after all, he could shut the door in her face. He could have someone up there with him. But she's willing to chance that he won't, and he doesn't, and this realization emboldens her. She rings the bell.

For a long moment there's no answer. Then she hears a voice from somewhere above. She steps back from the doorway and looks up, and there's Jack, leaning out of one of his windows.

"Hey there," he says with evident surprise.

"I was just driving around . . ." she says. Suddenly she wants to turn around and flee. "I guess it's too late."

"No, it's fine. Just a second, I'll come down." He disappears, and she stands there for a moment. Then she notices that the door isn't completely shut. She pushes it with the flat of her hand and it opens, and she steps inside.

Her footsteps echo in the wide, empty hallway. The overhead lights are dim. She keeps to the right side of the marble steps, sliding her hand along the smooth wooden banister as she makes her way upstairs. At the top she pushes through swinging wooden doors and walks straight into Jack. "Oh, my God," she breathes, clutching her hand to her chest, "you scared me."

"You scared me," he says.

"Sorry. The door was open, and I just—"

"Good," he says, wheeling around. "I like surprises."

Walking down the long hallway beside him, she says, "This is just like detention. Remember that feeling of being kept after school when everybody else has left?"

"Uh-huh." He nods.

"Did you ever even have detention?" she asks curiously.

"No," he admits. "But I can guess."

She shakes her head. "You were too good."

"You were bad," he says. "Getting detention. Skipping school. I remember you back then, Kathryn—making crib sheets for algebra. And didn't you get suspended once?"

"Oh, yeah," she says, remembering. "Mr. Tremble caught Rachel and me drinking Bud Light in her car before a dance. I think it was just one day."

"But your mom grounded you for life."

"Commuted to three weeks for good behavior." She smiles. At the end of the long hall, the door to Jack's apartment is ajar. Kathryn follows him inside and shuts the door. "Anyway, as I remember, you weren't so perfect either," she continues. "You were just lucky."

"I was charming," he says, heading toward the kitchen. "I got away with murder."

Jack's apartment is neat but homey, with a series of black-and-white photographs of weather-beaten houses lining the hall and a large, tattered Oriental in the living area. The two couches are worn and comfortable-looking; the television sits on an old leather suitcase, and a paint-spattered trunk serves as the coffee table. Thrift-store lamps cast a soft glow. The newest thing in the room appears to be the stereo system, which is black and shiny, with a dazzling array of tiny dancing lights.

"Want a Bud Light?" Jack asks, opening the fridge.

"Will I get detention?"

He grabs two long-necked bottles with the fingers of one hand. With the other, he rummages in a cutlery drawer and comes up with a bottle opener. Prying the tops off the beers—Samuel Adams, Kathryn sees—he hands one to her. "It depends."

He looks into her eyes only for a second, but she feels a flutter move through her chest. "On what?" she says.

"On how charming you are." He sits on the edge of the kitchen table, his arms folded, still holding the beer.

"Do you want to be charmed?"

He takes a sip of beer. "Everybody wants to be charmed," he says softly, "whether they know it or not."

She moves closer to him, takes the beer out of his hand, and puts it on the table, placing hers next to it. She looks into his gray-green eyes, and he stares steadily back at her, waiting to see what she'll do. Gently, she traces his cheekbone with her fingers, touching the hard brown stubble on his jaw and the soft fullness of his lips. When she leans forward to kiss him, she smells the beer on his breath and the grassy scent of his shampoo. He reaches up and pulls her toward him, his hand flat on the small of her back. Standing between his legs, holding his face in her hands, she runs her tongue over his teeth and senses his mouth opening, his tongue meeting hers, and then her head is back and he's kissing her ear, her neck, pushing her sleeveless vest off one shoulder and kissing that, too. She moves her hand down his neck to the soft top of his white T-shirt and slides her hand under it. His chest, with its small thatch of brown hair, is taut; she can feel his heart beating hard against her palm.

"Jesus, Kathryn," he breathes. "Are you sure—?"

"Don't talk," she says, closing her eyes and leaning her head against his. He slides his hands under her vest, touching the bare skin underneath, moving them up to her rib cage and higher, until it tickles and she squirms away. He pulls her forward, and she falls heavily against him, her head in his neck, the length of his chest warming hers.

"Just hold me," she whispers, and for a long moment that's all he does. His embrace feels familiar somehow, as if they're reuniting after a long absence instead of coming together for the first time. She is absorbed in the moment in a way she hasn't been in ages, years perhaps. The rest of the world feels very far away. "I know you," she says.

He threads his fingers through her hair, pushing it off her face, and his hand comes to rest on the back of her neck. "I know you, too."

In the dark of his bedroom they trip over her sandals and his jeans with the belt still in them, the buckle clinking against the zipper. His sheets and blanket are crumpled at the foot of the bed, and pillows are strewn on the floor. "I wasn't expecting company," he mumbles, and she doesn't answer; she pushes him onto the bed and climbs on top of him, pulling his T-shirt over his head and leaning down to kiss him, her hair falling in his face, getting in their mouths, until he pulls it back with one hand and topples her off him, rolling over so that she's underneath.

She stretches out, lifting her arms above her head, and he unbuttons her vest, then tries to peel it off, catching it on her shoulder, making them both laugh while he tries to untangle it from her limbs. "Mr. Smooth," he says. "I guess you can tell it's been a while." He traces his finger slowly along the satiny rim of her bra and then he leans down and kisses the top of her breasts, his breath hot on her skin. She runs her hand down the length of his chest and into his jeans, and slips her fingers under the waistband of his shorts. His abdomen is supple and warm—like a dog's stomach, she thinks idly, and when she strokes him he lets out a sigh from somewhere back in his throat, not unlike a dog sound. As he takes off her bra, slipping the straps down her arms, unhooking the back clasp with one deft move, she feels a wave of affection wash over her. Here they are, all wet tongues and noses, nestled together like two furry mammals in a soft, dark bed. He weighs her breasts in his hands and pushes them together, brushing his mouth over her nipples until they're hard, pulling gently on one and then the other with his teeth until she pushes his hand down between her legs and his attention shifts.

When his fingers move inside her she has to catch her breath. Everything falls away except the motion in the darkness. He shifts his hand and the feeling subsides; she moves her hips to show him how to sustain it. All at once her head is light, her limbs relax, she feels herself reaching for him like some deep-sea creature yearning toward the surface. When she comes, suddenly, before she expects to, she feels as if she's drowning, then riding a wave, riding it slowly all the way out, until it dissolves into the motion of the sea.

"One more," he murmurs after a moment, his lips brushing her stomach, but she pulls him up and kisses him, hard, on the mouth, moving her shoulder forward so he slides halfway off her. She shifts from underneath and then, quickly, climbs on top, feeling like a little kid in a tickle fight. She pushes his arms over his head and he smiles at her, amused, as if he thinks she's a little kid, too. As she bends over to kiss him, she feels his pelvis moving against her, his thigh between her legs, and she reaches down to push his jeans to his knees and then his soft jersey boxers. He kicks his legs, and the clothes fall to the floor, the belt hitting wood, coins scattering out of his pockets.

"Damn," he mutters, "I'll never find those quarters."

Moving against him slowly, she sits up on her knees. "Do you have—" she begins.

"I was just wondering the same thing," he says. Twisting under her, he reaches over to his bedside table and pulls out a drawer. "God knows, they've probably expired." She can hear him crinkling what sounds like candy wrappers. "Ah, it's all coming back to me. The impossible-to-open foil packet," he says, tearing it with his teeth.

She slides off him. He fumbles beside her as she waits for him to put it on—it seems too intimate, somehow, for her to help. Then he turns toward her and runs his hand along the curve of her hip. "Armed and dangerous," he says.

She laughs. "We'll see about that." She climbs on top of him again and guides him inside her, shifting her hips to find the easiest angle. She arcs her body over his and he pulls her forward, rubbing his face against her breasts, tracing them with his tongue. After a moment she sits back and he leans forward on his elbows, watching her. He puts his hands flat on her chest and runs them down to her thighs, and then he holds her steady, rocking her back and forth. She closes her eyes, letting her body fall into the rhythm, familiar and strangely foreign at the same time. It's been almost a year, but instinctively she senses how to work it, when to pick up the pace and when to slow it down. After a few minutes she feels him tense beneath her; "Oh—my—Kath," he breathes, pulling her toward him and away, and she watches him swallow, watches his eyelids flutter, feels him moving faster, straining against her, and her own heartbeat quickens and her mind goes blank and she's moaning with him, riding him, and he jerks up three times, four, and then the rhythm slows and she feels his body go limp. When his breathing steadies she sinks onto his chest, his bare skin slick against hers, and slides her shoulder under his arm.

Through the window, in the fluorescent glow of a streetlight, the sky is a deep, brilliant blue. Kathryn can't see the moon, doesn't remember if there is a moon tonight. The wall beside the window is lined with shelves piled haphazardly with books. A large poster hangs opposite the bed; she can make out the bold block letters, black on white, that spell out KANDINSKY. She wonders idly where he got it, if he ordered it from a catalogue or found it somewhere in town. Or maybe he saw the painting in a museum in Prague and brought the poster home with him in a cardboard cylinder. Has he been to Europe? She realizes that she has no idea.

Meeting him again, it feels as if the ten years have evaporated. She has known Jack since they were kids. She was with him the day after his mother walked out, when he was fifteen, and she was one of the first people he called when his mother came back a year later. She's been to his house and hung out with his little sister, who has Down's syndrome. But she knows little about who he has become in these ten years—what he's done, where he's been. He went to the University of Maine on a scholarship the fall after they graduated, and she heard through the grapevine that he had a column in the school paper and worked in the Bear's Den, a campus pub, to make up the difference in tuition. But she never heard from him directly, and she never wrote him herself. Their friendship wasn't like that. It was collective, part of the group.

Now, feeling his arm beneath her, she shifts and turns away, hugging the edge of the bed. Thinking about what she's done, she feels her face flush in the darkness. I am so stupid, she thinks, risking his friendship like this. My mother's right—I am self-destructive. Kathryn wants to creep out without his noticing, leave him sleeping in his bed. Maybe they can both pretend it never happened.

"Was I dreaming?" he says, as if reading her mind. He turns toward her, tracing her shoulder with his finger.

"Yes," she says.

"Am I dreaming now?"

"You're having a nightmare."

He laughs.

"I have to go."

"Shhh," he says, "I'm sleeping." He kisses her shoulder.

"Jack. I'm sorry." She flinches away from him and sits up, gathering the sheet around her. "This was stupid of me. I feel ridiculous."

"Why?" He props himself up on one arm.

"I came here to seduce you."

"Yeah."

She looks at him. "I don't want to jeopardize our friendship."

"What friendship? I'm your boss."

"Oh, God," she says, putting her face in her hand.

He looks over at her and grins. "Come here."

"No."

"Come here," he says, pulling on the sheet she's wrapped in until she lets herself be pulled over. "We don't have to decide right this minute what this is," he says. "We can take it slow. Okay?"

She sighs and looks at him.

He tugs on the sheet and it falls open. "Remember, it's just a dream," he murmurs. Leaning down, he kisses her collarbone, her rib cage; he circles her navel with his tongue.

She intends to resist, but his breath is hot on her stomach, and her will is weak. She closes her eyes and stretches out on the bed, feeling his hands encircle her waist, his fingers on the small of her back. "I remember," she whispers.

PART FOUR

RELEASE

Her mother is sitting at the kitchen table, sipping coffee, when Kathryn walks in the door the next morning.

"I was just about to call the police," her mother says, flicking her wrist to look at her watch. Then she looks back at Kathryn, and her mouth falls open. "Good Lord, what have you done to your hair?"

"Oh, this." Kathryn keeps forgetting how different she looks. Glancing in Jack's bathroom mirror this morning, she even surprised herself. "It wasn't me, it was Lena," she says, as if Lena had held a gun to her head.

Her mother's eyes widen, and she shakes her head. "I think Lena's getting a little too New York for her own good."

Kathryn gets a mug from the cabinet beside the sink and pours herself some coffee. "What are you doing here, anyway?" she says, trying to change the subject. "I thought you were at Frank's camp this weekend."

"I took a raincheck," her mother says, getting up. "I had a strange feeling about something, I didn't know what. Now I guess I do." She rinses her mug, puts it in the dishwasher. "Ed Gaffney called about an hour ago."

"He called you?"

"He's concerned about you. I am your mother," she adds, as if it's news.

Kathryn sighs. She hadn't wanted her mother to hear about the tapes—of course she's worried now.

"Don't be naive, Kathryn," her mother says sharply. "And don't play games. You could be in real danger."

Shrugging this off is not going to work. Kathryn reaches for her mother's hand. "I'm aware of that."

"Where were you last night?"

"At Jack's."

Raising her eyebrows, her mother leans forward, as if in slow motion. Clearly, this wasn't the answer she expected. "Well," she says.

"I didn't mean to stay out all night. I fell asleep."

Her mother nods, assessing the situation. "So what is this?" she asks finally. "Is this a relationship?"

Kathryn thinks of Jack's warm body next to her this morning, his arm curved around her hip, his breath hot on her neck. "Stay," he whispered as she left. She takes a long sip of coffee. "I don't know," she says.

Squinting, her mother scrutinizes her face. "You need to be careful, Kathryn. You need to look out for yourself."

"I thought you liked Jack, Mom."

"Not just Jack. All of it."

Kathryn can detect fear in her mother's voice, and she feels a sudden protective rush. "Nothing's going to happen to me," she says. "This is Bangor, for Pete's sake."

"Where eighteen-year-old girls vanish into thin air," her mother says. "I've worried enough about you over the years. Don't give me good reason."

"I won't, Mom. I promise," Kathryn says. But they both know from years of experience that this promise is a formality, an understanding that Kathryn will do what she must and her mother won't have to know. *I'll be back at midnight, I won't drive with anyone who's drinking, we're going to the movies, his parents are home.*

AFTER HER MOTHER leaves to show some houses, Kathryn calls Rosie's office to leave a message asking for an appointment later in the week. To her surprise, Rosie answers the phone herself. She's in the office doing some paperwork, and though it's a Sunday, she offers to see Kathryn at three. Her husband and son are at a baseball game, she tells Kathryn, so she has a little time to kill. "Besides, I like keeping odd hours," she says. "It makes this feel less like a job."

When she gets to Rosie's office, slightly stuffy and sour-smellling in the heat of midafternoon, Kathryn realizes that she doesn't want to talk about the reunion or sleeping with Jack; she doesn't want to go into the tapes. What she really wants to talk about is her hair.

You've become her, Hunter had said. And of course, though she hadn't done it consciously, he's exactly right. After all, isn't that what she always wanted? She distinctly remembers wishing she could jump inside Jennifer's skin and inhabit her body, to see the world through those light-blue eyes. In high school Kathryn memorized the list of products that were lined up in the Pelletiers' bathroom—Gee Your Hair Smells Terrific, Dove soap, Vaseline Intensive Care lotion, Johnson's Baby Oil, all-natural kiwi lip gloss, Cutex nail polish—and bought them for herself, as if using the same potions might transform her. Jennifer's jeans were faded to the perfect light blue; her shirts hung from her shoulders in a smooth silky drape. For a while Kathryn believed that if she bought the same clothes they'd have a similar effect, but she soon discovered that the magic was nontransferrable. On Kathryn those shirts were wrinkled and stained within minutes, and the jeans creased unattractively when she sat down. Even her laundry seemed to undergo a different process; her shirts shrunk and faded, buttons disappeared, her jeans never achieved that soft, sexy blue.

So now, all these years later, Kathryn has gone and dyed her hair blond, Swedish blond, Jennifer blond, just in time for her ten-year high-school reunion, where Jennifer would not be. And maybe part of her is trying to replicate Jennifer and part of her is trying to usurp her. Because even in her absence—especially in her absence—Jennifer's life has had more of an impact on the people around her than Kathryn's probably ever will. If this were a Bette Davis movie, Kathryn muses, it would probably turn out that *she* was the villain, the supposed best friend who got rid of her more beautiful and charismatic rival.

"I don't know," Rosie says. "Let's consider a different scenario. Maybe by looking like Jennifer, by, in a sense, becoming her, you're trying to find your way into the mystery. Maybe in order to find her, you have to get as close to her as you can."

On the way home Kathryn cranks the radio, and Bonnie Tyler's raspy voice, wailing "Total Eclipse of the Heart," fills the car. Closing her eyes, Kathryn lets the music soak in, saturating her pores. She is sodden, drunk on it. She hasn't felt this way since high school, when she would go into her room and sit on her bed in the dark with headphones on, absorbing the music into her bloodstream like a drug. She expected so much from it then. The music showed her a way through a thicket of emotions; it made sense of her confusion. It distilled her heart.

In college, older and more cynical, she made fun of the music she used to love. The lyrics were cloying, the arrangements sappy, the groups passé. Her friends from prep schools had listened to a different kind of music, more self-referential and cutting-edge. She amused them by describing school dances featuring a deejay with a handlebar mustache and a shiny red baseball jacket who played Whitney Houston and Sheena Easton and lots of Madonna. She quoted sappy lyrics from earnest, anthemic pop songs, and they doubled over with laughter. But a part of her, deep down, was loyal to that younger self. She had not forgotten the tremendous relief she'd felt at hearing her own emotions confirmed and explained at a time when they were such a mystery to her.

Now, driving up Broadway, she listens intently to the steadily rising anger in Bonnie Tyler's voice—"*Every now and then I fall APART*"—and she remembers Jennifer blasting this song as they drove to school on cold winter mornings. Nothing seemed to exist except the music; the moment was reduced to its essence, and that essence was pure feeling. At times like this, Kathryn realizes now, she was as close to Jennifer as she would ever be. Jennifer would select a tape, find the right song, and let the music say what she was unable to admit. Kathryn always felt as if the music was a code, and if she could only figure out what it meant, she'd hold the key to Jennifer's elusive personality. Sometimes she didn't try; she just lost herself in it. But usually there were two parts of her, one that existed purely in the moment and one that hovered above, watching, waiting, hoping somehow to find a clue that would yield an answer.

*　　*　　*

> *There's a message in the wild*
> *And I'm sending you the signal tonight*
> *You don't know how desperate I've become*
> *And it looks like I'm losing this fight . . .*

Kathryn is sitting at the kitchen table by herself that evening, listening to the tapes again, when the telephone rings. Absently, she goes over and picks it up. "Hello?"

There's silence on the other end.

"Hello?" she says again, her senses sharpening.

"Kathryn," a voice whispers.

"Who is this?"

"Leave it alone."

"What?"

"*Leave it alone.*" The voice is slow and distinct, but unidentifiable. Then there's a click, and the line is dead. Immediately, almost without thinking, she dials Star 69, as Paul had done. The phone rings and rings, but no one answers.

She replaces the phone on the hook and stands there for a moment, unable to move. When it rings again, seconds later, she lets the machine get it. "Kathryn, it's Jack. Just calling to say—"

"Hi," she says, picking up the receiver.

"Screening, huh?"

"I got a weird call," she says.

He listens silently while she tells him about it. Then he says, "I don't like this."

"It's probably nothing," she says. "Some high-school kid who read the article and wants to have a little fun."

"Those tapes weren't nothing." He draws in his breath. "I'm starting to get uncomfortable with all this."

"All what?"

"What this is turning into."

"What do you mean?"

"You know what I mean. You're basically live bait."

"Look," she says, reasoning with herself as much as with Jack, "this is exactly what we wanted. We're smoking this guy out."

"Is this what you thought it would be? That some psycho would come out of the woodwork to harass and threaten you? Because that wasn't my scenario."

"What did you think?"

He sighs. "I thought that maybe someone who saw something or heard something would come forward. Or—who knows?—maybe Jennifer would read the piece and decide to show herself."

She sits back in her chair and looks out the window into the darkness. The trees look soft and spongy in the light from the house. "Maybe it's time to give up that fantasy."

"Yeah, I guess it is," he says. "And maybe it's time to face the fact that this is turning into something you can't control."

Slowly, she winds the long phone cord around her hand.

"Gaffney has the tapes. He's on top of it," Jack says. "I think we should tell the police about Hunter and let them take over from here."

"And I should just drop it?"

"Yes."

She relaxes her hand, turning it slightly, and the phone cord slips off, resuming its coiled shape. "Okay."

"Okay?"

"Okay, if that's what you think."

He pauses. She can tell he's debating whether or not to believe her. Then he sighs again. "This wasn't even why I called. I wanted to ask you to dinner this week."

"Jack," she says, "I don't expect—"

"Listen, Kathryn. I don't think you expect anything. But I do. Call me old-fashioned."

"Okay, then," she says, "I accept."

"Good. How about Wednesday?"

"Fine."

"So what are you doing now?"

"Listening to those tapes again. Trying to see if there's anything there."

"Have you eaten yet?"

"No. What time is it?"

"Nine-thirty."

"Hmm. I guess I forgot."

"Well, I just ordered a pizza, and I have to pick it up. I could pick you up at the same time."

She laughs. "Would this cancel out dinner on Wednesday?"

"Think of this as an appetizer," Jack says.

WHEN THE RAIN begins, in the middle of the night, Kathryn gets up to close the window. Lightning rips through the sky like a cartoon bolt; thunder cracks so loudly that Jack, who's been sleeping soundly, sits up in a daze and looks around.

"It's just a storm," she says softly, as if to a child. "Go back to sleep."

He shakes his head, rubs the back of his neck. "I used to love these when I was a kid."

"Me, too."

Leaning back against the headboard, he reaches for her hand and pulls her toward him. His arms around her shoulders, she watches the rain falling in heavy sheets against the tall window. It's like being at a Laundromat, she thinks, or a car wash. She remembers going through the car wash at the Texaco station on Hammond Street with her father when she was a little girl—how frightened she was at first, and then how thrilled when she realized she was safe, the raging storm couldn't reach her. And soon they'd be back out in the sunshine, clean and dry. Lulled by the rain, Kathryn drifts to sleep in Jack's arms. She doesn't stir until the first faint light of morning tints the sky.

It's still raining later that morning when Kathryn drives up to the school. Formless clouds, heavy and gray, hang low in the sky. Holding a newspaper over her head like a pup tent, she dashes from the visitors' parking lot to the double front doors, which open with a vacuum-sealed whoosh and close slowly behind her.

Inside, the air is cold. Kathryn rubs her arms, suddenly covered with goose bumps, as she passes the glassed-in administrative offices. The school secretary, typing away at a computer, appears to be the only one there. Kathryn goes down a long hall to the main part of the building, and then up the wide ramp to Hunter's classroom.

The door is open and the light is on, but Hunter isn't there. Tentatively, Kathryn steps into the room. Despite the light, it's dim and shadowed. Fine rain sifts against the windows, blurring the view. The large black-and-white wall clock ticks quietly, its second hand a thin red needle inching around the face. Somewhere in the distance, a truck horn blares. Kathryn looks around at the posters of Martin Luther King and

John F. Kennedy, the Far Side cartoons taped to the board, the dusty apple-shaped candle on Hunter's desk—a gift from some grade-grubbing student, Kathyrn thinks, and a name pops into her head: Helen Duvall, a girl in her class who, over the course of the school year, brought Hunter apple magnets, apple pins, a tie with apples on it, and, finally, an apple pie he shared with the class. He made it clear that he was amused and slightly horrified by the attention: "Oh, no!" he'd say, covering his eyes when she approached his desk with yet another gift-wrapped trinket, but Helen just smiled blandly. It was hard to tell whether she was in on the joke.

"Miss Campbell." Kathryn turns around as Hunter is shutting the door behind him. Her heart leaps a little, but she tells herself to relax—what's she afraid of? Still, it feels a bit strange; she can't remember when she's been alone with a teacher in a classroom with the door shut.

As if reading her mind, he says, "I always keep this shut in the summer. There's no one else here, anyway."

"There are a few people," she protests feebly.

"Not up here. I have it all to myself." He grins, leaning back against his desk with his arms half folded, hands underneath, like a football coach. He's wearing a Nike T-shirt and black bicycle shorts, and Kathryn wonders if he biked into town this morning. She remembers that he used to do that kind of thing, hiking up mountains before school, training for marathons and posting his daily miles on the board for the class to keep track of. "I thought you might come by," he says. "Something about our conversation seemed . . . incomplete."

"Umm," she says, thinking, *All right, here we go*, with the vertiginous sensation of jumping off a high diving board, "there was something. I've been wondering why you didn't tell me you were involved with Jennifer when she was your student."

He gazes at her for a moment through narrowed eyes, as if he's having trouble seeing her. Then, biting down on the word, he says, " 'Involved'?"

"Sleeping with. Do I need to be more specific?"

His face is a mask of feigned shock. He laughs. "What a thought. What a fantasy."

"Come on," she says. "Jennifer must have told you I knew."

"You must have misunderstood."

"We all knew," she continues. "Abby, Rachel—everybody."

"They're lying," he says calmly. "Abby Elson is a drugged-out piece of trash, and Rachel lives in some kind of fantasy land." He nods, as if remembering. "She used to send me poems. You know—love poems. So I'm afraid your sources are shaky, at best."

Kathryn smiles. "They're not my sources. Jennifer was my source."

"Now you're lying."

Taking a deep breath, Kathryn says, "She used a code; she told people she was orienteering twice a week, and then she'd go to your place. She'd start out in the woods somewhere, and you'd pick her up in your car."

His eyes are trained on hers, but he says nothing.

"It began sometime in the fall," she continues carefully, "after the suicide attempt. Nobody else understood, but you knew what to say, how to help. You were almost like a father figure—"

"Not a father figure," he says.

Kathryn feels her knees buckle, as if someone has kicked them from behind. She holds her body rigid. "You helped her," she says.

Holding his hands up in front of his pursed lips as if he's praying, Hunter looks at her for a long moment. Then he sighs. "She needed help."

"I know."

"There was nobody she could talk to."

Kathryn feels a pain in her chest. *Come on, Jen. Don't get deep on me. We're supposed to be celebrating.* "I know," she says.

"What else do you know?"

Her mouth is dry. She swallows. "I know that she loved you," she says softly.

"Did she tell you that?"

"She didn't have to. It was plain to see."

And maybe it was, if she'd been paying attention. Maybe all of it was more obvious than she knew. Shared glances, a hand lingering on a shoulder, coded language and double entendres—Kathryn hadn't seen any of it; she'd missed whatever clues might've come her way. Where had she been when Jennifer was slipping out to see him? How could she have been so oblivious when they were in his class together every day?

"She told me you didn't know," he muses, as if talking to himself. "She said she was afraid to tell you."

"Afraid of what?"

"That you couldn't handle it—you might tell somebody. That it would be weird in class." He shrugs. "Who knows? But I guess she lied to me."

No she didn't, Kathryn thinks. You're the only one she didn't lie to. "She didn't mean to tell me," she says. "I kind of figured it out."

"Why didn't you say something earlier?"

"What was there to say?"

"So why do it now?"

Her hands, she realizes, are trembling. She puts them behind her back. "I've been thinking about what you said at the reunion—about how I was such a nothing in high school."

"I don't think I said that exactly," he protests mildly.

"But you were right," she says. "I was in her shadow. I have been for a long time."

"What does this have to do with—"

"I just wanted you to know that I know," she says. "I thought it might clear the air between us." She looks directly into his eyes. "You were right. I always envied what Jennifer had."

Without expression, he appraises her. There is a long silence between them.

"I . . ." She hesitates, raising her hand to her mouth, and shakes her head. Then she turns away, as if to leave.

He reaches out and puts his hand on her arm. "What?" he asks, pulling her back. His grip is firm, and she resists. He lets go, lifting his hands as if in surrender. For a moment neither of them says a thing. "What do you want from me?" he asks finally.

She looks at him steadily, calmly, though her heart is racing. "I want . . . to know you. I'm tired of playing games."

He gazes at her quizzically, tilting his head as if trying to see her a different way. "I don't know, Kathryn," he says finally. "I don't know if I believe you."

"If you're involved with Rachel . . ."

"Who told you that?" he says sharply.

"I'm not dumb. I saw that look between you at the reunion."

"We . . ." He hesitates. "There was something. Not anymore."

Now he's lying, she thinks, watching his Adam's apple bob slightly as he swallows. She wonders if Rachel has told him about their conversation. It's impossible to tell. All of a sudden Kathryn feels a wave of panic, like nausea, rise up in her. She doesn't know what is real and what is false; even if he acts like he believes her, she has no idea if he really does. She doesn't trust anything—her intuition, his cues. How foolish, she thinks, to imagine that she can play games like this with someone like Hunter. He knows all the tricks—he's spent his life playing games.

"Are you ready for this?" he says abruptly.

For what? She looks at him, at the small smile on his lips, at his dark, piercing eyes. Almost imperceptibly, something about him seems to have changed. He is gentler, somehow, his expression softer.

"Yes," she murmurs.

"Tonight, then," he says.

She nods.

"There's a diner off of Route 1-A, near the Hampden town line. It's called Raymond's."

"I'll find it."

"Seven o'clock."

She nods again. "Seven o'clock."

Walking out to the parking lot in the drizzling rain, Kathryn's head feels light, as if she's short of oxygen. It's so easy to lie, she thinks. You just say the words, and they might as well be true. She feels the same way she used to feel as a teenager when she deceived her parents and got away with it—disbelief mixed with fear that they'd be behind her in a second, that they'd figure it out. When she realized she'd pulled it off, she felt a thrill of relief, and then, some time later, deep in her bones, a sadness that she could deceive them so easily, that her omnipotent parents could be fooled. Because if that were true, then they weren't omnipotent anymore; anything could happen. They couldn't save her and they couldn't hurt her. She was on her own.

When Kathryn gets home there's a note from her mother on the kitchen table and a message from Jack on the answering machine. "I'll be out again tonight—sorry!" the note reads. "A party at Julie Spenwen's for work. Thanks for letting me know where you were last night. Hope it was fun. We need some groceries if you get a chance. Breakfast tomorrow? Love, Mom."

Kathryn pushes the button on the machine. "Hey, Kathryn," Jack says. "I'm wondering where you could be. Anyway, you know how we talked about moving you in other directions at the paper? Well, there's a concert tonight at the Maine Center for the Arts, an Appalachian bluegrass band, and I'd like you to cover it. You can interview the group afterward. It's not a unique story, but the director of the center has been pestering me for publicity about this event, and I'm thinking you might have an interesting take on it. Call me back." She hears him start to put the phone down, and then there's a clatter and he says, "Oh, hi to you, too, Mrs. Campbell."

Kathryn stands at the table for a moment, trying to figure out what to tell him. Then she dials Jack's number. "I'm having dinner with my mother tonight," she lies. "Maybe if I'd known about this earlier . . ."

"Can't you postpone it? I had to pull strings with the arts editor to get you this assignment."

"Sorry. It's important to her. But let me know if something else comes up, okay?" She feels a twinge of guilt; she can tell he's annoyed. But she shrugs it off. "Hey, I think I left my earrings at your place. I might have to pick them up later."

"After your mother-daughter bonding session?" He says it sarcastically, but she can hear a relenting in his voice.

"Maybe. I don't want to wake you."

"You can wake me," he says. "Just don't disturb my dreams."

It's early afternoon when the rain stops, when the gray cloud ceiling begins to break apart and glimpses of blue appear. Standing in the living room, looking out the picture window, Kathryn stretches her arms over her head, tugging her shoulders at the sockets. It's been nearly a week since she's gone running, and her body feels sluggish and stiff. She finds her running shorts in the dryer and an old cotton T-shirt of her mother's—FUN RUN OF '91—hanging on the line, and she slips them on quickly, inhaling her mother's floral perfume and a whiff of Tide detergent as she pulls the T-shirt over her head. Her mother doesn't actually like to go running; Kathryn suspects the T-shirt is for show, or some old boyfriend's. Or maybe both.

She starts out slowly, her feet squishing down the street. A block away, on Center Street, she can hear cars shushing by, but Taft Street is eerily quiet. On Montgomery she takes a left, past the older houses with peeling paint, the broad expanse of park made lush by the rain, past the newer houses of brick and siding that cluster together in a secluded inlet, and makes her way toward the Kenduskeag.

It's been years since she's been to the spot by the river where the five of them sat around the fire that night, watching Jennifer walk out into the darkness. For a while after it happened Kathryn had taken comfort in returning there, as if Jennifer might somehow be present, as if Kathryn might be close to her that way. But when the search parties dwindled and the investigation slowed, the place became a painful reminder of what they didn't do. *I'll be fine*, she'd said, and they believed her; they didn't stop her. They let her slip away.

Thinking back now, Kathryn can see how much she wanted to take at face value what Jennifer had told her—as if her words, even when spoken without conviction, were some kind of promise. Why had she been so eager to accept that Jennifer was fine, when every indication was that she wasn't? Why had she been so unwilling to read between the lines?

"*FINE*," Kathryn's sophomore-year college roommate, a psychology major, had yelled at her one time, frustrated at Kathryn's unwillingness to open up. "Fucked-up, Insecure, Neurotic, Emotional—yeah, you're *fine*, you lying bitch." Kathryn knew her roommate was right—it was a meaningless word, a cover. It hid what she didn't want others to see, and what she couldn't face in herself. She lived on the surface of that word, repeating it so often that she almost believed it.

She has been so afraid for so long. She was afraid that if she admitted to one thing, one genuine feeling, then she'd have to admit to it all; she'd have to feel everything. She didn't know if she could do it. She was afraid that she wouldn't be able to hold things together if they started to fall apart, that she would be unable to contain the chaos. Jennifer was right to keep things from her—her sadness, her neediness, her relationship with Hunter. Because what would Kathryn have done if she'd known?

The rain has started up again. It falls lightly on her face, her neck, her arms; it gets in her eyes and mixes with her tears, making the road ahead a blur. She's glad to be crying, glad for the rain; it feels like both punishment and absolution. All the tears she never shed, the pain she wouldn't let herself feel, the relief at admitting her own complicity. She may not be responsible for Jennifer's disappearance, but she is responsible for ignoring Jennifer's unhappiness, for refusing to face the fact that she might have been in trouble. She is accountable for that.

The Kenduskeag is swollen with the rain, its banks muddy and sodden. Avoiding the soupy trails, Kathryn runs on the slope of matted grasses, which are slick and squeaky underfoot. She feels almost drunk— or on some drug that makes things appear off kilter and unbalanced. Trees seem to be falling toward her, their leaves and branches heavy with rain.

The site, when she reaches it, is barren and nondescript. She stands for a moment breathing heavily, trying to get her bearings. To the left is the spot where they parked their cars. To the right, where there used to be a clearing, brambles and weeds have grown up. She had expected to be overwhelmed, to feel immensely sad, but instead she feels nothing. It's just a place.

She runs along the edge of the long dirt road leading back to the main road that parallels the river. At the fork she bears left, her feet slapping the pavement, following the route Jennifer took that night. In the ten years since, much has happened on this stretch of road. New developments have sprung up, streets have been paved, trees cleared. But somehow it still feels secluded; the infusion of people and activity seems less to have transformed the wilderness than to have been absorbed by it.

After a mile or so she comes to the intersection of Griffin Road, the place where Jennifer's gum wrapper was found and where the police dogs lost her scent. Kathryn stops and looks up and down the road. A logging truck rumbles by, its wheels sizzling in the rain. Several cars pass, and then a small black pickup heading north slows and comes to a stop in front of her with the motor running.

The passenger-side window scrolls down. "Are you all right? Need a ride?" a young woman shouts, leaning toward her across the seat. She's wearing a floppy straw hat and tortoiseshell glasses. Sodden bags of mulch are piled in the truck bed.

"No thanks," Kathryn says. "I'm in the middle of a run."

"In this weather?" The woman screws up her face.

"I'm almost home. But thanks anyway."

"Okay, whatever you say." She waves and starts to close the window.

"Wait," Kathryn says. "Where are you going?"

She shrugs. "I could drop you anywhere."

"No, I mean, where are you headed? What's up that way?"

"Oh." She looks out the windshield. "I live about eight miles from here, on Mud Pond. There's not much else but fish and bears up there."

"You anywhere near Pushaw?"

"Sure. Is that where you wanna go?"

"No, I just wondered." Kathryn smiles and steps back, waving good-bye.

Standing in the rain, she watches the pickup pull away, its red tail-lights glowing smaller until they vanish over a rise. She tilts her head up and closes her eyes, feeling the soft raindrops on her eyelids, tasting their metallic sweetness on her tongue. Then she turns around and heads for home.

Hunter is sitting on a round stool at the counter with his back to the door when Kathryn gets to the diner that night, a few minutes late. He's drinking coffee and talking in a low voice to the waitress, who's leaning against the ice-cream cooler and laughing in a familiar way, as if she knows him.

Kathryn takes the stool beside him. He doesn't look up. "I was beginning to wonder if you'd show," he says.

She slips off her jacket, puts it on the empty seat beside her, taps her wet umbrella on the floor and lays it at her feet. "I said I would."

He laughs. "I don't take much stock in what people say."

The waitress raises her eyebrows at him and slides a laminated menu toward Kathryn. "Coffee?"

"Do you have tea?"

"Lipton."

"Okay."

Turning to the shelf behind her, the waitress opens a box. Kathryn looks around. The diner is tattered but comfortable, with blue-vinyl booths and framed car ads from old *Life* magazines. Edsels, Fords, Chevys, Coupe de Villes. Two sixtyish men in flannel shirts are sitting at a booth in the back, playing cards. At another booth, an elderly woman with her hair in a net is daubing her face with powder and peering in a small compact mirror. "Runaround Sue" is playing on the jukebox. "I never even knew this place existed," Kathryn says.

"It's a local hangout."

"I grew up in this town."

He laughs again. "You're not a local."

The waitress sets a cup of hot water in front of Kathryn, a tea bag in an envelope on the saucer. Then she refills Hunter's coffee and moves away.

"You know each other," Kathryn says quietly, glancing at the waitress.

"I've spent some time in this place."

"She likes you."

"I like her, too," he says evenly.

"Are you dating her?"

"No."

"Are you 'involved' with her?"

He turns and looks at Kathryn. "You ask a lot of questions."

She tears open the envelope and pulls out the tea bag, then drops it in her cup. "I'm curious about you."

"What makes you think I'm going to give you a straight answer?"

I don't, she thinks, but she says, "Why wouldn't you?" She looks in his eyes, at the blackness of his pupils.

He takes a long sip of coffee. "Everybody holds something back."

"You could refuse to answer. You don't have to lie." She pauses, then presses forward. "Then again, I guess refusing to answer is basically a tacit admission."

"Not necessarily. Sometimes things are complicated. Not everything can be explained with a yes or no."

"I'm not talking about yes or no. I'm talking about articulating the complications."

He purses his lips. "All right," he says, shifting tack. "How about you? Aren't there things you'd rather not talk about?"

Lifting the tea bag out of her cup, she shakes it slightly and puts it on her saucer. "Not really." She raises the cup to her mouth, looking at him over the rim. "Ask me anything."

He smiles at the challenge. "Why did Paul leave you?"

She sloshes the cup against her lip, burning her tongue. "He didn't leave me. I left him."

"Why did he make you leave him?"

She smiles slightly. "I don't know."

"You're lying."

"Because I wasn't—I couldn't . . . engage." She puts down the cup. "He wanted more. I can't blame him."

"But you do blame him."

"I wasn't the only one at fault. He could be selfish."

"But you drove him away."

He's goading her. She furrows her brow, annoyed, trying not to show it. The small clock above the pastry case says 7:17 P.M. "Now it's your turn," she says. "Why did you put that envelope in my car?"

"What?"

"The tape, the photograph . . ."

"I don't know what you're talking about," he says.

"The message on my machine . . ."

Shaking his head, he says, "You may have a secret admirer, but it isn't me."

"These weren't love notes."

"Ahh," he says as if he understands.

"Why would somebody try to scare me?"

"Why do you think?"

"I assume it's to stop me from asking questions."

He shrugs. "You shouldn't assume."

"Why not?"

"Because once you start making assumptions, you'll ignore what's in front of you, and then you'll never find what you're looking for."

"You think I can find what I'm looking for?"

He drains his coffee cup and puts it down. Then he swivels on his stool so he's facing her. "How badly do you want to know?"

"I want to know," she says.

Sitting back on his stool, he crosses his arms and rubs his chin. "Ever been orienteering?" he says abruptly.

"Not really," she says.

"It teaches you a lot about yourself," he says. "How aware you are of the world around you. How in touch you are with your natural instincts."

She looks at him steadily.

"You have to stay sharp or you'll lose your bearings," he says.

"I think I lost my bearings a long time ago."

He smiles—a faint, ironic smile—and says, "You can follow the signs, if you know how to look."

"I'm not sure I do."

"I'm not sure you do either."

"What are we talking about here?" Kathryn asks in a level voice.

He reaches up and touches her face, running two fingers down her jawbone, and she flinches, lifting her chin. "What's the story with Jack Ledbetter?"

She swallows. "What do you mean?"

"Don't be coy, Kathryn."

She laughs, trying to keep her voice steady. "What do you want to hear, that I'm sleeping with him?"

He squints at her, waiting for her to continue.

"In his dreams, maybe," she says.

"Uh-huh." He says it slowly, and she can tell he's trying to decide whether to believe her. The waitress saunters over with a pot of coffee and fills his cup. "More water, honey?" she asks Kathryn, and Kathryn shakes her head.

When the waitress leaves, Kathryn turns to face him. "What's the story with Rachel?" she says.

"She's a nice girl," he says.

"But the two of you—"

"I told you," he says coolly. "There was something. Some time ago."

"For how long?"

"A few years. Off and on."

"How many years?"

He looks at her for a long moment, as if he's inspecting her. "A few."

"She's in love with you, isn't she?"

"Maybe."

"Are you in love with her?"

"No. She's been . . . convenient."

"What would she do if she heard you say that?"

He gives Kathryn a funny smile. "She won't."

Patsy Cline is singing "Crazy." The flannel shirts are standing to go, pulling change out of their pockets and counting it on the table. Over in the corner the old woman is hunched over a bowl of soup, patting her mouth with a napkin between slurps.

"What are you doing here, Kathryn?" Hunter asks.

"What?" Though she knows to expect it, his bluntness shocks her.

"Why are you here?" His voice is dry and cold.

She feels a panic rise in her chest. What does he want to hear? What might he be willing to believe? She doesn't answer at first; she looks into her cup and toys with the soggy tea bag. Then she says, "You know why I'm here—I told you before. Jennifer was always in the spotlight. It took a long time for you to notice me." Though she hates to acknowledge it, even to herself, there's a part of her that means it. She knows it's this part that will persuade him, if he's willing to be persuaded. "What about you?" she asks. "Why are you here?"

"I'm not sure yet," he says. "I'm trying to figure that out." He slides off his stool and stands close to her—a little too close. She resists the impulse to pull away. He takes out his wallet, riffles through it, and lays a five-dollar bill on the counter. "Don't play games, Kathryn," he says quietly.

She feels a spider of fear crawling up the back of her neck. "I'm not playing games." She looks up at him, her wide eyes full of deceit, and he returns her gaze.

"I'll need a better answer than that," he says. He turns to leave, then looks back at her. "I'll call you," he says, and he's gone.

IT'S ALMOST MIDNIGHT when Kathryn gets to Jack's. She rings his buzzer and then, finding the door open again, slips inside and makes her way upstairs. His door is open at the end of the long hall. When she gets there, the apartment is dark, lit only by a streetlight and a slice of moon outside the window. Beethoven is playing softly; Kathryn can see the small lights on the receiver at the end of the room jump and flash.

She shuts the door behind her and pulls her silk sleeveless turtleneck over her head. Then she unzips the long skirt she's wearing and lets it fall to the floor, stepping out of her sandals and the skirt and walking blindly to the middle of the room. Closing her eyes, she tilts her face upward. She's filled with some strange unfocused desire. Running her hands down her body, she catches her underwear in her fingers and bends to pull it off.

All at once Jack is behind her, his warm hands on her waist, his breath on her neck, the hair on his bare thighs rubbing the backs of her legs. She leans into him, and he pushes his hands under her bra, finding the clasp and unsnapping it and then pushing the straps off her shoulders. He slides his hands down between her legs and she moves them apart, sensing the wetness already, feeling him hard against her back, wanting him inside her, wanting him now. Reaching back, she pushes his boxer shorts down and takes him in her hand, trying to guide him, but he pulls away, grasps her hands in his and kisses the back of her neck, her ear, rubs his scratchy cheek against the side of her face. He begins to caress her again, willing her to follow his lead. She's never done this before, not with anyone watching, and she's self-conscious at first, timid in her movements. But after a few moments his hand rises to her breast and she continues, stroking herself the way he was doing, then letting herself enjoy the nuance of her own touch. When she starts to come, he braces against her and she lets herself fall back, writhing in his embrace, his body moving with hers as the motion subsides. Then he turns her around and kisses her hard on the mouth, maneuvering her back toward the kitchen table, where he sets her on the edge. "Just a moment," he murmurs. He disappears and then comes back; hearing him rip open the little foil packet, she smiles in the darkness. Then he pulls her toward him, hooking her knees around his hips, and pushes inside her. She's so wet now that there's no hitch; they slide together like two parts of a machine.

"I've always wanted to do this," he whispers, "You know, Jack Nicholson . . ." His voice trails off into ragged breaths. "Oh—Kathryn," he murmurs after a while, and she pulls him closer, lifting his chin to kiss him, touching his warm tongue with her own. When he shudders against her, she holds him tight with her legs, his head in her neck, smelling his fresh sweat, running her fingers through his coarse, thick hair.

After a moment he lifts his head. "Hello."

"Hello," she says.

"I hope you are who I think you are."

"I hope so, too," she murmurs, shutting her eyes against the dark.

LATER, LYING IN bed, she says, "Jack, I have to tell you something."

He props himself up on an elbow to look at her.

She sighs and fiddles with the sheet. "I wasn't bonding with my mother tonight. I went to meet Hunter."

"I know."

"You know?"

He scratches the back of his neck. "I had a nice chat with your mom earlier. Of course, she had no idea where you were. It didn't take a genius to figure it out."

She sighs. "Sorry."

"Oh, I knew something was up." He grins. "No good reporter gives up that fast." Then, slowly, his expression grows serious. "But if you're going to follow through on this, you've got to understand what you're doing."

She nods.

"This guy could be capable of anything."

"I know. I'm being careful," she says. "I met him at a public place." Down a long, wooded stretch of road in the middle of nowhere, she thinks, but keeps it to herself.

"Are you meeting him again?"

"I have to. I'm so close, Jack," she says intently. "It's like we're locked in this game together—like chess—and every move is loaded. And if I can just figure out where he's vulnerable . . ."

"Don't kid yourself, Kathryn," Jack says. "It's his game. You're just a pawn."

She doesn't answer. She remembers, after the divorce, when her parents would vie for her and Josh's attention by pointing out how the other was manipulating them: "Your dad's just bribing you," her mother would say; "She's using you to get to me," her father countered. The thing is, it was usually true—but it didn't help to know it. If she wanted their attention, then she had to play their game. So she learned to be cynical, and to take what she could get.

"Will you promise to tell me next time you see him? I want to know where you'll be."

"Okay," she says. It's not a promise and it isn't a lie, but something in between.

When Kathryn reaches Gaffney the next morning on the phone, he instructs her not to come to the police station. "Dunkin' Donuts, outer Main Street," he says. "I won't be in uniform."

She brings a newspaper and sunglasses—as if, in that bright yellow car with her platinum hair, she might possibly avoid notice—and takes a circuitous route from the east side to the west side, checking in her rearview mirror to see if she's being followed. She feels a little silly; it's a benign, sunny day in this sleepy little city, and people seem to be going about their business with ease and leisure. But Gaffney's caution alarms her—more than Jack's, which she can dismiss as over-protectiveness. And she can't shake the uneasy feeling that Jack is right: She doesn't understand the rules of this game.

Three semis are parked together in the lot, and inside three truckers sit on stools next to each other, wolfing doughnuts from a big open box. Kathryn sits at the other end of the counter and stares at the bewildering variety of pastries in the brightly lit display. The doughnuts are grouped by type: Kremes, Frosteds, Glazed, Jellies—and there are also muffins and sweet rolls and bagels. Bagels? When did that happen? Kathryn wonders. Then again, it's been years since she was in one of these places. She's found other ways to indulge her sweet tooth besides eating an entire box of Munchkins, as she and Jennifer used to do.

"What can I get ya?" demands the pimply-faced teenager behind the counter. His pink-and-orange-striped uniform looks like goofy prison duds.

"Umm . . ." She scans the selection. Boston Kreme, Bavarian Kreme, Chocolate Kreme, Kreme . . . "I guess I'll have a Honey Bran muffin," she says, and immediately regrets it. "No, no—change that. Wait." Her eyes move down the rows. "I'll have a Chocolate Frosted. And a Bavarian Kreme."

"Is that all?"

She shakes her head. "A coffee. Regular. No, hazelnut. With milk. And—a jelly donut." One more, what harm can it do?

"Strawberry, grape, blueberry," he says in a bored voice.

"Um—blueberry."

When Gaffney walks in her mouth is full of Kreme. She washes it down with coffee, burning her tongue in the process, and stands to greet him, brushing powdered sugar off her fingers and shirt onto her shorts.

Gaffney eyes the two remaining doughnuts on her napkin and smirks. "One of those for me?"

"Ah—sure," she says.

"Nah," he says, "I only eat the coffee rolls. Hard to stop at one, though, isn't it?" He sits on the stool beside her. Even out of uniform, Gaffney looks like a police officer, stiff and uncomfortable in his ironed jeans and button-down. "So," he says after he's ordered his roll and decaf, "tell me what's going on."

She tells him what she knows about Hunter—how she found out he was involved with Jennifer, how he's been spilling pieces of information each time she's seen him.

"Hunter," Gaffney muses. He shrugs. "Didn't spend much time on him. We could never find any link between them except that he was her coach. I do remember that he was smug—like he knew something we didn't. But we never had anything on him."

"You still don't," she says. "He hasn't confessed to anything."

"What about the tape and that picture?"

She shakes her head. "He hasn't told me anything concrete. But I have the feeling that he might. Little things he's said . . . I don't know. It's just a feeling. I think he's testing me to see what I'll do."

Gaffney tears open two Sweet'n Low packets and pours them in his coffee. "I don't like the sound of this. I think maybe we should bring him in for questioning."

Her heart sinks. Damn, she thinks, not yet, not when she's so close. "On what grounds?" she asks, trying to sound even and unbiased.

"New information about his relationship with Miss Pelletier."

"Information from me."

"We don't have to reveal the source."

She laughs. "Yeah, I'm sure he'll have no idea."

"Look," Gaffney says, putting down his roll. "If he's the one who made your friend disappear, you're probably in a lot more trouble now than you would be if we brought him in."

She knows he's right. But she also knows, or thinks she does, that Hunter is too smart to let himself be trapped by the police. "He won't tell you anything," she says. "This guy has flown under your radar before."

"What makes you think he'll open up to you?"

"I don't know," she says. "It's personal."

"What do you mean?"

She pulls at her jelly doughnut, tearing it into small pieces. Blue goo oozes over her fingers. "I'm Jennifer's friend, we were both in his class. . . . It's between the two of us, somehow."

With a skeptical look, Gaffney says, "Excuse me for being blunt, Miss

Campbell, but it sounds like he's got you just where he wants you. You think you're special—that's the first mistake."

"I don't think I'm special," she says. "But I do have special access. And I think I can get him to tell me what he knows, or what he's done."

Gaffney puffs his cheeks full of air and slowly exhales.

"Listen," she says, touching his arm. "He's been living with some kind of secret for ten years. I think he wants to share it, but not with just anybody. It has to be somebody he thinks would understand."

"And why is that you?"

She ponders this, absently biting her lip. Then she says, "Because he thinks I was jealous of her. He thinks I'm glad she's gone."

Gaffney shakes his head slowly. He takes off his glasses and rubs his eyes. "You're in dangerous territory," he says.

"I know."

He looks at her for a long moment. "What do you want from me?" he asks.

"I need some advice," she says. "I want to know what I have to do to trap him."

"By which you mean . . . ?"

"If he tells me what he did, would it hold up in court?"

"Maybe. It depends."

"What if I got it on tape?"

"That would be better."

"Could you hook me up with a body mike?"

"If it comes from the police, you'll have to read him his Miranda rights first," he says. "I'm guessing that might change the mood."

"Yeah," she says, considering this, rolling a piece of doughnut into a doughy ball. "What if I bring my own microcassette player, keep it in my bag?"

"You could. You'd be taking a risk. There's an audible click; you have to turn over the tape. And if he finds it. . . . The last thing you want to do is enrage him."

She nods.

"If you're right, and he had anything to do with Miss Pelletier's disappearance, this guy has a lot to lose—and he knows it. He may be dying to tell someone, but sooner or later his self-preservation instinct will kick in, and he'll come to his senses. And if it's too late, if he's already told you, you may be in serious trouble."

"I know."

Gaffney sighs. "You're determined to do this, aren't you?"

"I want to find out what happened."

He shakes his head. "This is not a game, Miss Campbell."

"I know," she says. Though her voice is resolute, her legs are trembling. She twines them around the cool metal pole and smiles at Gaffney. "I'll be careful," she says, but it's only a formality, and neither of them believes it.

Days go by with no word from Hunter. Kathryn begins to feel like a jilted lover, wondering what she said or did to scare him off. She finds herself checking her mother's answering machine several times a day, driving through the high-school parking lot in search of his black Jeep, which isn't there. She leaves her car doors unlocked, almost hoping he'll put something on the seat. She looks up his name in the phone book and finds it—Hunter, Richard, at an address on Birch Lane—and she copies it onto a piece of paper. But instinctively she feels it would be wrong to call him. She doesn't want to seem pushy; she's afraid it would make him more suspicious than he already is. When he's ready, she tells herself, he'll be in touch.

Her mother is happy to hear that Kathryn's foray into investigative reporting seems to be over. "I'm so glad you let that drop," she says. "Your father and I both thought it was getting a little dicey."

"You've talked to *Dad* about me?" Kathryn says, incredulous.

"Well, I was concerned about what you were getting into, so I called him for advice. Turned out we were on the same page." She smiles. "He can be very perceptive, you know."

"I can't believe I'm hearing this."

Her mother shrugs lightly. "Before we were bitter enemies, remember, we used to be best friends."

"No, I don't remember," Kathryn says pointedly.

When Jack proposes another story idea, a profile of an eccentric artist who lives on the coast and builds larger-than-life sculptures out of found materials, Kathryn takes the assignment. She drives down to Mount Desert Island one afternoon and interviews the woman in her Bass Harbor studio, then spends two hours walking through her sculpture garden on a sloping hill leading to the sea. The experience is magical; the massive figures, placed in a circle and facing each other, appear to be dancing in the mutable afternoon light.

Doing the story reminds Kathryn of what she used to love about covering the arts: The focus was on the work, not the person; the artists she interviewed were passionate about what they did, and that passion was contagious. She drives back to Bangor, to her mother's office, to use the computer, finishing the story at one in the morning in a rush of adrenaline. For the first time in a long time she's pleased with the work she's done. The next day Jack proposes an interview with a band called Tidewater that's being featured on the summer fair circuit, and she readily agrees. It's better than sitting around.

At the end of the week, as Kathryn is backing out of the driveway on her way to Borders to pick up a Tidewater CD in preparation for the interview, she notices a piece of paper pinned under the windshield wiper. It's folded in half, with her name neatly printed in block letters on the front. Opening it quickly, she looks around to see if anyone is watching, but no one's in sight.

I've been thinking about you, it reads in a small, vertical script—*about your idea that we articulate the complications. I'm not sure that's wise. Regardless, I think we're beginning to understand each other. I look forward to showing you how to find your way out of the woods.*

It's from Hunter, of course. Kathryn studies it for a moment, trying to make sense of it. *I think we're beginning to understand each other.* What does that mean? She turns off the car and goes into the house, scrounging in a kitchen drawer for the slip of paper she'd put there with his number on it. Then she picks up the receiver and dials.

The phone rings three times, four. Then a male voice says, "Hello?"

For an awkward moment she realizes she's never called him anything but Mr. Hunter. "Hello," she says finally. "This is Kathryn. Campbell."

"I know who you are. That was fast."

Shit, she thinks, closing her eyes, I should've waited. "I've got a lot going on," she says briskly. "I wanted to get back to you before my day fills up."

"Glad you could fit me in."

I sound ridiculous, she thinks. Calm down. Relax.

"I thought you might come by the school. I've been half expecting you."

"I didn't want to push anything. I figured if you wanted to see me, you'd call."

He laughs, a dry sound in the back of his throat. "I thought you said you weren't playing games."

"I'm not," she says. *But you are.* She pauses. "To tell you the truth, I'm a little afraid of you." She means it—she is a little afraid of him. But she also knows that by saying it she might take him off guard.

"Why?"

"You can be intimidating."

"Really? I don't mean to be."

"Oh, I think you do," she says.

For a moment he doesn't answer. Then he says, "There's something I want to show you. Let me tell you how to get to my place."

A FEW HOURS later, clutching in one hand the directions she scrawled on a napkin, Kathryn is in her car driving to Pushaw Lake with a microcassette player in her bag on the seat beside her. After ten miles or so the roads narrow, three lanes to two lanes to one. She turns onto an unpaved tributary that seems to have been carved haphazardly out of forest, identified by a wooden marker: Sunshine Way. This strikes her as funny; though it's the middle of a bright, cloudless day, trees shade the road so completely that little sunlight can get through. After what seems like miles but is actually, according to the odometer, just under one, the road forks and Kathryn bears left, onto Birch Lane.

The road is deeply rutted, as if an eighteen-wheeler had barreled through on a rainy day. But a big truck would never make it. The road takes sharp turns at odd angles; trees press close on each side. Kathryn begins to feel a creeping panic—where the hell is she? what is she doing here?—and she stops the car in the middle of the road, holding on to the steering wheel with both hands to calm herself. She's all alone, miles from anywhere, and no one knows where she is. She peers up through the lattice of leaves to the blue sky beyond. "What are you *thinking*?" she says aloud, and she laughs at the insanity of taking such a risk.

She'd called Jack before she left, but he wasn't at his desk. The message she left was vague and halting. She hadn't wanted to say too much; she didn't want him to try to stop her. "Hi, it's me," she said. "I'm going to be gone this afternoon, on old business. If you don't hear from me by this evening . . . But I'm sure you will. This is a good thing. I know what I'm doing." Now she wishes she'd been more specific.

She shuts her eyes and starts to reason with herself. She's being paranoid. She's never seen Hunter do anything remotely violent; why would she imagine he'd ever try to hurt her? It occurs to her that maybe this whole thing—this idea that Hunter had something to do with Jennifer's disappearance—is some kind of fantasy, a story she's concocted because she can't accept that Jennifer just vanished. Because she needs an answer, any answer, whether it's the truth or not. Maybe this is all a stupid, laughable mistake, and Rick Hunter is simply a charismatic young teacher who had a relationship with one of his students ten years ago.

So what? Kathryn thinks. He wasn't much older than they were—six or seven years, maybe. He might have been twenty-five when they were seniors. Jennifer was a wise child, older than her age. She wasn't about to share the details of her difficult life with some immature boy. If she loved this man, if he filled a need for her, what crime was there in that?

A horn sounds loudly on the road behind her, startling Kathryn out of her thoughts. Glancing in the rearview mirror, she sees a dirty white sedan and in it a man wearing tinted glasses, chewing on a toothpick. He nods and lifts his hand to get her attention. "You okay?" he hollers out the window.

"Yeah. Sorry," she yells back. She starts the car, and he follows behind her until she turns into a driveway marked by a small wooden plaque that says HUNTER'S LODGE. He beeps his horn again and keeps going.

Fifty yards down the drive the trees fall back, and Kathryn finds herself in a large, grassy clearing. Straight ahead and slightly to the left is a neat shingled cottage; beyond that the sparkling lake, a wedge of shoreline, and the deep-blue sky make a vivid terrine. She parks beside Hunter's black Jeep and gets out with her bag, experiencing the slight vertigo one can feel after an arduous journey to an unfamiliar place. She leans against her car for a moment to steady herself.

"You made it."

Hunter is standing by the door to the cabin. He's wearing a faded green T-shirt, khaki shorts, and tan hiking boots. Kathryn is struck again by how young he seems out of his teaching uniform of starched shirts and ties and pressed pants. He looks like anyone she knows, any of her friends from graduate school.

"I can't imagine what it's like to get out of here in the winter," she says. "How do you make it to school every day?"

"It's not bad. You just need four-wheel drive and a shovel." He smiles, and she smiles back. He seems different, somehow—more relaxed. It makes her feel more relaxed, too. "C'mon, I'll show you around," he says.

She follows him to the front of the cabin, which is surprisingly modern, a wall of glass opening onto a broad, high deck. "I'm facing south, so I get the sunrise and the sunset," he says. "I designed it so I'd be able to see both."

"This is not what I expected," she says.

"I used to live in a little shack on this same spot with a woodstove and no phone, but I got sick of roughing it." He laughs. "That's my dirty little secret, I guess. I like a good hot shower now and then."

"I won't tell."

"I knew I could trust you." Leading her up the steps and through the sliding glass doors into a big, sunny room with a high ceiling and exposed beams, he explains how he cut trees on his own property to build the cabin, selecting them carefully so there wouldn't be a gap in the woods.

Kathryn looks around at the simple furnishings: two Adirondack chairs, a Danish modern off-white couch, a wrought-iron lamp with a parchment shade, a coffee table fashioned from a tree trunk, Bose speakers. An old black rotary phone. Low, built-in bookshelves line the walls; interspersed among the rows of books are pieces of handcrafted pottery, old clocks, and some scattered Americana—an old Coke bottle, a handmade doll, a worn wooden shoe form. "You have good taste," she murmurs.

"Surprised?" he says, an amused lilt in his voice.

She walks through the living room, setting her bag on the couch, and peers into the immaculate modern kitchen at the far end. "I was envisioning a few deer heads on the wall, maybe a varnished fish." Wandering over to the fireplace, she scans the framed snapshots on the mantel. There's a close-up of a lily, a long shot of a woodpile, a mountain stream. "You don't have any personal photos," she remarks.

"No," he says. "I don't see much point."

"Why not?"

"I don't believe in fetishizing people. Photographs do that."

"Oh. I thought they just helped you remember."

"You don't need a photograph to remember," he says. "What's important stays in your head. In your heart."

The sentimentality of these words startles her, and she turns to look at him, but she can't read his expression. "Are you close to your family?" she asks.

"No," he says.

"Why not?"

He pauses before answering, a small reprimand for her nosiness. "My mother is unstable, and my father died when I was young."

Like Jennifer, she thinks. "Do you have any siblings?"

"Yes."

"Where are they?"

He shrugs. "It's not so much where they are as who they are. I have nothing in common with them."

"Have they ever been here?"

"No."

"Has anyone ever been here?" She smiles to show that she's kidding, but he takes the question seriously.

"I'm not a total recluse, but I'm also not afraid of being alone. What about you, Kathryn?" he asks abruptly. "How do you feel about being alone?"

She walks over to the wall of glass overlooking the water. Outside, the colors seem artificially heightened, like a colorized movie: a robin's-egg-blue sky, a navy-blue lake, emerald-green trees. "I used to hate it," she says.

"What changed?"

"I changed."

"Ah," he says, "back to our old debate about whether people change. I guess we have a fundamental difference."

"You don't think you've changed at all in the past ten years?" she asks, turning back to look at him.

He shakes his head. "People learn to tolerate things, or hide things. Our essential natures stay the same."

"So if you met Jennifer today—" she begins.

"Whoa," he says, stepping back. "Where did that come from?"

"I just wondered," she says quickly, her eyes innocently wide, as if the question had randomly occurred to her.

"Why?"

"I wondered if she's your type."

He studies her face as if trying to figure out how it works.

"Not that she's a type," she adds. "But if she came back—"

"Kathryn, she's dead," he says bluntly.

She blinks. "I—How do you know?"

"Everybody knows."

"What do you mean?"

He rolls his eyes. "C'mon. The girl vanished ten years ago and hasn't been spotted since. What'd you think, she ran off to be a movie star?"

"But there's no proof—"

"What proof do you need? At some point you just have to accept the empirical evidence."

Taking a deep breath, she says, "Okay, then. What happened to her?"

He shrugs. "Oh, everybody has a theory, don't they? I don't think it really matters. The point is"—he flips his fingers out aggressively—"she's gone. That fact alone renders idle speculation meaningless."

"I don't agree," she says. "It does matter."

"But there's nothing anybody can do about it."

"What they can do is find out the truth."

The corners of his mouth turn up slightly. "My. I never knew you were such a crusader."

That night by the river flashes through her mind. *Come on, Jen. Don't get deep on me.* "I never was," she says.

He stands there looking at her for a moment, with his hands on his hips. Then he rubs his chin. "Let's define our terms," he says. "I'm not sure I believe there is such a thing as the truth. There are facts. But truth is variable, open to interpretation."

"Facts, then," Kathryn says. "Facts would be enough."

"Ah," he says, "but facts will only take you so far. You can have all the facts and still not know what happened."

This is going in circles, she thinks; I'm not going to get anywhere this way. "Jennifer was in love with you," she says. "Is that a fact? Or is it the truth?"

"She was young. She didn't know what it meant to be in love."

"She didn't know," Kathryn persists, "so it wasn't true?"

"She wasn't in love with me," Hunter says abruptly, turning away. "If she'd been in love with me . . ."

"What?"

The telephone rings, a burbling, old-fashioned sound. They both jump.

"Just a minute," he says. He goes over to pick it up. "Hello?" Kathryn watches his face.

"Um. It's for you," he says with a questioning look.

"Me?"

He nods, holding the phone out.

She walks over, as if she's in a trance, and takes it from him. "Hello?"

"Kathryn? It's me, Jack."

"Oh." She looks at Hunter, who's watching her impassively.

"Are you okay? Is everything all right?"

Her head is light with panic, and she needs a moment before she can answer. She takes slow, shallow breaths. "How did you find me?"

"Give me a break," he says. "It was obvious where you were headed. I'd be pissed as hell right now if I weren't so concerned."

"Don't try to track me down again," she says.

"What?" She can hear the puzzlement in his voice.

"I told you it was over, Jack."

He's silent for a moment. Then he says, "Do you want me to come out there?"

"Not right now."

"Do you want me to call the police?"

"No."

"Has he confessed to anything?"

"I told you, no."

"Listen." He sighs. "Be careful. Don't say or do anything that might rile him up. I'm going to wait an hour, and then I'm coming. A guy here knows Hunter; he's been to his house to play poker. I'll get directions from him."

"You can talk all you want, but it's not going to make a difference," she says.

"I'll park at the end of his driveway. And I'll keep the lights on so you can see me. If I leave the car for any reason, the keys will be under the seat. Okay?"

Hunter's arms are crossed; he's leaning against the wall. Kathryn rolls her eyes at him. "This is embarrassing, Jack," she says. "Why can't you just accept the truth?"

"You mean that you're in love with me?"

She bites her lip, acutely aware of Hunter watching her. "Don't call me again," she says.

When she hangs up the phone, she smiles apologetically at Hunter. "Sorry about that."

"That's pretty odd," he says. "Calling you out here."

"Well . . ." She hesitates, her heart pounding in her chest. "I haven't been completely honest with you. Jack and I saw each other briefly, and it didn't work out. He's become kind of obsessive."

"Funny, I never thought of Jack Ledbetter that way."

"Neither did I." She shrugs. "The things you find out about people."

"How did he know you were here?"

"He must've guessed. I haven't made a secret of the fact that I'm . . . interested in you."

"In what way?"

She swallows. "I think you know."

He gazes at her for a long moment. Then he turns away. Glancing out the big window, he says, "The light is fading. If we're going on a walk, we should do it soon."

"We don't have to," she says.

"But you came all this way."

She nods. Then she turns to get her bag.

"Oh, leave that," he says.

"But—"

"Where we're going you won't need it," he says. "It would only get in the way."

THE WOODS ARE full of sounds. Hunter points out each one: the call of the whippoorwill, the pecking cuckoo, the low buzz of mosquitoes, the lapping of the water on the shore, the occasional rumble of a truck or car in the distance. He shows her how shadows fall according to the time of day, and how certain plants grow in specific conditions. He demonstrates how to move like a deer through the forest with a soft, sure step, how to move like sunlight, cloaking yourself in shadow.

She follows him silently, nodding now and then to show she's listening. She had thought she'd be scared to be alone with him like this, but she isn't. Instead she's remembering what a good teacher he was— how patiently he explained things in class, always checking with the students as he drew diagrams on the board to make sure they understood. He turned social studies into Trivial Pursuit; he delineated the structure of government with a dominoes game.

"Look," he's saying, "here—this is what I call a desire line. Strictly speaking, it's a landscape-architecture term for the paths people create when they cut across the grass instead of taking a prescribed route— people who follow their desires, if you want to be literal. But I just use it to describe any foot trail that's relatively new and hasn't been formalized by markers or maps."

At first she doesn't see it; she has to let her eyes adjust before she can discern the faint path of broken twigs and matted leaves. He bends to run his finger through a bald patch of dirt. "If you're lost, you can follow this line to safety. It will take you somewhere someone else has been."

"This must be yours," she says.

He nods.

"Where does it go?"

Straightening up, he says, "Why don't you find out?" He steps back and lifts his hand.

"Aren't you going to lead the way?"

"I know the way," he says. "This is your adventure."

She turns uncertainly and examines the area in front of her. It's hard to make out anything now. She glances from side to side, but it all looks the same. Suddenly the trees feel like people in a crowd, pushing and jostling.

"Relax," he says. "Take your time."

She shuts her eyes for a moment, then opens them. There, to her right, is the broken twig she noticed before. She looks beyond it and sees another dangling stalk and some matted leaves. Suddenly, as if she's looking at a picture that contains a hidden image, Kathryn's eyes adjust, and she can see the path. She traces the twig to a trampled leaf, and then, farther ahead, a patch of dirt and a heap of vines pushed aside by a careless foot. Slowly she begins to move forward, using each visual marker as a stepping-stone to the next. After several dozen yards something unexpected happens: she realizes that she can see the path stretching ahead, winding around to the left and out of sight. She begins to walk faster, her eyes traveling quickly from marker to marker as she makes her way through the woods.

Behind her, Hunter's step is so quiet that for a moment Kathryn forgets he's there. "You've got it," he says in a low voice, his praise warm on her back. This must have been what it was like for Jennifer, she thinks—this sudden ordering of the universe, this exquisite clarity.

All at once, without warning, Kathryn finds herself in a grassy clearing. She looks around at the pines ringing the perimeter, the birches poking up behind. It seems familiar, somehow, as if she's been here before. She breathes deeply, smelling the pine and the sour grass. Hunter steps into the clearing, and Kathryn turns to look at him. "I recognize this place," she says. Shutting her eyes, she turns slightly, listening to the sounds of the forest. "I must have been dreaming. I know it so well. I'm in the middle of this clearing, and I'm turning . . ."

In the distance, a train whistle sounds. Kathryn feels a chill through her. She stops and opens her eyes.

Footprints disappearing into the grass, an open window, an out-stretched hand, miles of highway, a shallow grave. It isn't until now, this moment, that she knows for certain. Jennifer is dead. She isn't hiding out somewhere; she didn't run away. She's dead, and she's probably been that way for a long time.

Ten years of waiting, and it comes down to this.

Hunter looks at Kathryn curiously. Everything is still. "I think I know what happened," she says.

He doesn't answer. His face is blank, expressionless.

"When she left us that night, she went to meet you," Kathryn says. "You picked her up on Griffin Road and drove her out here. And then . . ." She pauses. Vaguely, from the depths of her memory, Jennifer's words that night by the river float into her consciousness: *You know there's a path you're supposed to be following in life—but somehow, maybe because you wanted to, or maybe because it happened so slowly you didn't even realize it, you've moved farther and farther away from it. . . .*

"She brought her passport," Kathryn says slowly. "You must have been planning to go somewhere. But she changed her mind. It wasn't just going away. It was everything." She hesitates, watching his reaction. "She thought she could just leave, that she didn't owe you anything. After all you'd done for her," she says, her voice rising. "You had given her so much. And she was going to just walk away."

"It wasn't the way you think."

His words knock the breath out of her.

"We'd made all these plans," he says. "We were going to go to Mexico—I knew the International School needed teachers down there, and she wanted to take a few years off before college."

Frowning, Kathryn shakes her head. "But Jennifer wouldn't have done that. She wouldn't have done that to Will. She never said a word about going away."

"Will knew she was unhappy. He probably knew she wanted to leave. And it wasn't going to be forever, just a year or two. She'd written him a letter, explaining everything, that she was going to mail when we got there. She wrote you one, too, I think."

Kathryn feels a pang in her chest. "Really? Where is it?"

He shrugs. "I never saw it. She just told me about it. Who knows, maybe she was lying. Because when we got back here that night, it was clear she'd been thinking about the whole situation, and she wasn't going anywhere."

Kathryn nods. "So," she says haltingly, "you . . . got angry?"

He steps back with his hands up, as if he's been stopped by the police. "See, that's the thing. You're always jumping to conclusions."

"I'm not," she says. *Calm down, relax.* "I'm listening."

He looks at her, the muscles in his face twitching, and takes another step back, as if he might turn and go.

Kathryn reaches out and touches his arm. "Rick," she says in a low voice, "I'm sorry."

Slowly, he shakes his head.

"I am listening."

For a long moment neither of them says a thing. Then he looks at her intensely, his eyes probing hers as if he's searching for something specific. She resists the impulse to turn away. "I just don't know," he murmurs.

"Yes, you do." She pauses, trying to form the right words. "Remember how you said that Jennifer had an internal compass, that no matter how lost she was she could always find a way out? Well, you have that. You know."

He lifts his hand, and she recoils slightly, then steadies herself, hoping he didn't notice. Running his fingers through his thick, dark hair, he sighs loudly. "I don't want you to interrupt."

"Okay."

"I mean it."

She nods.

He takes a deep breath. "We did get into an argument," he says carefully. "She'd been drinking—we both had. Anyway, she took off; she ran out into the woods, and I followed her. It was pitch-dark and she was crashing through the trees and I was just trying to get her to slow down; all I wanted to do was talk to her, reason with her, but she was beyond that." He looks off into the distance, as if he's trying to remember how it happened. "It was like she was running from everything—everything she was afraid of, everything she couldn't control. There was no reasoning with her. She just . . . lost it.

"I didn't know about the asthma," he continues. "I mean, I knew about it—she'd mentioned it before—but I didn't know how serious it was. If I'd known what could happen, I never would have let her go. Because when I finally got to her, she was having a full-blown asthma attack. She didn't have an inhaler, and I had no idea what to—"

"Get her out of here," Kathryn breaks in; she can't help it.

He stares at her coldly. "It wasn't that easy," he says. "She was gasping like a fish, and we were in the middle of the woods. It was so sudden. By the time I got her out, it would've been too late. She was . . . dying, for God's sake."

"Of an asthma attack?" Kathryn says sharply. "That's absurd."

"I couldn't believe it either," he says.

"So what you're saying is, you just let her die."

"No. There was nothing I could do."

"Well, then, why didn't you tell someone what happened?"

"I almost did. I thought about it long and hard. But in the end, I just didn't see the point." He sighs, looking from side to side as if the trees might back him up. "She was my student," he says. "It didn't look good. I would've been blamed for it, when it wasn't my fault. . . ."

"They would've been able to tell if it was asthma," Kathryn says.

"Not necessarily. And even if they could, even if they proved it had nothing to do with me, I'd still have been implicated. It would've ruined my life."

"Ruined your life," she echoes, the cool neutrality she's aiming for undermined by a hostile edge.

"Listen, Kathryn." His voice is brittle and cold. "Nothing I could do was going to bring her back. Why should I pay the price for something I didn't do?"

"Didn't you care about the fact that all of us were going crazy looking for her? Jennifer's family spent months trying to find her. People's lives were torn apart."

"Would it have been better to know she was dead?"

"Yes. It would have been better."

"I don't know how to make you understand," he says. "And maybe I'm just a romantic. But you see, all the stuff that took place after the fact was meaningless. Jennifer was gone; she didn't exist anymore. What happened between Jennifer and me had nothing to do with anybody else."

Kathryn's head is spinning. The trees are closing in again. The sky is far away, a distant blue. It almost seems inevitable, being here like this with Hunter, circling the ring in a cautious dance, sniffing the air for Jennifer's scent. She tries to comprehend what he's saying, but his words don't make sense to her. The lyrics of that song on the tape he sent are running through her head: *"There's a message in the wild and I'm sending you the signal tonight. . . ."*

Slowly, she looks around the clearing at the patchy grass and small outcroppings of rock. One corner, across from where they're standing, is barren of trees and bushes and even grass. In the thin afternoon light, there are no shadows. The trees seem to be whispering, passing a secret around. "Jennifer is buried here, isn't she?" Kathryn says softly.

A plane buzzes overhead, and Hunter looks up. He watches it cut through the sky, trailing a faint line of white, until it's gone. Then he looks at Kathryn and shrugs. "She could be anywhere."

Something snaps inside her. She backs away, shaking her head. "This is bullshit," she says. "I don't believe you. I don't believe she just died like that."

"I don't need you to believe me," he says calmly.

"Then why did you tell me that story?"

"Because you seemed to want one so badly."

"But it's a lie." She can feel her heart beating in her chest. "I want to know the truth. I want to know why you killed her."

"I told you," he says, putting his hand up again, as if warding off her words, "you shouldn't jump to conclusions. That gets me very upset."

"Why did you call me and threaten me?" she asks, her voice rising in anger. "Why did you leave that stuff in my car?"

"I wanted you to leave it alone."

She tries to look in his eyes, but they're unreadable. All at once, she realizes how hard he's worked to keep this a secret. Rachel's unwillingness to say what she knows about him suddenly makes sense. "You've been sleeping with Rachel to keep her quiet, haven't you? You were afraid she'd tell what she knew."

"Rachel doesn't know anything about this."

"But she knows about you and Jennifer. She knows enough for it to be a problem."

"You shouldn't . . . do this," he says, his voice laced with warning.

"What are you going to do? Make me disappear?" She stares at him, her heart pounding. Then she turns recklessly, blindly, to find a way out, hitting her forehead on a branch. The leaves in front of her are a blur of green. She breaks into a run, moving forward without sense, tearing through brambles and stumbling over bushes, the sound of her feet pounding in her ears. All she knows is that the sun is to her left, sliding down the late-afternoon sky, and the cabin, and possibly Jack's car, are ahead of her in the distance. Her legs are strong; when she finds her gait she feels like a deer, slipping between trees and dodging branches with instinctive ease.

Hunter is behind her. She can hear his footsteps amplified in the quiet, thudding through the underbrush. He knows this forest; he will catch her if she slows, so she picks up the pace, working her way into the densest area she can see.

Suddenly she stumbles. She feels her foot give way and then splay to the side, and she sprawls forward, her leg stuck at an awkward angle in a rut of vines. She lands, hard, on the rocky ground. For a moment she just sits there, breathing hard. Struggling to stand, she puts weight on her foot, but pain shoots up her leg, making her head swim. She leans back against a birch, gripping her ankle.

All at once Hunter's hand is on her arm, his fingers digging into her flesh. He pulls her around, and she cries out in pain and sinks to the ground. He crouches over her, his face contorted in anger, his hands rough around her throat, and she turns her head away, feeling his grip tighten on her neck. There is a way in which this, too, feels inevitable, as if her worst fears were destined to come true, as if what happened to Jennifer must also happen to her. Why should she deserve anything different? Part of her almost welcomes this, doesn't care what happens next. It is tempting to imagine what it would be like to disappear, to escape herself, to leave everything behind. She looks up at the web of branches under a canopy of leaves, the flitting birds and specks of blue in the distance, and then turns her head, against the pressure of his hands, to look Hunter in the eye. She thinks of her mother and Jack and, strangely, randomly, something the Bass Harbor sculptor said as she pointed out the large window of her studio at the rocky Maine coastline: "This is life. This is all I need." She thinks of Jennifer's voice on the tape, pleading, *What do you want me to say?* She thinks of Jennifer laughing. And then, abruptly, she comes to her senses. Dying this way would be meaningless—another girl buried out here in the woods, and for what? She owes it to Jennifer, and to herself, to get out of here alive.

"Rick," she whispers, struggling to speak.

"No," he says through clenched teeth.

"Wait—"

He clamps his hand under her chin.

She tries to swallow. Saliva pools in the corner of her mouth, runs in a trickle down the side of her face. "Please," she manages. "I know . . . how . . . it happened." A branch is digging into her back and she attempts to move, but he has her pinned. "I know . . . why you told me."

"Stop," he warns.

"I—I loved her, too," she says.

He doesn't shift his position, but his hands loosen slightly on her neck. Wind moves through the trees, a chorus of whispers.

"I know how she was," Kathryn says. "How nothing you gave could ever be enough. You were only useful to her as long as you could help. And it was inevitable that sooner or later she'd figure out that you were no different from anyone else; you couldn't help her any more than anyone else had."

"I wanted to . . . help her," he says, almost inaudibly.

She nods slightly, as much as she can.

"You know too much. I never meant to tell."

Kathryn shakes her head. "She wanted to disappear. She would have found a way to do it. You were just the most convenient form of escape."

The words are so easy to say—just words, after all, nothing more. But even as she speaks them, Kathryn recognizes the cowardice behind them. They're the words of a rationalizing teenager, accurate enough in their own small way but in no sense true. Kathryn knows exactly what Hunter wants to hear because she wants to hear it, too: She wants someone to absolve her of responsibility for losing Jennifer. Blaming Jennifer for her own disappearance is easy enough, if you look at half the evidence.

He closes his eyes, and his head sinks onto her chest. Struggling against her own revulsion, she reaches up to touch his hair. It's softer and finer than she'd imagined.

"This is between us, Rick," Kathryn breathes. "No one else needs to know. Nobody else can understand what that means."

"I thought I was losing her," he says.

"You probably were."

"I never meant . . ."

For a moment she thinks he's going to say more, but he doesn't. She touches his neck with the flat of her hand, feeling the fine sandpaper of his skin, his strong jawbone, his pulsing jugular. "I believe you," she says. She's not lying; she does believe him. She believes him in the moment, knowing that a split second later it might not be true.

He lifts his head to look at her, then pulls himself up to sit beside her. "This is strange," he says. "I'm not sure what to do."

"You don't have to do anything," she says.

Reaching down, he traces the side of her face with two fingers, gently brushing the hair off her cheek. "You are . . . like her," he muses. "It's not just the hair. It's as if you had to go through the experience of losing her in order to find her in yourself—the part of her you always wanted to be."

She turns away. It's a grotesque justification. It may be true. *Which one of us is going to be famous? Who's going to be the alcoholic? Which one of you girls will ditch your husband for me when we come back for our ten-year reunion? Who's dying young?*

"You could stay here," he says.

She nods. "I could."

For a few moments neither of them speaks. The afternoon light is fading quickly now, the forest floor around them becoming dense and shadowed. "We should get back," he says finally.

Sitting up, she rubs her leg. "My ankle is killing me."

He prods her ankle gently, touching different places. "Does that hurt?" he asks. "Does that?"

She grimaces. "It all hurts."

"It's swollen," he says. "I can take a look at it at the cabin."

"Oh. Thanks," she says, trying to sound nonchalant, "but I need to get home. My mother is expecting me."

"You can call her."

"We have plans," Kathryn says.

"So tell her something came up." He smiles at her, a bland, steady smile, a challenge.

She shakes her head. "I can't. It's—it's her birthday." Her mother's birthday is actually in May, but it's the only thing Kathryn can think of.

"Really? Why didn't you say so before?"

She starts to answer, then realizes the question is rhetorical.

He reaches for her hand and pulls her to her feet. Gingerly she puts pressure on the hurt ankle and finds that she can limp-walk well enough. "I think I can make it," she says.

"No, let me help you." Hunter leans his shoulder against hers, coaxing her to put her arm around his neck. It's a high and uncomfortable angle, and Kathryn finds herself off balance, dependent on him for support.

They make their way slowly through the woods, and after a few minutes Kathryn realizes that Hunter has steered them back to a trail. It's easier to walk two abreast now; the branches and bushes have been cleared from the path.

When they get to her car, she turns to face him. Over his shoulder she can see the faint glimmer of headlights through the trees. *Jack*, she thinks, and prays silently that Hunter doesn't turn around.

"When will I see you again?" he asks.

"Whenever you want," she says, trying to keep the alarm out of her voice.

"Tomorrow." He moves closer.

Butterfly wings flitter in her stomach. "Fine," she says, inching back.

"Tonight."

"It is tonight."

"Later," he says.

"Let me go home first, see about this ankle." She smiles apologetically. "I'll call you."

He looks at her as if he's not sure whether to let her go. "You'll be fine," he says. "You don't need to worry."

"I know."

She opens the door to her car, and then remembers the bag. Her car keys and the tape recorder are in it, and it's sitting on his couch. "I—my bag," she says. "I need to get it."

"I'll get it for you."

"No," she says, a bit too quickly, "I know right where it is."

He grins. "The house isn't that big."

Her palms are sweating. "But—"

"Stay here," he says. "I'll be right back."

Watching him trot around to the front of the cabin, she is lightheaded with panic, as if terror has replaced the blood in her veins. She imagines him sliding open the glass door, entering the house, looking around for the bag, and spotting it on the couch, then picking it up. Curious. Looking inside. Pulling out the small black cassette player, turning it over, seeing the blank tape inside. Considering. Realizing exactly what it was intended for.

She might tell him that she is using the tape player for a story, or that she carries it everywhere she goes, or that she left it in the bag the day before and forgot about it. She could come up with all kinds of excuses, but he'd never believe her. He'd jump to conclusions; he'd assume she was planning to trap him, to get his confession on tape, and of course he'd be right.

She turns around and looks blindly at the tangle of evergreens, trying to make out shapes in the foliage. "Jack," she stage-whispers.

Ahead of her, somewhere in the trees, she hears her name. She narrows her eyes and limps forward a few steps, pausing to listen. She sees a dark form moving in the trees and then Jack steps forward. He gives her a once-over and glances up at the house.

"Oh, God," she breathes, relief washing over her. Looking hastily over her shoulder, she moves toward him. "We've got to get out of here, fast."

"Are you all right?" he asks, coming to meet her.

"I think so," she says. "We have to get to your car."

"What about yours?"

"I don't have the key."

He puts his arm around her waist, and they move as quickly as they can down the driveway to where Jack's car is parked. When they've almost reached it, they hear a yell.

"Hey!"

Kathryn turns to see Hunter's dark form poised at the edge of the cabin. The tape recorder is clenched in his hand.

"Hey!" He throws the tape recorder down and begins running toward them down the driveway.

Kathryn wrenches open the passenger's side door. She heaves herself inside, locking her door and the one behind it as Jack jumps into the driver's seat. He fumbles with the keys, dropping them on the floorboard and scrambling to retrieve them. Just as Hunter reaches the car, Jack starts the engine.

Finding Kathryn's door locked, Hunter pounds his fist on the windshield. His face is terrible, his eyes wide and his mouth contorted in fury. He presses his nose against the glass and Kathryn shrinks back in her seat. "You fucking bitch!" he spits, bashing his fist against the window, as if he's punching her in the face.

"Hang on," Jack says through gritted teeth. He pulls off the shoulder and onto the dirt and gravel road with Hunter close beside them, walking and then jogging and finally running to keep up. Kathryn watches Hunter's hand on her window, the white pads of his fingers gripping the glass and then sliding as Jack turns the wheel and the car veers to the left, cutting sharply across the road and sideswiping a cluster of bushes, the branches squeaking as they scrape along the side. Jack guns the engine and the car jumps and jostles over the rutted road. In the side-view mirrow, Kathryn sees Hunter looking after them as they drive away, his figure getting smaller and smaller until they go around a bend and it disappears.

AT THE POLICE station Kathryn gives a statement with as much detail as she can remember. "Her body is buried in that clearing," she says. "I'm sure of it. There's a path leading to it from the cabin, but it's hard to see."

"We'll find it," Gaffney says. "Now, are you going to be willing to testify against this guy in court?"

"Whatever it takes," she says.

"Good." Gaffney smiles broadly. "Now go get that bum ankle looked at, and we'll do the rest. I don't want to see you nosing around here again anytime soon."

In the car on the way to the emergency room, Kathryn leans back and closes her eyes.

"Tired?" Jack asks.

"No. Not tired." She looks over at him. "It's just a weird way for this to end. It feels . . . unfinished."

"You solved it, Kathryn. The mystery is over."

"But it isn't," she says. "We still don't know why."

Slowly, he shakes his head. "I hate to say it, but I doubt we ever will."

She gazes out at the streetlights gliding by her window. *Facts will only take you so far,* Hunter said. *You can have all the facts and still not know what happened.*

But maybe, she thinks, that's the wrong way to think about it. Maybe you have to have the facts before you can even begin to make sense of the story.

She turns to look at Jack, and he leans over and kisses her on the neck, keeping his eyes on the road.

"I do love you, Jack," she says.

He grins and lightly squeezes her knee. "You've had an exciting day," he says. "I won't hold you to that."

EPILOGUE

As summer draws to a close, the night air sharpens. Mornings are bracingly cool. Kathryn has a cast on her leg for the broken ankle, and she's getting quite adept at hobbling around. She spends a lot of time on the front porch of her mother's house, sitting in the swing and working her way through *Anna Karenina*, which she was supposed to read for a class in college but never got around to. After work Jack comes over and makes dinner for her and her mother, or they order a pizza, or they go down to the Sea Dog to sit on the deck and watch the boats go by. Inevitably, by the end of the evening they're back on the front porch of her mother's house again.

When the police went to Hunter's property to look for a body, Hunter was gone. An hour later they tracked him down at Bangor International Airport, where he was sitting in the TV lounge with a standby ticket to Mexico. He didn't seem surprised to see them, and he didn't put up a fight. He got up, gathered his bags, and led them all down the escalator and through the electronic doors to the police cars lined up by the curb.

They didn't even bother to handcuff him. People who witnessed the arrest said at first they couldn't figure it out; they thought maybe he was working undercover, he seemed so unfazed by it all.

Kathryn doesn't know if everything Hunter told her is true. But the police did find a body in the clearing, and dental records confirmed the identity as Jennifer's, so that much, at least, is known. Hunter isn't saying much; he's got a smooth-talking lawyer and even an alibi, the waitress from Raymond's, who swears she remembers that he took her home that night ten years ago after closing the place down at two.

So the truth about what happened will probably never be fully revealed. But for some reason, Kathryn finds, it doesn't matter so much to her anymore. Whatever Hunter's lies and distortions and backtracking, whether he panicked, letting Jennifer die out of negligence and fear, or whether he killed her with his own hands, at least they've found her. She's not missing any longer. They can lay her to rest.

AFTER THE FRONT-PAGE articles have been written and filed away, Jennifer's family holds a small memorial service at Mount Hope Cemetery, where her remains are buried under a simple stone marker. It's a clear, cool day; looking around as Will is speaking, an open Bible in his hands, Kathryn is aware of the sharp edges of things: the cut marble headstones, the dry, brittle leaves rustling overhead, the black spiky fence, the lines of age and grief etched on the faces around her. Jennifer's mother, usually so nervous, exhibits a strange, watchful calm. Rachel looks as if she's been crying for days.

As they were standing around before the service, Mrs. Pelletier came up to Kathryn and hugged her fiercely and wordlessly before taking her face in her hands and drawing her close. "I underestimated you," she whispered. "It's all right," Kathryn said, and Mrs. Pelletier just smiled sadly and took her seat. Will enveloped Kathryn in a full body hug. "This is tough," he said, choking back tears. "I hated what Rachel said that night at the reunion, but in a way she was right. This has consumed me." Rachel was icily cordial, as if she'd been deeply, gravely wronged.

Standing beside her at the grave site, Jack slips his hand into Kathryn's and laces his fingers through hers. "I never understood what it meant to say 'rest in peace,' " Will is saying. "Now I do. In burying my sister today I am finally letting go of the past, not because questions don't remain, but because I acknowledge that no one can ever adequately address the one question that matters: why she was taken from us, why her life had to end so early. As long as we need an answer, we will have no peace. So we make a choice, and that choice is to put to rest the questions that remain.

"So, Jennifer," he says, not looking down and not looking up, but somewhere in the middle distance, "rest in peace. And forgive us for not knowing you better."

At the end of the service the small crowd disperses, and the five friends linger behind. "We should be better about staying in touch," Brian says, and they all nod in wistful acceptance of the fact that their friendship, rooted in a specific time and place, will probably survive mainly in memory. Brian looks at his watch and excuses himself with promises of wedding invitations and pints of Geary's the next time any of them are in Portland. Rachel says she has mountains of papers waiting to be graded; she needs to get back to her desk. At the path toward the gate she turns back to look at the ones who remain. "I loved her too," she says, holding her chin out as if she's balancing something fragile on it, and there is a long pause before Will nods and Jack says, "We all know that."

Will, Kathryn, and Jack talk about logistics for a while. Will is going down to Florida for a few weeks to stay with his mother before heading back to Boston. Hunter's trial is scheduled for late January at the moment but likely, through defense maneuverings, to be delayed and even moved. "I don't even care when it happens," Will says. He clears his throat and looks at them, a small smile softening the intensity of his words. "I just needed for her to be found."

After a while they leave him standing there by the stone marker in the weak sunlight, tilting his head and leaning forward slightly on the balls of his feet as if engaged in conversation. "He'll be all right," Jack says as they make their way to his car, and Kathryn answers, a little quickly, "I know," though neither of them actually does. Their exchange isn't disingenuous, exactly; it's just shorthand for so many things. These discussions will come, but not today. For now they're content to keep things simple. This moment, they know, is fleeting, and they want to hold on to it as long as they can.

THE SKY IS the color of skim milk most mornings; at night the moon lights the sky like a giant strobe. Kathryn buys a green Polartec sweatshirt from T.J. Maxx and takes to wearing it every day. After a week of this, her mother says, "Let's go shopping. My treat," and pulls out a pile of catalogues. They sit on the living-room couch together and leaf through the pages, and by the end of it Kathryn has a new fall wardrobe for the first time in years, suitable for a long, cold descent into winter.

Her Virginia driver's license expires, and she renews it in Maine. She gets a check-cashing card at Doug's Shop 'n Save and transfers her checking account to Fleet Bank. When her mother offers to buy season tickets to the Bangor Symphony—something they can do together—Kathryn agrees. Frank repossesses the yellow Saturn, and she takes a loan from her father to buy a used Toyota from a lawyer in his firm. She starts to scan apartment listings in the paper. And though she tells herself she can leave anytime, it's getting harder to imagine doing so.

She calls her brother, Josh, and leaves a message on his machine telling him that she's staying in Bangor longer than she'd thought, and she hopes he'll come up for a weekend. He calls back with a date: the first week in October, will she still be there? "It looks that way," Kathryn tells him. "I don't have plans to leave."

"Face it, my dear," her grandmother says one afternoon when Kathryn begins to make noises about moving to a city—Boston, maybe, or Washington, D.C.; she has a friend there who writes for the *Post*—"you're not going anywhere." She gestures toward a pile of books Kathryn has stacked on a chair. "You have a library card, for goodness' sake. If that's not a sign of permanence, I don't know what is. But I'll just say one thing," she says, leaning closer. "If you do intend to stay in this town, you must make a commitment to it. None of this moaning about other places and missed opportunities. I don't want to hear it, and neither does anybody else. If you stay here, it should be because you want to, and not out of a failure of nerve or imagination."

"What a *ridiculous* thing to say," Kathryn's mother says, dramatically rolling her eyes, when Kathryn reports her grandmother's view. "This does not have to be a lifetime decision. It's the end of the twentieth century, for God's sake—we're not homesteaders roaming around in covered wagons looking for a place to put down roots for generations. You can stay here for a few months or a few years, even," she says, shrugging lightly, "and then go somewhere else if you want to. Last time I heard, you didn't need to sign a long-term contract to live here!" She laughs, but Kathryn finds her words unsettling. She imagines herself ten years from now, still restless, still uncommitted, telling herself that Bangor is okay for the time being, but one day she'll discover the place she really wants to be and move on. She wants to feel like she belongs somewhere, that there's a place she can be that will become a part of her.

"How did you know you wanted to stay here?" she asks Jack, in different ways, again and again, and the answer is always the same: "This is home." He shrugs, his certainty a given, like air. "I never had any desire to live anywhere else." His assuredness both fascinates and repels her. What's wrong with him, that he doesn't dream of a different life, that he can be so easily contented in this small corner of the world?

Early one morning, just after dawn, Jack takes her to Ebemee Lake to go fishing. Mist rests on the surface of the lake like meringue; the trees behind are distant smudges of gold and green and red. A loon sounds its low and mournful call, another echoes back. In the soft gray light Jack's face is sharp and clear, like a studio portrait. Kathryn watches him bending over his rod, concentrating on his line, his careful hands gently threading the lure into place. She looks at the red-checked wool scarf wound around his neck, his fleece-lined jacket, the gray ragg socks pulled up to his shins under thick leather boots. Glancing up, he catches her eye.

"What are you thinking?" he says.

"I'm not thinking. I'm watching."

"You're always thinking," he says, going back to his reel. "Tell me."

In another part of the lake a motorboat starts up, tinny and low, like the hum of a mosquito. The air smells like cold, wet stones. Kathryn remembers this lake. She's been here before. The summer after seventh grade, she and Jennifer spent three weeks here at Camp Keonah. Kathryn had detested every minute of it—the wake-up call at dawn, early-morning swim practice in the frigid water, the hokey Indian-themed art projects featuring beads and feathers and Elmer's glue. But Jennifer was in heaven. She woke up before the trumpet to go on long nature hikes; she starred in the camp musical and taped the satiny blue ribbons she won in canoe races to the rafters of her bottom bunk. When it was time to leave, both of them cried—Kathryn because she was so relieved it was over, and Jennifer because she dreaded going home.

Thinking back, Kathryn realizes that something was already happening to them then. Their lives were moving in different directions. It would have been easy to let circumstances come between them; they shared so few interests or desires. But for some reason it didn't matter. They were two young girls struggling to make sense of a world they didn't understand—a world that would only become more complicated and less comprehensible as they grew older—and they needed each other. Whatever else happened, that simple fact remained.

"Look," Jack says, breaking the silence, and Kathryn follows his gaze to a flotilla of geese several hundred yards away. As the geese glide across the lake, they fan out in a V, their heads and bodies perfectly aligned, like synchronized swimmers. The lake seems different to her now. It might as well be bottomless, the woods around it stretching to infinity. It occurs to her that she could go on searching for the rest of her life for something that can never be found—a promise, an answer, a sign. For so many years she's been waiting, hovering above the moment, that she barely knows how to be.

Closing her eyes, Kathryn smells the pine and smoke in the distance, listens to the water as it laps the sides of the metal boat. She feels a strange quiet, the heat of her restlessness evaporating into the cold morning air. If Jennifer were anywhere, Kathryn thinks, this is where she would be. In her mind's eye Kathryn can still see her. She's leaning forward in the canoe, lifting an oar and then pausing, the oar poised over the water. She turns her head. She's smiling. Has she forgotten something? Is she coming back?

"Hey, you didn't answer my question," Jack says. "Where are you?"

Kathryn opens her eyes. In the distance the geese rise out of the water, squawking and flapping, skimming the surface as they lift into the sky. She twists the gold ring on her finger, and then, almost without thinking, slips it off and puts it in her pocket. She stretches out her hands and looks at them. Her fingers are bare, unadorned; they look naked in the morning light. Reaching out, she touches the rough denim of Jack's knee. "I'm here," she says. It may not be much of an answer, but for now it's the best one she can give.

ACKNOWLEDGMENTS

My husband, David Kline, and my agent, Beth Vesel, were indispensable in the writing of this book. My editor, Claire Wachtel, kept me going through the thick of it. I am grateful for the support and guidance of my parents, Bill and Tina Baker, and my sisters, Cynthia, Clara, and Catherine. Mark Trainer, Katie Greenebaum, Elissa Schappell, and Cathi Hanauer gave generously of their time and advice. Special thanks to Alicia Anstead, Tom Webber, and Jeanne Curran of the *Bangor Daily News*, Lieutenant Edward Geissler of the Bangor Police Department, and Bangor High student Maggie Beiser, who should receive much of the credit for the details I got right.

Finally, I want to acknowledge Danny Staples, Bangor High School Class of '81, whose spirit pervades this book.

About the author

About the book

Insights,
Interviews
& More . . .

Read on

Meet
Christina Baker Kline

CHRISTINA BAKER KLINE is the author of five novels. Born in England and raised there as well as in the American South and Maine, she studied at Yale, Cambridge, and the University of Virginia, where she was a Hoyns Fellow in Fiction.

In addition to the #1 *New York Times* bestseller *Orphan Train*, Kline's novels include *Bird in Hand*, *The Way Life Should Be*, *Desire Lines*, and *Sweet Water*. She is coeditor, with Anne Burt, of *About Face: Women Write About What They See When They Look in the Mirror*. She commissioned and edited two widely praised connections of original essays, *Child of Mine* and *Room to Grow*. She is coauthor, with her mother, Christina Looper Baker, of a book on feminist mothers and daughters, *The Conversation Begins*. She has taught creative writing and literature at Yale, New York University, and Fordham, among other places. Her essays, articles, and reviews have appeared in the *San Francisco Chronicle*, *Psychology Today*, *More*, *Coastal Living*, *The Literarian*, and others. She lives in an old house in Montclair, New Jersey, with her husband and three sons, and spends as much time as possible on the coast of Maine. ∽

Reading Group Guide

1. "Desire lines"—the paths we take in life—play a major role in the narrative. Each character has an idea of where his or her path will lead. How does the reality differ from the paths they imagined in high school?

2. Kathryn and Jennifer are very different. Jennifer is mercurial, beautiful, and self-centered, while Kathryn is quiet, unassuming, and lacks a strong sense of self. Why do you think they were drawn toward each other?

3. Hunter tells Kathryn that she is better off with Jennifer gone. Is this true? How might Kathryn's life have been different if Jennifer never disappeared? What did she gain from the experience of loss?

4. The author does a fantastic job of detailing the complex and nuanced interpersonal dramas of high school, and how they continue to influence us into adulthood. Can you recall an incident or a person from high school that still affects you?

5. The music of Kathryn's adolescence resonates throughout her emotional journey. What effect does this have on you, the reader? How does the author use music to evoke a sense of time and place? Why do you think music is so important during our formative years? ▶

6. How does Kathryn's relationship with her mother evolve over the course of the book? Do you think the shift in their dynamic has anything to do with Kathryn's investigation?

7. Do you think Kathryn's burgeoning relationship with Jack signifies a positive change or a return to bad habits? How will this relationship be different from those she's had in the past?

8. Rosie, the therapist, believes that Jennifer's disappearance put Kathryn in an arrested state of development. She has been afraid to make any choices, or move on, because moving on means giving up. Do you agree with this assessment? Why or why not?

9. We don't spend many pages actually observing Jennifer in scenes, but the interviews Kathryn conducts paint an intriguing portrait. At the end of the book, what impression of Jennifer are you left with?

10. Of the six friends, who do you most identify with, and why? Do you agree with Hunter's theory that people don't change? In what ways have you changed since high school?

11. The choices we make, and the consequences they have, are a

major theme in the book. Which of Kathryn's choices do you agree with? When do you think she should have chosen differently?

12. Just for fun: if you had to come up with yearbook superlatives for each of the characters in the book, what would they be? ❧

Sweet Water

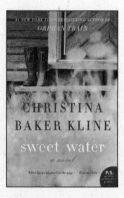

When Cassie Simon, a struggling artist living in New York City, receives a call telling her she has inherited sixty acres of land in Sweetwater, TN, from her grandfather, whom she never knew, she takes it as a sign: it's time for a change. She moves to the small Southern town where her mother, Ellen, grew up—and where she died tragically when Cassie was three. As Cassie delves into the thicket of mystery that surrounds her mother's death, she begins to discover the desperate measures of which the human heart is capable.

THE WOMAN from the Sweetwater courthouse said she thought I could get good money for the land.

"That's a pretty piece of property your granddaddy's left you. Developers have been itching to get their hands on it for years," she said. Her name was Crystal. Her voice was slow and sweet. "We're not exactly a booming metropolis, but people come and go."

"What's the house like?"

"Well, it's not much to look at, but the location's great. About five minutes outside of town, running parallel to the highway. Easy to get to. That's why I say you won't have any trouble getting rid of it. They can chop it into three or four subdivisions, pave roads all through it, and even the farthest houses won't be more than ten minutes from town.

"But I don't imagine you'll get much for that old house. They'll probably tear it down and start from scratch. Too much of a pain to work around it. I'll tell you what, though, you ought to get somebody to help you if you've never handled land before. You'll get swindled if you're not careful."

It was quiet in the gallery, a typical weekday morning. A blond, Nordic-looking couple in their thirties were the only visitors. I smiled at them politely, cradling the phone on my shoulder with my chin, and wrote down the names

Crystal was giving me. To my surprise, the list included my uncle Horace, a local real estate developer.

My grandfather had left me sixty acres. Sixty acres—I couldn't even visualize it. The land stretched across my imagination like a continent, a universe of dying grass and scrubby hills, with an old abandoned house at the center. Crystal, who seemed to know everybody, told me that Clyde, my grandmother, hadn't wanted to live there. She thought it was inconvenient, too remote and old-fashioned. She lived in a modern housing development closer to town, with electric garage doors and access to cable TV. Horace and Elaine, my mother's siblings, lived with their spouses near shopping malls. Their children were grown and out of the house.

"I wouldn't call your uncle first on this one," Crystal was saying. "To be honest with you, it was a surprise to everybody that old Mr. C. left you that land. Not that you don't deserve it, seeing as you're Ellen's daughter and all, but I think people had just plain forgot about you."

In his will, my grandfather had said he wanted to leave his three children sixty acres each but since my mother was dead her share would be passed on to me. From what I could get out of Crystal, it seemed that Horace and Elaine had thought it would be theirs to divide.

It occurred to me that I had absolutely no idea what the property was worth. Thousands of dollars? Five, ten, fifty? ▶

Crystal said she had no idea either. She gave me a name to call for an estimate. "And after you talk to him, take some time to think it over," she said. "You don't have to decide what to do right away. That land ain't going nowhere."

When I hung up the phone, the blond woman looked over at me. "Such an interesting collection you have here," she murmured, tapping one long fingernail on the wall next to a dark abstract acrylic. "Vietnamese. Quite unusual, no?"

I handed her a flier about the artist, and she rolled it up and used it to point out features of the painting to her friend.

I looked around the gallery. The place seemed absurdly small, despite all the work Adam and I had put in trying to make it feel larger: eggshell walls, track lighting, bare, polished pine floors. Geometrically arranged paintings and drawings, each separately lit, lined the walls. The current exhibit—attenuated wire sculptures that resembled cyclones—hung from the ceiling on long wires or rested on butcher-block pedestals we had retrieved from a defunct meatpacking plant. Brochures were stacked on an old wooden desk near the entrance next to an open guest book and cards that read:

> Rising Sun Gallery Contemporary Vietnamese Art
> 304 Hudson Street, NYC
> Adam Hemmer, Owner

with the hours and a phone number.

In the seven years I'd known him, Adam had always wanted his own gallery. In college he studied Asian languages and art history; his mother was a collector of Vietnamese art, so he had a ready field of interest. When he came into some family money in his early twenties, all the groundwork had been laid.

I was with him from the beginning. The two of us spent countless hours finishing the floor and arranging the lighting and seeing to hundreds of details. On opening day we worked through the early hours of the morning, completing final touches as the opaque slice of sky outside the window became transparent: gray, then misty yellow tinged with rose. At five o'clock, as the sun was edging around the corner of the building and spilling in shards across the canvases, over the sculptures, he reached for me in the stillness and we made love for the first time, on the hard wood floor. I remember the smell of paint and polish, the sounds of us echoing in the high-ceilinged room. I thought at the time it was like making love in a church.

That was a long time ago. I can barely recall, now, what drew me to him in the first place. I think it had something to do with the fact that unlike most of our friends, he had a plan for himself and seemed bent on achieving it. He was witty; he was smart. And working for Adam, I knew, would be valuable experience. When it got so that we were barely communicating except to talk business, I repeated those words to myself—valuable experience—like a mantra.

Somewhere along the way, I suppose I must have fallen in love with him. When he reached for me that first time, that early morning in the gallery, it seemed inevitable. The air around us had been charged for weeks. And for a while he was so sensitive to me, so gentle, that I confused the touch of his fingers with love, though a whispering voice in the back of my head warned me not to trust him, even then. So when I found out that he had been seeing other women, I was devastated at first and then philosophical, as if they too were somehow inevitable.

I continued to work with him and even, occasionally, to sleep with him. But as time went on I began to feel a strange silence breeding inside me, a void as tangible as anything I could devise to fill it. I could feel it hollowing against my ribs, inching higher and higher, corroding into itself like a hill of sand.

The blond couple signed the guest book before leaving. I could hear them conversing in some guttural language as they clomped down the stairs to the street. At the bottom of the stairs they paused, letting somebody in, and I cocked my ear to listen. This was what I liked least about being in the gallery alone: you never knew who might be on the way up; you just had to wait, defenseless.

It was Adam. "Oh, hey," he panted, coming into view. He was lugging a large canvas. "Help me here. Meet Veronica." He tilted his head toward a tall hazel-eyed woman following behind him. "She's cataloguing this stuff." ▶

9

"Don't get up. I'll help him," she said in a posh English accent.

Adam raised his eyebrows at me. "Did that couple buy anything?"

"No. They looked around for a while, though. They took a card." I pretended to straighten some papers on the desk. "If you don't need me, I've got some errands to do."

"Well, actually—"

"Let her go," Veronica said. "I'm happy to stay."

I smiled evenly at her. "Great." I went back into the office and got my bag. When I returned, Adam and Veronica were deep in conversation about the oil painting propped against the wall.

"I think it's quite marvelous, really," Veronica was saying, nervously glancing at Adam. She waved her hand in front of the canvas. "All that . . . movement."

"You think?" He sounded dubious. He was silent for a moment, his hand on his chin, and then he said, "No. It hesitates. Nok could see it, but he couldn't do it."

"Hmm." She stepped back, squinting.

"Maybe he should've settled for being a gallery owner, then," I said.

Outside, the West Village was crowded with people heading for lunch, meetings, health clubs. Despite the heat, the air was damp. As I walked along the mazelike dead-end streets, I thought about the winding streets of Venice I had wandered the summer before; there were so many of them, and they all seemed to lead nowhere. But in New York, unlike Venice, people walked with a sense of purpose. They had appointments to keep, problems to solve, deals to make. Just thinking about it made me tired.

I drifted up Hudson Street, buying a salad from a Korean grocery along the way, heading toward the concrete playground where Hudson and Bleecker intersect. A homeless woman followed me, and I gave her my change. After that I was approached three or four times, and every time I turned away I felt a part of me harden and steel itself. This happened every day, and every day the process was the same.

I felt that familiar hollowness, the gnawing space inside me that seemed to be growing. I thought about the gallery, the flawed painting, Adam's hand on Veronica's back.

All at once I was overcome with anxiety at the narrowness of my routine. My days had become numbingly predictable. Every morning the clock struck seven and the alarm drove me toward it—back to the city, into each day, the minutes ticking one after another, time that loitered but wouldn't stand still. Up and showering, soap, shampoo, orange juice by the sink, scanning the paper for fatalities in the neighborhood, hesitating over my umbrella—would it rain? Applying lipstick, nude, the color for summer, at the mirror in the hall. Locking the door behind me once, twice, three times. Swinging shut the iron gate out front, walking in the sun or wind or rain and descending into darkness, tokens, the smell of urine. On the subway folding screens—the *Daily News,* the *Times*—hid blank faces the shades of New York: boredom, mistrust, ennui.

As the clock struck nine we'd be open for business, for pleasure. Hot Brazilian coffee and bagels delivered by Julio, tip included. Inventory. Phone calls. Mail: exhibition at the Sonnabend Gallery, opening at Elena's; the Philadelphia Museum requesting a piece for its collection, but the artist and his work were nowhere to be found.

Time would speed up for a deadline, quickly slow down again: the clock would strike one and it'd be time for lunch. Adam seducing a collector on the phone in the office, me eating turkey on rye, reading the *Voice.* As the day heated into afternoon, Adam might leave for a late lunch with a dealer, and suddenly the gallery would be full: twelve Japanese tourists who speak no English and want to take pictures of the pictures; a couple with three little children; two skinheads who tell me they're from Milwaukee. A headache pounding against my brain. Three o'clock. Four. Adam would return smelling of bourbon and cigarettes.

Evening overpowered afternoon. Long shadows would fall across the butcher block as we shuffled papers, locked the office, straightened the desk. At seven the street was eerily deserted, trash dancing across the gutter. At eight I'd be in the White Horse Tavern with Drew, nursing a seltzer with lime.

The silence consumed me like a parasite, making me high-strung and nervous. Nothing was happening. Tomorrow would be the same. In the bar I'd eat a bowl of olives and watch ▶

the lights come on. Nine o'clock. Ten. Then we'd be out on the street: perhaps now it was raining. I wouldn't have my umbrella. My hair would be plastered down in strips around my face. The rain would be soft, radioactive, bringing the refuse of the city back to itself. We'd split a taxi to Brooklyn, and Drew would tip the driver. It would already be tomorrow. I was almost twenty-seven. The silence whispered in my head. Other faces in other taxis turned and looked at me, and I looked back; I saw myself. The silence grew.

At the park I slipped off my shoes and sat on a bench with my knees up and my arms wrapped around them. All of SoHo and all of the Village probably didn't amount to sixty acres. ᦖ

The Way Life Should Be

I CLICK ON A PHOTO, and the profile is revealed. Chuck, thirty-four, is an actuary who knows how to have a good time. He has been burned before but remains confident that the woman of his dreams is out there. Robert, thirty-one, wants a mutually satisfying relationship with a fellow bodybuilding enthusiast from the tristate area. Colin, a thirty-nine-year-old firefighter, is looking for a red-haired beauty who is ready to start a family and would be happy living on Staten Island. It doesn't take much reading between the lines to spot the guys who live in the same house with or next door to their parents.

As I consider these options, my gaze strays from the computer screen to the bulletin board on my wall. Tacked to the gray synthetic fabric is a photo, torn from a magazine, of a weathered elfin cottage on the Maine coast. Several times a day my glance strays to this photo; the image has become totemic, as unreal a place as Middle Earth. Just looking at it soothes me, the way sound machines of waves or rain can calm your nerves. I have never been to Maine, but in my imagination life there isn't so complicated. I picture a lump of dough rising under a tea towel on a kitchen counter; pansies spilling from a window box; seagulls the size of small dogs, circling in slow motion overhead.

Impulsively—perhaps recklessly— I widen my search, inching up the East ▶

Angela is single in New York City, stuck in a life that seems to have, somehow, just happened. On a hope and a chance, she decides to pack it all up and move to Maine, finding the nudge she needs in the dating profile of a handsome sailor who loves dogs and Italian food. Far from everything familiar, Angela begins to discover the pleasures and secrets of her new small-town community and, in the process, realizes there's really no such thing as the way life *should* be.

Coast. Near Boston I find fewer Italians and bankers, more Irish Catholics and lawyers. Curiously, my qualms about serial rapists and ax murderers diminish the farther north I go, as if all the miscreants and deviants in the northeastern U.S. have confined themselves to the New York area, and the rest is safe.

Moving up the coastline, the pickings get slimmer. Maybe there's a dating website specifically for Mainers, or perhaps Internet dating hasn't really caught on there yet. There is a grand total of six profiles. Most of the head shots feature guys wearing baseball hats with obscure local slogans. Then, all at once—hey! I am gazing into the ice blue eyes of a thirty-five-year-old with the screen name "MaineCatch." His opening teaser is "Sail away with me . . ." No baseball cap, a nice tan, a full head of slightly tousled blond hair, navy blue tennis shirt. I sit up straight in my desk chair and click on his picture.

". . . in the night, and all day, too," the teaser ends. As I read the profile I have to remind myself to breathe. It turns out that Rich, thirty-five, runs a sailing school in a coastal town on Mount Desert Island (*Where?* I must Google it immediately). Five eleven and 180 pounds, he has never been married, is a nonpracticing Protestant, loves Italian food and shellfish. Besides sailing, his interests include curling up with a good book, "my dog Sam (short for Samantha)," hiking, and . . . cooking.

My heart thumps.

I click a button that says "Register for free!" I can post my profile and picture, and receive and respond to inquires, but if I want to contact someone, I'll have to pay the monthly charge of $29. There's a feature called "tagging" that allows you to comment on someone's profile without joining by using one of ten canned lines they provide ("You're hot! Check me out—maybe we can start a fire together").

I fill in the blanks:

Name: Angela (no last name).

Age? Am tempted to lie, then realize that it might lead to a potentially unpleasant spurning scenario. 33.

Religion: Nonpracticing Catholic.

Profession: Event Planner.

Hometown: New York City.

Vital statistics: Hmm. Tempted to ignore or minimize, but realize that this is risky. How is it that most people on this web-site describe themselves as "slim" when most Americans are overweight? I check "medium height, medium build." Then, reconsidering, change it to "slim."

Hobbies /activities: Watching old Lifetime movies in bed, drinking vodka tonics, going out with friends, reading the Styles section, trolling the Chelsea flea market, eating out. Going to the gym every four or five days and trotting on the treadmill for the duration of *Access Hollywood*.

My fingers hover over the keyboard.

Had I the kind of lifestyle wherein one might actually cultivate interesting hobbies, what would they be? Not that I have ever actually done it, but if I did exercise in a nongym way, I think I might enjoy hiking.

So—"Hiking."

The one time I went sailing, with friends at a time share in the Hamptons, I threw up over the side of the boat, but I'm sure I could grow to love it. I like everything except the water part. The beautiful wooden vessels, the salt-crisp nautical wear, picnics on deck with a glass of wine. The shiny, curving wood in the cabin and the rounded windows belowdecks.

"Sailing."

When I was little I wanted a dog. I begged for years, and finally got a mutt named Rusty. He didn't take well to house-training and tended to snap, and when he was almost a year old he met an unfortunate end after ingesting rat poison left in the garage by my dad. But I have no doubt that I could grow to love someone else's adored dog, particularly a Lab named Sam.

"Dogs."

And then there's cooking. For this one I don't have to lie or fudge. I write, "Enjoys cooking Italian food and shellfish with friends, al fresco dining under a clear, star-filled sky." The lyrics of that oldies song about piña coladas and getting caught in the rain waft through my head.

So call it coincidence, call it kismet, call it what you will, but my interests dovetail quite nicely with those of MaineCatch.

Several months ago the publications director of the museum ▶

took a picture of me for the annual report. It's like a yearbook photo—stiff smile, white blouse—but it's all I've got. I fish it out of a drawer and hurry down the hall to the industrial-strength printer/scanner, scanning it through before I have time to second-guess myself. On the computer screen, I am cheered to see, I look a little better than in real life.

I finish filling out my profile and hesitate over the screen name. It should convey cool nonchalance as opposed to sluttish desperation. What would appeal to Mr. Catch? I try out a few. "Ready2Sail"? Too obvious. "NewYorkCatch"? Erk. I flash through a few possibilities—SpicyGirl, LemonLover (like my grandfather, I do love lemons, but—no)—before trying out NewYorkGirl.

NewYork . . . Girl. I think about it for a moment. It's a stretch, but anyone can see my age on the form. It's breezy. I'm going with it.

Since I am disinclined to pay for this, I scroll through the short list of generic options and fix on the one that seems most neutral: "I'm intrigued! Check me out."

I send my profile and the canned tagline to MaineCatch and get a confirmation notice from the website. I feel a flash of regret, and then a tingle of hope. It's the same feeling I had when I was ten and stuffed a message in a bottle and tossed it off a pier into the ocean. Now that I remember it, the bottle kept washing up onshore with the tide and I finally gave up—but still. My message is out there, and now all I can do is wait and see. ∽

Bird in Hand

IT HAD BEEN A RAINY MORNING, and all through the afternoon the sky remained opaque, bleached and unreadable. Alison wasn't sure until the last minute whether she would even go to Claire's book party in the city. The kids were whiny and bored, and she was feeling guilty that her latest freelance assignment, "Sparking the Flame of Your Child's Creativity," which involved extra interviews and rewrites, had made her distracted and short-tempered with them. She'd asked the babysitter to stay late twice that week already, and had shut herself away in her tiny study—mudroom, really—trying to finish the piece. "Dolores, would you mind distracting him, please?" she'd called with a shrill edge of panic when three-year-old Noah pounded his small fists on the door.

"Maybe we shouldn't go," she said when Charlie called from work to find out when she was leaving. "The kids are needy. I'm tired."

"But you've been looking forward to this," he said.

"I don't know," she said. "Dolores seems out of sorts. I can hear her out there snapping at the kids."

"Look," he said. "I'll come home. I have a lot of work to do tonight anyway. I'll take over for Dolores, and then you won't have to worry."

"But I want you there," she said obstinately. "I don't want to go alone. I probably won't even know anybody." ▶

NEW YORK TIMES BESTSELLING AUTHOR OF *ORPHAN TRAIN*

CHRISTINA BAKER KLINE

bird in hand

a novel

On the drive home from a rare evening out, Alison collides with another car running a stop sign, and—just like that—her life turns upside down. Exquisitely written, powerful, and thrilling, *Bird in Hand* is a novel about love and friendship and betrayal, and about the secrets we tell ourselves and each other.

"You know Claire," Charlie said. "Isn't that what matters? It'll be good to show your support."

"It's not like she's gone out of her way to get in touch with me."

"She did send you an invitation."

"Well, her publicist."

"So Claire put your name on the list. Come on, Alison—I'm not going to debate this with you. Clearly you want to go, or you wouldn't be agonizing over it."

He was right. She didn't answer. Sometime back in the fall, Claire's feelings had gotten hurt—something about an article she'd submitted to the magazine Alison worked for that wasn't right, that Alison's boss had brusquely criticized and then rejected, leaving her to do the work of explaining. It was Alison's first major assignment as a freelance editor, and she hadn't wanted to screw it up. So she'd let her boss's displeasure (which, after all, had eked out as annoyance at her, too: "I do wonder, Alison, if you defined the assignment well enough in the first place . . .") color her response. She'd hinted that Claire might be taking on too many things at once, and that the piece wasn't up to the magazine's usual standards. She was harsher than she should have been. And yet—the article was sloppy; it appeared to have been hastily written. There were typos and transition problems. Claire seemed to have misunderstood the assignment. Frankly, Alison was annoyed at her for turning in the piece as she did—she should have taken more time with it, been more particular. It pointed to something larger in their friendship, Alison thought, a kind of carelessness on Claire's part, a taking for granted. It had been that way since they were young. Claire was the impetuous, brilliant one, and Alison was the compass that kept her on course.

Now Claire had finished her novel, a slim, thinly disguised roman à clef called *Blue Martinis*, about a girl's coming-of-age in the South. Alison couldn't bear to read it; the little she'd gleaned from the blurb by a bestselling writer on the postcard invitation Claire's publicist had sent—"Every woman who has ever been a girl will relate to this searingly honest, heartbreakingly funny novel about a girl's sexual awakening in a repressive southern town"—made her stomach twist into a knot. Claire's story was, after all, Alison's story, too; she hadn't been asked or even consulted, but she had little doubt that her own past was now on view. And Claire hadn't let her see the manuscript in advance; she'd told Alison that she didn't want to feel inhibited by what people from Bluestone might think. Anyway, Claire insisted, it was a novel. Despite this disclaimer, from what Alison could gather, she was "Jill," the main character's introverted if strong-willed sidekick.

"Ben will be there, won't he?" Charlie said.

"Probably. Yes."

"So hang out with him. You'll be fine."

Alison nodded into the phone. Ben, Claire's husband, was effortlessly sociable—wry and intimate and inclusive. Alison had a mental picture of him from countless cocktail parties, standing in the middle of a group with a drink in one hand, stooping his tall frame slightly to accommodate.

"Tell them I'm sorry I can't be there," Charlie said. "And let Dolores know I'll be home around seven. And remember—this is part of your job, to schmooze and make contacts. You'll be glad you went."

"Yeah, okay," she said, thinking, oh right, my *job*, mentally adding up how much she'd earned over the past year: two $50 checks for whimsical personal essays on smart-mommy Web sites, $500 for a parenting magazine "service" piece called "50 Ways for New Moms to Relieve Stress," a $1,000 kill fee for a big feature on sibling rivalry that the competition scooped just before Alison's story went to press. The freelance editing assignment with Claire had never panned out.

"The party's on East End Avenue, right?" he said. "You should probably take the bridge. The tunnel might be backed up, with this rain. Drive slow; the roads'll be wet."

They talked about logistics for a few minutes—how much to pay Dolores, what Charlie might find to eat in the fridge. As they were talking, Alison slipped out of her study, shutting the door quietly behind her. She could hear the kids in the living room with Dolores, and she made her way upstairs quietly, avoiding the creaky steps so they wouldn't be alerted to her presence. In the master bedroom she riffled through the hangers on her side ▶

of the closet and pulled out one shirt and then another for inspection. She yanked off the jeans she'd been wearing for three days and tried on a pair of black wool pants she hadn't worn in months, then stood back and inspected herself in the full-length mirror on the back of the closet door. The pants zipped easily enough, but the top button was tight. She put a hand over her tummy, unzipped the pants, and callipered a little fat roll with her fingers. She sighed.

"What?"

"Oh, nothing," she said. "Listen, Dolores will feed the kids, you just have to give them a bath. And honey, try not to look at your BlackBerry until you get them in bed. They see so little of you as it is." She yanked down her pants and, back in the closet, found a more forgiving pair.

When Alison was finally dressed she felt awkward and unnatural, like a child pretending to be a grown-up, or a character in a play. In her mommy role she wore flat, comfortable shoes, small gold hoops, soft T-shirts, jeans or khakis. Now it felt as if she were wearing a costume: black high-heeled boots, a jangling bracelet, earrings that pulled on her lobes, bright (too bright?) lipstick she'd been pressed into buying at the Bobbi Brown counter by a salesgirl half her age. She went downstairs and greeted the children stiffly, motioning to Dolores to keep them away so she could maintain the illusion that she always dressed like this.

She went out to the garage, got into the car, remembered her cell phone, clattered back into the house, returned to the car, remembered her umbrella, made it back to the house in time to answer the ringing phone in the kitchen. It was her mother in North Carolina.

"Hi, Mom, look, I'll have to call you later. I'm running out the door."

"You sound tense," her mother said. "Where are you going?"

"To a party for Claire's book."

"In the city?"

"Yes. And I'm late."

"I read her book," her mother said. "Have you?"

"Not yet."

"Well. You might want to."

"I will, one of these days," Alison said, consciously ignoring her mother's insinuating tone. Then the children were on her. Six-year-old Annie dissolved in tears, and Dolores had to peel Noah off Alison's legs like starfish from a rock. Alison made it out to the car again, calling, "I'll be home soon!" and madly blowing kisses, and realized when she turned on the engine that she didn't have a bottle of water, which was annoying, because you never knew how long it would take to get into the city, but fuck it. There was no way she could go inside again. Halfway down the driveway she saw Annie and Noah in the front window, frantically waving at her and jumping up and down. Alison pressed the button to roll down her window and waved back. As she pulled the car into the street she could see Noah's cheek mashed up against the glass, his hand outstretched, his small form resigned and motionless as he watched her drive away. ∽

Orphan Train

The #1 *New York Times* bestseller that has captured the hearts of readers everywhere. . . . Between 1854 and 1929, so-called orphan trains ran regularly from the cities of the East Coast to the farmlands of the Midwest, carrying thousands of abandoned children whose fates would be determined by luck or chance. When seventeen-year-old Molly Ayer is tasked with helping an elderly widow clean out her attic, she uncovers not only a little known part of American history, but also an unexpected friendship.

STANDING BEFORE the large walnut door, with its oversized brass knocker, Molly hesitates. She turns to look at Jack, who is already back in his car, headphones in his ears, flipping through what she knows is a dog-eared collection of Junot Díaz stories he keeps in the glove compartment. She stands straight, shoulders back, tucks her hair behind her ears, fiddles with the collar of her blouse (When's the last time she wore a collar? A dog collar, maybe), and raps the knocker. No answer. She raps again, a little louder. Then she notices a buzzer to the left of the door and pushes it. Chimes gong loudly in the house, and within seconds she can see Jack's mom, Terry, barreling toward her with a worried expression. It's always startling to see Jack's big brown eyes in his mother's wide, soft-featured face.

Though Jack has assured Molly that his mother is on board—"That damn attic project has been hanging over her head for so long, you have no idea"— Molly knows the reality is more complicated. Terry adores her only son, and would do just about anything to make him happy. However much Jack wants to believe that Terry's fine and dandy with this plan, Molly knows that he steamrollered her into it.

When Terry opens the door, she gives Molly a once-over. "Well, you clean up nice."

"Thanks. I guess," Molly mutters. She

can't tell if Terry's outfit is a uniform or if it's just so boring that it looks like one: black pants, clunky black shoes with rubber soles, a matronly peach-colored T-shirt.

Molly follows her down a long hallway lined with oil paintings and etchings in gold frames, the Oriental runner beneath their feet muting their footsteps. At the end of the hall is a closed door.

Terry leans with her ear against it for a moment and knocks softly. "Vivian?" She opens the door a crack. "The girl is here. Molly Ayer. Yep, okay."

She opens the door wide onto a large, sunny living room with views of the water, filled with floor-to-ceiling bookcases and antique furniture. An old lady, wearing a black cashmere crewneck sweater, is sitting beside the bay window in a faded red wingback chair, her veiny hands folded in her lap, a wool tartan blanket draped over her knees.

When they are standing in front of her, Terry says, "Molly, this is Mrs. Daly."

"Hello," Molly says, holding out her hand as her father taught her to do.

"Hello." The old woman's hand, when Molly grasps it, is dry and cool. She is a sprightly, spidery woman, with a narrow nose and piercing hazel eyes as bright and sharp as a bird's. Her skin is thin, almost translucent, and her wavy silver hair is gathered at the nape of her neck in a bun. Light freckles—or are they age spots?—are sprinkled across her face. A topographical map of veins runs up her hands and over her wrists, and she has dozens of tiny creases around her eyes. She reminds Molly of the nuns at the Catholic school she attended briefly in Augusta (a quick stopover with an ill-suited foster family), who seemed ancient in some ways and preternaturally young in others. Like the nuns, this woman has a slightly imperious air, as if she is used to getting her way. And why wouldn't she? Molly thinks. She *is* used to getting her way.

"All right, then. I'll be in the kitchen if you need me," Terry says, and disappears through another door.

The old woman leans toward Molly, a slight frown on her face. "How on earth do you achieve that effect? The skunk stripe," she says, reaching up and brushing her own temple.

"Umm . . ." Molly is surprised; no one has ever asked her this before. "It's a combination of bleach and dye." ▸

Orphan Train *(continued)*

"How did you learn to do it?"

"I saw a video on YouTube."

"YouTube?"

"On the Internet."

"Ah." She lifts her chin. "The computer. I'm too old to take up such fads."

"I don't think you can call it a fad if it's changed the way we live," Molly says, then smiles contritely, aware that she's already gotten herself into a disagreement with her potential boss.

"Not the way *I* live," the old woman says. "It must be quite time-consuming."

"What?"

"Doing that to your hair."

"Oh. It's not so bad. I've been doing it for a while now."

"What's your natural color, if you don't mind my asking?"

"I don't mind," Molly says. "It's dark brown."

"Well, my natural color is red." It takes Molly a moment to realize she's making a little joke about being gray.

"I like what you've done with it," she parries. "It suits you."

The old woman nods and settles back in her chair. She seems to approve. Molly feels some of the tension leave her shoulders. "Excuse my rudeness, but at my age there's no point in beating around the bush. Your appearance is quite stylized. Are you one of those—what are they called, gothics?"

Molly can't help smiling. "Sort of."

"You borrowed that blouse, I presume."

"Uh . . ."

"You needn't have bothered. It doesn't suit you." She gestures for Molly to sit across from her. "You may call me Vivian. I never liked being called Mrs. Daly. My husband is no longer alive, you know."

"I'm sorry."

"No need to be sorry. He died eight years ago. Anyway, I am ninety-one years old. Not many people I once knew are still alive."

Molly isn't sure how to respond—isn't it polite to tell people they don't look as old as they are? She wouldn't have guessed that this woman is ninety-one, but she doesn't have much basis for comparison. Her father's parents died when he was young; her mother's parents never married, and she never met her grandfather. The one grandparent Molly remembers, her mother's mother, died of cancer when she was three.

"Terry tells me you're in foster care," Vivian says. "Are you an orphan?"

"My mother's alive, but—yes, I consider myself an orphan."

"Technically you're not, though."

"I think if you don't have parents who look after you, then you can call yourself whatever you want."

Vivian gives her a long look, as if she's considering this idea. "Fair enough," she says. "Tell me about yourself, then."

Molly has lived in Maine her entire life. She's never even crossed the state line. She remembers bits and pieces of her childhood on Indian Island before she went into foster care: the gray-sided trailer she lived in with her parents, the community center with pickups parked all around, Sockalexis Bingo Palace, and St. Anne's Church. She remembers an Indian corn-husk doll with black hair and a traditional native costume that she kept on a shelf in her room—though she preferred the Barbies donated by charities and doled out at the community center at Christmas. They were never the popular ones, of course—never Cinderella or Beauty Queen Barbie, but instead one-off oddities that bargain hunters could find on clearance: Hot Rod Barbie, Jungle Barbie. It didn't matter. However peculiar Barbie's costume, her features were always reliably the same: the freakish stiletto-ready feet, the oversized rack and ribless midsection, the ski-slope nose and shiny plastic hair . . .

But that's not what Vivian wants to hear. Where to start? What to reveal? This is the problem. It's not a happy story, and Molly has learned through experience that people either recoil or don't believe her or, worse, pity her. So she's learned to tell an abridged version. "Well," she says, "I'm a Penobscot Indian on my father's side. When I was young, we lived on a reservation near Old Town."

"Ah. Hence the black hair and tribal makeup."

Molly is startled. She's never thought to make that connection—is it true?

Sometime in the eighth grade, during a particularly rough year—angry, screaming foster parents; jealous foster siblings; ▶

a pack of mean girls at school—she got a box of L'Oreal ten-minute hair color and Cover Girl ebony eyeliner and transformed herself in the family bathroom. A friend who worked at Claire's at the mall did her piercings the following weekend—a string of holes in each ear, up through the cartilage, a stud in her nose, and a ring in her eyebrow (though that one didn't last; it soon got infected and had to be taken out, the remaining scar a spiderweb tracing). The piercings were the straw that got her thrown out of that foster home. Mission accomplished.

Molly continues her story—how her father died and her mother couldn't take care of her, how she ended up with Ralph and Dina.

"So Terry tells me you were assigned some kind of community service project. And she came up with the brilliant idea for you to help me clean my attic," Vivian says. "Seems like a bad bargain for you, but who am I to say?"

"I'm kind of a neat freak, believe it or not. I like organizing things."

"Then you are even stranger than you appear." Vivian sits back and clasps her hands together. "I'll tell you something. By your definition I was orphaned, too, at almost exactly the same age. So we have that in common."

Molly isn't sure how to respond. Does Vivian want her to ask about this, or is she just putting that out there? It's hard to tell. "Your parents . . ." she ventures, "didn't look after you?"

"They tried. There was a fire . . ." Vivian shrugs. "It was all so long ago, I barely remember. Now—when do you want to begin?" ∾